WHEN THE SWEET TALKING'S DONE

. . . tells of a passionate love affair between Philip, an aristocratic young Englishman, and Sabine, a beautiful half-Siamese Countess who bewitches him with her animal sensuality. Sabine was born to privilege and riches; but she has the soul of a whore, and the raging flames of her sexual hunger have been fanned by a cloistered upbringing.

Sabine's father is a French aristocrat and diplomat whose second wife, a dominating bitch of a woman, resents her stepdaughter's attractiveness. Like the monster she is, she steps in to prevent Sabine marrying Philip. Sabine's hopeless promiscuity and the stepmother's determined opposition together subject Philip to continual humiliation. But Sabine has entered the pores of his skin. . .

This powerful erotic novel unfolds against a vivid background of modern London.

Also by Robin Douglas-Home

SINATRA

HOT FOR CERTAINTIES

Blues in the Night (author Johnny Mercer, composer Harold Arlen, copyright 1941 by Harms Inc, USA) is reprinted by permission of Chappell and Co Ltd

When the Sweet Talking's done

Robin Douglas-Home

But when the sweet talkin' done
A woman's a two-face,
A worrisome thing who'll leave ya t'sing
The blues in the night

—BLUES IN THE NIGHT (Mercer, Arlen)

LESLIE FREWIN : LONDON

First published in 1968
by Leslie Frewin Publishers Limited
15 Hay's Mews, Berkeley Square, London W1

Set in Baskerville
Printed by Anchor Press
and Bound by William Brendon
both of Tiptree, Essex

09 086920 6

I

The BEA Comet soared into the sky, leaving in its wake Gibraltar harbour, the cluster of Royal Navy destroyers round the boom, the terraced white houses climbing up the side of The Rock. Philip Rodolphin unfastened his seat-belt.

Leaving the battalion after six years had been, when he had come to face it, a surprisingly painless business. There had been only two really emotional moments for him. One was when the Pipes and Drums had beaten Retreat the evening before: he realised, as he watched the swishing drumsticks and the swinging kilts, that from that day on he would watch as an outsider, that no longer would he feel part of the scenery of the Beating of a Retreat. The realisation hurt him: the magic of the pipes was in his veins and he could never hear them or the tattoo of the side-drums without a primitive tingle at the back of his neck.

The other emotional moment was when he went to say goodbye to his platoon. All forty-four of them had gathered in the platoon stores to present him with a leaving-present – a cigarette-dispenser in the shape of a football inscribed with all their signatures – and he had had to make a short speech. His voice had broken in the middle of saying what a fine lot they had been, and he had had to cough loudly and look down at the ground, swallowing hard to stop the tears coming. When they had sung 'Will Ye No Come Back Again?' the tears welled unashamedly in his eyes. But, he noticed, there were tears in some of their eyes too, which pleased him a lot. He had wanted to mean something to them, something more than just their platoon commander.

Saying goodbye to his brother officers had been a mere formality: the only one he would miss was Fergus Menzies, and as he was on leave their farewells had been taken two weeks previously, after a boisterous tour of Gibraltar's more sleazy night-spots.

Even up till the last minute the CO had tried to make him change his mind about resigning. 'The regiment can ill afford to lose an officer of your calibre, Philip,' he had said that morning when Philip visited his office to bid a formal goodbye. 'Remember – if things don't turn out as well for you in Civvy Street as you hope, we'll always gladly welcome you back.'

'Thank you, sir.'

'I mean that quite sincerely. Have you got a job of some sort lined up?'

'No, sir. I've made no plans at all.'

What he had not told the CO was that he had not even confessed to his family that he had resigned his Regular commission. His father would be furious: he had been overjoyed when Philip signed on as a Regular: 'The Army's the only fit life for a young chap these days. I was in it for twenty-six years and don't regret a day of them. You can at least live like a gentleman which nowadays you can't do as a damned civilian.'

The only regret his father had expressed was that Philip had chosen to join the infantry and not the cavalry. But, as Colonel Jasper Rodolphin had lived and breathed horseflesh since his childhood, that was understandable. On his retirement he had almost automatically become Master of the Rodolphin Hunt, which he ran as if he was still in the Army. He reprimanded people for not being correctly dressed or on time for the Meet, and bellowed his head off in fury if someone were so misguided as to interfere with the running of the hounds. When he roared at some terrified offender 'You ought to be horse-whipped!' it was no idle suggestion: Colonel Jasper really meant it.

Yes, thought Philip, telling Father is going to be no easy task. What on earth was he going to give as his *reason* for resigning? He would work that out after he had spoken to his mother. She would be delighted: she had always hated the idea of him being a Regular soldier. Her aim for him had been to join Rodolphin's Bank, like his cousin Gerald had done, with the assured prospect of a directorship at a reasonably early age. But to Philip the idea of being a bank-clerk in the City, in a stuffy hide-bound old firm, albeit wealthy like Rodolphin's, was anathema. That was about the only point where he agreed with his father: his father's elder brother Marcus, Gerald's father, was managing director of Rodolphin's and the two brothers had always been at loggerheads.

Gerald was the same age as Philip. He lived in reasonably lavish style in a mews flat in Pavilion Road, Chelsea, where Philip had stayed during his embarkation leave before sailing for the Far East. Philip assumed that Gerald got a fat allowance from his father to enable him to live in that style; because, after all, Uncle Marcus was an eminent City figure and obviously earning a very high income. But Philip's father, having refused point-blank to have anything to do with Rodolphin's Bank at a very early age, had been forced to live on his Army income and now his pension, with perhaps a small token allowance from Philip's grandfather, the senile chairman of Rodolphin's.

Philip had telephoned Gerald from Gibraltar to ask if he could stay in the flat. Gerald had said Yes, of course. Philip had given no indication of how long for: he intended Gerald to assume it was just for a few days' leave. In fact he hoped to stay with Gerald until he had sorted out his future and got a flat of his own – if he could afford one. He had his Army savings, £465, to tide him over, and after that – nothing. He had never had any allowance from his father and he knew that he would certainly not get one now that he had resigned his commission.

He wondered what London would be like for him without Annette. Ever since he could remember, she had been the focal point of his stays there on leave. He had fallen in love with her during his last year at Winchester when she came down to visit her brother one Sunday. Right from the start she had always made it clear to him that she did not, and could not, return the strength of his love. But Philip went on hoping she would eventually change her mind. He would pour out his heart to her in passionate letters – latterly from Hong Kong, and then Southern Arabia; they had got so passionate that Annette had written back rather coldly saying he must really control himself because what *would* happen if her mother or someone chanced to read one of his more sensational passages. Philip had been very hurt – his letters to Annette had been his only outlet, and he forced into them all the repressed ardour of his very ardent nature. Ironically, it had been the very fact that he had seen so little of the beautiful Annette over the years that had allowed him to retain an idealistic passion for her, unaffected by the more carnal affairs he had had in Germany and on the troop-ship sailing out east. Ironically, too, he had never even kissed her, though he had tried often enough. She would never give in to him, saying it would only encourage him unfairly to think she loved him when she knew she didn't.

Then came the bombshell of her last letter. It had

4

arrived in the parachute drop on the day before the trip up to relieve the beleaguered garrison in the fort at Majaid is South Arabia. 'Darling Philip, I wanted you to know from me before you read it in the papers – that is, if you do *get* papers where you are. But I am getting engaged to someone you know very well called Freddie Mallard-Penge . . .' Philip read no further – he crumpled up the letter and hurled it into the scrub.

Freddie Mallard-Penge – how on earth could a marvellous girl like Annette be marrying someone like *him*? Philip had known him at Winchester where he was nicknamed Penge the Polecat because of his legendary BO. People who had to sit next to him in school used to chew peppermints or sniff Benzedrine inhalers in their efforts to neutralise the lethal 'Penge pong' as it was called.

Anyway, Philip reflected, she would be Mrs Mallard-Penge by now: perhaps Freddie had learnt to wash since his Winchester days. In a way, he had to admit, Annette getting married had cleared the air for him: though he felt he could never love anyone in quite the same idealistic way again, he knew in his heart that his romantic vision of Annette had always been destined to come to an unfulfilled dénouement – better, really, that it had happened in this sudden way than for him to have had to watch the malodorous Mallard-Penge stealing her away in front of his very eyes.

* * *

He was feeling extravagant, so he took a taxi from London Airport to Pavilion Road instead of waiting for the coach. Gerald would be still at his office in the City, but he had promised Philip he would see that his daily woman Mrs Drinkwater was there to let him in.

5

'Welcome home, Mr Philip,' beamed Mrs Drinkwater at the door.

'Thank you. It's good to be back.' He heaved his two heavy suitcases and his guitar-case into the narrow doorway and up the steep staircase.

'Is that all your luggage, sir?'

'No, the rest, the heavy stuff, is coming by sea and should be delivered here sometime this week.'

'I see you've got your guitar with you, anyway, sir. Be nice to hear you strumming away again. Can I fix you a bite to eat?'

'No thank you, Mrs Drinkwater. I had lunch on the plane.'

Philip went into the little room at the end of the passage that he had used on his last leave. As he unpacked to change he suddenly realised, not without a pang of regret, that when he took off his uniform that time, it would be the last time, in his life probably, that he would ever wear battledress. The end of a very significant chapter in his life.

Mrs Drinkwater called to say that she was going home and would be back in the morning. Philip went into the sitting-room and mixed himself a vodka and Canada Dry. He knew what he must do before Gerald got back – telephone his parents and get over all the explaining he would have to do. With a gulp of his drink and a long sigh he picked up the telephone.

'Hello, Mother? This is Philip...'

'Philip? *Darling*. Where are you – not in Gibraltar?'

'No, in London, in Gerald's flat. I've just arrived.'

'Darling, how *terribly* exciting. What is it – a bit of unexpected leave or what?'

'No. I'm back for good. I've resigned my commission.'

A pause, then: 'You've *what*, darling?'

'I've resigned. I'm out of the Army.'

'Darling, this is simply *wonderful* news. But it's all so sudden.' Her voice suddenly changed from a hysterical crowing into a more guarded tone: 'You didn't get into any trouble or anything awful, did you? I mean, there was no scandal or anything you haven't told us about, was there?'

'No, no. I just resigned. I got fed up and thought I'd like to become a civilian and get a job. I don't exactly know what, but——'

She was effusive again: 'Oh, it's *wonderful* to have you back again. You know I *hated* you being so far away all these years. And I'm sure it didn't do your health any good living on that *atrocious* food in all that heat——'

'I've never felt fitter.'

'Oh *good*, darling. Dear, what a delicious surprise, though it's a pity in a way you won't be wearing your uniform any more. You looked so adorably handsome in it. Now don't worry about getting a job, darling. I'll get working on that right away. I've got lots of friends who'd simply *love* to give you a job. Will you be coming down to see us?'

'Well, I thought I'd stay here with Gerald for a bit until I get a job fixed. Then I could come down for a weekend.'

'Oh wonderful, darling.' Again her tone of voice changed: 'What do you want me to tell your father? He's out at the kennels just now.'

'Just tell him I'm back and that I've resigned my commission to start in civilian life. There's nothing more to it than that.'

'No, I suppose not. But you know what he's like – I don't think he'll be terribly pleased, darling, I do warn you. But I'll do my best to get him to see it's all to the good from your future point of view. He must see that, mustn't he, darling?'

'I hope he will. It's done now anyway, so there's no point in him getting angry.'

'No, I'm *sure* he won't.' She sounded totally unconvinced. She repeated, more softly: 'I'm sure he won't . . . Are you *deliciously* brown, darling?'

'Quite tanned, I suppose.'

'I just can't *wait* to see you. Shall I come up to London this week for a jaunt and we could——'

'No, I really wouldn't bother to do that. I'll be pretty well occupied hunting for a job. I should wait till I can come down to you.'

'All right, darling. But I'll get on to people like Ronnie Basildon and Hugo Brushworth straight away about helping you over a job. They should be able to pull a few strings.'

He knew it was pointless to try to deter her: 'That might be a help. They might know the right people to go and see, anyway. But I haven't really made up my mind about what *kind* of job I want yet.'

'No, no, darling. Don't worry. That'll all sort itself out. The main thing is you are here, back with us, gloriously *near* again. Dear, I can't get over it . . .'

They talked for a few minutes longer, then Philip pretended there was someone at the door to give him a chance to get off the line, otherwise – knowing his mother – she would have gone on talking all afternoon.

As he continued his unpacking, he realised with surprise that his mother had not mentioned Annette's marriage. She must have been really and truly knocked off balance to forget that: she had been matchmaking between him and Annette ever since she heard from one of her gossipy circle of friends that Philip was interested in her. Philip had never mentioned Annette to her himself: he couldn't stand her proneness to interference in his personal life. Indeed to get away from his mother's possessiveness had been one of the main factors in his decision to sign on in the Army.

'Annette would make me such a *proud* mother-in-law, darling,' she had cooed at him once. Yes, he said under his breath, because she's an only child and her father's got pots of money, that's why, you predatory old money-grubber!

An hour later the telephone rang. He knew who it was before he picked up the receiver: 'Hullo?'

'Philip? What the hell's all this balls about you resigning your commission?' His father's speech was blurred, but then afternoon drinking was no new habit for him.

'Oh hullo, Father. Yes, I've resigned, that's all. I'd had enough of the Army and thought——'

'*Enough*, boy? God, you've only had a measly six years. Mere chicken feed. Only just got your knees brown. *Enough?* Come on, there must be more to it than that!'

'There isn't, Father. I enjoyed it very much while it lasted, as you well know. But I thought the time had come——'

'Have you been gambling in the Mess?'

'Just a few games of bridge. Nothing more.'

'In debt?'

'No, Father.'

'Woman trouble? Any scandal?'

'No, Father. Nothing like that. I——'

'When did you actually resign?'

'When we were still out in Southern Arabia.'

'After that ambush you wrote to your mother about?'

'Yes.'

'I see, I see. So *that's* it. As soon as a few bullets started

9

flying around, you turned tail and ran and resigned your bloody commission.'

'*No*, Father.'

'God Almighty, boy, it's staring me in the face. Don't come the old bally-hoo with me about wanting to start a fresh life as a civilian or any of that balls. You were just plain *yellow*, that's all it was, plain yellow——'

'Father, listen——'

'Don't interrupt. You're a disgrace to your family name and a disgrace to me. Christ Almighty, can you imagine what it's like to have to face up to the fact that your only son is a snivelling, yellow-bellied coward who gets the wind up——'

Philip slammed down the receiver. His hands were shaking. He poured himself another vodka and Canada Dry, stronger this time, and sank into an armchair, eyes closed, lip quivering.

The telephone rang again almost immediately, but he left it ringing and ringing. When it eventually stopped, the silence was halcyon.

2

Philip spent the next few weeks getting in touch with as many Old Wykehamist friends as he could trace, lunching with them, drinking with them, finding out as much as possible about their jobs. They fell neatly into two categories: the lucky ones who had moved effortlessly into family businesses – usually stockbroker firms – with the prospect of a substantial income and a directorship or partnership fairly soon, and the unluckier ones – a smaller group – who had had to start from scratch, usually earning a pittance, and who one and all complained about the boringness of their jobs and of the people their jobs brought them into contact with.

'But why are you hunting for a job, old man?' most of them asked Philip incredulously. 'Surely you could walk into Rodolphin's Bank tomorrow and find a specially warmed-up seat waiting for you.'

'I just couldn't stand working there, in a bank, in the City,' Philip would answer. Gerald was always trying to sell him the idea of Rodolphin's, too. But Gerald's own description of a typical week in the place was enough to confirm Philip's innate dislike of the idea. He had been taken round Rodolphin's Bank once, in the school holidays, and he loathed the memory of the dark, poky little offices, the smell of dust and musty books, the wizened, hunched, bespectacled little men scurrying everywhere, the cathedral-like atmosphere of the austere, panelled board-room with its huge portraits of past Rodolphins. No, he would never work in Rodolphin's whatever they paid him – and he knew very well that at the start they paid almost nothing. It was reckoned by Rodolphin's to be a privilege to be *allowed* to start work there, a privilege that should really be paid *for*. How Gerald stuck it, he couldn't understand: but then Gerald, being the eventual heir, had been groomed for it since birth. And anyway he got a nice big allowance as well from Uncle Marcus.

The first time Philip's ears pricked and his interest was fully aroused was when he had lunch with Greville Whitfield. Greville had edited the *Chronicle* at Winchester and now worked as a copy-writer in an advertising agency called Baker, Digby and Pollstein – BDP for short.

'The thing I most like about advertising,' said Greville over a steak in the Tiberio, 'is that you don't get bogged down in one sphere of operation. For instance, I'm involved at the moment in a campaign on Radio Luxembourg for a breakfast cereal, a TV test campaign for a new soap, a press campaign for a tipped cigarette, and a piece of depth research on why people buy certain headache remedies. Pretty varied, you must admit. And hard to get bored with all that going on. No set routine, every day is different, and the people in advertising are so much more alive, so much *younger*, than in a place like the City or industry. Smashing secretaries. Mini-skirts all over the place. But you wouldn't believe the hidebound stuffiness of most of the clients we have to deal with. That's the only rub – the clients. But they're footing the bill, so you just have to put up with them.'

'Sounds interesting. Is it hard to get into BDP? I mean, would they take someone like me with no experience of any business dealings at all?'

'They have a trainee scheme which lasts for 6 months. You do a month in each department and at the end they tell you – and you tell them, too – whether it's on or not.

To get on that you have to pass lots of tests and be interviewed by a few directors and a psychiatrist——'

'A psychiatrist?'

'Yes, they've picked up that idea from the New York office. It's only to decide two things – one, if you're ambitious, and two, if you're queer.'

'Oh.'

'You always used to draw a lot at school. Have you got anything you could show them to whet their appetite? They're always on the lookout for new artists?'

'No, but I've got a lot of photographs I took in the Middle East. Oh, and some things I wrote for the Regimental Magazine.'

'That'd do fine. Make up a sort of bullshit folder of all your best photographs and all your writing, then you could produce it to show what a creative chap you are. Throw in some old drawings if you can find any. The more variety, the better.'

'What do they pay?'

'Well, while you're on the trainee scheme not very much. But I've only been here for 3 years and I'm getting £1,400 – which isn't bad at all, is it? If I were a bank-clerk, I'd still be around the £800 mark. Do you want me to tell the Personnel people you'd like to come for an interview?'

'Yes, I think I would like to. It certainly sounds a good deal more interesting than most of the other jobs I've been hearing about. Oh, one thing – what's their attitude to Old Wykehamists?'

'You can never tell really, because they base everything on these tests. But in the interviews it should help because the Chairman's an Old Wykehamist and they all want to make advertising a more respectable profession than it's thought to be at the moment. I shouldn't wear your old school tie, though – that would be going a bit too far.'

'No, I wouldn't dream of doing that. Haven't worn it once.'

'Oh, and tell them you play the guitar. You still do, don't you?' Philip nodded. 'That'll help. You have to write a short autobiography, so throw it all in. Being called Rodolphin won't exactly be a hindrance, either, let's face it. Probably think they'll get the Rodolphin Bank account.'

Greville chuckled as he finished his glass of Margaux.

*   *   *

Two days later, a typewritten letter arrived for Philip from the Personnel Officer of BDP asking him if it would be convenient to come in for tests and interviews the following Thursday at 9.45 am. He noticed with interest that the Personnel Officer was a *woman* called Doris Maple. Enclosed was an elaborate form which he was asked to fill in and return as soon as possible, including a 600-word autobiography.

'So you're thinking of becoming an ad-man,' said Gerald that evening. 'You'll certainly rake in the old cash, but I couldn't stand the people.'

'That's exactly what *I* couldn't stand about the City,' retorted Philip.

'Nonsense. At least people in the City are gents usually.'

'That's exactly what I mean.'

'What, what?' said Gerald, nonplussed.

Gerald had taken quite kindly to the news that Philip wanted to stay in the flat more or less permanently, or at any rate until he had got a job fixed and the prospects of some income. Philip was grateful to him for that. He was also grateful for the fact that because Gerald led a very active social life the two of them saw comparatively little of each other. Gerald went away every weekend, so the only times they met were at breakfast, when they both read the papers in silence, and in the early evenings, when Gerald returned to change before going out to dinner, which he seemed to do every night of the week. He had to face up to it – he and Gerald just didn't speak the same language or take the same attitude towards life at all, and the friends that Gerald invited back to the flat for drinks might have been from another planet for all Philip found in common with them. Even the girls – oh, they were mostly pretty enough, but that was all. Philip found them silly, immature, a caricature of the English deb type, which is exactly what they were usually. On his own evenings out he went alone to a movie and then on to the Sunset Jazz Club, where he could sit and drink and listen to the music. He had picked up one or two girls in the Sunset – and in particular one Chinese girl who said she was in love with him because he looked like Richard Widmark – and found them much more interesting than Gerald's debby set. One night the band had let him sit in with them on guitar for a jam session on 'There'll Be Some Changes Made' which had given him a great thrill.

On the nights he stayed in, he watched television or practised on his guitar, cooking himself an omelette in Gerald's kitchenette.

On the night before his interview at BDP he went to bed early. Next morning, in his best blue suit and a new white shirt bought specially from John Michael, and clutching his folder of photographs, drawings and articles, he took a bus to Park Lane where BDP had one of the new office blocks. At 9.45 sharp he walked into the room marked Reception. A very pretty girl with long blonde hair sat at a desk behind a huge vase of red roses and white carnations. She flashed him a wide smile: 'Good morning, can I help you?'

'I've come to see Miss Doris Maple.'

'Mr Rodolphin, is it?'

Philip, surprised: 'Yes it is.'

'Oh I was expecting you, Mr Rodolphin. Do sit down and I'll tell Miss Maple you're here.'

Philip sank deep into a comfortable armchair next to a table covered with copies of *Queen*, *Vogue*, *Playboy*, *The Economist*, *Look* and *Life*.

The blonde girl dialled on the internal telephone. 'Mr Rodolphin in Reception to see Miss Maple. Right. I'll tell him. 'Byee. Miss Maple will come down for you herself, Mr Rodolphin.'

'Oh, thank you.' He looked at the blonde's legs: they were very long, and crossed with a great deal of thigh displayed under the tight blue mini-skirt. Her telephone rang.

'Hello, Reception? Oh it's you, honey. Good morning, how do you feel today? . . . Oh nonsense, you didn't have *that* much to drink . . . I feel perfectly fine . . . No, I can't tonight . . . No, sorry, I'll have to say no tonight . . . No, it's NO, honey, and that's that.'

Philip looked at her left hand: she wore no wedding ring. A tall elegant woman with her black hair swept back in a bun and pince-nez dangling from a cord round her neck came through the door. The blonde promptly put down the receiver without saying goodbye.

'Mr Rodolphin? I'm Doris Maple. How do you do.'

'How do you do.' With a last furtive look at the blonde, who looked back at him with an outrageously flirtatious smile, Philip followed Miss Maple into the lift and up to her office on the 3rd floor. She waved to him to sit down at the desk facing her.

'Thank you for sending your form and biography back so quickly. They're in with the Chairman now. He will see you after I've finished with you.' Miss Maple made it sound like some medical examination. 'Now you'll do three tests with me, all timed.' She brandished a stop-watch. 'One is to test the quickness of your reaction, one for your knowledge of words and elementary logic, and one for your powers of visualisation. 100 questions in each, and you will have two minutes for each test.' Philip whistled. She went on: 'Yes, speed is very necessary, so I advise you not to waste time if you get stuck on one question but to carry straight on to the next. It's better to complete the test than lose possible marks by racking your brains. Ready for Test Number One?'

She handed him a ball-point pen and a printed form with odd-shaped diagrams all over it. He nodded. 'Right then, go,' she yelped.

At the end of the three tests, she said briskly: 'That's very good. You managed to finish all three before your time was up. It shows you have a *quick* mind anyway. Now I'll take you in to see the Chairman. While you are talking to him I'll be correcting your papers and I'll bring them in when I've totted up the marks.'

She led Philip along the passage, past several flashy-looking secretaries clacking away at their typewriters, to a door at the end. She knocked and put her head round the door: 'I have Mr Rodolphin to see you.' Then to Philip: 'Come in, please. The Chairman will see you now.'

Philip shook hands with a tall, distinguished-looking man with greying hair and a suntanned face. He wore a discreet, double-breasted grey suit and an Old Wykehamist tie. He waved Philip to an armchair beside a TV set opposite his desk: 'Sit down, Rodolphin. Make yourself at home. Cigarette?' He held out a large wooden cigarette box with tipped on one side and plain on the other.

'No thank you, sir.' Philip felt it better not to smoke. The Chairman took a tipped cigarette, lit it with a gold Dupont lighter, and plumped heavily down in his armchair facing Philip. 'Tell me now, what relation are you to Lord Rodolphin?'

'He's my grandfather, sir.'

'So Marcus Rodolphin is your . . . ?'

'My uncle, sir.'

'Oh yes. So your father is . . . ?'

'Jasper, sir.'

'Oh Jasper, yes. He's a MFH somewhere, isn't he? Of the Rodolphin, I suppose?'

'Yes, sir.'

'I met your grandfather once. Heard him speak at a City dinner. Very impressive he was, too. Must be getting on a bit now, though, isn't he?'

'Yes, sir. He's 78.'

'Mm. Fine figure of a man. Most impressive speech. It was at the time when they were talking of devaluing the pound and all that nonsense. Speech made a big splash in all the City pages, I remember. Talked to him afterwards. Always meant to ask him out to lunch and meet some of my directors here. But never got round to it. Then he'd retired. See much of him nowadays?'

'No, sir, I haven't seen him for some time.'

'Keeps himself cooped up in the old country seat, I suppose?'

'Yes, sir.'

'Sensible fellow. Wouldn't come near London if I

had my way. Terrible place to have to live in. . . . Met Marcus once, too.'

'Oh yes, sir?'

'Yes, met Marcus shooting partridges in Norfolk with the Smith-Dugdales. Very fine shot he was, too. Still I suppose he gets a lot of practice. Remember him getting a right-and-left in front, then changing guns and getting a right-and-left behind. Joy to watch. Had a brilliant dog, too. What was it called, Scruffy, something?'

'Scuffles, sir.'

'Yes, Scuffles, that's it, Scuffles. Most brilliant gun-dog I've ever seen. Met your father Jasper once, too.'

'Did you, sir?'

'Yes, met him at a meet of the Rodolphin. We were staying nearby with the Bell-Thompsons. He wasn't Master then. I think he was still in the Army – what was it, fourteen, fifteen years ago? He would have been in the Army then, wouldn't he?'

'Yes, sir.'

'He never went into the Bank, did he?'

'No, sir.'

'Marcus runs it now that your grandfather's retired, then?'

'Yes, sir.'

'Fine brain, Marcus. Read an article by him in *The Director* not long ago. Talked a lot of sense . . . Very distinguished family . . . Should be proud of your name. What do you want to come into a profession like advertising for when you could walk into Rodolphin's Bank?'

'I wouldn't like to work in the City, sir.'

'Oh by the way, do you know your Uncle Marcus' wife Eleanor is related by marriage to my daughter-in-law? Very distant, but she is.'

'No, sir.'

'Yes, I can't quite remember how we worked it out but she is related. So that makes us sort of distant cousins-in-law, doesn't it, eh?' The Chairman guffawed.

Miss Maple popped her head round the door: 'I hope I'm not interrupting, but I've got the results of Mr Rodolphin's tests.' She beamed at Philip as she walked across to the Chairman's desk: 'As you see, these are some of the highest marks we've ever had.' She beamed at the Chairman, too. He pulled across the forms and scrutinised them: 'Damn good show, Rodolphin, damn good show.'

Miss Maple tiptoed out with a sly grin at Philip.

'Damn good show, damn good show. So you'd like to join us, would you?' The Chairman pushed the forms to one side.

'Yes, sir, I've brought these along' – he held out the folder – 'to show you. Some examples of my work, photography, drawing and writing.'

The Chairman grunted: 'Let's have a look then. Mmm. What regiment were you in?' He looked quickly through the folder.

'The Royal Scots, sir.'

'Know a chap called Pongo Burberry?'

'I knew of him, sir. He was on the staff somewhere. SHAPE, I think.'

'Pongo and I went all through Normandy together. Fine chap, Pongo. Brave as a lion. Got three DSO's and two MC's. Can't do much better than that, can you? So you'd like to join the advertising profession, then, eh?'

'Yes, sir. I think it would be a fascinating——'

'Some of these photographs are damned good. Haven't got time to read your articles but you're obviously a creative fellow. Saw in your biography that you play the guitar, too.'

'Yes, sir.'

'Not that awful pop garbage they churn out nowadays?'

'I like playing almost anything, but jazz most.'

'Mmm. So you'd like to join our trainee scheme, eh?'

'Yes, sir.'

'Well, I've been into the situation and we won't have a vacancy for three months. Can you wait till then? Shall we keep it for you?' Philip hesitated.

'You needn't make your mind up now if——'

'Yes, sir, I'd like to wait till then.'

'Sure? Quite sure?'

'Yes, sir.'

'Good, good. I'll tell Miss Maple to keep it for you. Anything you want to ask me?'

'Er——'

'Good, right. Nice meeting you, Rodolphin, and I'll look forward to you joining us in three months.' The Chairman stood up and made for the door. 'Now I'll take you along to be vetted by our tame trick-cyclist. No problems in that for you, I'm sure. Healthy, clean-living chap, aren't you?' The Chairman chortled with laughter as he led the way down the passage. 'No pronounced Oedipus Complex, eh, what?' He chortled again.

*　　*　　*

As soon as Philip got back to Pavilion Road, he dialled BDP's number.

'Good afternoon, BDP.'

'Reception, please.' . . . A pause. Then:

'Reception. Can I help you?'

'It's Philip Rodolphin speaking. I was in this morning.'

'Who? Oh *yes*, Mr Rodolphin. Can I help you? Did you leave something behind?'

'No, it's nothing like that. I wondered if you would . . .
like to come out to dinner with me . . .'

'Er . . . good heavens, what a surprise, er——'

'I mean, I know you can't this evening because I
heard you say so when I was in there, but perhaps another
evening——'

'Well, it so happens that I *could* make this evening after
all—that is if you're *asking* me for this evening. I mean
I'm not suggest——'

'Yes, this evening would be fine for me. Is that all right
for you then?'

'Yes fine. Gosh, what a surprise. Do you always ring
up girls out of the blue like this?'

'Where shall I pick you up?'

'I live in 14 Lennox Gardens. Just behind that church
in Pont Street.'

'Fine. About eight o'clock then?'

'Lovely.'

'And – oh——'

'Yes?'

'Er, what's your name?' She laughed:

'Oh yes, I'd forgotten. Shirley.'

'Shirley what?'

'Shirley Snow. OK?'

'Fine. See you at eight. 'Bye, Shirley.'

' 'Bye, *Mister* Rodolphin.' She giggled.

'Hey,' said Philip. But she had put down the receiver.

*   *   *

'How did the interviews go?' Gerald asked when he
returned to his flat about 6.15 pm.

'Easier than I thought, really,' said Philip. 'First I had
to do these tests——'

'Tests? Did you pass?'

'Yes, three different tests. One with a lot of shapes where you had to fill in the missing one, and draw what a certain shape would look like reflected in a mirror and so on. Oh, and "complete this sequence" and that sort of thing.'

'Sounds quite easy to me.'

'Then another the same sort of idea only with words. "Which is the odd man out among these five words?" Or "If Apple equals Five and Pear equals Two what do five apples and two pears equal?" That sort of thing.'

'Not very difficult, was it?'

'Well, the point was you had 100 questions to answer in 120 seconds, so you had to move pretty rapidly to get through them all.'

'Oh, I see. What about the interviews? Are you getting a job there?'

'Yes. In three months' time. That's the earliest they can fit me in. I only saw the Chairman in the end and he spent most of the time saying he'd met Uncle Marcus partridge-shooting in Norfolk. The psychiatrist was a very different matter, though.'

'You saw a *psychiatrist*?' Gerald's jaw dropped.

'Yes, he asked me what I thought of my mother and father and as I didn't dare lie I had to confess I found them both pretty tricky. He just made little notes on a pad and stared hard at me through thick bifocal lenses. Weird little chap he was. Then he showed me lots of coloured blots and asked me what shapes I saw in them. I kept seeing the same thing – a conductor waving a baton, masses of rabbits and birds and butterflies, and whole galaxies of tits.'

'*Tits*?'

'Yes, I saw a tit in every blasted corner of the blots.

Dread to think what that means—probably because I wasn't breast-fed or something. But I had to be truthful. I dared not lie, can't you see?'

'God, what a bloody silly rigmarole. What on earth do they think they'll find out by it?'

'It's to see whether you're ambitious and queer.'

'What, you mean they *like* taking on queers?'

'No, to weed them out, you fool.'

'Well I've met some ad-men who were as queer as a load of clockwork oranges.'

'But they probably weren't at BDP. They say the system works.'

'Perhaps a queer would make a damned good ad-man.'

'Well anyway, at BDP they don't seem to think so. I can't say I actually broached a discussion on the subject. Oh look, I wonder if I could ask a great favour of you?'

'Go ahead. What?'

'Are you using the E-type tonight?'

'What, you want to borrow it? God Almighty, heaven preserve us. No, I'm not actually using it tonight. I'm dining with the Rossiters and they live just round the corner in Cadogan Square. Why do you want it?'

'I'm taking a new bird out, and it's so much better than going everywhere by taxi.'

'All right, all right, yes you can have it.' Gerald threw across the ignition key. 'But if there's *one mark* on the bodywork, one minute little scratch, or anything dirty like footprints on the dashboard upside down, I'll sue you for a million pounds.'

'Thank you, Gerald. I'll guard it with my life.'

3

At five past eight Philip drew the white E-type to a halt outside 14 Lennox Gardens. He rang the top bell marked 'Snow, Bridge, Connor'. A voice erupted out of the grille above the bell: 'Who's that?'

'Philip Rodolphin. I've come for——'

'It's me – Shirley. I'll be down in a second.'

'My, you're punctual,' she said when she appeared. She wore a neat black mini-skirt, a dress with a low neck-line and gold chain belt, and she carried a small gold bag. Her blonde hair fell straight down on her shoulders and seemed longer than it had in the Reception room of BDP. She wore little make-up.

Philip opened the car door for her. She climbed in, showing a lot of thigh as her dress rucked up round her hips. She pulled it down quickly, not without a grin at Philip's overt interest.

As they drove off, Philip said: 'Who's Bridge and Connor?'

'Two air stewardesses I share the flat with. They're away at the moment. It's very convenient because they're both very seldom there together. So it's really like sharing with just one other girl in a flat big enough for three.'

'How long have you been at BDP?'

'Six months. Daddy said I had to get a job and——'

'Who's Daddy?'

'He's a Tory MP.'

'Oh *that* Snow. Yes, I've heard of him.'

'Well after I'd come out last year and spivved around sponging off Mummy and Daddy for a bit, Daddy said

I'd have to *do* something. So in return I said OK if I do something can I have my own flat, so he said Yes if I shared with someone else. He wouldn't let me live on my own, you see. He obviously didn't trust me. Poor old Daddy. Probably he was quite right. Anyway, then I got this job at BDP. It's super. Better than dreary old typing, anyway.'

'Did you have to pass any of these weird tests?'

'No no, of course not. Not just to be a receptionist. All they want is a girl who looks reasonably presentable, talks the Queen's English, has a nice pair of legs for people like you to ogle at while they're waiting, and knows how to butter up people on the telephone. I spend most of my time reading magazines and doing crossword puzzles – or chatting up randy clients. Where are we going to eat?'

'I thought the Trattoo. Is that OK?'

'Super. I've only been there once and Peter O'Toole was at the next table. I couldn't take my eyes off him all dinner.'

'Well I can't promise to lay on Peter O'Toole but the food's usually good.'

'Why did you ask me out so suddenly like this?'

Philip hesitated. 'Because . . . because I wanted to find out all about BDP. I'm joining in three months' time.'

'Oh good. So you passed all those silly tests then? How super. Well I don't really know much about what goes on *inside* the agency because I'm there all day perched on that Reception stool. Still, I suppose I can tell you a bit.'

'Why did you agree to come out with me, anyway?'

'What?' She tossed her head and laughed: 'Oh well, my date for this evening fell through and I thought I might as well, you know . . . I mean, I figured you'd be joining the agency and wanting to know a bit about things and . . .'

She trailed off. She sounded unconvincing and she knew it. Philip looked across at her. She said: 'Why, you're not regretting asking me, are you?'

Philip laughed: 'Not at all. I'm just beginning to realise what a sensible decision I made – to telephone you.'

'Oh.' She sounded relieved.

During dinner, she prattled on answering all Philip's questions about BDP with a collection of gay and usually scurrilous anecdotes about various members of the staff. Then Philip suddenly said: 'Now let's stop talking shop. I want to hear about you. All about you.'

She looked momentarily surprised: 'About me? There's nothing much to know about me.' She sipped her glass of white wine, and said: 'It's me who's done all the talking. I'd far rather hear all about you.'

'That can come later. You first. Now you're a very attractive girl. Yet what are you doing coming out with me on a blind date like this? You should be booked up weeks ahead.'

She looked down at her glass: 'It's a long involved story and I really don't particularly want to go into it just now.' She looked up at Philip, smiling, and he was suddenly very conscious of her mouth and the swell of her full breasts that pushed themselves up over her low neckline. He put his hand on her thigh. Her own hand clasped his and pushed it down.

She said: 'Tell me about you. Just for the moment. I'd like to hear it. Then I'll tell you about me later. When we're not with people . . .'

He told her about Winchester, the Army, Annette.

She said: 'So you've not been seriously involved with anyone since Annette, then?'

'No.'

'What you say is strangely similar to what I was going

27

to say to you,' she said, fingering her glass of Cointreau. 'I mean, about my love life. You see, I was in love with this man for ages, then last month he suddenly went and got engaged to my best friend. It was hard to take——' Her voice faltered. Philip squeezed her hand. She closed her eyes and took a deep breath, then a long sip of Cointreau.

'I'd given him everything. It was foolish of me, I suppose, because he had never committed himself. I just sort of assumed . . . Just as you had with your Annette.'

'Well, I'd never really assumed anything. I'd just hoped.'

'Ah – that's where men are more realistic than women.'

'Not more realistic – more blind.'

'No, no, don't you *see*?' She banged her fist lightly on the table.

He leaned over and kissed her on the mouth. She did not resist. The kiss was a long, lingering one that grew in intensity.

'Take me home and do that again – lots of times,' she said, looking at him and folding up her napkin. 'Sorry, but I was never one for kissing in public places. My Puritan upbringing, I suppose. Not that it seems to have done me much good.'

Philip asked for the bill, then squeezed her knee under the table. He said quietly: 'It's funny how when you meet some people you can tell instantly that there's going to be a flash of some sort between you. I felt it this morning when I walked into Reception.'

'Does it happen often to you – this feeling about a flash . . . ?'

'Yes, I suppose it does. Mind you, I've been wrong a good many times, more often than I've been right. In fact I've got into some tricky situations because of it.'

'Well you *are* a bit impulsive. Never in my life have I

been out with a man I only met that morning and then let him *kiss* me – in public! Good Lord, what on earth would Daddy say? Mummy wouldn't say anything – she'd have quietly fainted. I'll have to admit, I felt a sort of certain something this morning when you walked in, too. But I never thought anything like *this* would happen.' She squeezed his forearm. 'I suppose you've caught me on the rebound, you crafty bastard. But who cares?'

She tossed her head and laughed. The waiter brought Philip's change. They left.

In the car she said: 'I'd just have to go for a man with a car like this anyway. Record-player and everything. The perfect seducer's equipment.'

'I must confess to you – the car isn't mine. It's my cousin's. He lent it to me.' She snuggled up to his left side:

'As far as I'm concerned it's all yours. It's the car I'll always imagine you in from now on.'

'Who are you on the rebound from?'

'Oh please, Philip, I really don't want to talk about it. It would just rake up all the mouldy past and spoil my evening. You do understand, don't you?'

'Yes, of course. I just thought you might like to get it out of your system.'

'Talking about it won't get it out of my system. Only time can do that. And you, perhaps . . .'

'Me?'

'Yes, you. You've already helped a lot just by being there.'

'But you must have hundreds of men after you?'

'Yes, quite a few, but none that I particularly *like* being after me.'

'I'll do my best. I'm flattered.'

'I think I must be a bit drunk to be saying all this. It

was all that wine and Cointreau. Don't take any more notice of me. Because tomorrow morning I'll flatly deny I said any of it.'

Philip pulled the car sharply into the verge and kissed her. Her mouth opened and her tongue jabbed at his teeth. Eventually she pulled away and said:

'I'm not one for car sex much, either. The gear handle's digging into my leg and I want to get closer to you but I can't. Take me home and tuck me up in bed. Lord, I must be crazy . . . crazy . . . crazy . . . You're the first man I've kissed since . . .'

'Since who?'

'Oh forget it. *Forget it*,' she shouted and fiercely switched off the car radio.

At her flat door neither of them spoke. She opened the door and Philip followed her upstairs in silence. She led him into a small sitting-room with pink *toile de joie* wallpaper and red curtains. The gas fire was on. She threw off her wrap, sank into the sofa with a sigh, and rested her head on the back, eyes closed, legs stretched straight in front of her. She kicked off her shoes.

'Say something to me,' she said softly.

Philip knelt on the sofa beside her and kissed her. The only sound was the muffled drone of the gas fire. He slid his hand down over her plunging décolletage inside her dress. She flinched as he touched her nipple and kissed him more passionately, biting at his lower lip.

'Carry me next door. To my bedroom,' she whispered between kisses.

He picked her up, carried her down the passage and kicked open the first door. 'Don't put on the light – there's enough,' she said. There was a street lamp outside the window which lit the room with a grey light diffused through the muslin curtains. He laid her on the bed.

'Unzip me,' she said, rolling over on to her stomach: 'Throw the clothes on to that chair.'

Soon she lay on her stomach on the eiderdown, naked, her hands up round her head, her long blonde hair spilling down over her bare shoulders. She was breathing quickly. Philip felt his heart hammer. It was weeks – no, *months* – since he had seen a girl naked – since that nurse on the troopship. He gazed eagerly at the full lines of her naked body. He said softly: 'Turn over.'

She obeyed, keeping her hands up over her head. She seemed to flaunt her nakedness at him. Philip began undressing, throwing his clothes on to the armchair on top of hers. She said: 'What are you doing?'

'Undressing.'

She got up with a start: 'Listen: I want you beside me naked, I want you to *sleep* beside me naked, but there's one thing you mustn't do – and that's make complete love to me. Do you promise?'

'Yes yes, of course.'

'No, really promise, because I mean it. I really mean it.'

'Yes. I promise. Get into bed now. You'll catch cold.'

She spoke from under the sheets: 'You won't try anything on while I'm asleep now, will you? Because I'll wake up. You really *promise*?'

Philip got into bed beside her, feeling her cool body alongside his own: 'Yes, I promise.'

'You can do anything you like to me – except *that*. She grasped him under the sheets. 'You promise me you won't, don't you, because——'

He muffled her words with a kiss. She said breathlessly:

'Do you understand? Please understand me . . .'

'I promise. I promise.'

The two naked bodies writhed and wrestled together,

groping and panting, each longing for the other, yet reluctantly accepting that a complete union on that night must not be. There will be other times, thought Philip . . . she wants me, I can *feel* she wants me.

* * *

'Where the *hell* have you been?' Gerald was standing on the doorstep when Philip returned. 'It's ten past nine. I nearly called the police.'

'Sorry,' said Philip, handing over the ignition key. 'I got a bit held up.' He grinned at Gerald.

'It's no laughing matter. I won't lend you the car again if you're going to stay out all night like this. You look a positive mess. Like a partridge pulled through a hedge backwards.' Gerald scanned the car for dents.

Philip said: 'It's virgin, I can assure you. Not a scratch.'

'Huh – more than can be said for your bird, no doubt,' said Gerald sarcastically, climbing into the driver's seat. 'And, by the way, your mother's already been on. I had to say you were in the bath. Will you call her back immediately. See you this evening.'

Gerald started up the E-type and disappeared down Pavilion Road.

My mother? thought Philip. What on earth could *she* want that was urgent? He had only had sporadic and stilted conversations on the telephone with her since his father's outburst. He had never called her, it was always she who called him – and always when his father was out. And the idea of him going down for the weekend had never been mentioned again – thank goodness!

He went upstairs and dialled her number on STD: 'Hello? It's Philip.'

'Darling. Lovely to hear you. Sorry to call so early but

32

I wanted to be sure to catch you. Did you have a lovely bath?'

'What? Oh yes, thanks.'

'The thing is this: Rodney Stafford, a great friend of mine, as you know, owns that firm called British Building, which is the biggest building firm in the Midlands. And Rodney says you might be *just* the man they're looking for.'

'But, Mother – '

'And Rodney has mentioned your name to the managing director, a man called Hector Busby, who's frightfully interested in the idea of you joining them. He's already got a training course mapped out for you and he's simply longing to meet you.'

'But, Mother, I've already——'

'This Hector Busby's a frightfully busy man and very difficult to pin down, and this evening was the only evening he could do for months and months. So I said you could dine with him this evening, darling. I do hope that's all right. You simply *must* cancel everything else. It's frightfully important for your future.'

'But, Mother, I've already passed the tests at an advertising agency and said I could join them in three months' time.'

'An advertising agency? Darling, *do* get your priorities right – this is the biggest building firm in the Midlands. You might be a director in no time at all, making pots of money. Anyway, I've said you'll meet Mr Busby at 7.45 tonight in the foyer of the Waldorf Hotel. Don't let me down, darling, *will* you? It's so important for us *all*. The advertising agency can wait – after all, they can't be very keen to have you if you have to wait three months, can they? Just meet this nice Mr Busby and see what he's got to offer. That's all I ask.'

Philip had made another date with Shirley that night,

but he said: 'All right, mother, I'll do it. 7.45 at the Waldorf – Mr. Busby.'

'Oh darling, how wonderful of you. I'm sure you won't regret it. *Such* an opportunity for a bright young man. Let me know how it all goes. I can't wait to hear *all* about Mr Busby.'

* * *

As Philip walked into the Waldorf foyer, a small dumpy man aged about fifty-five with pink cheeks and sleek white hair, wearing a dark-blue double-breasted pin-stripe suit, rose from an armchair, folded up his evening paper and came across to him:

'Mr Philip Rodolphin?' The voice had a slight North Country accent.

'Yes. You must be——'

'Busby. Hector Busby. Pleased to meet you.' They shook hands. 'Fancy a cocktail?' Philip nodded:

'A very good idea.'

'Lead on to the bar then.' Philip ordered a vodka and tonic, Mr Busby a Martini 'very dry'.

'It's very good of you to see me like this, Mr Busby.'

'Oh not at all. Not at all. We're always on the lookout for promising young types. Lord Stafford, our Chairman, mentioned you as being interested, and as I was down in town for a few days I thought I'd kill two birds with one stone, as you might say.'

Mr Busby finished his Martini in one gulp.

'You're nursing that drink a bit, aren't you, Philip? Mind if I call you Philip? So much easier than the formal Mr Rodolphin, don't you think?'

'Please do.'

Mr Busby ordered another Martini. 'So you're interested in joining the building trade, eh?'

'Well——'

'Fine trade for anyone these days. Been in it thirty-five years myself. Never regretted a moment of it. Got to the top, too, all on my own, without any of your fancy public-school background. Oh, no offence meant, but you get my point, don't you, Philip—eh?'

'Yes of course.'

Mr Busby gulped down his second Martini and beckoned the waiter to bring another. Philip still had half his drink left; he said: 'What would I have to do to start with? I have no experience at all, you see. Just six years in the Army.'

'No problem. No problem at all. We'd send you to Derby for a year. To start at the bottom just like anyone else. Working in all the different departments. You'd get your hands dirty just like everyone else. Best way to learn. I like you, Philip.' Mr Busby patted Philip's knee. 'You'd do far worse things than join us, I can tell you. The sky's the limit for a bright ambitious young fellow, especially with the right background like you've got. Always helps, you know, always helps. Might as well admit it – it always helps and I'd be a fool to deny it.' He patted Philip's knee again and ordered another Martini.

Two Martinis later, they went into the restaurant to dine. During dinner Philip tried to get Mr Busby to expand on what he would have to do during his first year in Derby, but to no avail. Mr Busby was much more interested in finding out about the Rodolphin family, or in telling Philip about his wife Martha and his two teenage daughters Avril and Muriel.

'Avril's the extrovert type, Muriel's the opposite. Amazing how different two daughters can be. And there's only eighteen months between them, too. Avril wants to be a model, Muriel wants to be an architect . . . I don't know

35

why I'm telling you all this, Philip. It's just that I feel at home with you, you know. Do you understand me?' He patted Philip's knee again.

'Yes, of course. But tell me a little more about what I'd have to do when I started, what I'd get paid and so on.'

'Oh come off it, Phil, don't let's talk shop and spoil an excellent dinner. You'd walk it in the firm, I'll tell you that. No problems. A year or two of dirtying your hands and you'd walk it. On the board in no time. With the Chairman behind you what else can you expect? Whereas the likes of me – now I slogged away for twenty years, right from nothing. And look where I am now. I made it to the top, so God's grief *you* ought to be able to – with all the advantages you start out with.'

Mr Busby drained his glass of claret and said: 'Now for some brandy, eh, Phil?'

'I'd prefer some Kummel on the rocks, please.'

'Kummel? OK then. Kummel it will be. I'll stick to brandy myself.'

'Thank you very much for the excellent dinner.'

'But the evening's only just started. What say you to coming along to some night spot with me? – showing me the ropes, you might say.' Philip look disconcerted: the idea of accompanying Mr Busby to a night-club filled him with dread. He was bored stiff, and quite convinced that the last thing he would do would be to join Mr Busby's firm.

Then Mr Busby rambled on into a series of reminiscences about his early days with the firm. Philip nodded politely at the right moments, but his thoughts were with Shirley. He wondered what she would do with herself that evening: she had not been too pleased when he telephoned to say he couldn't make it.

'Have I done something wrong?' she had said.

'No, no. It's just that my mother has fixed some blasted dinner with some tycoon of industry. Trying to get me a job. I'll have to go.'

'Oh. That's really all it is?' She had not sounded convinced.

Eventually Mr Busby and Philip were the last two diners in the restaurant. The head waiter stood nearby and pointedly looked at his watch.

'We seem to be outstaying our welcome, eh?' said Mr Busby with a rumbling laugh. 'Waiter – please send a bottle of Hines and a bottle of Kummel and some ice up to room 217, will you?'

'No no,' said Philip hastily. 'I really mustn't keep you up too late. I must be getting home.'

'Nonsense, Phil. The night is young and you are so beautiful, eh eh?' He roared with laughter, slapping Philip on the thigh and squeezing his kneecap.

He signed the bill and led Philip to the lift, ushering him gently by the elbow. As they left the lift on the second floor, he flamboyantly pressed a pound note in the lift-boy's breast pocket, saying loudly:

'Don't spend it all on sweets, my boy.' Mr Busby guffawed. Philip was convinced that after all that drink Mr Busby must be very drunk indeed, and his behaviour did nothing to dispel Philip's opinion. After all, the man had had *four* large brandies, let alone the Martinis and the wine beforehand.

Mr Busby fumbled for his door-key. He found it, but couldn't get it in the lock.

'Let me help,' said Philip, taking the key and unlocking the door.

'Thank you, Phil, thank you, Phil,' said Mr Busby, laughing to himself. 'A little bit of what you fancy never does you any harm, don't you agree, Phil, eh?'

Mr Busby closed the door with a slam and waved Philip to a chair. He himself pulled up another chair close beside.

'The drinks 'll be here shortly,' he said, leaning forward and putting both hands on Philip's knees. His eyes would not focus. He reached in his breast pocket and pulled out a pair of black horn-rimmed spectacles, which he put on slightly askew. 'Ah, now I can see you properly, Phil. Phil, has anyone ever told you – ' he looked drunkenly at Philip's face – 'what a very handsome fellow you are, eh Phil?' His hands squeezed Philip's knees. Philip sat quite still.

Mr Busby leaned forward till his face was inches from Philip's. He said quietly, slurring his words: 'Phil, I like you very much. Do you mind?'

His face lunged forward. Philip ducked his head. Mr Busby's mouth brushed his hair. Philip sprang up from the chair. With all the force of his right fist he struck Mr Busby across the jaw, knocking the horn-rimmed spectacles into the corner of the room where they hit the tin waste-paper-basket with a clang. Mr Busby lay on the floor rubbing his jaw with his hand, a dazed expression in his eyes. He said slurringly and lamely: 'Now, Phil, don't take it bad, don't get me wrong . . .'

Philip threw open the door and collided with a waiter carrying a tray on which were two glasses, a jug of ice, a bottle of brandy and a bottle of Kummel. The tray fell to the floor with a crash, the waiter looked stunned. Philip did not stop. He ran down the passage and pressed the lift-button viciously.

4

'Darling, tell me *all* about your dinner last night. How did it go?'

It was his mother on the telephone at 8.45 am the next morning.

'It was fine.'

'Did you fix anything?'

'No. I don't really think I want to join that firm.'

'Darling, do think carefully before you decide. It's a wonderful opportunity. Rodney Stafford's a very powerful figure, you know.'

'I would much prefer to go into advertising. That's all there is to it, really. I heard what Mr Busby had to say and it hasn't altered my opinion. But it was useful to see him. It clarified things for me.'

'Was he a *nice* man?'

'Oh yes, very nice. That's not the point, though.'

'You didn't have a row or anything ghastly, did you, darling?'

'No, no. But I've just decided that I would prefer to go into the advertising business. That's all. There's nothing more to it.'

'Rodney said Hector Busby was such a nice man——'

'He was. He was perfectly nice. He gave me an excellent dinner.'

'But you've made your mind up – even though Rodney says you could be a director in no time?'

'Yes. I prefer the idea of the advertising business. Apart from anything else, I don't want to go and live in Derby.'

'But, darling, it's only for one year. And think of the opportunities *after* that. Don't let a year in Derby put you off. Did you say you'd get in touch with Mr Busby? How did you leave it with him?'

'I think he understood my point of view perfectly.'

'You didn't offend him or anything, darling, did you? You weren't offhand, were you? Because it was very nice of him to spare the time to give you dinner.'

'No, I just made it quite clear to him that I didn't want to join his firm, that's all.'

'Oh darling, I do hope you did it *tactfully*, after all the *trouble* he's taken. And Rodney, too.'

'Yes yes, stop worrying. Oh, by the way, what does Father think of . . . me getting a job and all that?'

'Darling, he hasn't said a thing. He's still livid that you left the Army.'

*　　　*　　　*

Philip thereafter began seeing Shirley almost every day. When the day was warm enough and she was free for lunch, they would lie together on the grass in Hyde Park, eating sandwiches and apples. On the evenings she was free, they would go to the cinema and eat a hamburger afterwards, then go home to her flat. Even when she had another date for dinner, she would usually insist on meeting him at her flat at some early hour of the morning, so they could sleep together. Although they both now seemed to accept it as quite natural that they slept together at every available opportunity and behaved outwardly as lovers, she would still not allow him to make complete love to her.

'I'll do anything you want me to do – to you,' she would say sweetly but firmly. 'And you can do anything you like to me – except that. You'll have to understand me. Please, Philip – it's not so hard to bear when I give you everything else, is it?'

She would never explain her reason further than to say enigmatically that she had learned her lesson once before and she wasn't going to make the same mistake again.

Although he knew he wasn't really in love with her, he found her an increasingly amusing companion, quite apart from the obvious delight she took in appealing to him physically. She was never moody, always sympathetic, laughed readily, and was unrepentently flirtatious. She was especially proud of her breasts and took every opportunity of drawing his attention to them. They were, Philip admitted, very beautiful and deserved every bit of attention he could give them.

One sunny day at lunch in Hyde Park he brought along his private collection of poems and bits of his favourite prose that he had written into a red-leather-bound volume he had carried with him wherever he had gone in the Army.

'I want you to read some of it,' he said. 'See, there's a lock on it and nobody else except you has ever read it. I used to read bits of it at night by torchlight in the desert.'

She took the book tenderly, noting his initials stamped in gold on the front: 'What a wonderful idea to copy out all your favourite things. It's like carrying round a complete library in one book.'

'I know most of them by heart,' he said. She flicked through the pages:

'What beautiful handwriting you've got. What's that here?'

'It's Greek.'

'What does it say?'

'It's the bit from the Odyssey when Odysseus returns home in disgrace after years of absence and his old dog Argos, lying neglected and flea-ridden outside the house, recognises his master and has just enough strength to wag his tail before dying.'

'Oh what a sad story. Translate it for me line by line.'

Slowly he translated the hexameters. When he had finished, there were tears in her eyes. She squeezed his hand: 'You must have a very soft heart to have put in that particular bit. Read me some more.' She lay back with her eyes closed and her long blonde hair tumbling over the grass, holding one of his hands between both of hers lying on her breast. 'Read me some Keats – is there some?'

He read her a Keats sonnet. She suddenly said quietly: 'Philip, it's my birthday next week. Do you feel like giving me something I'd really love for ever?'

He nodded: 'Tell me what.'

'A book with a lock and my initials on it just like yours, so I can start writing in all my favourite things. But I'd like mine to be green, not red.' She sat up and looked at him, her hair almost covering one eye. He kissed her. She slowly pulled him down on the grass on top of her and put her hands tight round his neck . . .

When he left her to return to her office, he went straight to Hatchard's in Piccadilly and ordered a green calf-bound volume with a lock and the initials 'SS' in gold on the spine.

*   *   *

That evening, when Gerald came home to the flat from his office, he said to Philip: 'Hello, stranger. Never see you these days now you've found this bird you're keeping so secret. Why don't you ever bring her round here?'

'I will, I will. But she's got a flat of her own.'

'Listen, there's a charity bollock next Tuesday and I've got a party of chums together for it. Why don't you and she join us for it? Should be a bit of a mob. I'll sock you two tickets so you can go free.'

'Oh thank you. I think that's her birthday night, so that might be fun. I'll ring and check if she's free.'

'What, you let her go out with other chaps, do you? You don't exercise a monopoly in that direction yet?'

'I don't *stop* her going out if she wants to.'

'Broadminded and big-hearted of you, old man. Probably pay off in the end. Nothing like giving them a bit of the old rope. Are you dead keen on the bird then?'

'Fairly interested. I'd put it like that. You'll like her. She's very what you might call well built.'

'I should damn well hope she is after all the time you've been spending with her. *And*, I might add, I wouldn't lend you the old E-type for you to take out some scruffy old bag in. Give her a ring now to check if she's free on Tuesday. We'll all meet here for drinks at 7.30. Tell her she'd better wear a long dress.'

Philip telephoned Shirley who said she'd love to come.

'That's fixed then,' said Philip.

'Well done, old man,' said Gerald. 'By the way, Tuesday'll also be a bit of a last celebration for me. I've got some news for you.'

'What?'

'They told me today they want me to go to the New York office for two years. To learn the ropes in Wall

43

Street. I go in ten days' time. All a bit sudden, but it's been simmering a bit for some time off and on.'

'But, Gerald, what'll happen about the flat?'

'Well I've decided already about that. I don't want to let it to anyone else, so if you'd like to stay on in it on your own, you're more than welcome.'

'That's extremely kind of you, but I don't think I could afford the rent——'

'Don't worry about rent or anything like that. Father's taken care of all that. If you can just do the rates and Mrs Drinkwater, and keep it in good sort of order, that'll suit me fine.'

'Gerald, that's more than generous of you.'

'Not at all, old man, not at all. Now I must fix up my own little dolly for this bollock.' He thumbed through his Hermes address-book, musing: 'Now which lamb shall I lead to the slaughter on Tuesday, eh, eh?'

*   *   *

On the next Tuesday evening at 7.15 pm Philip borrowed Gerald's E-type to go round and pick up Shirley. She wore a long, low, yellow satin dress. Her hair was swept back in a chignon.

'My, you look beautiful. I've never seen you this dolled up before.'

'Thank you, love. Come to think of it, I've never seen you in a dinner-jacket. And you don't look so dusty yourself.'

He took her arm and guided her down the steps to the car: 'Gerald said I really ought to be wearing white tie and tails. But I haven't got any and I couldn't be bothered to hire some just for some old charity ball.'

'You look smashing. I wouldn't worry a damn. I hate

dancing with men in stiff shirts, anyway. It's so hard on my bosom.'

In the car she said: 'Love, you don't think I'm showing too much bosom, do you? Not that I can do anything about it, but I'd just like to know.'

She arched her back and held out her breasts: their slopes were full and prominent over the low neckline which stopped only just above the nipples. He gently kissed each slope: 'They look proud, defiant, utterly dishy. Gerald's eyes'll pop out of his head when you walk in.'

'What I'm worried about is that *I'll* do the popping out. I'll have to dance very carefully. I haven't worn this dress for ages and I must have added several inches to my most vital statistic. You see, if I bend down I'm sure a nip will pop out. Mustn't drop my napkin, but if you see me looking too décolletée, for God's sake say something, love, won't you?'

'Don't worry. You'll slay them all. If you've got something worth showing why not show them, that's what I say. Though I don't want you to cause a stampede – I might get killed in the rush.'

She laughed. 'Who else is going to be there? I mean, in Gerald's party? No one too frightening, I hope.'

'I've never met any of them. But there's Toby and Belinda Caterham——'

'You mean the Marquess and Marchioness of? The Duke of Surrey's son – no chin and thick glasses, who's always in the gossip columns?'

'Exactly.'

'She looks a right little minx. Deb of the Year my foot. Her mother just had the best publicity agent.'

'Now, now, don't be catty. She landed a Marquess

anyway. She may be perfectly charming.' Philip laughed. 'Then there's Gerald's girl Jennifer Pendennis——'

'What, Lord Chief Justice Pendennis' daughter who did a strip-tease at the Commem Ball? The leading light of the pot-smoking Chelsea set?'

'I presume so. I'm not as up in these social backgrounds as you are.'

'Well I just read William Hickey, that's all. You'd have to have been blind and deaf last year not to have heard about Jenny Pendennis. Well, I can see we're in for a wild night. I hope I can compete with this glittering company. Sure I won't let you down? The only way I can compete for sensation is with my neckline. Perhaps I'd better actually *arrange* for my bosom to fall out——'

'You can arrange for that as soon as I take you home – but not one moment sooner . . .'

* * *

At the flat the others were all waiting with drinks in their hands. Philip introduced Shirley to Gerald, then Gerald introduced them both to Toby and Belinda Caterham and Jennifer Pendennis. Philip noticed the Marquess eying Shirley's neckline in unabashed amazement as he shook hands, his lanky bespectacled figure drooping over Shirley like a wilting tulip. He was in white tie and tails, and his high collar together with his hooked nose accentuated the impression of having no chin: his mouth seemed to go straight to his Adam's Apple, which bobbed up and down like a yo-yo over his butterfly tie as he spoke.

The Marchioness, a neat, nervy, spindle-thin figure with short chestnut hair and a rather horsy face, wore a long pink tulle dress with a large bow on her bottom.

Jennifer Pendennis had a pert nose and a face like a hedge-sparrow with straggly black hair; she wore a long black dress with white shapes all over the skirt like a jigsaw puzzle.

Philip noted with pride that Shirley, with her chignon, her bare creamy shoulders, slim waist and plunging neckline, made the other two girls look like a couple of also-rans. Gerald's approval was evident in his face as he brought her a vodka and tonic. The Marquess was still surreptitiously ogling Shirley through his thick spectacle lenses.

'So you're defying convention, are you?' Belinda said rather bossily to Philip, who looked surprised. 'I mean, you're not bothering to put on a white tie?'

'I haven't got one. Anyway, one feels so much more comfortable like this.'

'I hope Mummy doesn't see you,' retorted Belinda. 'She's on the Committee for the ball and she forced Toby at gun-point to wear *his* tails. She'll be furious with you for letting the side down when *we're* all wearing long.'

Bugger Mummy, said Philip under his breath, smiling sweetly at Belinda.

'Gerald says you play the guitar quite beautifully,' she continued. 'I *do* hope we can hear you sometime. Perhaps you should have done the cabaret at the ball. I *wish* Mummy had known. Toby darling——' she shouted across at Toby who had pinned Shirley in a corner – 'What little tiny fools we were not to think of telling Mummy about Philip.'

'What, darling? Philip? Mummy?' Toby came lankily over.

'Yes, about his divine guitar-playing. He'd have been simply perfect for the cabaret at the ball.'

47

'Oh yes, cabaret at the ball, I see, I see, darling. Perfect. Been playing long?'

'About twelve years,' answered Philip.

'Should be OK by now then, eh? Ha ha. Lots of practice and all that. Scales and things, like on the piano?'

'Yes. Scales and chord sequences, harmonic progressions and so on.'

'Oh yes yes, harmonic progressions. Sounds quite the expert, doesn't he, darling?'

'But Gerald says he's simply *brilliant*, darling. *Do* let's get him to play. Gerald, is there time for Philip to play before we go?'

'No no,' said Philip hastily, shaking his head at Gerald who was talking quietly to Jennifer.

Jennifer came across to Philip and said: 'Will you give me lessons? I'd love to be able to play. Just a few chords to accompany myself singing.'

'You sing then?' Philip asked.

'For my sins. I warble the odd folk ditty.'

'I'll certainly teach you. It's very easy to pick up enough chords to get by on.'

'Come on,' shouted Gerald. 'Down drinks. We must be getting on, otherwise Belinda's ma will be after my hide.'

Belinda said: 'Yes, for God's sake. I promised Mummy we'd be punctual.'

'Toby,' said Gerald. 'Can you possibly give Philip and Shirley a lift? There isn't room in the E-type.'

Toby answered: 'If they don't mind sitting on top of each other 'cos there isn't much room in our job either.'

'We'll squeeze in,' said Philip with a wink at Shirley, who was watching the group with ill-concealed amusement.

48

'Mustn't squash your delightful dress, must we?' said Toby archly, patting Shirley on the bottom like a horse.

Belinda said loudly: 'Darling, will you fetch my coat? Hurry.'

Jennifer stretched her arms to the ceiling, put her head on one side, and said with a sigh: 'Oh, I feel like going quite and utterly *mad* tonight.'

Gerald said: 'Oh God, hoist storm-cones and seal down hatches, everyone. We know what that means. Jennifer, now you're to behave yourself. Remember Belinda's ma will be watching.'

'Bugger Belinda's ma,' said Jennifer.

'What, what?' said Toby, blinking at her. Belinda was putting on her coat, so she had not heard.

'Nothing, nothing,' said Jennifer, prancing to the door and taking Gerald's arm. 'Come on, honey-bunch, fly me to the moon in that dishy car of yours. Cloud Nine, here I come . . .'

*   *   *

Philip and Shirley bent double and crawled into the back of the Caterham's blue Lancia. 'Watch your hair on the roof,' warned Philip.

'Sure you're all right in the back there?' said Belinda from the front seat. 'Couldn't Shirley squeeze in between us in the front, darling?'

Toby said: 'Darling, it'd be absolutely impossible to change gear without the most obscene things happening to poor Shirley. If you can stick it in the back——'

'Yes, we're fine,' said Philip, nudging Shirley.

'Anyway it's only to Grosvenor House. Think you can last out?' asked Toby, turning his head round.

'Darling, do look where we're going and stop looking round at . . . the back seat,' ordered Belinda.

Chastened, Toby peered ahead, hunched over the steering wheel like a giraffe. Belinda turned round just as Philip was going to kiss Shirley's cheek. He pretended to be adjusting his position. Belinda said to Shirley: 'Are you a model or something?'

'No,' Shirley said. 'I wish I was. I'm only a sort of receptionist-cum-secretary.'

'With what people?'

'With an advertising agency.'

'What, in Paddington or somewhere?'

'No, in Park Lane – just next to Grosvenor House.'

'Oh, my dear, how frightfully grand.' Belinda sounded impressed. She went on, to Philip: 'Gerald said something about you looking for a job in advertising.'

'Yes, I've got one. In two months' time. In the same firm as Shirley.'

'How frightfully cosy. Did you hear that, darling?' She nudged Toby. 'Philip's going to work for the same firm as Shirley.'

'Oh, smashing, splendid, good idea.' Toby started to look round at Shirley, but Belinda snapped: '*Darling*, will you keep your eyes on the *road*.'

'Sorry, darling. Doing the old level best. Don't worry – I'll get you all there in one piece, what?'

Philip nudged Shirley who burst out laughing. Belinda swivelled round: 'What's the joke? Philip, what did you say? Come on, let us in on it.'

Shirley said: 'It's nothing. Philip just tickled me, that's all.'

Belinda said: 'Oh!' She sounded unconvinced.

Toby said under his breath: 'He'd be mad if he didn't . . .'

'What, darling?'

'Oh nothing, nothing. Here we are. Safe and sound at Grosvenor House.'

The doorman rushed up to the car and opened Belinda's door with a flourish.

' 'Evening, my lady. 'Evening, my lord.'

5

The dinner was for 600 guests in the huge Grosvenor House ballroom. Each party had its own table. Gerald efficiently led his party to a round table for six just beside the dance floor.

A string quartet was playing soft music on the dais, completely drowned by the chatter of the guests trying to locate their right tables. Waiters bustled to and fro, clanking trays and flourishing bottles of white wine. Then, when nearly everyone was seated, at some given signal another army of waiters descended on the tables from the kitchens, bearing plates of sole in white sauce.

Philip was placed between Belinda and Jennifer, Shirley between Gerald and Toby. Toby immediately engaged Shirley in conversation, while Gerald turned to Belinda. Philip said to Jennifer: 'I was abroad last year, but I hear you did a famous strip-tease dance at the Commem Ball.'

'Oh dearie me,' Jennifer said, 'and what a lot of hot water it got me into. I even got into *Time* magazine, in the "People" section. Of course I suppose people don't really *expect* a Lord Chief Justice's daughter to strip in public, do they?'

'No, probably not.'

'But, you see, I have this fantastic urge to show off my body. I mean, I'm proud of it, it's quite a *good* body, and I want people to *see* it. I mean, Philip, I've been shedding my clothes ever since I came out of cotton wool two years ago. And the thing is, at the parties in Chelsea with *my* set, *my* friends, nobody takes a blind bit of notice when I prance about in my underwear, and eventually in the nude, which is so much more satisfying. I mean, my friends just go on talking or snogging or whatever they're doing, and let me carry on with no fuss, no bother. Yet when I shed one measly top garment at the Commem Ball, all hell breaks loose. Christ, I thought under-graduates were *used* to that sort of thing.'

'They may have been, but the Press probably wasn't.'

'Oh, it's all so silly. Just because Daddy's a Lord Chief Justice they all expect me to be some sort of sheltered blue-stocking. I mean, there's girls stripping day and night in clubs all over London, Manchester, Birmingham and Newcastle. And nobody writes a word about *them* in the papers. Yet when measly Miss Jennifer Pendennis starts unzipping her skirt at a Commem Ball, there's a major international crisis. Crazy, isn't it?'

'I can vaguely understand why, I must admit. But tell me how you got to know Gerald. Because he's not the Chelsea Set, is he?'

'Gerald?' She laughed loudly. A waiter filled her glass with white wine for the third time. 'Gerald's always trying to *rescue* me from pot and the Chelsea set. Do you want to know how we met? It was terribly romantic. Or it would have been with anyone but Gerald. I'd gone to this afternoon wine and cheese party in Palace Street, just behind Buckingham Palace. At someone's flat, I can't remember who now, but he had this wild collection of Stan Getz records, and Stan Getz sends me wild. The others were all dancing and snogging round the place, and I did my strip-tease. Right down to nothing. Then I had to rush to the loo, and when I came out they'd locked the door on me so I couldn't get back to my clothes. They all thought it a big joke, you see, me being stuck on the landing, starkers. So I thought Ha Ha, I'll fix them, and

I pinched a black mackintosh that was hanging up and put it on. No shoes, no nothing, just a black mac over a bare body. I walked down Constitution Hill with my thumb up for a hitch-hike and it was the rush hour and there was a traffic jam, and I said to myself "The first car that stops with only one man inside I'm going to get into." And it was Gerald in his white E-type.'

'You mean you just got in?'

'He stopped, I opened the door, got in and sat down. He looked at my bare feet and said "Good God, my dear girl, you'll catch your death of cold." And I opened the mac to show I had nothing on underneath, and he said "My dear girl, I don't know who you are but you could be arrested for going about like that. Right outside Buckingham Palace, too." And I just burst out laughing. Then he took me to his flat and gave me some brandy and some Anadin, to keep off flu, he said. I told him what I'd been doing and he had to give *himself* some brandy. Do you know, from that day to this he's never made a pass at me. He's like a brother to me. I'll miss him when he goes to New York.'

'Maybe I could take over his role.'

'You? You're much too sexy-looking to be a brother. Admit it now – if I got into *your* car in Constitution Hill wearing nothing but a black mac, you wouldn't just give me Anadin and brandy, *would* you?'

'No. Probably not.'

'There. I knew it. Anyway you've got that gorgeous blonde girl. She's looking at you now.' The waiters were clearing away the chicken plates.

Belinda shouted peremptorily over the table: 'All change now.' To Toby: 'Darling, talk to Jennifer. I'm going to talk to Philip. You've been doing very well with Miss Pendennis.'

Philip said: 'A very interesting girl. No lack of conversation there.'

'You just bring it out in her skilfully, that's what it is. Now do the same to me.' Belinda did her best to look coquettish, fluttering her false eyelashes.

Philip laughed with embarrassment: 'Well, that's a challenge. I don't quite know how to begin.'

'I'll tell you: you probably want to know why I married so young. Everyone does. After all, I'm only just nineteen. And we've been married nearly a year.'

'Yes, I must confess it would interest me to know that,' Philip lied: he was much more interested in carrying on the conversation with Jennifer that Belinda had so abruptly and officiously stopped.

'People will probably tell you, because people are such bitches, that I married Toby for his title and his money. I can tell you, the last thing in the world I want to be is a Duchess. But as I'm going to be one, I might as well accept it and treat the whole thing as a lot of fun, don't you think? Enter into the spirit of the thing? It's the only thing to do. I could so easily become smug and bossy and officious, but I'm jolly well not going to. Toby and I have a perfect understanding. I married him because I know he's the only man for me. I just know it in my bones. We understand each other so completely.'

To Toby: 'Darling, *darling*, please get that silly old waiter back here with the wine. I'm *dying* for another drink. So is Philip. Darling, *wave* for him, *shout* for him, don't just *sit* there. *Do* something.'

Belinda waved, the waiter rushed up, then she said to Philip again: 'You must think I'm very precocious for my age. But Mummy always said I was sort of . . . well . . . advanced, you know.' She looked across at Shirley and said quietly: 'You know, I simply *wish* I had a bosom like that girlfriend of yours. Somehow I feel it's the only thing I lack. Toby's mad on bosoms——' She checked herself – 'but I think he's grown out of that now. I told him it was a silly adolescent thing to need a girl with a large bosom and I think he's accepted it. After all, you really can't judge a girl just by her bosom, *can* you now?'

'No no, of course not,' said Philip enthusiastically.

Confrey Phillips' band struck up 'The Lady is a Tramp'. Gerald leaned across to Belinda and said: 'A dance, Marchioness? I believe it's the correct thing to do for the host to dance with the lady on his right.'

'Thank you, Gerald, I'd love to.' Philip looked quickly across at Shirley and nodded towards the dance floor. She rose straightaway.

'How have you been getting on?' Philip asked as they danced.

'Well, it's been quite an ordeal. I looked across at you several times and you were so engrossed you never even noticed me.'

'Nonsense. I looked across at *you* several times and you were so deep in conversation that you never even noticed *me*.'

'Oh well,' she laughed. 'Obviously we've both been huge successes with our dinner partners. Gerald, I must say, is sweet and kind. A bit pompous, but sweet and kind all the same. It's jolly nice of him to let you have the flat while he's in New York.'

'I know. I've told him so often.

'Well, don't you forget it. I'm amazed at his kindness. He's very fond of you.'

'I can't think why. I've done nothing but be a bore to him.'

'Well he is, anyway. But that Toby – honestly. He's a

right hard case, if you ask me. He spent most of the time staring down my cleavage.'

'I know. Belinda told me he was keen on it.'

'Yes, but when you *talk* to a girl you usually look her in the eyes, not in the nipples, don't you? Honestly, I thought his great hooked nose was going to disappear down my dress once or twice.'

'What did he talk about?'

'Oh, he went on and on about being married so young – what is he, twenty-three? – and how he couldn't get used to the idea of having only one woman for the rest of his life but how lost he would be without Belinda and her mother who were the only women who'd ever tried to understand him. *She's* a little minx, my God: *she* knows which side of her bread is buttered. Acting the Duchess already. She treats him *abominably*. I wouldn't stand it if I were him.'

'She's probably the only girl ever to have taken any interest in him.'

'Nonsense. The son and heir of a duke, especially a rich duke, always gets the girls *and* the mothers interested – even if he looks as goofy as this one. He asked me if I could ever have lunch with him.'

'What did you say?'

'I said No because I always had lunch with you whenever I was free. How about that for loyalty! I'll bet you wouldn't have said the same thing about me if Belinda had asked *you* to lunch.'

'Well, that's different.'

'Why?'

'Anyway, I wouldn't *want* to have lunch with Belinda. Come on – let's go and sit down and hear some more laughs. They're all going back to the table.'

Philip and Shirley were the last to rejoin the group.

57

As they sat down, a salvo of bread rolls descended on the table like a hail of bullets.

'Oh lord,' said Belinda, looking round for the source of the salvo. 'Oh, it's Buster Pomeroy. It *would* be. Trust *him* to start a scene.'

Toby was gathering up the bread rolls and hurling them back at Buster Pomeroy's table. 'Darling, *don't*,' Belinda shouted. But Toby did not hear over the cheers from the tables round him. He hurled bread roll after bread roll at the Pomeroy table. When he had exhausted his supply, he reached for a soda-water siphon on the table. Just as he turned to level it at his target, a bread roll struck him hard on the nose and dislodged his spectacles. He checked, swivelled, and levelled the siphon at the nearest figure to him – which happened to be an imposing, elderly matron with grey hair and a long pink dress who was advancing towards the table.

The jet of soda-water hit her straight on the chin. A look of intense anger passed over her features, immediately followed by a look of sheer delight. 'Why, Toby darling, it's ME, Mummy-in-law,' she shrieked, as Toby prepared to fire another burst. Belinda rushed up to Toby and put his glasses back on his nose.

'You've hit Mummy, you *fool*,' she spat.

'Oh God, I'm sorry, I really am sorry,' bleated Toby.

'It couldn't matter less,' said Belinda's mother, wiping the soda-water out of her eyes. 'Just as long as you're all enjoying yourselves. Toby, darling——'

A bread roll hit the back of her neck. She winced, then caught sight of Philip in his dinner jacket. She winced again. Bread rolls were still flying between the Pomeroy table and Toby.

'Mummy, this is Philip Rodolphin.' Philip rose. 'He hasn't *got* a tail-coat.'

'Hasn't he heard of Moss Bros?' said Belinda's mother acidly. Then another jet of soda-water hit her on the forehead. Toby had lost his glasses again and had mistaken her for one of Buster Pomeroy's party. She grinned manfully, the soda-water dripping from her chin down her dress.

'Darling, stop it *at once*,' yelped Belinda. 'This is *too much*. Tell Buster we'll all meet up later at the Romeo. And put down that bloody soda-water siphon.'

Belinda grabbed it from him. In so doing she accidentally pressed the lever which unleashed a jet straight between Toby's eyes.

'You silly little *idiot*,' said her mother furiously, picking up a napkin to mop Toby's face with tender affection.

*　　*　　*

The Romeo Club was a plush night-club in Curzon Street, 'in the heart of Mayfair' as it proudly proclaimed in red lights over the door. Philip had often heard Gerald talk of the place, but he had never been there before.

When the Caterhams' car, with Philip and Shirley again squashed in the back, drew up outside the Romeo's door, there was the same instant recognition and attitude of respect from the doorman, the same deferential tone of the ' 'Evening, my lady. 'Evening, my lord.'

Belinda swept in as if she owned the place.

In the foyer – which had red velvet walls like every other room in the Club – Belinda was greeted effusively by a short, fat, bald man wearing a dinner jacket and white shirt much too small for him, holding the longest cigar Philip had ever seen. He bent low and kissed Belinda's hand.

'Ah, my favourite Marchioness, the most beautiful

Marchioness in Europe,' he said in a strong Italian accent. He turned to Toby: 'And my favourite Marquess in the whole of *Debrett*'s.' He embraced Toby round the waist and kissed his shirt-front with a loud smacking noise: 'How grateful I am that you have deigned to patronise my humble little establishment yet again.'

He kissed Belinda's hand again with a breathed 'Ah, Marchioness, but you are so irresistibly beautiful tonight.'

'Randi,' said Belinda, quite unmoved by this display of Continental gallantry. 'This is Mr. Philip Rodolphin and Miss Shirley Snow.'

'Ah, any friend of the Marchioness is immediately a friend of mine. Welcome to my humble little establishment. Are you related to Mr Gerald Rodolphin, sir?'

'I'm his cousin. He's coming any moment.'

'Ah, Mr Gerald – one of my most loyal customers.' He picked up a form from the table and handed it to Philip. 'Please, sir, would you do me the honour of filling in this form so that I may make you an honorary life member immediately.'

Philip folded up the form and put it in his pocket. Randi clapped twice loudly and spoke in strident Italian to the head waiter, who guided the four of them to what was obviously the best table in the room. A discotheque was blaring out the latest pop records. A few couples were dancing closely in the dim-lit room. Almost as soon as they sat down, two waiters came running up with champagne bottles in silver chalices.

'Did we order champagne, darling?' asked Toby.

The head waiter interrupted: 'Excuse me, mi'lord, this is with the personal compliments of Mr Ravello.'

'Oh really, how damned generous,' said Toby.

'Darling, you know he always does this every time we come and he just puts it down on someone else's bill when they're too drunk to notice,' said Belinda in her most strident voice.

'Don't be so bloody ungrateful, darling,' said Toby.

Gerald and Jennifer joined them with much flurrying of waiters.

'Randi Ravello seems quite a character,' Philip said to Belinda.

'Don't you know Randi?' she asked with surprise. 'He's the most charming night-club owner in London. It was really because of him that Toby and I got married. One night when I was in here with someone else he didn't really approve of, he whispered to me he'd found the perfect man for me. So he put Toby, who was out with some awful bird, at the next-door table. We made eyes at each other all through dinner and that was that. Randi gave him my telephone number and he rang first thing the next morning. So romantic, don't you think? Darling –' She shouted across at Toby who was deep in conversation with Shirley – 'do ask Randi over to our table for a drink so Philip can get to know him.'

Toby stammered: 'All right, darling' and summoned a waiter. In a few seconds, Randi Ravello appeared, long cigar in hand, and bowed low to Belinda: 'Marchioness, I am indeed honoured.' The waiter brought a chair for him and placed it next to Belinda, between her and Philip. Another waiter appeared with a huge goblet of brandy and handed it to Randi, who grasped it with both hands and swilled the brandy around. 'To your delectable beauty, Marchioness.' He raised his glass to Belinda and drank a deep gulp.

Belinda said, nudging Philip: 'Randi, tell Philip all about yourself.'

'Ah, Mr. Rodolphin,' said Randi, 'you want to know about me? I am the last of the long line of Ravello princes.

My full name is Prince Randolph Ravello. But as my title is not officially recognised by Her Majesty, I have dropped it. And anyway I do not consider it fitting for a prince of noble blood to run a humble –' he gestured round the room – 'little establishment such as this. Although, if I may say so myself – ' his voice rose to a crescendo – 'it is the outstanding night-club in swinging London. No other place can touch it for elegance, beauty, panache, class, taste.' A waiter came up and whispered in his ear: he listened, then replied in a flow of loud jabbering Italian, banging his fist on the table as he spoke. The waiter retreated in dismay.

'Forgive me, Marchioness. A little domestic trouble.' He raised his glass to Belinda and drank again. 'I am doing *fantastic* business these days. Last night we were packed: I could not have fitted even you in at all, Marchioness. We had the Duchess of Kent, Prince Rainier and Princess Grace, Gregory Peck, Sophia Loren, Michael Caine. Last week it was just the same. Every night jam-packed. We had the Shah of Persia——'

Belinda interrupted: 'I didn't know he was over here.'

'Secret visit, secret visit,' Randi said confidentially. 'Then there was the Aga Khan, the Snowdons, the Duke of Bedford – ah, Marchioness, I could go on for ever. Business is *fantastic*.'

'You don't seem to be very full tonight,' said Belinda chirpily.

'Ten minutes ago you couldn't *move* in here. And in ten minutes' time it will be the same. You mark my words.'

'Tell Philip what you did in the war, Randi.'

'Ah, the war. I was a major in the Life Guards. I went with them right through Alamein, Sicily, up Italy, then Normandy and right through to Berlin. Sonny Blandford and David Westmorland, they were under me as my troop commanders. Fine boys they were, fine boys. See, look at this – ' he pulled up his right trouser leg to show a bandage with a red slash on it. 'I was shot in the leg at Anzio. It still bleeds. I have not been able to dance since that day. My wound plays me up very badly but the doctors say there is nothing to be done.' A waiter came up and whispered in his ear. He launched into another tirade, banging his fist again on the table. Belinda whispered to Philip: 'He spent the war in a camp for undesirable aliens near High Wycombe. The bandage is for his varicose veins.'

Philip said: 'What about the blood though?'

'Blood?' whispered Belinda. 'That's not blood. It's red ink. He puts it on every day.'

'Ah, Marchioness,' Randi went on, having dismissed the waiter with a shout, 'I am having such trouble. The pianist in my bar has walked out on me. He has given me a week's notice, the fool. And I pay him *fifty* pounds a week. *Fifty* pounds, the best money in London.'

Belinda nudged Philip: 'Randi, I have an idea. Why don't you replace him with a guitarist. Guitars are all the rage now, and so are folk-songs.'

'Ah, Marchioness, if I could find the right one, a good one, I would. The only bar in Mayfair to have a guitarist to play and sing for you. It would be good, you are right, Marchioness.'

'I know the perfect man for you.'

'Tell me where I can find him.' Randi produced a pen and pad from his pocket. 'With your recommendation, Marchioness, I would take him without an audition.'

'He's sitting right beside you – Philip Rodolphin.'

Randi swung round to Philip: 'You play the guitar and sing?'

'Yes.'

63

'He's brilliant,' said Belinda.

'You play and sing for me then? Fifty pounds a week?'

'Well I'd like——'

'Philip, you *must*, you *must*,' shouted Belinda.

Randi put out his right hand to shake Philip's hand: 'It's fixed then. I will make you the most famous guitarist in England. When can you start? Monday week?'

Philip laughed helplessly: 'Yes, I suppose I could.' He shook Randi's hand.

'You wear dinner-jacket and play from 7 till 11. Then I give you dinner. And you can invite any of your friends in to have dinner – free on me.'

'That's very kind of you.' Belinda smiled glowingly at Philip.

'Come, I show you the bar where you will play.' Randi stood up. Philip followed him down a passage to a dim-lit bar, the walls of which were dark wood panelling and hung with what looked like ancestral portraits in gilt frames. A huge chandelier of cut glass hung from the centre of the ceiling. Randi pointed to the piano: 'That's where you will stand.' He indicated the microphone and loudspeakers. 'All the latest equipment. Nothing but the best.' He tapped the microphone to show it was working.

'Fine,' said Philip. Randi grasped his elbow. 'My boy, I will make you the most famous guitarist in Europe. What relation are you to Lord Rodolphin?'

'Grandson.'

'Good, good. Will he come in to hear you?'

'I think he's really too old for night-clubs.'

'Too *old*? Never. I will count it a great honour to give him a dinner of caviare, grouse, champagne, anything – as my guest. Tell him.'

'I will, but I don't think he'll come.'

'My boy.' Randi guided him back to the dancing room.

64

'This could be an important stepping-stone in your career. Anyone who works for me is made. They become a household word. And anyone the Marchioness recommends I would be a fool not to take on. She is my favourite customer. Now she will come every night. *Every* night.' He cackled with glee.

As they entered the dancing room, Philip saw that a group was playing loud beat music on the stand and all the spotlights had been turned up on to one lone figure on the dance floor. Everyone else was standing round, cheering and clapping hands in time to the music.

It was Jennifer Pendennis, dancing a wild dance, throwing her legs and arms all over the place. Then she began undulating slowly, rhythmically, and her hands went behind her back. Suddenly her blouse flew off, exposing a small black bra. The onlookers cheered and shouted 'More.' Randi was puffing excitedly on his cigar, standing on tiptoe, craning his head over the crowd to see what was going on.

Then Jennifer threw off her skirt, leaving herself only in a pair of transparent pink pants and a black suspender belt. The cheering and clapping rose to a crescendo. People crowded round the dance floor to look. The band played louder and faster.

Jennifer undid her suspender belt, threw it off into the crowd and began unrolling a stocking.

'That girl is with the Marchioness, is she not?' shouted Randi. 'Who is she?'

Philip shouted back: 'Jennifer Pendennis.'

'Jennifer *Pendennis*, the Lord Chief Justice's daughter?'

Philip nodded.

Just as Jennifer was about to unhook her bra, having taken off both her stockings and flung them into the crowd, Gerald rushed out on to the dance floor, picked her up bodily and carried her, kicking in fury, back to the table. The crowd laughed and booed good-naturedly. There was a roll on the drums and a lot of clapping.

Over the noise Philip heard Randi shout at a waiter: 'Get me William Hickey on the telephone. Fast, boy, *fast*.'

6

'Well, I must say,' said Shirley. 'Old Horse-face Belinda certainly turned up trumps fixing that job for you at the Romeo. Fifty quid a week. That'll solve all your problems.'

Philip said: 'Yes. Just when my Army savings were running out, too. I'll have to practise a bit though. I'm a bit rusty, and I don't want to let Belinda down after the big build-up.'

They were lying naked in bed together in Shirley's flat. It was an hour after Jennifer's strip-tease at the Romeo. They had taken a taxi to avoid the crush in the back of the Caterhams' car.

On the bedside table lay the green leather book with the lock and her initials on, which he had given her earlier that day. She leaned across and picked it up. 'Philip, will you write the first poem in it for me? The one that will remind you most of me?'

'I'll have to take it back with me. I can't remember a whole poem these days. My memory's going.'

'All right. Take it away with you and don't tell me which poem you're going to choose—so it will be a surprise.' She put back the book, then leaned down and kissed him thoughtfully.

'And another thing,' she said after a long kiss, 'I've been thinking – now you're going to be playing seven nights a week in the Romeo bar, next weekend'll be your last free weekend. And I wondered – would you like to come home with me for the weekend?'

'Up in Northumberland? Yes, I'd love to.'

'Oh Philip, it would be such fun. I'd love you to meet

my father and mother. They're so easy – nothing like Belinda's ghastly mummy.' They both laughed. She went on: 'We'll go up on Thursday afternoon and down on Sunday night. I'll get time off from the agency. They always give it to me – they're very good about that. Is that a deal?'

'It's a deal.' Philip pushed her head down on the pillow, looked at her lovingly for a moment, then their mouths met. He felt her thighs squirm under the pressure of his. If only she would let him make love to her completely ... what a *waste* it seemed. After all, they were both naked and what was the difference? Still, it was a difference she seemed to value, and he had to respect her wishes. He couldn't really complain, after all, considering the way she gave him – and *loved* giving him– all of the *outside* of her body. And what a voluptuous body it was ... But still he wanted it all. And he knew that sooner or later he would get it. He knew, he knew . . .

* * *

That Thursday Philip and Shirley caught the midday train from King's Cross to Newcastle. At Newcastle Station they were met by Evans, the Snows' chauffeur-gardener-handyman, in a Humber shooting-brake. Evans drove them at a hearse-like speed the twelve miles to Farrow House where Shirley's parents lived.

Farrow House was an old rectory standing in a large walled garden, with a short crescent drive in the front, and a white wooden gate at each end leading on to the main road.

When Philip and Shirley arrived, they were ushered straight into the dining-room where Shirley's parents had already started their soup.

'We do hope you don't mind us starting,' said Lady Snow as Shirley introduced Philip. 'But we're so used to the trains being late. And Lancelot's a stickler for punctuality, aren't you, darling?'

Sir Lancelot grunted, shook hands with Philip, kissed Shirley, and then went straight back to his soup, which he drank extremely noisily. He was a tall, well-built man with a ruddy face, a moustache, and greying hair that curled up round his ears and round the back of his head in little ducks'-tails. He wore a crimson velvet smoking-jacket with a white carnation in the buttonhole.

Shirley had told Philip all about her parents on the train journey. Sir Lancelot Snow, MC, TD, MP, had been Tory member for his Northumbrian constituency for twenty-one years. He was one of the most respected and flamboyant Tory back-benchers – and also one of the most eccentric. He was a director of no less than twenty-three different companies ranging from an electronics firm to a chiropodists' instruments business – though what he did in his capacity as director nobody quite knew. Certainly he had a large and extravagantly furnished office-flat in Mount Street, Mayfair, where he held court during the week and always employed the prettiest of secretaries, whose mini-skirted bottoms he would flagrantly and jocularly pinch in the presence of the most august visitors. Lady Snow was kept strictly at home in Northumberland except on occasions of great social or domestic importance, when she was allowed to pay a fleeting visit to the capital, and then be sent packing off home again. 'Your place is in the constituency, Dolly,' Sir Lancelot would boom. 'Nursing it while I'm in London.'

During the war Sir Lancelot had been a major in the Life Guards seconded to the Special Air Service. On an airdrop he always defied custom by making his batman jump first, so that the batman would be on the ground to fold up his parachute for him. He was also an amateur pianist of some ability who had had lessons from Carroll Gibbons. During the Italian campaign he had 'requisitioned' a grand piano and a chandelier from an Italian mansion and had them both fitted into the back of an Army 3-ton truck. He used to don his dinner-jacket even when shelling was on, have the chandelier lit by a generator, and play cocktail music to his soldiers on the grand piano. Rumour had it that this was how he earned his MC and that the citation had read that his bravery included 'deliberately diverting the enemy artillery from more important targets'.

Lady Snow – or 'Dolly' as almost everyone seemed to call her – was a tall, wide-hipped matron with a loud, strident voice and a prominent aquiline nose. Her grey hair fell loosely down to her shoulders or was swept back in a bun. She was a staunch Roman Catholic, madly in love with her husband, and stoically overlooked all his obvious faults.

At dinner Shirley and her mother did most of the talking, with Philip answering the occasional question from Lady Snow. Sir Lancelot let out the odd grunt or guffaw, and spent most of his time seeing that both his and Philip's wine-glasses were kept well filled.

At the end of dinner there was an ear-splitting screech from the hall, suggesting that a woman was about to be strangled. Philip looked up in concern.

'Don't worry,' said Lady Snow quickly. 'That's only Cocky complaining that no one's paying any attention to him.'

'Cocky is Daddy's cockatoo,' explained Shirley. Sir Lancelot rose from the table. As he left the room, Philip saw that the back of his crimson velvet smoking-jacket was spotted with white stains.

'Let's play some bridge. Shirley says you're very good,' said Lady Snow. 'Lancelot's mad about bridge.'

They all moved into the sitting-room across the hall to find Sir Lancelot playing 'Tea for Two' on the piano with a large and ferocious-looking white cockatoo sitting on his left shoulder. Every so often the cockatoo would let out a terrible shriek, at which Lady Snow would quietly say: 'There, there, Cocky, we all love you *very* much.'

'He doesn't like strangers,' roared Sir Lancelot at Philip as the cockatoo let out a series of shrieks in Philip's direction. Lady Snow busied herself arranging the card-table: 'Let's play bridge, darling.'

They drew for partners and Philip found himself playing with Sir Lancelot against Shirley and her mother. Sir Lancelot offered Philip brandy.

'Thank you, sir.'

'Don't call me "sir" whatever you do,' growled Sir Lancelot.

When the game of bridge started, Philip found himself unable to concentrate because each time he had to play a card Cocky the cockatoo would dance up and down on Sir Lancelot's shoulders, raising and lowering his crest, letting out the most terrible shrieks. Consequently Philip played extremely badly and the ladies won both the rubbers. Sir Lancelot said nothing. By now his left ear-lobe was bleeding profusely where Cocky had pecked it playfully, and the blood frequently splashed on to the cards as he played them. Some drops had even landed on his white carnation.

'Time for bed now, Cocky,' said Sir Lancelot, getting up from the table at the end of the second rubber. The cockatoo shrieked. As Sir Lancelot left the room, Philip saw that the shoulder and back of his smoking-jacket was covered with fresh droppings.

'He really loves that bird Cocky,' giggled Lady Snow. 'I often think Cocky's the only reason he ever comes home. I sometimes wish he'd choose something a bit quieter – like a canary or a budgerigar.'

*   *   *

When they all went upstairs to bed, Philip found that his bedroom was next door to Shirley's. He undressed, washed, cleaned his teeth, then tiptoed out into the passage in his pyjamas and knocked softly on Shirley's door.

'Come in,' he heard her say quietly. She was in bed with her bedside light on: 'Oh, it's you. I thought it was Mummy.'

Philip stood by the side of her bed caressing her hair on the pillow: 'What a terrifying man your father is. I couldn't play a single hand properly with those eagle eyes on me.'

'He's not really a bit frightening. It's all an act.'

'And that cockatoo.'

'Oh, Cocky. Just one of Daddy's minor eccentricities. I think it's rather lovable.'

'Lovable it may be, but with that damned bird shrieking at you every time you play, do you wonder I didn't play a card right? I even forgot to count trumps.'

'Daddy didn't mind.'

'He looked livid when we lost.'

'No, no, that's all an act. He loved you.'

'He never spoke.'

'That means he's taken to you. When he doesn't like

someone, he never draws breath. Making needling little remarks.'

Philip leaned down and kissed her mouth. She wound her arms round his neck. He broke away and lifted up her bedclothes as if to get in beside her. She said quickly: 'No, no, you can't do that.'

He looked amazed: 'Why not?'

'No, no. Please. Not here. Not at home.'

'But why not?'

'Because . . . because I don't want to. Not here at home. Anyway, Mummy might come in to say goodnight and that would be awful.'

'She won't come in now. She said goodnight to you already.'

'She might. You never know with her. Anyway, Philip, I don't want you to. Not here. Not in my own home. I wouldn't feel it was . . . well, *right*. Do you understand?'

'Not really. I mean, every night we've——'

'Well, please try. I don't want to. So be a darling and go back to your own room. Don't make a scene now. Sleep well.' She blew him a kiss and snuggled down under the sheets.

He closed her door and tiptoed back to his own room, wondering at her decision, but accepting it nonetheless.

*　　*　　*

The next three days were, for Philip, especially pleasant and relaxing. Apart from breakfast and dinner, when Sir Lancelot and Lady Snow were present, he had Shirley completely to himself. She took him all round the estate in the Land Rover, and when it was sunny she took him up The Law, the highest point for miles around, to see the

73

view. The Law was a gently sloping hill covered with long grass which overlooked the surrounding countryside.

They would lie together on a tartan rug under the clear blue sky, hidden from everything by the long grass. It was an oasis of privacy. She would delight in letting Philip strip her. First the sweater, then the brassière, leaving her naked from the waist up. Then Philip would catch her as she made a mock attempt to run away, and unzip her skirt. She had already taken off her shoes, and she wore no stockings, so that left her completely naked except for her frilly underpants.

'Take them off me,' she would say. And Philip would slide them down over her thighs and down her legs to leave her completely naked in the sunlight. She would dance around the little clearing they had made in the long grass, jumping and throwing herself about, revelling in the joy of utter nakedness in the open air. Then Philip would catch her again, pin her to the ground and kiss her.

'Why won't you let me sleep with you while we're here?' he would say softly.

'Oh, Philip, don't let's go into that. Let's enjoy ourselves *here*.' And she would kiss him again more passionately.

But her passion was confined to their meetings on The Law. She would never relax her rule about him not joining her in bed at her home, however much he questioned, however much he objected. In the end he gave up, no longer expecting anything from her in her home. He still didn't understand why, but he knew he must accept her ruling.

Sunday evening came. 'We haven't booked a sleeper,' said Shirley to her mother, 'but I'm sure we'll be able to get one once we get on board the train.'

'Darling, don't be too certain,' said her mother nervously.

'Typical of you – leaving everything to the last minute,' growled Sir Lancelot, shaking his head as Cocky took another bite out of his ear-lobe.

Evans the chauffeur drove Philip and Shirley to the station after dinner. As the London train drew in, Shirley said to Philip: 'Leave it to me.'

She accosted a sleeper attendant who was looking out of the window: 'Can you let us have two sleepers, please?'

'Come in, miss, and we'll see what we can do for you,' said the attendant. Philip and Shirley boarded the train with their luggage, having said goodbye to Evans. Shortly after the train had started, the attendant came up and said to Shirley: 'Sorry, miss, all I can do is to let you have a double second-class.'

Shirley said: 'Oh, that's fine,' looking at Philip for acknowledgement. She picked up her vanity case and made to follow the attendant. The attendant picked up their suitcases and led them to a double sleeper, one berth above the other, in the next carriage. He switched on the light and ushered Shirley in. 'You're sure this is all right, *miss*?' he asked pointedly.

'Yes,' said Shirley, laying her vanity case on the lower bunk. 'That's just what we wanted.' She pressed a ten-shilling note into his hand. 'Call us at seven o'clock, will you please?'

Philip followed her into the sleeper door. The attendant squeezed past Philip and said goodnight. When he had gone, Philip said to Shirley: 'That was pretty cool of you.'

'Come on. You take the top bunk, I'll take the bottom.' She began to take off her clothes. Philip climbed up into the top bunk and began to get undressed. When he was in his pyjamas, he leaned over to look at Shirley. She

75

was in her short Baby-Doll night-dress, looking at herself in the mirror, putting cream on her face. Her nipples showed through the night-dress. He said:

'I hope you're not going to be as stand-offish as you have been for the past three nights.'

'Wait and see,' she said. The train rocked and sent her gripping for the door-rail to keep her steady. She continued to cream her face. Soon she put the cream-pot down on the shelf and climbed into bed. Philip leaned over from the bunk above: 'Don't I get a goodnight kiss?'

'If you come and get it,' she said coquettishly, switching off the main light and leaving only the blue light on.

The train lurched as he climbed down to her in the lower bunk.

'Take off your pyjamas,' she said in a whisper as he stood beside her.

He obeyed. 'Take off your night-dress.'

She moved about for a minute, then threw the night-dress out at his feet. She lifted the sheet for him to climb in beside her. The sleeper was so narrow that he had to lie half on top of her.

She moved under him sensually as the train lurched from side to side. They kissed and explored each other with slow hands. Eventually she said, in a low whisper: 'Philip, I want you now. All of you.'

He said: 'You've said that before.'

'No, but this time I mean it.' He laughed into her hair: 'You've said that before, too.' The train swung again from side to side.

'This time you see I mean it. This is the time I've been waiting for.'

He said quickly: 'No, you mustn't.' He raised his head to look at her. There were tears in her eyes.

'Yes,' she said. 'I want you.' She pushed him, groaned

and whispered: 'That's marvellous. Keep it like that, keep it like that. Just like *that*.' She swung to and fro with the rhythm of the train. She was warm and wet. He whispered back:

'But you've never let me before. Why *now*?'

'Just keep it like that, like *that*. Give it all to me. All, all, all.'

*   *   *

They did not speak after they had made love. Shirley lay naked on the bottom bunk, her right arm over her eyes, her head turned to the wall. She was breathing quickly, heaving up and down with each intake of breath. Philip climbed the ladder to the top bunk, put on his pyjamas and got under the bedclothes. He leaned down to look at her: she was still exactly as he had left her. He said: 'Don't catch cold. You'd better pull the clothes up over you.'

Without moving her right arm from where it was shielding her eyes, she pulled the blankets up over her with her left hand. Philip said: 'Are you all right?'

Again, without moving her right arm, she nodded twice. Philip lay down. It was a long time before he went to sleep.

*   *   *

When he awoke, the train was stationary. He looked at his watch: 6.30 am. This must be King's Cross. Then he heard the muffled sounds of her crying. He leaned down: 'What's wrong?'

She didn't answer. He climbed down the ladder. Her face was buried in the pillow. He touched her bare shoulder. She shrugged his hand off: 'Don't touch me, don't touch me.' She was sobbing.

They each got dressed in total silence. At seven o'clock

the attendant knocked. 'Thank you, we're awake,' said Shirley through the door.

When they were both dressed and ready, Philip said: 'Come on, we'll go and get a taxi.' He took her by the elbow. Again she shook his hand off saying: 'Please – I've already asked you: don't touch me.'

They walked to the taxi rank in silence. Philip gave the taxi-driver her address first and then Pavilion Road. In the cab she nestled into the corner of the seat, as far away from Philip as she could get.

'What have I done?' he said eventually.

'It's not what *you've* done, it's what *I've* done,' she started sobbing again. 'You wouldn't understand, but the last time I did that, behaved like that, it ended up with me having to have an . . . abortion.' She put her head in her hands and cried uncontrollably. He patted her shoulder. Again she spat: 'Don't touch me, don't touch me. If you touch me again, I'll get out of the cab at the next lights.'

When the taxi arrived at her flat, she grabbed her suitcase, wiped away her tears with her other hand, and said to Philip over her shoulder: 'Don't get in touch with me. I'll . . . I'll write to you. Wait for me to write. Sorry about . . .' Then she slammed the door and ran up the steps.

Philip called out through the window: 'Thank you for a wonderful weekend.' The taxi-driver let out the clutch. Philip's last view of her was fumbling in her bag for her keys, wiping her tears with her arm.

*　　　*　　　*

At lunch-time, he got a letter from her, delivered by hand from BDP. 'Darling Philip, Please forgive me for my behaviour this morning. And, for that matter, last night. I should not have let you make love to me. I don't know why I did. I must have been crazy. I suppose it was because I thought I loved you, and I suppose I do in a way, but love is wrong when it leads to this. Ours has been a brush-fire romance which has burst and crackled, and when the fire dies there will only be ashes. It is best for both of us if we stop seeing each other now, before we reach the ashes and have an even bigger disaster. Believe me, I know where this can all lead to. Don't call me, don't write, forget me completely – though I will never be able to forget you. Even so, it is better for us both that I try. Good luck at the Romeo. Love and xxx's – S.

P.S. I will still love your book of poems even though I mustn't love *you*.

P.P.S. Do try to understand me just a *little*. I *know* I'm doing the right thing. But sometimes it's *right* to do the wrong thing.'

7

It was fortunate for Philip that he was starting to play at the Romeo Club that Monday evening: the expectation of it served to distract him from brooding too much over Shirley. What had he done wrong? he kept asking himself. Surely she must have accepted all along that sooner or later they would make love together completely? It just couldn't have gone on on that basis, all the time nearly but not quite. She had never told him about the abortion before, but he supposed that that had a lot to do with her behaviour. A residual guilt complex? Or was it all just an excuse because he had proved to be a great disappointment as a lover? After all those weeks of looking forward to it, had she been terribly let down by the reality when it had eventually happened? He couldn't get it out of his mind that he had been, in some significant way, a terrible failure. After all, if he had been a success, would she have behaved as she was doing? No, obviously not. That was the way his logic ran, anyway – right or wrong.

He decided it was pointless to try to telephone her in her present mood, so he spent most of the day practising on his guitar. At 6 pm he changed into his dinner-jacket. Just before he was about to telephone for a taxi, Gerald returned: 'My dear old man, I'll take you. Must be in on the opening night. Toby and Belinda are turning up, too.'

On the way to the Romeo Club in Gerald's car, Gerald asked: 'Well, old man, how did the weekend chez Snow go? Spiffing?'

'We had a very relaxed time,' said Philip, guardedly.

Gerald said teasingly: 'Shirley as come hitherish as ever, eh?' Philip laughed.

'She was sweet – as she always is.' He was determined not to reveal to Gerald a trace of the impasse that had developed between him and Shirley.

'Is she coming to see you tonight?'

'No, I don't think so,' muttered Philip. 'She has another date fixed.'

'Good God, I should have thought the least the wench could do would be to turn up to lend you her support on your opening night.' Gerald sounded disapproving.

When they arrived at the Romeo, Randi Ravello was there on his doorstep to greet them, dinner-jacketed, brandishing the inevitable king-size cigar.

'Ah, Philip, my boy,' he put his arm round Philip's shoulders. 'Between us we're going to make the Romeo bar THE THE THE place in London. I tell you, you are the biggest thing to happen to the Romeo in the twelve years I have had it. Do you know that?'

'I'm sure Philip'll do you proud,' said Gerald.

They walked through the foyer, down the passage into the bar.

'See,' said Randi excitedly, 'I have bought you a brand-new microphone. And look.' He pointed to the cards laid on each table and picked one up to show to Philip. The card read 'Entertaining in the Romeo Bar— PHILIP RODOLPHIN on the guitar.'

'See, I have everything beautifully organised for you,' Randi went on. 'I tell you, boy, this is a big night for the Romeo. *And* for you. You will be the biggest attraction in London by the time I have finished with you, boy. You mark my words, boy.'

At the moment the bar was empty except for the barman, who was polishing glasses and putting out crisps and olives in saucers.

'I have asked everyone for 7.30 – to give you a chance to warm up,' said Randi, as if sensing his thoughts. 'By 7.30 the joint will be – how you say it? – jumping. Now, Philip – I call you Philip from now on, OK, boy? – you start away, you start away.'

Philip tuned his guitar, tapped the microphone, then sang two songs. Randi and Gerald, who were now sitting together at a table drinking Martinis, clapped loudly as he finished.

'Joe, give the guitar-player boy a drink,' roared Randi at the barman. 'Go on, Philip, keep going! Get warmed up, boy!' He waved his cigar about like a conductor's baton. A long piece of ash fell off the end of it into the saucer of olives. 'Here, boy – here,' he shouted at the barman, holding out the saucer towards him. 'I have stuffed these olives. Ho ho, ho ho, ho ho.' He slapped Gerald on the back just as Gerald was sipping his Martini so the whole drink flew across the table, splashing into the saucer of crisps. 'Oh I am so sorry, so very sorry,' roared Randi. He held out the saucer of crisps to the barman: 'Now I have stuffed the crisps, too. Ho ho, ho ho, ho ho. What a night, what a night. Never a dull moment at the Romeo, is there?' He leaned confidentially over to Gerald: 'I have asked everyone who is *anyone* here to-night: Princess Margaret and Tony, the Duke and Duchess of Kent, Prince William of Gloucester——'

'I thought he was in Lagos, Randi,' interrupted Gerald.

Without the flicker of an eyelid, Randi went on: 'Yes, but he's flying back specially. Lady Docker, Twiggy, Onassis, Charlie Clore, Paul Getty, the Countess of Dartmouth, Jean Shrimpton——'

The list would have gone on for ever if Toby and Belinda Caterham had not appeared in the doorway. 'Aha,' said Randi, leaping up and kissing Belinda's hand effusively, 'my favourite marchioness, the most beautiful marchioness in the world. Welcome to my humble little establishment. Barman, champagne.' He clapped his hands twice.

The Caterhams sat down beside Gerald with a wave at Philip who was playing and singing, fortified by the large vodka-on-the-rocks that Joe the barman had brought him on Randi's orders.

Gradually the bar filled up until all the tables were occupied and people were standing along the bar itself. Needless to say, none of the celebrities Randi had mentioned appeared, but there was certainly a good turn-out. Randi's public relations had been effective all right. It was only later that Philip learned that a large proportion of his audience consisted of representatives of the gossip columns and their girlfriends. As Philip was sipping his vodka in an interval between his numbers, his guitar resting on top of the piano, a man detached himself from the group at the bar and walked over to Philip. He was stocky, thick-set, with almost no neck. Brown greasy hair hung low over the collar of his white shirt which was a dirty brown where his hair had rubbed it. The collar of his grey suit was liberally flecked with dandruff. He had sunken eyes in a grey, pockmarked face. There was a small boil with a yellow pus-filled top on the side of his nose. His suède shoes were worn and scruffy, and one of the laces was undone. The knot of his brown knitted tie was very tight.

'Good evening, Mr Rodolphin,' he said in a smooth, silky voice. Philip noticed that he never once looked him directly in the eye. 'I'm Mervyn Twankey. I write for the Samuel Pepys Diary on the *Daily Echo*. Have you got a moment to talk now?'

'Well, I'll have to start playing again in a few minutes——'

'This won't take a second. Just a few questions.' Twankey's voice became even silkier. 'Randi did ask me along personally, you know.' Twankey had still not looked Philip directly in the eye. He offered Philip a cigarette out of a crushed Rothmans' carton from his pocket which Philip declined, and then lit one himself from the stub of his old one. His fingers were badly stained with nicotine, and his fingernails were long and black with dirt. There was a large wart on his right knuckle.

'You are Lord Rodolphin's grandson, aren't you?'

Philip nodded.

'If it's not a rude question, why exactly are you playing the guitar here?'

Philip looked nonplussed.

'I mean, Mr Rodolphin, your grandfather's known to be a profitable banker and you can't exactly be doing this for the money, can you?'

Philip said, a trifle angrily: 'I am certainly doing it for the money. I get no money from my grandfather. I am doing it because I like playing the guitar to people and Mr Ravello was kind enough——'

'OK, Mr Rodolphin, let's skip the soft soap, shall we? We all know that kindness was the last thing Randi had in mind when he offered you this job. It's just one big publicity stunt. I'm agreeably surprised, I must admit, that you can play the guitar and sing as well. In fact you play very well.'

Philip said brusquely: 'I can't see what publicity he thinks he'll get out of me.'

'Oh come come, Mr Rodolphin, don't let's be so naive,

84

shall we. Lord Rodolphin's grandson playing the guitar in a night-club bar? It's a great story. Has his lordship cut you off without a penny?'

'I've already told you, my grandfather doesn't give me any money anyway. He never has done.'

'Tell me, you're currently escorting Miss Shirley Snow, Sir Lancelot Snow's daughter, aren't you?'

Philip stared at Twankey in amazement. Twankey continued to look at Philip's stomach but never higher. Twankey went on: 'Any chance of an engagement there?'

'I – I am not escorting Miss Snow,' Philip stammered.

'But you were last week. You were a weekend guest at her home in Northumberland.'

Philip stared incredulously. Then he blurted: 'I am *not* escorting Miss Snow.' He took a quick gulp from his vodka.

'So the romance has broken up, has it?' Twankey persisted, the cigarette bobbing in his lips as he talked. His voice remained as silky as ever.

Philip said nothing. He picked up his guitar and fiddled with the tuning. Twankey purred on: 'I think I should tell you that I talked to Miss Snow on the telephone before coming here.' Philip looked up quickly. 'She confirmed,' went on Twankey, 'that your romance had ended. She did not say why, though. Would you care to tell me?'

'No, I would not. Look, I'll have to start playing and I——'

'Your father doesn't approve of your playing here, does he?'

'I really don't know——'

'I've spoken to him on the telephone this evening, too,' Twankey smirked. 'His reaction was, shall we say, hostile to the whole idea. By the way, Mr Rodolphin, why did you resign your commission in the Royal Scots?'

Before Philip had time to reply, Randi Ravello intervened with a loud: 'Now, Mervyn, my boy, see you write something nice about the Romeo's brilliant new guitar-player, eh? Marvellous, isn't he, eh, eh?'

'Yes, Randi, he's fabulous,' Twankey purred with an acid giggle. 'I think he should do the Romeo proud.'

*   *   *

Philip's stint ended at 11 pm. Randi was effusive in his praise and on the strength of Philip's success offered the Caterhams, Philip, Gerald and Jennifer Pendennis (who had turned up later) dinner on the house. The party was ostentatiously ushered to the table of honour, already laden with silver chalices containing champagne bottles.

During dinner Belinda said to Philip: 'What *were* you doing talking to that odious Mervyn Twankey?'

'You *know* Twankey?' Philip said, amazed.

'*Know* him? I should think we do. He's caused Toby and me more trouble than anyone else in the world. But he's clever, devilishly clever: he's always just within the law, so one can never sue.'

'He asked me some extremely awkward questions. He'd been on to Shirley, and my father, and he seemed to know everything about me.'

'Oh you can bet your boots if you're hiding even the teeniest skeleton in your cupboard, Twankey will sniff it out.'

'What kind of things has he done to you and Toby?'

'From the moment we started going out together he was on our trail night and day. I mean, I know Toby's a

86

duke's son and I was Deb of the Year, but we're not all *that* interesting. Yet you'd think that twelve million readers of the *Daily Echo* were rushing to their letterboxes every morning desperate to read the latest instalment in the Great Caterham Romance saga. It drove Mummy and Daddy up the wall. Twankey used to ring up almost hourly. And if no one would speak to him he'd appear on the doorstep. I remember once just after our engagement I got flu. Mummy and Daddy were out and Toby was visiting me. Twankey saw Toby go in, waited a few minutes, put on a long black overcoat and rang the bell. He was carrying a small black case and had a stethoscope round his neck. So Albina (that's our Spanish maid who had only just come over from Spain and was a bit goofy) she naturally thought he was the doctor when he said "I've come to see Miss Belinda." So she showed him into my bedroom. It was too awful because Toby was lying on the bed kissing me. Suddenly I looked up and there was Twankey scurrying to get his camera out of the little case. I screamed and both Toby and I jumped under the bedclothes, Toby fully clothed, dirty shoes and all. I screamed at Twankey that I'd call the police but I couldn't reach the telephone from under the bedclothes. So in the end, after pleading with us for a picture in that horrible smooth voice of his and us refusing point-blank, he left. He sent me a copy of the picture he took of Toby and me under the bedclothes – two huge lumps – saying he'd keep it and publish it during our honeymoon. But he never did. Obviously the paper didn't dare.

'Then there was our wedding rehearsal. Daddy was absolutely adamant that there should be no photographers allowed inside the church. Twankey kept on asking and asking but Daddy refused point-blank. So we went through the rehearsal and were walking down the aisle when the organist must have played the deepest note on his pedal. Anyway, there was a terrible noise like a deafening fart and the whole organ fused. Everyone looked up at the bass pipes and there sticking out of the slit in the biggest pipe was a long telephoto lens. It was Twankey. He had hidden *inside* the pipe and photographed the whole thing.

'Daddy was puce with rage and made him hand over the roll of film which Daddy then pulled out of the cassette. Daddy's language, in church *and* in front of the bishop, was *quite* appalling. I heard him say "fucking" twice and a whole host of "bloodys". I've never been so embarrassed in my life.

'Twankey plagues the life out of the Royal Family too. He stopped the council dust-cart one morning as it left the Kensington Palace driveway saying he was a detective and that Her Royal Highness had lost an ear-ring and had asked him to search the rubbish for it in case it had got thrown out by mistake. So the dustmen let him search right through the complete load looking for intimate stuff about Princess Margaret – which he would then have pieced together and sold for a fortune to some foreign magazine. He spent *five hours* searching that dust-cart while the dustmen just sat around drinking endless cups of tea.

'But there's one extraordinary thing about Twankey. You saw how revolting looking, how unattractive and how *dirty* he is?'

'Yes. Repulsive.'

'Well even so he always manages to have some pretty bird in tow.'

'What sort of bird?'

'Oh, some top model. Or starlet.'

'I suppose they're keen to get their pictures in his newspaper then?'

'Yes, there's always that angle. But he manages to *keep* them in tow quite successfully. He had one glamour number there with him tonight.'

'Yes, I saw her. Drinking like a fish. And laughing much too loudly.'

'I think she's a model called Tamara Reno.'

They had finished dinner. Suddenly Jennifer stood up, flung her arms high and wailed: 'Darlings, I feel like doing a simply *crazy* dance.'

That was enough for Gerald. He pulled her by the arm towards the door while she screamed: 'Randi adored my dance the last time.'

'But I didn't,' yelled Gerald back.

'I think Gerald's in love with that girl,' said Belinda primly.

'Mad chump if he is,' said Toby. 'She'd probably do a strip at the altar on her wedding day. Anyway, Gerald'll have seen so much of her body by now that there'd be little point in a honeymoon.'

'Darling, don't be bitchy,' said Belinda. '*You* were watching her closely enough last time.'

'Me? What, what?'

'I was watching you. Your spectacles steamed over.'

'Balls. Absolute balls.'

*　　*　　*

Next morning Philip rushed to open the *Daily Echo* at the Samuel Pepys Diary page. Under a huge headline of 'A RODOLPHIN SINGS FOR HIS SUPPER – After Romance Break-up with MP's daughter', the story ran: 'You never know who you're going to meet in Mayfair these days. Take Randi Ravello's Romeo Club. There, strumming a guitar and crooning his sad little ditties about love and life, is that epitome of aristocratic panache, Mr Philip Rodolphin, 25-year-old grandson of Lord Rodolphin, head of the famous banking family.

'Why are Philip's ditties so sad? For two very good reasons. "My family doesn't give me a penny," Philip told me as he sipped a vodka between numbers. "The damned fellow ought not to have resigned from the Army," thundered his father, Colonel the Honourable Jasper Rodolphin, from his country seat where he is Master of the Rodolphin Foxhounds. "Damned disgrace singing disgusting pop stuff in some bar or other. Letting down the family."

'And the other reason? Philip now sees no more of his recent lady-love, glamorous blonde Shirley Snow, 19-year-old daughter of Sir Lancelot Snow, Tory MP for Hesketh North. "Philip and I had a row about something, I'd rather not say what," Shirley confided in me yesterday tearfully. "We are not going steady any more. But I think he still loves me. There is no one else for me."

'One of Philip's favourite numbers? "Jealous Heart, oh Jealous Heart, stop weeping."

'The only member of the cast who appears to be pleased with this situation is Randi Ravello himself. He positively gloats over the sound of the cash-register clicking up cocktails for blue-bloods like the Marquess and Marchioness of Caterham who flock to hear Philip sing and strum of his lost love and his lost pounds, shillings and pence from the Rodolphin family coffers.'

8

During his first week playing at the Romeo Club, Philip quickly found that playing the guitar in a Mayfair night-club was a very different business from entertaining the battalion at concerts with adaptations of pop songs using scurrilous lyrics about the Regimental Sergeant Major and other prominent battalion figures such as Selma, the battalion whore (or 'bicycle' because everyone 'rode' her). In the Army he had known his audience exactly and could plot their precise reactions to a song or a joke. And consequently he had been the star turn at the battalion concerts and an automatically requested guest-performer at all the Company 'smokers', as the smaller concert evenings were called.

But in the Romeo he rapidly discovered that each night the audience were quite different. He could tell how different by the amount of attention they paid to him, by how much they talked during each particular song – and by the amount of drinks they bought him. It was lucky for him that he had a repertoire of about 300 songs of varied types – ballads, folk-songs, pop songs, traditional airs – which allowed him to chop and change his pro-gramme as the moods of his audience suggested.

He found that, while he was actually playing and singing, people either listened to him intently or ignored him completely, treating him like part of the furniture. People sitting near him seemed to think that while he was playing he was deaf to their conversation. Hence during the first week couples within earshot of him dis-cussed their most intimate problems, like marriage, divorce, illicit love affairs, and in one case an abortion. As soon as he stopped playing, the conversation would be abruptly switched off – and would not start again until he began playing once more.

When he arrived in the bar on his second night, he found a man sitting alone drinking at the table closest to the piano. At his feet lay a very mangy, ancient, brown bulldog, snorting through its teeth each time it breathed. The man was almost bald. A large hooked nose dominated a gaunt sun-tanned face. His eyes were very close together. He wore a check shirt, black tie, an elegant tightly-cut brown tweed suit, with very narrow trousers, and pointed, highly-polished brown shoes. He rose from his seat as Philip approached the piano with his guitar.

'May I introduce myself, Mr Rodolphin,' he said in a high-pitched mincing voice. He held out a thin freckled hand. 'I'm Kieron Phelps. Of no fixed employment.' He tittered nervously.

'How do you do,' said Philip distantly. The bulldog sniffed loudly at Philip's trousers.

'Oh, don't mind Clementine. She's just getting to know you.' Phelps tittered again nervously, swivelling at the hips as he did so. '*Do* have a drink with me before you start playing.'

'Thank you very much, but I have to start in a few minutes and——'

'Oh *come* on, Randi won't mind. And there's only me and Clementine in here at the moment. Joe, bring Mr Rodolphin the drink of his choice.'

Joe the barman nodded. Philip had no choice but to sit down at Phelps' table. He laid his guitar on top of the piano.

'I read *all* about you in the papers,' said Phelps in a crowing voice, putting his hand on Philip's knee and squeezing it. Clementine continued noisily sniffing Philip's trousers. Philip felt beads of sweat on his brow, although the bar was quite cool. Joe put a vodka-on-the-rocks down beside Philip.

'Why I came in to see you, Mr Rodolphin – oh, Mr Rodolphin is *so* formal, can I just call you Philip and you call me Kieron? – why I came in is because I have a lovely flat two doors away from here and I thought you might like to use it to change in, into your dinner-jacket, you see. I mean, you could leave your clothes there, there's simply *masses* of room because there's only me and Clementine' – he gave the bulldog an affectionate kick – 'and you could bathe there and everything. I mean, simply *everything* you needed. Perhaps, who knows?' – He bent his hooked nose close to Philip's face and squeezed his knee even harder – 'you might even want to take a nice little dolly back there one night. And *we* wouldn't mind, *would* we, Clementine?' He kicked the bulldog again, and giggled, while Clementine growled.

Philip felt a strong desire to rush from the bar. But he checked himself and stammered: 'That's extremely kind of you, Mr Phelps – '

'Oh come now, Kieron, *please*.'

' – Kieron, but I have a flat of my own not far from here where I can change. It's really quite convenient.'

'But I mean, dear Philip, one day you might be in the most dreadful rush and be desperate for a place to bathe and change nearer by. I'll tell you what, I'll give you the key – my name's on the door, number 86 – and then you can just drop in when you like.' He pulled a bunch of keys out of his pocket on a gold chain and began to take one off the key-ring.

Philip protested: 'No, really, it's most kind of you but –'

Phelps pressed the key into Philip's hand and closed his fingers round it.

'There, there, there. Remember any time you like. We'll expect you, won't we, Clementine? Now tell me all about yourself. Have you got some new devastating popsie tucked away somewhere? Is that why you ditched that poor Snow girl?' He tittered again, obviously relishing the idea of Shirley being 'ditched'.

Luckily for Philip, a couple entered the bar, so he didn't have to answer.

He got up, saying: 'I must start playing now. Thank you for the drink.'

Phelps gave a little wave of his fingers. 'Don't forget. Number 86. *Any* time you like. And I'll be listening to you, so play simply *beautifully*.'

Philip found it hard to play and sing that night, because every time he looked up he met Kieron Phelps' piercing, narrow eyes focussed on him, leering in the most unpleasant way.

Halfway through his stint, Philip followed Joe the barman out to the Gents'. 'Joe, who on earth is that Kieron Phelps?'

'Mr Phelps? He's an old customer. Rich as Croesus, queer as a coot. Keep your back to the wall when *he's* around, that's what I say. One night I was serving him a drink and he was a bit squiffed and he put his hand in my crutch, felt my balls and said "Hmm, Joe, quite a nice pair." I nearly crowned him with the tray, I did. But he's an old customer and he tips well, so I just forgot it. He's obviously got his eye on you, though.'

'I'll say he has. I can hardly play a note, the way he keeps staring at me.'

'Do you want me to get rid of him for you?'

'I'll say I do. But can you do it tactfully?'

94

'You just leave it to me.'

Phelps gave Philip a leering, toothy smile as he returned to his guitar and began playing. Philip wondered what Joe was going to do.

Suddenly he saw Joe crouch down beside the end of the bar and throw a stuffed olive along the carpet straight under the table of an elderly couple sitting in the middle of the room. They were obviously going to a ball as the man was in white tie and tails and the lady in a long white satin dress. Just as the stuffed olive rolled under the lady's feet, Clementine the bulldog shot out from under Phelps' table and tore snorting across the room right under the lady's long dress. The lady shrieked. Her escort jumped up. Clementine knocked over their table, then rushed back to Phelps chewing the stuffed olive.

Phelps ran over to the couple: 'I'm most *terribly* sorry. Clementine never usually does that sort of thing.'

'Take that beastly animal out of here,' screamed the old lady, fanning herself with her handkerchief. 'Take it out of here at *once.*'

'Yes,' said her escort loudly, very red in the face. 'You shouldn't be allowed to bring an uncontrollable dog like that into a place like this.'

'Come here, Clementine,' said Phelps meekly. 'I do apologise.'

Joe the barman was setting the table to rights. As Phelps left the bar with Clementine back on her lead, Joe winked at Philip. Later he came across to the piano: 'I told you I could fix it, didn't I?'

'Yes, but how?' said Philip, laughing yet incredulous.

'That bleeding dog has a passion for stuffed olives. As a barman you have to learn these little tricks of the trade.'

*   *   *

On the third evening, halfway through Philip's stint, Mervyn Twankey walked in through the door with a striking-looking, tall, willowy girl with long straggly, reddish hair and a lot of beautiful leg showing under a green and white striped mini-skirt. Twankey came straight up to Philip.

'Good evening, Mr Rodolphin.' Just the same silky voice. 'I do hope you didn't object to my little piece about you in the Diary.'

'I can't say I liked it. But you didn't expect me to, did you?'

'Oh *dear*. Oh, can I introduce Miss Tamara Reno.' The redhead stepped forward. Philip was struck by her wide mouth and huge black-rimmed eyes sunk in a tightly thin face. The arm she stretched out seemed almost devoid of flesh. She looked starved.

'How do you do,' said Philip, shaking her hand.

'Pleased to meet you,' said Tamara Reno, fluttering her false eyelashes and brushing the long hair out of her eyes with her other hand.

'Anything interesting been happening here since Monday?' asked Twankey.

'Nothing at all,' said Philip guardedly.

'Oh, well, we'll just have a drink and watch the action. Come, Tamara baby, the grog calls.'

*   *   *

Joe the barman had given Philip some valuable bits of advice when he had started playing in the Romeo bar. One tip was this: 'Occasionally Randi blows his top about something. If this happens, all hell breaks loose and the best thing you can do is to play and sing as loud as possible and try to drown the noise.'

On the fourth evening there was a loud roar from the

direction of the restaurant. Philip looked up the corridor and saw Randi and a young waiter standing by a table on which lay a whole smoked salmon. Randi was gesticulating wildly, his cigar throwing out sparks as he whirled it around.

'You, boy!' Randi roared, 'you don't cut smoked salmon like it was a piece of roast lamb. You shouldn't be working at Randi Ravello's Romeo Club. You should be working at a fucking Corner House. I'll cut your little balls off. Aaagh.' With this he picked up the thin, lethal-looking knife used for carving the smoked salmon and shook it in the waiter's face. The waiter, terrified, ran down the passage towards the bar with Randi wielding the knife in hot pursuit. The waiter skeltered through the bar and out of the Emergency Fire exit at the back. 'I'll cut your balls off. Get back to Bournemouth——' Randi's voice was cut in mid-sentence as he saw there were several customers in the bar who had all turned round as the waiter hurtled through. Philip had been playing as loud as he could, but he could not drown Randi.

Randi's expression immediately changed from one of fury to one of obsequious greeting: 'Good evening, my lords and ladies, may I welcome you to my humble little establishment.' He caught someone looking at the carving knife, and quickly hid it behind his back, walking out backwards and bowing low from the waist. The customers looked amazed: Joe winked at Philip.

The waiter did not reappear till the following evening. Apparently he had run the whole way home to Baron's Court. And the scurrilous rumour propagated by Joe was that he turned up for work that evening wearing a cricketer's box to protect his genitals – just in case Randi tried to carry out his threat.

* * *

The next morning Philip got a telephone call in the flat from Greville Whitfield at BDP. Greville said: 'See you're filling in time at the Romeo Club, old man.'

'Yes. Quite long hours, but quite good fun and very good money.'

'Good for you. Look, old man, what I rang up about is this – I've got two foreign birds on my hands tonight and I wondered if I could bring them along to listen to you for a bit, and then after you've finished maybe we could all join up and have dinner. I mean, I know it's a blind date for you and all that, but you'll have to rely on my judgement when I say they are a good pair of dollies and you won't be lumbered. That is if you're free, of course. How about it?'

'Yes, I'm free. But who are these birds?'

'Ha, ha, ha, ha. I'm keeping that a secret till you see them.'

'What nationality are they?'

'One's half French and half Siamese, the other's some sort of French mixture, and blonde.'

'And which of them is *your* bird – just so that I know.'

'Neither of them, my dear fellow. Neither of them. They both happen to be friends of the family, and as they are strangers to London I said I'd take them out. And you, my dear chap, would make the ideal member of the quartet.'

'All right, Greville. You've sold me. But don't mob things up while I'm playing.'

'No, of course not, old chap. We'll be as good as gold and pretend not to know anyone so lowly as the bar guitarist.'

As he played that evening, Philip wondered what he had let himself in for. Since his row with Shirley, he had not been out with another girl. And the idea of a new

98

girlfriend certainly intrigued him, especially a French one who was half Siamese.

At 10.30, half an hour before Philip's stint was over, Greville appeared with two girls. Philip gave Greville a cursory nod as he came in, then continued playing without looking in the direction of Greville's table. But after a few moments his curiosity got the better of him, and during his songs he stole furtive glances to see what the two girls were like.

One was a tall, athletic-looking girl with short blonde hair. She wore a cherry-red dress that did not conceal a pair of rather stocky legs. The other one – obviously the half-Siamese girl – was very different. She had expensively-coiffured jet-black hair surrounding a definitely Oriental, slightly dusky face – not technically beautiful, but unbelievably provocative, with dancing blue eyes that slanted upwards slightly, a tip-tilted nose and a full-lipped mouth that opened with her frequent shy smile to show perfectly white, regular teeth. She wore a blue satin dress with a low neckline narrowing down to a tiny waist and then flowing out again over her exceptionally long, neat legs. She was the epitome of Oriental sex appeal with French chic added.

Philip found himself unable to stop looking at her – she was like a magnet. He was sure, too, that he had seen her somewhere before, but he just could not remember where or when.

She looked at him, caught his eye, smiled, then lowered her eyes demurely to the ground as if she were shy at such overt behaviour. Philip felt a glow in the pit of his stomach. One look from her had been enough to tell him that a strong magnetism already existed between them.

She caught his eye again. Again the same demure, almost shy, look down to the ground while she busied herself with her pearl necklace. The other girl was talking to Greville.

At the end of his song Greville and the two girls clapped loudly. Philip bowed, embarrassedly, in their direction, catching the girl's eye as he did so. What a flirtatious look she could give! There was such hidden promise, such coquettishness in her glances!

Eleven o'clock came. Philip laid his guitar on the piano and went over to join them. Greville rose to greet him:

'Ah, the maestro himself. Philip, this is Nicole Lassage' – Philip shook hands with the muscular blonde – 'and Sabine d'Alsace.' He shook hands. She gave him a delightful smile, then dropped her eyes again demurely, just as she had done before.

Of course! Sabine d'Alsace. He remembered a photograph and a paragraph in last Sunday's Town Talk column in the *Sunday Express*: 'The Comtesse Sabine d'Alsace, 23, only daughter of the Duc d'Alsace, French Ambassador to Denmark, and the late Princess Tsai of Thailand, has arrived in London for a 3-month course to learn nursing at St Stephen's Hospital, Fulham. Sabine's step-mother, Duchess Beatrix, a great-niece of the Kaiser, is the daughter of the Margrave von Wolfenbuttel-Schleswig, who owns a vast estate and schloss near Hamburg in West Germany. Comtesse Sabine will stay with the French Ambassador Henri Lassage and his wife, long-time friends of the Duc, in their Kensington house. The Ambassador has one daughter Nicole, the same age as Sabine. As the Duc has no other children, Sabine is heiress to the Alsace vineyards, estates and fortunes and the fabulously beautiful Château Tropez in the Loire valley.'

As Philip sat down Greville said: 'We all thought you played quite marvellously.'

'Oui, oui,' said Nicole, laughing.

'I loved your choice of songs,' said Sabine with a wonderfully attractive accent. 'Do you plan ahead or just sing them as the – how do you say it? – mood takes you?'

'Just as the mood takes me,' said Philip, laughing.

'Well, you must be in a very good mood tonight,' said Sabine. They all laughed.

Philip thought: What a wonderful voice she has got – *anything*, even reciting from the telephone directory, would sound provocative in that marvellous accent.

Greville said: 'Well I expect the maestro is hungry. Let's finish up the drinks and go in to dinner.'

'What are you drinking?' Philip asked Sabine as she lifted her glass to drain it.

She looked at him with a question in her mercurial blue eyes: 'Why do you ask?'

'I was just interested.'

'Whisky and water. I always drink the same. It is the best, don't you think? I get a bit bored with wine in France. What do you drink, Philip?' She made his name sound more romantic than he had ever heard it sound.

'Vodka usually.'

'Ah, for having none of the hangovers, yes?'

Philip laughed again: 'Yes.'

Greville rose and led the way into the dining-room. They sat at a round table in the corner. Greville started talking to Sabine, so Philip had no choice but to talk to Nicole who, in close-up, was even less attractive than she had appeared from a distance. She reminded Philip of a lacrosse mistress at an English girls' school. And the way in which she seemed to boss Sabine about reinforced that impression. She had told her to finish up her drink, told her where to sit, and almost dictated to her what she should order for dinner. But Sabine seemed to accept it all as quite normal.

Philip said to Nicole after they had ordered from the menu: 'So Sabine is staying with you, is she?'

'Oui. Her mother and my parents are great friends for a long time. And I am really, what you call it, her chaperon.' Nicole laughed.

Philip asked: 'How do you mean?'

'Well, we both do this nursing course together. And she is not allowed out in the evenings without me. And I just have to look after her all the time.' Nicole looked across to see if Sabine was listening, then leaned closer to Philip and said softly: 'You see, she has led a very sheltered existence up till now in France in her father's château. She has not led the life of a normal girl. Out there she is treated almost like royalty – because she is the heiress to the château and estates and everything. And her step-mother – ach, she is the most formidable woman. She will not let Sabine do a single thing on her own. I tell you – ' Nicole leaned even closer to Philip – 'she was only allowed over to England to get her away from some boyfriend she had who her step-mother disapproved of. So my parents have been told that on no account must they let her get involved with some Englishman here. So that is where I come in. That is my job – to act as chaperon and lady-in-waiting all in one.' Nicole laughed again.

He said provocatively: 'Do you think you make a very good chaperon?'

'Mais oui, oui.' Nicole went off into uncontrollable giggles. 'You ask the difficult question. Well, I am a very good girl myself, you know.'

Philip said to himself: I bet you never get offered the chance to behave otherwise, you French bag. 'How long have you been in London?' he asked Nicole.

'Six months.'

'And you haven't got a boyfriend yet?'

'Oh, si, si. Si, si.' Nicole exploded with laughter. 'Honestly, your questions are of the most extraordinary kind. Si, as a matter of fact I *do* have a boyfriend. A very nice boyfriend. But he is not in London at this moment.'

'But surely you wouldn't *stop* Sabine having a boyfriend if she found one she liked here?'

'No.' She paused thoughtfully. 'No – not as long as I approved of the man. No, I wouldn't.'

'Then you'd be disobeying orders, wouldn't you?'

'Oui, oui. I would. But I don't like the Duchess, so I wouldn't care at all.'

'What about your parents?'

'Why should they know? Sabine and I would keep it secret. We are a real pair of devils, I can tell you. *She* may be innocent, but I am not. Do I *look* innocent?'

'Not really, no.'

'Ah, you have judged me right. But I must protect Sabine — because she *is* innocent. When you talk to her and maybe dance with her, you will see just how very innocent she is. And I don't want her to lose that innocence. Because it is a beautiful thing in a girl, oui?'

'Oui, oui,' said Philip, hiding a smile behind his hand.

*   *   *

Eventually Greville and Sabine got up to dance. Philip watched them closely: they immediately started dancing cheek to cheek. Sabine, her eyes closed, had her left arm high round Greville's neck. Philip realised, with some astonishment, that he already actually felt jealous of Greville: in fact he even felt slightly angry with Sabine for allowing herself to be so close to Greville and for seeming to enjoy it.

Philip said to Nicole: 'Is Sabine keen on Greville?'

'Non, non, pas du tout,' Nicole laughed. 'Sabine always dances like that. You will see when you dance with her. She is the same with every man. She looks the big flirt, yet really she is so innocent. She knows nothing.'

'But I thought you said she was sent over here by her mother to get her away from some boyfriend?'

'Oui. But she hardly ever *saw* this man. She was so closely guarded and chaperoned. She was never alone with him or anything like that. Sabine knows nothing, I can tell you. Why do you talk so much about Sabine?'

'I'm sorry. I'm just interested. She seems to have had such an unusual background. Almost medieval. Doesn't she long to escape?'

'Yes. I think she does. Here we go again – talking about Sabine.'

'Oh I *am* sorry. Let's talk about you then.'

'Non, I am used to it. Always when I am out with Sabine the men want to know all about her. But I am not the jealous type, so I don't mind.'

'Tell me about this boyfriend of yours.'

'Him I keep a big secret. I never talk about him, except to Sabine. She knows all my secrets, big and little. Here they come back now.'

Philip stood up as Greville and Sabine returned from their dance. All four talked about the band and about the general set-up of London's night life. Of the two girls Nicole did most of the talking. Sabine mostly sat and listened. Philip knew that, according to etiquette, he should first ask Nicole to dance. But he was determined to have his first dance with Sabine.

Fortunately, Nicole herself saved him from any embarrassment. While Sabine was hunting in her bag for something, Nicole whispered in Philip's ear: 'Now you ask her to dance.' She grinned mischievously and turned to Greville. Thank God for that, thought Philip: he did not fancy the idea of treading a measure locked in Nicole's muscular arms. He said to Sabine, laying his hand on her bare elbow: 'Would you like to dance?'

'Yes, I would love to. Thank you.'

He had never danced with anyone in that way in his life. Her cheek was firmly against his, and he could feel the caress of her eyelashes on his cheek as she blinked. Her breasts pressed into his chest: he could feel the twin points distinctly. Lower down, she seemed to push and swivel her stomach into his loins in time to the beat. Then she locked his right leg tightly between hers. They moved as one. It was the most bewitching sensation. He felt himself getting hot and excited, so he broke his face away from hers and looked at her. With her slanted eyes wide and her curved mouth slightly open, she was the picture of allure. God, what an exciting woman, he thought. She said softly and huskily: 'What were you and Nicole talking about while we were dancing?'

'About you.'

'What did she say?'

'She told me about your life in France.'

'What else?' Philip paused, then looked her in the eye: 'She said how innocent you were.' A smile spread slowly across her beautiful face until it became a full laugh. Philip explained: 'No, you see, I was very jealous about the way you were dancing so close with Greville. And Nicole said I shouldn't worry because you danced like that with everybody. And that you were really very innocent.' Sabine went on laughing to herself.

Then she said: 'And you – do *you* think I am innocent?'

'I don't know yet.'

'Would you like me to be innocent?'

'Not *too* innocent. But a little bit . . . ' Her hand on the back of his neck pulled his head close to hers again. Out of the corner of his eye he saw Greville start dancing with Nicole.

'So you were jealous of me dancing with Greville, then?'

'Yes.'

'Why?'

'Because . . . because I find you a very exciting woman and——'

'And?'

'And I wanted you to dance with me like that.'

'Now I am dancing with you much closer than I was with Greville, am I not?'

'Yes.' He twined his fingers into hers. She squeezed his hand. He almost had a pain in his stomach where she was pressing him: his right thigh gripped between hers was almost numb with the pressure. He whispered: 'I must see you again, Sabine.'

'You have no real girlfriend then?'

'No. Not now. Until last week. But not now.'

'What happened?'

'We had a row.'

'Was she pretty, beautiful?'

'Yes.'

'Will you tell me about her some time?'

'Yes, of course. You promise that I will see you again?'

'I promise.'

'And you will tell me all about this man you have in Germany.'

'So Nicole told you that, too, did she? You find out a lot, Philip.' She chuckled into his ear. 'Yes, I will tell you about him.'

'You're not upset at leaving him then?' She said quickly:

'Don't let's talk about him now. Let's dance together and forget everyone else in the world.' Her fingers stroked the back of his neck. He thought: She could say the most mundane things in the world and with that wonderful accent they would sound romantic and sensuous . . . she *can't* be 'innocent', can she?

He whispered: 'I don't think you are very innocent, you know.' She chuckled again.

'As long as the right people think I am and the right people think I'm not, that is all that matters. Philip, I love dancing with you but I think we should go back now, otherwise it's rude.'

'Will you dance with me again, once – before we go?'

'Yes. But do dance with Nicole just a little bit, will you?'

Philip nodded: 'Greville's been dancing with her just now.'

'Oh has he? I didn't notice . . .'

He led her back to the table, hand still entwined in hers. Greville and Nicole were just sitting down.

'Oh don't sit down, Nicole,' said Philip. 'Come and dance with me.' He wanted to get this chore over so he would be free to ask Sabine once more.

'Oh thank you, Philip, I'd love to,' said Nicole loudly.

On the dance-floor she tried to clasp him tightly, but he used all his strength to keep her at arm's length.

'Well, did you enjoy your dance with Sabine?'

'Yes. Loved it.'

'You certainly looked as if you were enjoying it. See, I told you – she dances like that with everybody. Yet she is so innocent. It is a joke, non?'

'But you, Nicole, now *you're* not innocent, *are* you?'

Nicole smirked coquettishly: 'I know my way around, oui. But then a woman should do at my age.'

Philip looked round at the table and caught Sabine's eye intently on him.

The band played a Bossa-Nova so loud that it relieved Philip of the burden of trying to make conversation to Nicole. At the end of the dance he led her back to the table where Greville was relighting a cigar and Sabine was looking rather bored. Her face lit up as Philip approached.

There was general conversation for a few minutes, and then Sabine nodded at Nicole. The two girls rose saying they were going to the Ladies'.

When they had gone, Greville said: 'Well, you certainly seem to have made a hit.'

'Why?'

'While you were dancing just now, Sabine was pumping me with questions about you. She couldn't take her eyes off you.'

'I hope you gave me a favourable report.'

'I was most complimentary, old man, even to the point of telling diabolical falsehoods. There was I, putting on my best bib and tucker, trying to charm the girl, and all she wanted to hear about was crummy old you. God, I just don't know. It must be the age-old appeal of the wandering minstrel, the heiress in the tower and all that nonsense. What did you *do* to her on the dance-floor, for God's sake?'

'I did absolutely nothing.'

'Nonsense. You were twined around each other like ivy.'

'Well *you* can't talk. So were you.'

'Nothing like as close as you, old man. I have my reputation to consider. Talking of reputations, I think

I'm rather drunk. Do you think I'm fit to drive these two birds home?'

'Yes, of course.'

'Well, I'd better be. 'Cos I'm not leaving them in *your* foul clutches.'

Sabine and Nicole reappeared. The two men rose while they sat down. Sabine leaned across to say something to Greville. Nicole nudged Philip, and whispered: 'You promised her another dance. Ask her now. She wants you to.' Nicole winked, cleared her throat and turned to Greville.

Philip reached under the table for Sabine's hand. She gave it to him. He pressed it to his thigh. She looked deep into his eyes with a half-smile playing round her wide mouth. He raised his eyebrows in question. She nodded, put her bag on the table and rose to dance.

On the dance-floor they went straight into a tight embrace. Once again he felt the intoxicating brush of her fingers on the back of his neck. She pressed into him with all her strength. She whispered: 'I think I must have drunk a little too much brandy.'

'Why?'

'Because I shouldn't behave like this. Not on the first evening.'

'Nor should I. But you make me *want* to behave badly. I can't help it. You have the most incredible effect on me.'

'So do you on me. But maybe it's the brandy. I will know for sure in the morning.'

'I wish I could take you home.'

'So do I. But Greville brought us and I think it better that he should take us both back. Don't you?'

'No.'

'Yes, the first night it is better. Another night – well, who knows?'

'All right, if you say so.'

'Don't be angry, Philip, *please*.'

'I'm not angry. Can't Greville take Nicole and you come with me?'

'No. Not tonight. I would love to. But – not tonight.'

He kissed her ear, letting his tongue roam round the lobe.

'Do that more,' she whispered. 'I love you doing that.'

He made as if to kiss her mouth, but she turned her face away, saying: 'No, Philip, not here, not here. You do understand, don't you?'

Some time later, in a daze, Philip stood on the doorstep of the Romeo and waved goodbye as Greville drove away with Sabine and Nicole.

As he got into the taxi to take him home, Philip Rodolphin said to himself: You silly mug, you've gone and fallen in love well and truly – and *what* a girl to pick, for God's sake . . .

9

Philip found it hard to sleep that night. Sabine's face was vivid in his mind's eye, her voice in his ears, her scent still lingered on his cheek and hands. Looking back on the evening, he supposed he had known the first instant he saw her in the bar that she was the kind of girl he would find inordinately attractive. The way she moved, every gesture she made, her voice, the way she challenged you with her eyes, her touch while dancing – all these were carried out with a sort of careless, animal grace that was at the same time innocent yet intensely sensuous. The magic of the Oriental woman, he supposed. He understood how Nicole could be deceived into thinking Sabine was so 'innocent'; because Nicole, let's face it, was nice and well-meaning but pretty stupid where nuances of sex appeal were concerned. She had a brutish, callumphing approach to everything: yet, Philip realised, it was important for him to keep in with Nicole if he wanted to succeed with Sabine; if Nicole turned against him, in her role as chaperon, confidante and unofficial lady-in-waiting she could make life very difficult for him – and for Sabine, for that matter, assuming that Sabine was as keen as she had seemed to be and as he hoped she was.

He realised, too, that Nicole got a definite vicarious pleasure out of the fact that he and Sabine had been so obviously attracted to one another right from the start. He passingly wondered who on earth this boyfriend of Nicole's could be, the one that she insisted on keeping so secret. Some mole-like, downtrodden little fellow, no doubt, whom Nicole would envelop in her all-embracing

aura of possessiveness, and thus bolster up, prop and
succour; a spotty, frightened youth with boils on the
back of his neck, perhaps a stammer. No – Philip checked
himself: he was being too unkind. Yet that was the only
sort of man he could visualise falling for Nicole who, for
all her dominant overbearingness and heavy-handed
coquetishness, had about as much sex appeal as a plastic
alligator. Although, Philip conceded, she hadn't got a
bad body – a bit on the big side perhaps, but still curvy,
wholesome. He wondered if she had ever put it to good
use . . . Unlikely.

Just after Gerald had left for his office, the telephone
rang. It was Nicole.

'Philip? How *are* you this morning?'

'Fine, thanks. How about you?'

'Oh, we're very well, thank you. Though we stayed up
almost till dawn.'

'Oh? What doing?'

'Talking. And you'll never guess who about?'

'Who?'

'About you, Philip. Yes, I mean it, about you!'

Philip felt for words: 'What on earth could you find
to talk about . . . about *me*, for Heaven's sake?' Secretly
he was pleased – it meant that Sabine was interested.
Decidedly interested.

Nicole lowered her voice: 'I tell you, Philip, you have
made a big hit. Believe me, I know it when I see it.' A
pause. Then: 'Philip, you won't hurt her, will you? She
is so innocent.'

'No, of course not. How could I hurt her, anyway?'

'Well, there are ways. But listen – this is not why I
telephoned you. Can you come to lunch with us here on
Sunday? Mama and Papa will be here but nobody
else. Can you?'

Philip thought quickly: 'Yes. I'd love to. Thank you. What's the address?'

'5 Holland Park Mews. A white house with green shutters. You can't miss it. About one o'clock then?'

'Fine.'

'See you then, Philip. Good luck at the Romeo tonight.'

'Thank you, Nicole.'

'Goodbye. Sabine sends her love.'

'Goodbye. Send mine back to her.'

'I will. She is still asleep. Au revoir.'

*   *   *

Gerald was staying away for the weekend, so he had very kindly lent Philip his E-type again. At five to one Philip drew up outside 5 Holland Park Mews and rang the bell. While he had driven there, he kept wondering whether Sabine would seem as attractive to him in the cold noonday light of a set luncheon as she had in the dim midnight light of the Romeo Club – and whether he would seem as attractive, as he had evidently then done, to her.

Nicole opened the door: 'Ah, Philip, so punctual. Come in.'

The house was in fact three mews houses knocked into one, beautifully decorated, with expensive chintzes, curtains, murals and *trompes l'œil*.

Nicole saw Philip looking in admiration at the luxurious décor in the hall: 'That is all Mama's ideas. Beautiful, don't you think?'

Philip agreed. Nicole led him into the sitting-room where he saw Sabine with a fat, short man with a bushy black moustache and greying hair, and a slim, elegant woman with brunette hair in a chignon and a proud,

113

well-sculptured face. She was wearing a tight grey tweed suit and tinted spectacles and was smoking a cigarette through a long black holder.

Nicole said: 'This is my father and mother. Sabine you know.' Philip shook hands with the Lassages and nodded at Sabine. Sabine glanced down at the ground coyly, smiling. She was wearing a tight-fitting black sweater, a wide black belt with a brass buckle round her tiny waist and a splayed grey and green tweed mini-skirt. The moment he saw her, Philip knew for sure that her potent attraction of the other night still held good. He thought to himself: How could she be 'innocent' and wear a sweater as provocative as that?

They all moved into the dining-room. At lunch Philip did not get a chance to talk to Sabine. He sat between Afdera Lassage and Nicole. Sabine was opposite, on the Ambassador's right. Philip said to Afdera: 'I do admire the way you've done up this house. I think it's beautiful.'

'Ah, thank you,' she said. 'But, you see, I have taste. I am not one of these bloody Frogs. I am a Moroccan. And so I have taste. Don't I, darling?' – she shouted at her husband.

The Ambassador looked at her with a faintly pained expression: 'What is that you say, my darling?'

'I was just saying that I am not a bloody Frog, so I have taste. Is that not true?'

The Ambassador smiled pathetically as if he had had to answer that particular question many times before: 'Yes, my darling.' He nodded at his wife politely. A footman took round the first course, a delicious dish of whipped egg and shrimps.

'Of course,' went on Afdera, 'we only live here at the weekends. During the week we have to live at the Em-

114

bassy. Too bloody pompous: I can't stand it.' Philip laughed nervously: he did not know quite how to cope with this turbulent woman who was so obviously embarrassing to her suave husband. But he found himself warming to her in spite of her outrageousness. There was something very appealing about her. Apart from anything, she was still a very attractive woman. Afdera said: 'So you play the guitar at the Romeo?'

'Yes,' said Philip.

'Don't your family mind that?'

'I expect they do. I haven't talked to them about it.'

'I thought the Rodolphins were one of the most aristocratic families in England.'

'I suppose they are. But——'

'Well, they cannot like you playing in a night-club surely?'

'They haven't said anything——'

'Philip, I wish you'd fock Nicole.'

'What?'

'I said, I wish you'd fock Nicole. Oh, I know it's Sabine you are keen on, but Nicole needs someone to give her a good fock. She's not her father's child, you know. Oh no. Henri was at the Embassy in Copenhagen before the war and I had an affair with a good-looking but stupid Dane. Henri knew all about it, but he couldn't complain because he can't have children. Nicole is the child of that Dane. And her brother, my son Emile, is the child of a Spaniard I was madly in love with during the war.' Philip looked surprised. Afdera went on:

'Don't look embarrassed. Henri knows all about it and he doesn't care a bit. Not one bit.' Philip looked quickly at the Ambassador: he was conversing in French with Nicole and Sabine. Afdera said:

'But I do wish you would fock Nicole. Or, if not you,

someone else. She really needs badly to be focked.' The footman serving her the roast beef did not turn a hair.

Philip said loudly: 'I thought she had a boyfriend.'

'A boyfriend?' said Afdera incredulously. 'That miserable fellow she goes on about is a figment of her imagination. He has never focked her in his life. I despair, I really despair. Have you focked Sabine yet?'

Philip stammered: 'But – but – '

'All right, you haven't. But you soon will, I expect,' said Afdera confidently. 'Sabine will get all the focking she needs. And she certainly needs it, like we all do.' She shouted: 'Don't we, darling?'

The Ambassador looked up calmly and said: 'What, my darling?'

'I said all we women need the focking.'

'Yes, yes, of course,' said the Ambassador with an embarrassed laugh.

Sabine looked nonplussed, Nicole looked desperate. Nicole said: 'Oh Mother, do stop interrupting.'

Afdera said: 'Sabine, do you know what is the focking?'

Nicole interrupted: 'Mama, don't be ridiculous. Of course she doesn't know.' Sabine looked from one to the other. The Ambassador quietly said in French: 'Sabine, tell me how your nursing course here is going.' Sabine answered back in quiet French.

Nicole sat back relieved. She gave an angry look at her mother: Afdera laughed impishly. Then she said to Philip: 'If I were you, I would stick to Sabine. She is the better bet. Nicole? She is hopeless. Absolutely hopeless.' Afdera leaned under the table and squeezed Philip's knee. She laughed loudly: 'If I were younger, after lunch we would go upstairs and have a damn good fock, no?'

Philip said, desperately trying to change the subject: 'You know Sabine's father and step-mother well?'

'I don't but Henri does,' said Afdera. 'In fact he was the Duchess's lover for a long time. Though what that old tart saw in him I cannot imagine. But then she had so many lovers that I think she doesn't expect too much from any one of them. She is bitch. Real bitch. Don't you think so, Sabine?'

Sabine, interrupted from her conversation with the Ambassador, looked as if she had not understood: 'What did you say?'

'Don't you think your step-mother's a real bitch!' said Afdera.

'Oh *Mother*,' said Nicole. '*Don't*——'

Sabine laughed nervously: 'I do not understand——'

The Ambassador said quietly to Afdera: 'Darling, I think we should go next door to have coffee.'

They all got up from their chairs: Philip gave a sigh of relief.

*   *   *

After coffee and liqueurs the Ambassador left the room, apologising to Philip that he had some work to attend to. Afdera left soon after, saying that she had an appointment upstairs with her masseuse.

'I should have warned you about my mother before-hand,' said Nicole, laughing, as soon as Afdera had left the room. 'She is always saying the most *terrible* things. And the awful thing is that she always gets away with it. I don't know how my poor father stands it.'

Philip said: 'Oh don't worry. I find her very amusing. I just hope she doesn't say that sort of thing' – he laughed – 'at some pompous diplomatic reception.' Nicole screeched:

'Oh, she doesn't care a *bit* what she says to anyone. You should have heard some of the things she's said to your Prime Minister at a lunch once. I wouldn't dare tell you in front of Sabine. She'd be shocked to death.'

'Nonsense,' snorted Sabine. 'Come on, Nicole, tell us.'

'No, no, absolutely not. I refuse. It even embarrasses me to think about it. But I *do* wish she would stop saying things about your step-mother, Sabine. I've asked her to, but it's no use – she never listens to anyone.'

'I'm used to people saying things about my step-mother,' said Sabine with a sigh. 'No one likes her. At least no woman, anyway.'

Nicole said quickly to Philip: 'Please excuse me for a short time, will you, Philip? I have some things to do.'

'Yes, of course,' said Philip, pretending not to notice the knowing look that passed between Nicole and Sabine. Nicole closed the door. Sabine and Philip were standing rather awkwardly in the middle of the sitting-room. Philip said, in an attempt to break the tense silence: 'I did enjoy the other night. I do hope you'll come and visit me at the Romeo again.'

'I loved it. And that crazy man, Ravello, is he called? What's he like as a boss?' Sabine sat down on the sofa. Philip lit a cigarette, then sat down beside her and gave her the best of his knowledge, scurrilous anecdotes and all, about the legendary Randi Ravello. Sabine laughed and laughed. He found the sound of her laughter very provocative: when she laughed, her whole face lit up, and her generous mouth opened wide to show the two rows of perfectly white teeth. He suddenly realised that, when she was not laughing, her face, though very attractive and even beautiful, was a sad face, stamped with a sort of wistful longing for something that must have always eluded her. He could sense some deep unhappiness within her, but it served to make her all the more attractive to him.

Her hand was lying on the cushion just beside her knee. It was a beautifully shaped hand, long elegant fingers, clear varnished nails. As she laughed at his last story about Randi Ravello, he placed his hand gently over hers. She laughed on for a moment, then looked at him and dropped her eyes. But she did not take away her hand. He gently kneaded her fingers. He looked at her and said softly:

'You mustn't mind what Nicole's mother says.'

She did not look at him. She slowly put her other hand on top of his and said: 'I don't mind, really. Afdera is very kind underneath it all. She just says that sort of thing for effect, to embarrass Henri. Henri used to be . . . a great friend of my step-mother's, and I think Afdera resents that. But then most women resent Beatrix. She is a very attractive woman.'

'Do you get on well with her?'

Sabine caught her breath. She raised her eyes to look at Philip, both eyes exploring Philip's face, with a kind of hunted look, darting from his eyes to his nose and mouth and back again. Her two hands were almost desperately clasping Philip's hand between them, feeling his knuckles and stroking his fingers. She was breathing quickly. Still she did not answer, still she looked deep into his face, as if she were searching for something.

Then suddenly she pulled her hands away and stood up. She said rather loudly as she walked across the room: 'Tell me what's been happening in the world today. I have not read the papers.' She picked up a *Sunday Express* from a table and brought it to Philip: 'What's going on?'

Philip took the paper and unfolded it on his knee as she sat down again beside him. 'Pretty dull stuff. I don't think you've missed much by not reading the papers today.'

'Read me out something interesting,' she said. Philip felt for her hand again. She willingly gave it to him. He scanned the front page: 'I don't think there's much interesting there.'

'There must be something. What's that about Princess Grace?'

'Just that she's going to have another baby, that's all. Here – you read a story to me.'

'Why?' She looked at him questioningly, seemingly frightened.

'Because I love your accent. It's terribly attractive. It makes even the most ordinary English words sound appealing and amorous.'

'Amorous? What does that mean?'

'Well, to do with love.'

'Love?'

'Yes.'

She looked at the paper and began reading slowly: 'Princess Grace of Monaco is——' She stopped and said: 'No, I can't go on.'

'Yes, please do. I would love to hear you reading.'

'Is expecting another baby in March. She – No, I can't go on, I really can't go on.'

'Please do,' said Philip.

'She – No, please let's stop this.' She took her hand quickly away from Philip's.

Philip urged: 'Go on, go on.'

Sabine looked again at the paper, then put her hands quickly up to hide her eyes. She began to shake slightly. Philip gently pulled one of her hands away from her eyes. He was amazed to see she was crying. 'What's wrong?' he said softly. 'What's wrong?' He put his hand lightly round her shoulders.

She sobbed. Then she rose quickly from the sofa and

ran out of the room, leaving the door open behind her. A few minutes later, Nicole came in. Philip asked:

'What's wrong with Sabine?'

Nicole quietly closed the door behind her and said: 'She is upset. You see, the thing is, she has great difficulty in reading. The doctors have been trying to help her for years. But they say it is some form of neurosis because she is so terrified of her step-mother.'

'Her *step-mother*?' said Philip, incredulously.

'Yes, I'm afraid so. Her step-mother has always bullied her – her mother died when she was one, you see, and her father married again very soon afterwards. And this has produced some sort of emotional blockage which has prevented her from reading properly. It is kept as a secret outside the family and close friends. But by chance you have discovered. Please do not ask her to read again. Then all will be all right. She will come down in a few minutes, and you must just forget the whole thing. Don't mention it or ask her about it, *please.*'

'No, of course, I won't. But how does she read her letters?'

'She doesn't, except very slowly. Usually I have to read them out for her. Now – please forget it. I can hear her coming down the stairs.'

*　　*　　*

The next morning at breakfast, Gerald said to Philip: 'Look, old man, I'm off to New York on the 11th so I thought I'd better give some sort of farewell do.'

By midnight that Thursday night, the flat was a bedlam. Gerald had moved all the furniture and pulled back the carpet in the sitting-room to allow for dancing.

The food and drink was in the kitchenette, the coats in Gerald's bedroom.

Between them he and Philip had asked about a hundred people. But at midnight it seemed as if half the population of London was in that flat. If you wanted to dance, it meant fighting and struggling for your place on the small bit of floor used for dancing, squashed between necking couples or dancers wildly gyrating in the weirdest clothes – the men in shirts, sweaters, frilly ruffs, white suits, the girls in pyjamas, trouser suits, long dresses, almost topless dresses, jeans. The smell of scent and sweat was already formidable. Every so often one of the more wildly jiving couples would bang into the table on which the gramophone stood, so the needle would jump several grooves with a jarring squawk. The volume control, needless to say, was at its maximum.

There were couples spread on the floor all along the passage, and even in Gerald's bedroom. They had thrown the coats off Gerald's bed and were sitting and lying around in semi-darkness, lit only by the light in the passage. Every so often someone on the floor would kick the door shut, leaving the room in total darkness – then conversation would come to a halt, and the only sounds would be giggles and sighs and heavy breathing as the couples necked and kissed on the bed and on the floor.

Philip's own bedroom, being at the far end of the passage round the corner from the bathroom, had, he was glad to find, so far escaped the notice of the party-goers. To make quite sure, after changing out of his dinner-jacket into sweater and jeans, he locked his door and pocketed the key, then returned to preside, at Gerald's request, over the gramophone and choice of records, most of which Gerald had borrowed from a collector-friend.

Philip had not yet danced with either Nicole or Sabine. As soon as they had all arrived together by taxi, the two girls had been swept into the maelstrom of dancers by two total strangers. The girls had looked quite happy, so it was then that Philip had stolen away to fill himself with sausages and so on, as he had eaten no dinner.

One by one the lights in the sitting-room were being put out, until the dance-floor was lit only by the light in the passage. Philip could barely see to read the labels on the gramophone records. Glasses were being knocked over and trodden on; the butler and maid whom Gerald had hired for the evening were scurrying about mopping up spilt drinks and broken glass which was quite a danger as several girls were dancing in bare feet.

Gerald loomed out of the gloom: 'Going quite well, isn't it, old man?'

Philip shouted back: 'Going like a bomb. Where on earth did you find some of these people?'

'I have my contacts, you know. Not an unattractive girl in the room, is there, you must admit?'

'No. From what one can see, the standard is very high.

'Are your two birds all right?'

'They seem to be dancing quite happily. I haven't seen them since we arrived.'

An attractive dark girl in tight yellow trousers suddenly broke away from her partner on the dance-floor, threw both her arms round Philip's neck, and kissed him hard on the mouth. Then, without saying anything, she returned to her partner. Philip had never seen her before in his life.

'That's success for you, old man,' shouted Gerald, laughing.

'Who is she?' said Philip.

'Couldn't see, it's too dark. Keep going with the magnificent music, old man. The joint is positively jumping. You'd make a great disc-jockey.'

'Hell,' shouted Philip, 'I want to dance sometime.'

'Well, put on a great stack of LP's and leave them.'

'I can't really because people keep asking for requests, and if I'm not here they'll try to put them on themselves, and that's a sure way of ending up with a bust gramophone. And we don't want that, *do* we?'

Gerald shrugged his shoulders: 'Just keep the hot music going, otherwise we'll have a mixture between a riot and the rape of the Sabine on our hands.' Gerald disappeared to get another drink, chuckling at his own pun.

Philip could just see, through the murk and smoke, Nicole doing a wild jive with a frail-looking dark youth in a black leather jacket, tight jeans and high black boots. She looked as if she was enjoying herself. Then he saw Sabine. She was dancing cheek to cheek, eyes closed, with a tall blond man with long sideboards wearing a frilly white shirt and a wide black leather belt round the top of his pale blue hipster pants. He felt a momentary twinge of jealousy that anyone else should be enjoying the potent sensation of dancing close to Sabine.

'Can you play some Rolling Stones stuff?' said a girl in a shrill voice, extricating herself from her partner's embrace with some difficulty.

Philip said: 'Yes, certainly. Coming up next.'

Just after the Stones record had begun playing, Sabine appeared in her pink satin trouser suit: 'You promised you'd dance with me. Are you not going to?'

'Yes, of course. But my job at the moment is to look after the records. I can dance with you now though.' He was secretly flattered that Sabine had come up to him on her own accord when she had seemed to be enjoying herself so much on the dance-floor with that other man.

He took her in his arms and they advanced into the smoke of the dance-floor. Immediately she embraced him tightly to her, pressing herself to him with her body, stroking the back of his neck with her left hand. Her cheek was hot. His hands felt her back delightedly, and then he kissed her long and sensuously on her ear-lobe. He could feel her wriggle with pleasure. He whispered in her ear: 'You seemed to be having a good time with that fellow, so I didn't want to interrupt.'

'Ah, mon Dieu, but he was a bore.'

'Why did you dance so close to him then?'

'Is there any point in dancing any other way? If you're with a man, you might as well be close to him, yes?'

Philip laughed, then kissed her ear again, more savagely this time. She arched her head so that she could reach his ear with her own tongue.

After a long, long time she said: 'Philip, I don't want to be a nuisance, but I have a terrible headache. I think it must be the noise and all this smoke. Have you got some aspirins and a place where I could lie down for a little time?'

'Of course. How awful for you. We'll get some codeine in the bathroom and then you can lie down and rest on my bed until it's gone.'

'That would be wonderful. Sorry to be such a bore.'

He led her to the bathroom, past Gerald's bedroom in which there was a knotted mass of couples sprawled all over the floor and bed. The bathroom door was locked. They waited outside for a few minutes, then heard soft giggles coming from the other side of the door. Philip knocked loudly. The door opened and a young man and girl walked rather sheepishly out. Philip raised his eyebrows at Sabine, who laughed outright and said: 'Pity we have to spoil their fun.' Philip took two codeines from the cabinet: Sabine took them with a tumbler of water.

He guided her to his bedroom door, unlocked it, and led her in. She stood in the doorway as he switched on the bedside table lamp. She said with a chuckle: 'I don't wonder you keep it locked tonight.'

'Here, lie down and let those pills get to work.' He pointed to the bed. She lay down, kicked off her shoes and closed her eyes. She looked beautiful. He stood gazing down at her:

'Don't you want to get properly into bed? Under the sheets?'

She shook her head. He switched off the bedside lamp, and then, on a sudden impulse, leaned quickly down and kissed her mouth. She did not move her face away: instead, she opened her mouth wide and let her tongue jab and glide round the inside of Philip's mouth. Her arms went up and round his neck, pulling him down until he was lying on top of her. She gasped as the full weight of him fell upon her.

They kissed: one of his hands crept down her neck and began to knead her breasts. She breathed more quickly.

'Wait a minute,' she whispered. He felt her undo the buttons on the back of her jacket, which fell away leaving only her brassière. She unhooked that, too. With a swift swoop Philip placed both hands on her breasts, moving them gently from side to side, feeling the nipples stiffen in his palms as he did so.

With one hand she was undoing the buttons on his shirt, then she let it slide inside to stroke the hair on his chest. He kissed her again. She rose to him, bare-breasted, breathing fast, whispering just as her mouth closed on his: 'Oh Philip, oh Philip – I need you, I need you . . .'

Suddenly the bedroom was plunged into light by the switch at the door. The metallic voice of Belinda Caterham said: 'Oh, so sorry to interrupt you, Philip dear, but Toby and I were just leaving and I wanted to say goodnight.'

Philip rose quickly from the bed, while Sabine covered up her naked top with her hands. He said: 'Sabine's got a headache. She's just lying down for a bit.'

'Oh poor dear,' said Belinda, the most flagrant insincerity in her voice. 'I do hope it goes. That's certainly one of the best treatments for a headache.' Belinda turned off the light as Philip followed her out of the room. He closed the door behind him.

'Sorry to interrupt your snogging session with the beautiful heiress.'

Philip laughed embarrassedly, doing up his shirt buttons. 'I was just settling her down, that's all.'

'If you ask me,' retorted Belinda, 'you were trying to *unsettle* her in the biggest possible way. Still, don't worry about me. Get back to the good work.'

'No, no, I have to get back to tend the gramophone.'

'Not quite so much fun, I have no doubt, as tending the glamorous Sabine. I've never seen any two people dance so obscenely as you two were doing.'

'Oh nonsense. We were behaving like the Puritan Fathers compared to most of the couples in that room.'

'Not from where *I* was looking, dear Philip. Anyway, it's all in a good cause. I hope you land the fish: she'd make a good catch.'

Philip kissed Belinda goodnight, then went back to the gramophone. Nicole came up to him, her blonde hair disarrayed, her lipstick smeared round her mouth: 'Where on earth is Sabine, Philip?'

'She's lying down in my bedroom. She's got a bad headache.'

'Oh, good – I mean how *awful* for her, but it's nice to know she's all right, oui?' She leaned closer to Philip and whispered: 'This man I've got hold of is rather interesting. He wants to take me home. I want to go with him. A bird in the hand, oui?'

'I'll take Sabine. Don't you worry. You go.'

'I'd better just go and see her.'

'All right. It's the room at the end of the passage.'

Some minutes later Nicole reappeared, saying: 'That's all right. Sabine says I'm to go home on my own, and that you'll take her back. Take care of her now, Philip.'

'Of course,'

The frail-looking youth in the black leather jacket grabbed Nicole's arm and pulled her away. She shouted: 'Good night, dear Philip.'

He waved back as she was pulled almost bodily through the door.

He turned his concentration back to selecting records: there was still a large crowd of very bemused and amorous dancers in the room. Another strange girl leaped up to kiss him and then swung back to smooch with her partner. Gerald had completely disappeared in the near-darkness. But Philip had to find him. He went round the dancing couples looking in vain. Then he found him in a dark corner of the room lying on the floor beside Jennifer Pendennis.

'Sorry to bother you, old man, but——'

Jennifer said drunkenly: 'Oh Philip, can't you see this is no moment to start some family discussion?' She was wearing only a bra and panties.

'Gerald, I couldn't borrow your car, could I?'

'Terribly sorry, old fellow, but I'm afraid I'll need it to take Jennifer home. Can't you take a taxi?'

'Not quite the same thing, is it?'

'No, I suppose not. What, you've got one of your birds on the plate, raring to go, have you?'

Philip nodded. Jennifer giggled and said: 'Goodee goodee.'

'Well, look, Towser Farringdon is absolutely blotto and has passed out in my bedroom. If I get his keys – he drives a Mercedes – will that do? Because he'll have to stay the night here, anyway.'

'Yes, that would be fine.'

'What a bore you are,' said Gerald, getting up from the floor. Jennifer screamed: 'Spoilsport' at Philip. Gerald led Philip into his bedroom. There in the farthest corner was a huddled figure asleep on the floor. Gerald felt in his pockets and produced a bunch of keys: 'Here you are. It'll be one of these.'

'Thank you,' said Philip. 'Now you'd better get back to Gypsy Rose Lee Pendennis.'

'She's been very restrained tonight,' said Gerald chidingly. 'Only down to her underwear. Not enough light for her to strip in, she said. Thank God. Though it might have made the party. But she'll come up with something, you *bet*.'

'What colour is Towser's Mercedes?'

'Light blue. Coupé. I saw it earlier on. Parked right outside the door.'

Philip took the keys and went along the passage to his bedroom. He went in, leaving the door open to give some light. On the near end of the bed he saw a man and girl in a passionate embrace: tucked up at the far end was Sabine. In another corner on the floor was a second couple, oblivious to the discomfort of lying on the carpet.

He whispered to Sabine: 'Come on, I'll take you home.'

'Philip, I didn't know what to do when these people came in and started making love all round me.'

'You did very well. Now get ready, and I'll take you home. I've borrowed a car.'

'Has Nicole gone?'

'Yes.'

'Good. I mean, I didn't want her to wait for me.'

Sabine dressed, then Philip led her out of the bedroom and closed the door, leaving the couples in total darkness. With difficulty they found her coat in Gerald's bedroom, scuffling among the couples lying round the room in various postures.

They went downstairs and found Towser's Mercedes right outside the door. Philip opened the front door for Sabine. 'No,' she said. 'No, thank you. I'll squeeze in the back.' Philip looked surprised but allowed her to do as she asked. He himself got into the driver's seat, switched on the engine and drove away.

'Did you enjoy yourself – apart from your headache?'

'Oh yes,' she said. 'A marvellous party. So many beautiful girls. Did you dance with any of them?'

'Not one.'

'Oh come, come, I don't believe you. What were you doing all that time, then?'

'Putting on gramophone records.'

'Nicole said she saw a girl run up and kiss you.'

'Yes, but I didn't know who she was.' He heard a rustling noise from the back seat and looked in the rear-view mirror. But he could see nothing.

'You expect me to believe that? You must have known who she was. Girls don't just kiss a man like *that*.'

'This one did. So did another.'

'Did you like it then?'

'Yes. Loved it. Who wouldn't? They were very attractive girls.'

More sounds of rustling and movement from Sabine

in the back seat. As he drove into the mews where the Lassages' house was, Sabine said: 'Don't park outside the house. Go further along where it is dark, to the end.'

Philip obeyed. She said, as he drew to a standstill: 'Now switch off your lights.' He did so. Only the dim lights of a street lamp some twenty yards away illuminated the inside of the car. She said softly:

'Now look at me.'

He switched off the engine and turned round. She was lying full-length across the back seat with her coat over her. As he looked, she threw off the coat. Underneath she was completely naked. He looked for her clothes: they were bundled down on the floor. As she breathed, her stomach moved provocatively up and down. He had never seen such a beautiful naked body in his life. There was no modesty, no shame, no inhibitions about her.

'*Look* at me, Philip, *look* at me. Then come to me.'

He started to climb over the back of the front seat.

'No,' she said softly but firmly. 'I want *you* naked. Like me. But first, I want to see you naked. Then I want to *touch* you naked. Then I want to *have* you naked. Philip, quick.'

10

After the intricate tableau of their love-making, the two naked bodies lay quite still, face to face, legs entwined, on the narrow back seat of the Mercedes. The windows and windscreen had steamed over, making the light inside the car a ghostly grey.

'Philip, say a little something to me.'

Philip rose on one elbow and looked down at the finely-chiselled, beautiful face framed by a tousled mass of black hair. Her eyes looked up at him, darting unspoken questions into his own. He said quietly:

'I have never in my life made love like that with anyone before. I feel completely drunk with it. You have somehow put a spell on me and I find a magic in even just touching your arm. You make the whole thing so lyrical, so beautiful, even on the back seat of a car. My enchantress – ' he kissed her shoulder – 'I rather think – I don't know for sure – but I rather think I love you. Who could not love you after *that*?'

She put one hand quickly up to cover her eyes. Then her body began to heave. He thought at first she was laughing at his banal attempts to tell her how wonderful he thought her. Then he heard a stifled sob and realised she was crying. He gently prised her hand away from her eyes: the tears made her eyes shine like headlights in the grey light. Her whole face seemed to be asking him a desperate question.

'What on earth's the matter? What did I say wrong?' He gently stroked her forehead. The tears rolled down her face to splash on the seat.

'Philip,' she said between sobs, 'you mustn't love me. You can do this to me as long as you promise not to love me. As much as you like you can make love to me, but promise never to love me. Never, never.'

'What *are* you talking about?'

'You wouldn't understand. But I ask you, Philip, *please* never be in love with me.'

'Why? Why on earth not, that is if I wanted to be?'

'Because . . . because I am hopeless. I am really wicked. I can't help it but I am. It is like a disease I have. Oh Philip, help me – I don't know what to do about me. Please help me to do something about it.'

'Of course I will, but what is it I've got to do something about?'

'About *me*. The *whole* of me. It eats me through and through. I can feel it sometimes gnawing at the inside of me. And I behave like this when I know I shouldn't. But I just can't *help* it. I really can't. I've tried, but I can't, I can't, I *can't*.' She sobbed again.

Philip gently lifted her up till she was in a sitting position. He put her coat over her and sat beside her, his arm round her neck. He said gently: 'Now stop crying and tell me exactly what is wrong. And I'll see what I can do to help. Stop crying, just tell me the whole thing.'

She gulped several times to hold back new tears. Then she said: 'Give me a cigarette, will you, please?' He lit her one in his mouth and handed it to her. She said: 'It's the way I have to . . . have a man, Philip. I *have* to have a man make love to me. Not just sometimes, but almost all the time. At nights, Philip, when I haven't had a man that day I can't get to sleep unless . . . unless I do it to myself – you understand? I know how to do it to myself— otherwise I just can't sleep. It's as if I had something burning in me down there. So I have to make my fingers do it for me. And then I sleep. Even in the mornings when I wake up, sometimes I have to do it again.'

Philip was staring at her in amazement: was this the girl who seemed so controlled and aristocratic, whom Nicole had said was so 'innocent' about anything to do with men?

'But Nicole said you were so innocent. I never thought...'

'Oh, I keep it a secret from Nicole. I don't tell anyone. It suits me for Nicole to think I am innocent. The only person who knows me well enough to guess is Beatrix, my step-mother. Because she is like that, too. That's why she has such a bad reputation. Philip, I've only told one other person this before. So you must keep it a secret. You promise?'

'Of course I promise. But . . . but you haven't had a man since you've been in London, have you?'

'No, no. That is why I so desperately needed you tonight. I was nearly going mad. Philip, I *had* to have you tonight otherwise tomorrow I don't know what I'd do – probably go out into the Park and find someone.'

'Have you ever done that before?'

She looked down, ashamed: 'Yes, I have.'

'Often?'

'Sometimes.'

'When did this . . . this feeling start?'

'When I was seventeen at home. I was never allowed to go out to parties or to dinner with boys unless I was chaperoned and escorted and almost guarded by some older member of the family or my mother's staff. Then one evening at a party in a big schloss near Hanover belonging to one of Mama's cousins we were playing a sort of Hide-and-Seek game. And I was hiding in the linen-cupboard with Heini, and——'

'Who is Heini?'

'He's very handsome, very rich, a sort of playboy, but he pretends to work as a doctor in Hanover. Anyway, he started to undress me in this linen cupboard and I loved it so much, before I knew what I was doing he was making love to me on the piles of linen. After that I had to see him as often as I could. While I stayed at the schloss. Every day, every night. If I could think up enough lies to get out of the house. A girlfriend used to come and pick me up and we used to say we were going shopping or something, and I used to go to Heini's flat and she would wait outside. Or at parties I used to say I felt ill and go home early and then go out again and spend all night with Heini. He was awful to me, though. Sometimes there'd be other girls there with him and he would make me allow them to share the bed with us and do things to me – and the awful thing is I didn't mind. In fact I rather enjoyed them being there. Though I was a bit jealous of him having them when I was *not* there. Heini told me all sorts of tricks, and so did some of his other girlfriends. I couldn't have lived without him. He taught me everything. Did you think I made good love?'

'Yes, very good.'

'Well, you must thank Heini that I know so well what to do. He was famous in Hanover because he has this big thing – how you say it, cock? – and all the girls tried to get him to make love to them. But really he is awful and I hate him now.'

'Didn't your step-mother find out?'

'Yes. You know how people gossip. One night when I was with Heini instead of being at a party she found my bed empty at 3 am, and she rang Heini's flat. Like a fool I answered because Heini was in the shower at the time and she recognised my voice. When I got back she was waiting for me in my bedroom, packing my clothes into suitcases. She hit me in the face. The next day she sent me back home to the château. And Heini never wrote to me *once*. Not *once*. But I still got into trouble back home in France.'

'How?'

'He was about forty, married – staying nearby for the summer with his four children. His wife was in Paris. One night he came to dinner and we stayed up late alone and he came into my bedroom and – I don't know, but I was so upset at losing Heini that I just couldn't refuse him. He stayed all night with me. And even when his children went back to his wife in Paris, he used to drive one hundred miles after work to come and sleep with me, and then leave first thing in the morning to drive back to Paris. What his poor wife must have thought!'

'And you let him make love to you completely?'

'No, no. Every day I used to have to have clean sheets. What could the housemaid have thought about that? Jean said I was the best mistress he had ever had. He still writes to me. He even wanted to marry me, which Heini never did.'

'Did your step-mother find out about Jean?'

'I think she suspected something in the way Jean always came back from Paris when there was no good reason to do so.'

'What happened then?'

'This I am a bit ashamed of, but I'll tell you, Philip, just to show how wicked and difficult I am. I had been going mad because I had no Heini and no Jean. And I was walking in our woods one day when I came on one of the gardeners raking up leaves. He was young and good-looking in a James Dean sort of way. I talked to him for quite a long time and then he suddenly kissed me. Then I just fell back on to the pile of dead leaves and let him make love to me. I felt so much better after that. Just having someone *in* me was enough.'

'Did you see him again – the gardener?'

'Oh yes, several times. We met in the woods. He was so romantic. He used to write me poems. But then the silly fool began giving the housemaids letters to give to me. And Beatrix opened one of them. The poor boy was sacked on the spot and I never saw him again. And that's why I'm here in England: she sent me here to get me away from that boy. I never even knew his name. We hardly spoke.'

'Are you still in love with Heini?'

'Don't be silly, I've *never* been in love with Heini. I just need him because there's no one else. I'm never allowed to meet anyone or see anyone now. I'd have gone mad without Heini and Jean. But I hate Heini, I really hate him. He's evil. He's evil.'

She leaned down. Philip felt her lips weaving down his stomach.

'Love me, Philip,' she whispered. 'Heini always said the second time's so much better than the first. Love me, Philip. Then I won't *need* anyone else.'

Her lips were on him, and he moaned and shuddered with delight. After a while, she raised her head and said: 'If I have you like this, Philip darling, then I won't need——'

He squashed her mouth with his own.

*   *   *

'Heini was right: the second time *is* much better than the first time, isn't it?' She lay in the crook of his arm. Her face looked quite serene, relaxed like a baby sleeping.

Philip said: 'I think you still love Heini.'

She pounded his chest softly with her fist. 'I don't, I don't. I tell you, I have never loved him. I once thought I did, but I don't. He is wicked and bad, I tell you . . . You won't tell Nicole about us tonight, will you, Philip? You see, she must go on thinking I am the innocent maiden. You know, in spite of all her big talk, she is a virgin. She has never had a man?'

'Really? What about her boyfriend?'

'I don't believe he exists. She won't say his name or anything about him.'

'Maybe that man she has got hold of tonight will do the trick.'

'That blond man with the long hair?'

'Yes.'

'No, no. I can tell – he is all talk and no go. Believe me.'

Suddenly there was the sound of shoes clacking down the mews. Philip wiped clear enough of the rear window for him to see out. In the dim light of the street lamp they could see Nicole, her hair dishevelled, go to the door and put the key in the lock.

Philip said: 'Don't say she's had to *walk* back.'

'Looks like it,' said Sabine. Then she burst into tears again.

'Oh Sabine darling, not *again*,' said Philip. 'What is it this time?'

She said between her sobs: 'It's just that Beatrix would so hate me to have made love to you twice, and to have so enjoyed it. She would hate it. And she would *hate* me for it.'

'Forget Beatrix. Put on your clothes' – he said that as if to a child, helping her on with her clothes while she snuffled and sobbed – 'and then I'll take you home.'

At the door of the house she clasped him suddenly to her and said: 'Philip, you will be there when I need you, won't you? You will, won't you?'

'Yes, I will.'

'And you know how much I need you?'

'Yes, I know.' They kissed on the doorstep. Then she went in.

On the way home he was still tingling from her touch. He could smell the scent of her body on his face and hands. He sighed and shook his head: he was in love now more than ever before. He saw himself as the protector of Sabine, saving her both from her step-mother and from herself. And how she needed to be saved from those two evils! He would release her, he was *determined* to release her . . . to succour her, to nourish her so that she thrived and was happy . . . He so wanted to make her happy, happy, just happy.

*   *   *

When he got back to the flat, he could not go to sleep because there was still one couple on his bed and another on the floor. Gerald was nowhere to be seen, nor was Towser. A few pairs lay around the sitting-room while the gramophone played a Count Basie LP set at 'repeat'. He slumped into an armchair in the corner and dozed off.

He woke up as it was growing light. The gramophone was still playing the same Count Basie record. The couples were all still asleep on the floor and on the sofa. The room was in complete disarray, cigarette ends everywhere, upturned glasses, bras, bits of clothing. The smell was heavy, thick with smoke and drink and sweat. He opened a window. The sleeping couples did not stir at the noise.

He went along the passage and softly opened Gerald's door. Gerald was in bed, just waking. 'Hello,' he said. He felt his forehead. 'God, I feel like a fart in a thunderstorm. What time is it, old man?'

'Quarter to eight. Where's Towser? I've still got his car key.'

Gerald pointed to the curtains, underneath which two feet were sticking out. 'Last time I saw him he was dreaming technicolour dreams over there.'

'I'll leave the keys on your dressing-table for him when he comes to.'

'Get on all right with the beautiful countess?'

'Fine.'

'Suppose you must have done if you're only just back.'

'No, I've been back for some time. Had to sleep in a chair in the sitting-room because there are people lying all round my bedroom.'

Gerald laughed, then groaned, holding his head.

Philip said: 'I'll get you some coffee and Alka-Seltzer.'

The bedclothes beside Gerald began moving and a head peered out from under them. It was Jennifer Pendennis: 'Oo golly, what time is it? Where on earth am I? Who on earth are all these men?'

'Shhhh, sweetie, go back to sleep. It's still bye-byes time,' said Gerald, patting her head. She collapsed on the pillow and almost immediately began snoring. Gerald raised his eyebrows and winked: 'I could do with that coffee and Alka-Seltzer. My mouth's like a Saudi-Arabian taxi-driver's jockstrap. I must have eyes like a bull-terrier's balls and breath like a buzzard.' He sank back on to the pillow.

Philip closed the door and went to the kitchen to put on the kettle. He heard the letter-box snap as the postman delivered the mail. He went downstairs to find one letter, typed, addressed to him, with the letters 'BDP' on the envelope. It read: 'We now have an unexpected vacancy on our trainee scheme and will be able to take you on on Monday week, the 10th. Please let me know by return or by telephone if you still want the vacancy. Yours sincerely, Doris Maple.'

11

Philip's beginning with BDP was completely governed by the fact that, come hell, high water or group meetings, he had to speak to Sabine on the telephone at least three times a day. The arrangement was that, if he didn't call her, she would call him, giving a fictitious name. In Philip's first week at BDP she had run out of her stock of aliases: so Philip had to think up some new ones.

Ever since the night of the party, the night they had made love in Towser's Mercedes, they had been seeing each other twice or maybe three times a day. Sabine could not afford to let even Nicole in on the secret – so she had to invent all sorts of spurious reasons why she was going where she was: hairdresser (that ran out on the first day), palm-reader, dentist, chiropodist, wig-maker, dress-maker, astrologer – and so it went on. Sometimes Nicole would demand to come, too – in which case Sabine would say No, she had to go alone. Nicole never persisted, never suspected. For on each occasion Sabine would meet Philip either at the flat, where they would make love, or outside his office, in which case they would go for a coffee in one of the Park Lane bistros.

'I feel like an escaped convict on the run,' Sabine would say from behind her dark glasses and coat pulled up round her ears to prevent her being recognised. One afternoon they went to a re-showing of the film 'High Society', sitting in the top dress circle seats.

'Do you know,' said Sabine as she ate an ice-cream in the interval, 'this is the first time I have been to the cinema alone with a man? The music of *High Society* will always bring back this moment, darling Philip. Will it for you?'

'Yes, my love,' said Philip, kissing her cheek.

He was completely besotted with her. He had scarcely noticed Gerald's departure for New York, leaving him the flat and the E-type all to himself. He had scarcely noticed his start at BDP. Everything he considered was in terms of Sabine. If she did not call him in the office at the appointed time, he fidgeted and fretted until he was nearly beside himself with anxiety. She had rendered him, as a trainee, almost useless.

What worried him most was the lying that had to be done to Nicole. Sabine had to lie herself black to get rid of Nicole. And when Nicole rang Philip – which she did from time to time – Philip had to lie again and say that he hadn't seen Sabine at all.

'We must not let anyone in on our secrets,' said Sabine emphatically.

Philip believed her, and obeyed her.

One afternoon when they were in bed together at the flat, Sabine suddenly burst into tears. Philip asked:

'What's the matter now?'

'You wouldn't understand,' Sabine sobbed.

'Tell me, come on – tell me. Get it out of your system.'

'It's Beatrix.'

'What about Beatrix?'

'I'm enjoying myself so much with you, Philip darling, and she would hate it to happen. She hates to see me enjoy myself. She would do anything to stop it. She hates it. She hates *me*.'

She sobbed violently: 'I know she does. I know she does.'

Philip said softly: 'Now don't get into a state. Your step-mother doesn't hate you——'

'She does, she *does*.'

'Of course she doesn't. Relax and forget all these silly notions. Your step-mother isn't here and she can't ever destroy what has gone on between us.'

'But I feel her *here*. Right *here*. Coming between us. She will spoil everything for us, I *know* it, I *know* it.'

'How can she spoil what has happened already? And what we know about each other? Do not get in such a state, little love. Your step-mother is miles away and powerless to come between us.'

'She will, she will, I *know* it – she will.' She sobbed into his shoulder, clutching him fiercely. She went on: 'You do not understand. Beatrix has always hated me. I want to give it all up, the château, all the money and everything. I don't want a bit of it. But Beatrix will not listen. She says it is mine by right and I must have it. I just want to leave it all and marry someone else far away who knows nothing about my family and my money and my château. Someone who will look after *me*, *me*, *me*. I want a *man*, *my* man, just for me and me alone. Do you understand me? You *must* understand me, Philip. It is too easy to understand, yes? I must have a man who will stop this ... this wickedness in me and make me not want other men all the time. You could do that, Philip, you could do it – if you wanted to. Please want to do it, Philip, please, *please*?'

One night she said she couldn't see him because she was going out in a party to the theatre with Greville Whitfield. Because there were other people going to be present, she was allowed to go out without Nicole as chaperon. She didn't call Philip the next morning, so he called her from his office:

'How did you enjoy the evening?'

'It was fine,' she said. 'Just fine.' There was something in her tone of voice which made him instantly suspicious. He asked:

'Who were the other people there?'

'Philip, I don't know. I really don't know.' Again her tone of voice put him on his guard.

'You must know who *some* of them were?'

'I don't. I know none of them.'

He tried a long shot, but his hunch proved right. 'You mean, there was nobody else there?'

A long pause: 'No, Philip, there was nobody else there,' she said. 'I was furious with Greville for telling lies. It was unforgiveable of him to do that. But he said they had rung at the last minute saying they couldn't come. And how was I to know he wasn't speaking the truth?'

'What did you do after the theatre?'

'We had dinner.'

'Alone?'

'Yes.'

'Where?'

'In his flat. He cooked it.'

'And when did you get home?'

'Philip, why do you ask so many questions?'

'When did you get home?' He was speaking forcefully now.

'After midnight.'

'What time?' A long silence. Then she said quietly:

'About half-past two.'

'And what were you doing all that time?'

'Oh, Philip, really——'

'Come on, tell me, what were you doing from eleven till half-past two?'

She said nothing. He barked:

'Did you go to bed with him?'

'No.' A pause, and then a very faint 'Yes'.

Philip closed his eyes and pursed his lips in anger. His hand tightened on the receiver. He shouted: 'You bloody

145

little tart. You bloody little *whore*.' He slammed down the telephone and wiped his sweating brow. Then he banged his clenched fist several times on top of his desk till the pencils jumped.

*   *   *

Half an hour later, the telephone in his office rang. It was Shirley in Reception. He had not seen her since joining BDP. In fact he studiously avoided going near Reception on his way in and out, and until this moment she had had no cause to telephone him. She said in an official sort of voice:

'Mr Rodolphin? There's a Mrs French in Reception to see you urgently.' The way she said 'Mrs French' suggested a caustic disbelief. 'Mrs French' was one of the code-names Sabine and Philip had agreed on for her to give whenever she rang him at his office.

'Oh, please tell her I'll be right down,' said Philip hastily.

What on earth is Sabine doing coming here? he thought angrily on his way down in the lift. He was still furious with her for her behaviour with Greville Whitfield the night before. He had for a second considered refusing to go down and see her, pleading the excuse of an office meeting. But he dismissed the idea straight away because he thought she might do something mad like find out where his office was and burst in.

She was sitting in Reception reading *Queen* magazine. Shirley gave him a cold look that suggested she knew that Sabine was no more 'Mrs French' than she was Eliza Doolittle. Sabine rose without speaking and he led her out of the door, through the hall into the street. He said frostily: 'What on *earth* are you doing turning up here?'

146

'Philip, don't be angry with me. I had to come and see you after you were so furious on the telephone. I had to explain about last night. Here, I have a taxi waiting.' She pointed to a cab.

'But I just can't leave the office just like that. I might be needed for something.'

'Oh, Philip, just for a short time. I must explain and stop you being angry with me.'

'Hello, hello, hello,' said a loud voice behind Philip. It was Greville Whitfield, presumably returning from a meeting, with a pile of lay-outs under his arm. 'Good morning, Sabine, good morning, Philip,' he said with a hearty smile. He kissed Sabine on the cheek. She gave Philip a guilty, hunted look as he did so. She said:

'Thank you for last night, Greville. I did enjoy it.'

'So did I, by Golly, so did I,' boomed Greville. 'Must do it again some time. Still, I mustn't delay you two. Where are you two off to?'

Sabine said quickly: 'To the hairdresser. Philip is going to ride with me.'

Greville looked up at the windows of BDP: 'Hope none of the directors see you playing truant in office hours, old man. But the best of luck. 'Bye.'

As Greville went in the door, Sabine and Philip got into the taxi.

'But where *are* we going?' said Philip.

Sabine leaned forward and spoke to the driver through the glass partition: 'Please take us to the Zoo.' She closed the glass window and sank back.

Philip protested: 'But the Zoo's miles away.'

'Philip, I must talk to you now. To get this business about last night straight. I had to tell Nicole I was going to have my hair done, to get away from her, as I'm not allowed out on my own, as you know. And that girl in your Reception. She never took her eyes off me. Looked me up and down.'

'There's nothing to *get* straight about last night. You went to bed with Greville and that's all there is to it.'

'No, but don't you *see*, Philip, I did and I didn't?'

'What do you mean? Did you get into his bed?'

'Yes.'

'Were you naked?'

'Yes.'

'Well, there you are.'

'But I didn't let him go *in* me, Philip. Don't you see? I didn't because I was thinking all the time of *you*.' She repeated: 'I didn't let him go *in* me. Don't you see? That makes it all right, doesn't it, Philip?'

Philip stared straight ahead without answering. Secretly he was heartened by this revelation.

'Philip darling.' She kissed him on the mouth: he tried not to respond but the ardour of her kiss aroused him in spite of himself.

'Philip darling, I want you to make love to me now. Here. Now.'

'Are you mad? In a taxi in broad daylight?'

She lifted herself up and took down her panties. Then she lay on the floor and put her legs up on the back seat, pulling up her dress to show a bare stomach. She said: 'Philip, I must have you, I want you now. All the way.' She opened her legs wide.

He noticed the little Jacob's ladder of hair that ran up to her navel. He said: 'Have you gone mad? Supposing the driver looks round? Or what happens at the traffic lights? Sabine, don't be ridiculous.'

'So you don't want to make love to me?' She sat up and began frenziedly undoing his trouser buttons. He did not resist. Her head lay in his lap. After a while she said:

'I know what we will do. Sit back on the edge of the seat and I will sit on top of you.' She sat astride him and pushed him avidly inside her. She pulled her skirt down and said: 'Now nobody can see anything. I am just sitting on your lap. But oh! how wonderful it is to have you inside me.'

Philip said softly: 'What happens when we get to the Zoo?'

'We turn round and come back. Oh how I need you, Philip. Especially after last night. Never let me go out with anyone else again. Do you forgive me?' She pressed her full weight down on him.

He closed his eyes at the enjoyment of her love-making and breathed: 'Yes.'

She leaned down and kissed him on the forehead.

Soon the driver pulled down the partition and said over his shoulder: 'At the Zoo now, Madam.'

Sabine shouted over her shoulder, 'Thank you. Now please go back to BDP in Park Lane.'

The driver shrugged his shoulders without turning round and let out the clutch.

*　　*　　*

That evening as he dressed to go to the Romeo Philip switched on the TV. Sabine had said that that afternoon she was making a speech at the official opening of the National Festival of the Wines of France, and she had been warned that TV cameras would be there.

Sure enough, in the 'Day by Day' magazine programme after the six o'clock news, there was a long feature on the wine-tasting session. It showed Sabine making a speech, talking to the French Ambassador and the President of the Board of Trade, and sipping the first glass of wine. The announcement referred to her as 'that beautiful heiress the Countess Sabine d'Alsace, daughter of the Duc d'Alsace, who is over here for a few months to learn nursing.' Sabine looked a picture of beauty and innocence. Philip could not quite believe that the last time he had seen her she was lying semi-naked on the floor of a taxi-cab.

*   *   *

For the next month he saw Sabine almost daily. The main problem was to find a suitable and discreet partner for Nicole. The lanky, blond youth she had picked up at Gerald's party had turned out to be a failure because he had wanted to go to bed with her and she had refused to let him. So each night it was a problem of finding an escort for her.

The pattern of their outings was the same. Either they would all meet Philip after the Romeo, the girls and the other man having been to a play or cinema, and then have dinner and go back to Philip's flat and play the gramophone with all the lights off. Or else they would go back to the Lassages' house when Nicole would tactfully say Goodnight and retire to bed, leaving Philip and Sabine alone in the sitting-room where they would make love on the sofa to the accompaniment of Sinatra's 'Songs for Swinging Lovers' or 'High Society' or 'Sergeant Pepper'.

One night there was a ball given in the River Room of the Savoy. Sabine was to dine with the Lassages who had both been asked, and the arrangement was that Philip would join them after he had finished at the Romeo.

When Philip arrived at the Savoy, the party was in full swing. There were hundreds of guests, and it was some time before he could find the Lassages. Eventually he located them sitting with Nicole at a table behind one of the pillars. He greeted them all and sat down.

'Sabine is dancing,' said Nicole to explain Sabine's absence. 'With some man none of us know.' Philip looked at the dance floor, but it was too crowded for him to pick out Sabine.

'You have been seeing a lot of Sabine,' said Afdera Lassage, looking stunning in a tight white satin gown with a huge diamond necklace round her neck. 'You are in love with her?'

Philip shrugged his shoulders: 'I don't know.'

'Oh come now, you must *know*. Have you focked the girl?'

'Really, Ambassadress, I can't——'

'Just tell me if you have focked the girl.'

'I cannot tell you, really I can't.'

'Then I presume that you have. At least I *hope* that you have. Good for you. If ever a girl needed focking, it is Sabine. Come and dance with me.'

Philip got up and led Afdera to the dance-floor. She danced beautifully, very close, intently observing all the other couples, making comments like: 'Not so good-looking a man. Pretty girl.' Or: 'Handsome man but a tramp of a girl.'

Eventually they saw Sabine, looking beautiful in a pink and white dress with low-cut neckline. 'There's your lady-love. Look how she's behaving.' Sabine was dancing in her usual close way with a tall dark-haired man with a prominent aquiline nose. 'Spanish or Italian, I'd say,' Afdera commented. 'Look how close she dances. Doesn't it make you jealous?'

'No,' lied Philip. He caught Sabine's eye: she immediately danced further away from her partner.

Afdera said: 'She is a tart, that girl. I'm convinced of it. No wonder that bitch her step-mother is worried about her going out alone. Her step-mother is just the same.

Always was. A complete tart. Couldn't resist anything in trousers. Has Sabine told you about Paul?'

'No,' said Philip.

'You ask her about Paul d'Estainville sometime,' said Afdera cryptically.

Sabine was going back to the table. Philip led Afdera off the floor. As soon as they got to the Lassages' table, Philip asked Sabine to dance. She said Yes with alacrity.

It was the same closeness, the same magic. To dance with Sabine was both a revelation of what dancing can become and a delight in intimacy of bodies.

'What was Afdera talking to you about?' she said.

Philip paused. Then: 'She told me to ask you about Paul.'

Sabine froze for a minute, then said: 'Paul? Ah, that is too terrible. Paul has a wife called Ulla who used to be Beatrix's best friend in Germany. She brought them both to the château. She was beautiful and nice. Then one night after a party Paul by mistake ran her down in the car. Now she is a cripple and has to go about in a wheel-chair because she cannot walk. And Beatrix has this terrible permanent affair with Paul. He comes almost every day to see her in the château, and they go on holiday together. It is awful for Ulla, but Beatrix is terrible like that. I feel so sorry for poor sweet Ulla, who is divine and never complains. But it must hurt her terribly. Philip, you will help me never to do anything as cruel as that?'

'I will try.'

'It's because Papa and Beatrix are no longer in love. He sleeps in a different room. They rarely see each other. So Beatrix has to have other men to keep her happy. Oh it is too awful. I hate it, I hate it. Please never let that happen to me.'

They danced closely for a long time, exploring with their hands each other's bodies. Then Philip said: 'I think we had better sit down.'

They walked off the dance-floor to the Lassages' table.

They all sat talking for several minutes, then a grey-haired, red-faced man came and said something to the Ambassador, who got up and followed the man into the throng. When he came back some minutes later, he said to Afdera: 'We have all got to go now.'

Afdera, Sabine and Nicole looked at him in amazement.

'Why, Papa?' said Nicole.

'Nonsense,' said Afdera.

Sabine clutched Philip's hand under the table. The Ambassador whispered something to Afdera and Nicole. They all got up. Sabine followed them with a quick goodnight kiss on Philip's cheek.

'What is it?' Philip asked Nicole as he said goodnight.

'It is silly but we have to go,' Nicole said. 'Some woman has complained that when Sabine was dancing with you she was behaving in a shocking manner. So my father thinks it better that we go.'

'How ridiculous,' said Philip angrily. 'We weren't doing anything wrong.'

'But this woman thinks so,' said Nicole.

Afdera came up to say goodnight to Philip: 'Typical focking English middle-class prudishness. But my stuffy old husband thinks it better we go in case it causes more talk. He says we can't have Sabine the centre of some scandal. Though *I've* been the centre of millions and it's never done *me* any harm. Nor her step-mother. Goodnight, Philip. You'll have to find yourself another bird for the rest of the evening. That shouldn't be difficult for a sexy fellow like you, should it? . . .'

12

In those early days at BDP, Philip found it almost impossible to concentrate on learning about typography and market research. He was – and he fully realised it but was powerless to do anything about it – completely obsessed with Sabine. Never before in his life had any girl made it so clear that she needed him so much; never before had any girl literally bloomed and thrived on him and appeared to wilt away without him.

'Sabine has never looked so pretty as she does now,' Nicole had said. 'And she says she has never been so happy in her life – and I can believe her. If she doesn't see you for a time, or if you don't ring her up, she immediately gets depressed. She withers like a picked flower that needs water. Yet as soon as she sees you or you telephone her, she blossoms into life, her eyes shine, and she looks a new person.' Of course Nicole did not know about most of the times that Sabine met Philip secretly in the daytime, because Sabine did not want her to know in case she told her father or felt hurt at being so obviously left out. And Nicole never suspected that Philip and Sabine actually made love.

Philip felt much the same about Sabine as she evidently did about him. He relied on her completely for sustenance; he spent most of his working hours at BDP dreaming of the last time he had made love to her, or about the next time he would see her. At the Romeo his songs would be played and sung to an imaginary Sabine, sitting worshipfully before him. She did not come to the Romeo because he did not want the waiters, or Randi Ravello, to recognise her and start gossiping – although there was plenty of gossip going round about him and Sabine already. This unfortunately was inevitable after they had been seen together on several occasions, Sabine having been previously a much-publicised figure and a natural target for gossips speculating about her romantic life.

The morning after the Savoy ball, Philip and Sabine arranged to meet at his flat in the lunch-hour. Again she said she would tell Nicole that she was having her hair done. After they had made love, they made plans to meet that evening, when Philip had finished at the Romeo, at a party at Annabel's.

As they danced in Annabel's, Philip said: 'Sabine darling, it's no good: I can't go on like this. I shall have to have all of you or nothing of you. I am too much in love with you to continue with this secrecy and these furtive meetings, terrified of people finding out, terrified of your step-mother. Sabine, I want to marry you. Will you marry me?'

She looked at him for a long time, then buried her head in his shoulder and shook with sobs. Luckily the dance-floor was too dark and crowded for the other dancers to see. He put his hand on her head and said: 'What's wrong? You must have known I would ask you sooner or later.'

Her only answer was to sob more. Eventually she choked: 'It's the music. Tell them to change that music.' The record being played at that moment was Paul McCartney singing 'Yesterday'.

'What's wrong with it?'

'Tell them to change it. It was Heini's favourite song.' The record came to an end. She said, controlling her sobs: 'You see, Heini is there wherever I go. I will never get rid of him. It is an omen that just as you ask me to marry you they play Heini's song.'

'Nonsense. Don't be so silly. Do you want to marry me?'

'Yes, Philip darling, of *course* I do. I have thought about nothing else for weeks. I want to have your children and to have you beside me for ever, and never go back to that château again in my whole life. But Beatrix——' She choked on another sob – 'What will Beatrix say? Philip, I am frightened about Beatrix. Papa won't mind, but Beatrix——'

'Listen – you write to Beatrix tomorrow and tell her you have become engaged to me and want to get married as soon as possible. After all, you are over twenty-one and she can't do anything to stop you. It's not as if she was your mother.'

'You don't know Beatrix. She will not like me being happy, Philip, I know she won't. She will stop me, I know it, I know it.'

'She *can't* stop it if you really want it. It is up to *you*. Now listen – tomorrow you're going to do two things. The first is at lunch-time when we're going to a jeweller's to find an engagement ring for you.'

She looked into his eyes lovingly, smiling through her tears, and kissed him quickly on the mouth: 'Thank you, darling Philip. I would love to wear your ring.'

'And the second thing – you are going to write to your step-mother, explaining the situation, and saying you want to get married to me as soon as you can. Then we'll announce it so that we don't have to go on meeting in secret, and everything will be all right.'

'Oh, Philip, you make it all sound so easy. I wish it was going to be like that in real life. But you don't know Beatrix. She hates me to be happy. And she will know

how happy I am with you. Oh Philip, tell me it will all
be all right. I am so frightened.' She clutched him: 'And
nothing in the world will make me lose you. Because
you are everything to me. With you I never need anyone
else.' Again she kissed him, this time passionately: 'Philip,
you are the love of my life and I adore you. You will
give me lots of babies, oui?'

* * *

The next day in the lunch-hour (she had told Nicole
she was going to the dentist) he took her to Collingwoods,
the family jewellers in Conduit Street. A dignified
gentleman in stiff white collar, dark grey suit, and wearing
thick-lensed spectacles, greeted them as they entered
somewhat embarrassedly: 'Can I help you, sir?'

'Yes,' said Philip nervously. 'We are looking for an
engagement ring.'

'Come this way, sir. I will show you our stock.' Sabine
clutched Philip's hand for reassurance. The man pulled
a tray out of a cabinet.

'These are our diamond specimens, sir. Is that what
you had in mind?'

Philip looked inquiringly at Sabine. She whispered:
'Rubies and diamonds.'

'Rubies and diamonds,' repeated Philip.

The man pulled out another drawer: 'Here is our stock
of ruby and diamond rings, mostly antique Victorian but
including some very fine stones.'

Sabine hesitated, then pulled out a Victorian ring of
rubies and diamonds in a gold setting. She tried it on her
engagement finger: it fitted exactly. She smiled delightedly at Philip. The man said: 'If you'll excuse me saying
so, sir, that smile alone was worth the price of the ring.'

He clasped his hands in a priest-like way as if to bestow a blessing.

Philip said, producing his cheque-book: 'I'd like to pay for it now.' Sabine went down the shop to look at the ring on her finger in the long mirror beside the counter. Philip said quickly: 'How much is it?'

'Er, £135, sir. That is less a discount of £15 for so important a client as the Countess.' Philip looked up, surprised.

'Oh yes,' said the man smugly, 'I recognised her from the newspaper photographs as soon as you came in. May I be the first to wish you, sir, a long and happy life together with all God's blessings.'

'Thank you very much,' said Philip, writing out the cheque and thinking: well, there go most of my savings from the Romeo.

Outside the jewellers she held up the ring for him to admire. Then she kissed him and gave him a package wrapped in brown paper she had been carrying. 'Don't open it now,' she said quickly.

She could hardly take her eyes off the ring, holding her hand this way and that to observe the effect. 'Now I am really yours,' she said lyrically, 'and I don't care who knows it. I will never never never take this ring off.' She kissed the ring. 'Never, never, never . . .' She danced down the street . . .

Back in his office after lunch he unwrapped the package. It was a 12 by 10 photograph of her head and shoulders in a red leather frame. She had written on it in her large, childish writing: 'To darling Philip from your very own S. XXX'

He kissed her through the glass.

*　　*　　*

That night Sabine and Nicole were going to an official white-tie-and-tails dinner at the Persian Embassy in honour of the French Prime Minister. So when they had talked on the telephone in the afternoon and he had thanked her for the photograph, Sabine had said she wouldn't be able to meet Philip that evening.

Just after he had got back to the flat after the Romeo at about 11.45 pm, as he was admiring the photograph of Sabine on his dressing-table, the telephone rang. Who could it be ringing at that hour?

'Philip?' It was Sabine. 'Look, darling, I'm at the Embassy but I can't stand it any more and I need you, darling, desperately. I've told Nicole I've got a headache and want to go home. She wants to stay here as she is having fun. I'm getting a taxi and coming to you now, darling.'

'Are you sure Nicole won't go home and find you not there, darling?'

'No. She won't go home for hours and anyway she won't go into my room. They're talking of going on in a party to Annabel's. See you in a few minutes then, my darling?'

'Wonderful.' Philip always felt a deep hollow of excitement in his stomach at the prospect of seeing Sabine alone. And the feeling came now. Probably because their moments alone had to be snatched furtively and each one was like an escape. And to make love to Sabine was the most thrilling experience of his life: each time became more thrilling, because somehow their love, instead of cloying with familiarity, blossomed anew and more vigorously each time.

Soon the doorbell rang. He ran down the stairs, his heart racing with excitement at seeing her again, even though he had seen her at lunch-time and talked to her on the telephone twice since then.

She was looking stunning in a full-length ice-blue satin dress with a low square-cut neckline and a tight waist, and elbow-length white gloves. Her hair was swept up in a chignon on top of which she wore a crescent-shaped diamond tiara. She carried a small silver-encrusted evening bag. He stood gaping in wonder at this breath-taking sight: he had never seen her looking more beautiful.

'Aren't you going to let me in?' she said with a laugh.

'Sorry.' He kissed her on the cheek. 'I was just looking in adoration at this vision who has just rung my bell.' They went up to the sitting-room. She began taking off her gloves, dancing round the room, chanting: 'We're alone, alone, is it not too wonderful?'

'Darling, you look absolutely terrific. Weren't the men clustering around you in droves? A drink?'

'Yes please, darling. Whisky and water and ice. Yes, I did have a little success. But oh they were *so* boring, those pompous men. I kept thinking of my wonderful adorable Philip with the naughty twinkling blue eyes.' He handed her the drink and kissed her for a long time on the mouth.

She threw her gloves on the sofa and held out her hand to display the ring: 'Doesn't it look marvellous? It shines so beautifully at night. Everyone was admiring it, asking if I was engaged. But I said no, it was a family ring and I just wore it on that finger to put off undesirable men.' She laughed: 'They all thought that very funny.'

'Darling, I want . . . '

She looked at him intently, her eyes shining, her mouth slightly open and her breath coming fast: 'Yes, darling, I was thinking of you making love to me all through dinner.' Philip took her arm. She drank a long gulp of her drink, then put the glass down and leaned her head on his shoulder as he led her into the bedroom.

She said softly: 'Let me undress in front of you.' Only the bedside light was on: the red lampshade diffused a pink glow round the white walls. 'Sit down and watch me.'

Slowly, garment by garment, she undressed till she was completely naked except for the tiara. She stood in front of him, undulating her body, smoothing her hands down her flat, hairy stomach and up again to cup her breasts. He leaned forward to kiss her stomach.

'Get into bed,' he whispered. 'And wait for me.' She lay on top of the bed, raising one knee and then the other, as if trying to assuage some desperate inner yearning, squirming, sighing quietly to herself, her hands clenching and unclenching, her eyes closed.

'Philip darling, come to me soon . . . I do so need you . . .'

*   *   *

They lay still and silent for a long time. Then Philip said: 'My love, I'm obsessed with you. I think about making love to you every day and every night, in the office, at the Romeo, in bed at night so that I can't sleep.'

'It's the same with me, darling Philip. I can't live without you. Tonight at dinner I couldn't even make conversation because I kept looking at my ring and thinking of being in bed with you. And now we are each other's it is so wonderful. Nicole saw my ring.'

'What did she say?'

'She guessed you had given it to me. I made her promise not to tell her parents until I have written to Beatrix.'

'Haven't you written yet? You promised you would do it this evening before you went out to dinner.'

'Darling, I started to write but then I couldn't finish it

and I tore it up. I started again but I tore that up too.' She clutched him tightly, stroking the hair on his chest. 'Darling, I'm so frightened about Beatrix, what she will say. But if I say I love you and want to marry you, there is nothing she can do, is there?'

'Well, at the moment I'm earning, with the Romeo and BDP, over £3,000 a year. And she can't say that's too little for two to live on, can she?'

'And we can start off living here until we find a house of our own, can't we? Gerald would let us, I'm sure. I'll have some money of my own which we can use to buy a house. I do so want to live in London. I never want to go back to France and that château. I wish we could just go out tomorrow morning to a registry office and get married there and then, with no fuss and bother, no people, no relations – except perhaps Papa.'

'Well, we can always keep that as a trump card up our sleeve if your step-mother starts being difficult.'

'Yes, all right. I'd rather love to get married right away and start having babies. We'll have wonderful babies.' She began to cry.

Philip said: 'What's wrong now?'

'I'm so unhappy when I think of Beatrix,' she sobbed. 'Beatrix will hate me marrying you, I know she will. She has always hated me to be happy. She says I am no good and don't deserve to be happy. Philip, you won't leave me, you won't let me down, will you? I'd die if you did.'

'Of course I won't. But you'll have to stand firm if your step-mother is difficult.'

'Of course I will. I will never let you go, never in my life.' She tried to raise her head but her tiara caught in the pillow and she had to extricate herself. Philip said: 'Why don't you take that thing off?'

'No, I must keep it on in case anyone sees me going home, then they will never think I've been in bed with you. Philip, I want to sleep the whole night here with you.'

'I want that, too. As long as you're sure the Lassages won't worry.'

'As long as I get home before breakfast it will be all right. Nicole never goes into my room. It is right that we should spend the whole night together on the day we get engaged, isn't it?'

'I'd like to spend every night with you from now on.'

'I wish I could live with you like other people do.'

'You will write to your step-mother tomorrow, won't you?'

'Yes, darling. I promise . . . Philip?'

'Yes?'

'I want you again . . . '

*　　*　　*

Some time later the telephone rang. Sabine was asleep in the crook of his arm. He crept out of bed without waking her and went naked into the sitting-room.

'Hello?'

'Hello, Philip? This is Nicole. I'm so sorry to ring you at this time but I'm terribly worried about Sabine. I got back from the Embassy and she's not here. She left hours ago saying she was going home with a headache. Her bed's not been slept in.'

Philip weighed up the situation quickly: 'Oh, she came to see me. We've been talking.'

'Oh thank God for that. I thought she'd been kidnapped or something. Is she all right?'

'Yes, she's fine. I'm bringing her back now.'

'Can I speak to her?'

'Yes, hold on. She's just in the loo.'

He put down the receiver and ran next door to wake Sabine. She took some time to come to her full senses. He shook her.

'It's Nicole on the telephone. She's been to your bedroom and found it empty. I've said I'm taking you back now. She wants to talk to you.'

Sabine got sleepily out of bed and wandered into the sitting-room, naked except for her tiara.

'Hello, Nicole? . . . Yes, I'm fine . . . Yes, he's bringing me back now. My headache was so bad I had to come and lie down at Philip's for a short time. Then we got talking, you know how it is . . . Oh Nicole, please don't tell your parents . . . Thank you . . . See you soon. Goodbye.'

She put down the telephone and fell on Philip's shoulder: 'Oh darling, what a bore she is. I wanted to wake up beside you and cook your breakfast in the morning. I can actually boil an egg . . .'

'I know, but it's better you go back now. She seemed quite happy with your story, didn't she?'

'Oh yes. Being a virgin herself she would never suspect me of anything. Anyway she thinks I am so innocent! Come and talk to me while I dress.'

As she dressed, she said: 'I like where you have put my photograph. Now I can watch over you in bed every night even when I am not here.'

Soon she was dressed and, after making up her face and tidying her hair, looked as fresh, as stunning, as she had when she arrived at the door.

His last words to her as he dropped her at the Lassages' house were: 'Now promise you'll write that letter to your step-mother today.'

'Yes, darling, I promise.' She gave him a full-mouthed goodnight kiss.

As he drove home he could still smell her animal scent on him.

*   *   *

A week later, she had still not written to her step-mother. Philip was by now getting angry with her.

'Don't be angry with me, darling,' she would plead. 'You don't know how difficult it is to write to Beatrix.'

They had seen each other almost every day or evening.

Then one night after he had returned from the Romeo she telephoned him. He had not seen her that day. She was crying: 'Darling, I must tell you something. I don't know what to do about it.'

'Tell me, what is it?'

'It's my days. They haven't come.'

'Your days?'

'Yes, you know my monthly days. They are three weeks late. And they still haven't come. I must be having a baby.'

'Why didn't you tell me before?'

'Because they've been late before. But never as late as this.'

'Have you told anyone else?'

'No. Not even Nicole.'

'Have you written to your step-mother yet?'

'Yes. I posted it this evening. I said I wanted to get married to you as soon as possible. Especially now with this baby.'

'Did you say about the baby?'

'No, darling. But I'll have to tell her sooner or later.'

'You could get rid of it if you——'

'Darling, nothing on earth would make me get rid of it. It is ours, yours and mine, and I love it already. I want to have it. Even if we can't get married before it comes, I want it, I want it, and no one will take it away from me. It is mine, all mine, and I will keep it. I love it because I love you, Philip my darling. It makes me feel all warm and complete to have it inside me . . . A part of *you* always with *me*.'

13

Three days later Philip was telephoned in his office by the French Ambassador: 'Philip, can you please come to the Embassy and see me when you finish work today?'

'Yes, of course, Excellency. Is it urgent?'

'Yes, it is urgent. And it is private. And I'm afraid I must ask you not to call Sabine between now and then.' Philip had not spoken to Sabine that day because he had spent all the morning in meetings, but he knew she had rung because his secretary had left a note on his desk saying 'Mrs French' had rung.

'I must not call Sabine?'

'No. I must ask you to follow my request. I will explain why this evening. I will send a car to pick you up at your office, when? At 5.30?'

'Yes, that would be fine, Excellency.'

As he put the telephone down, his palms were wet with sweat, his stomach felt hollow. He could not concentrate all afternoon. What could the Ambassador want? It must be important, else why at the Embassy and not at his house? And why was he sending a car? He dared not break his word and telephone Sabine. But he wished *she* would ring him. No call came.

At 5.30 a chauffeur-driven black Citroen was waiting at the door of BDP. 'Mr Rodolphin?' said the chauffeur.

Philip nodded. The chauffeur opened the rear door for him.

At the Embassy a liveried footman escorted Philip straight into the Ambassador's study. He rose from his desk to shake hands. The only light in the room came from an Anglepoise lamp on the desk. The walls were lined with bookshelves full of books with ornate leather bindings. He beckoned Philip to sit down in one of two armchairs beside the crackling fire. He himself sat in the other, almost hidden in shadow. The light from the fire glinted on his half-lensed spectacles.

'I must explain all this secrecy and air of intrigue,' he said. 'This morning I had a telephone call from the Duchess of Alsace, Sabine's step-mother. She had received a letter from Sabine saying that she wanted to get married to you as soon as possible. Naturally this threw her into some state of confusion as she does not know you or anything about you. Of course I was able to say that I had met you and explain a certain amount about you. But the Duchess demanded that before the romance could proceed any further she should have the chance of talking to Sabine herself about it. As the Duchess cannot herself come to London, Sabine must go back to France to her home. The Duchess emphasised that she has nothing against her step-daughter marrying whom-ever she wants to, but she insisted that she must see Sabine personally at this stage because she has always more or less acted as Sabine's mother. I gather that Sabine is already wearing an engagement ring that you gave her?'

'Yes.'

'I think perhaps it would have been more diplomatic to consult me before the romance developed quite so far. Then I could have advised you on the best way of handling things. Marrying Sabine, as you can perhaps see, is not quite the same as marrying any girl. She is the heiress to a very old title and to a château and a considerable fortune in France and——'

'But she doesn't want any of those things,' Philip burst

out. 'She wants to become a normal wife living in London. She wants her step-sister to inherit all that stuff in France.'

'Ah, perhaps that is what she has told you. But she seems not to have told her step-mother the same thing. I must be brutal with you, Philip, but the Duchess told me that this is not the first time Sabine has written to her from abroad saying she wanted to marry someone.'

'So Sabine has to go home. When?'

The Ambassador paused, lighting a small cigar. He threw the match into the fire and said quietly without looking at Philip: 'She has already gone. On this afternoon's flight.'

Philip started up from his chair, then sank back into it, staring amazed at the Ambassador, who said: 'The Duchess did not want any scenes. And she did not want either of you to do anything rash. Privately, I think she was afraid that you might elope, as I gather Sabine has made some sort of veiled threat to that effect in her letter.'

'And Sabine didn't resist at all?'

'She was most upset. But her step-mother had asked me to tell her not to tell you she was going home. At first, she refused. In tears. Then I managed to persuade her that her step-mother only wanted to *discuss* the marriage with her, and that she would probably be back very soon. On the basis of that promise she agreed to go. She left a note for you which I will give you. The Duchess did ask me to ask you (although I am sure you need no asking) not to mention a word about this to anyone else. Imagine if the Press, for instance, got wind of it . . .'

'No, of course, I won't mention it to a soul.'

The Ambassador rose: 'Thank you, Philip, for being so understanding. I can assure you that patience is the best course. If at any time you want advice or help do not hesitate to call me.' He picked up an envelope from his desk and handed it to Philip. 'This is Sabine's note to you. All I beseech you is don't do anything rash, because no good will come of it. And I speak with the interests of you and Sabine at heart, and especially with the knowledge of the Duchess, who *can* – I emphasise *can* – be a most formidable woman. Goodnight, Philip.'

'Goodnight, Excellency. And thank you for your help.'

Philip was near to tears. The Ambassador patted his shoulder:

'My car will take you wherever you want to go.'

'Back to my flat to change for the Romeo.'

'Ah yes,' said the Ambassador. 'The Romeo.'

In the car Philip switched on the interior light and read Sabine's letter through his tears: 'Darling, my darling. I have to go back to Beatrix and they won't let me call you. I *knew* she would do something like this when she got my letter. I will just tell her we want to get married and that is that. She won't be able to stop us because I won't let her. Oh I miss you so much already and I am crying terribly but your ring is still on my finger and when I look at it everything comes all right. I will telephone tonight when I get home and have spoken to Beatrix. And soon I will be back to love and love you with a million kisses for ever. My darling, I do so much adore you and you are with me all the time in my heart and in my head and inside me. Don't forget me. Everything will be all right, I promise you. Your very own and terribly loving S. XXXXX.'

*   *   *

That evening in the Romeo he could hardly concentrate on a single song. There was a hearty, drunken party of loud-voiced people in there who kept asking him to play requests, and it was all he could do not to throw down his guitar in a fury and walk out of the bar. He drank far too much, too, to lull his anxiety and quieten that nagging feeling inside him that he had lost Sabine for ever. At 11 pm when he had finished, he hurried home without having any dinner so as to be in the flat when Sabine called.

He waited for what seemed ages, drinking vodka after vodka. At five minutes to midnight the telephone rang.

'France calling,' said the operator. 'I have a call for you.'

'Hello?' It was Sabine's voice.

'Yes, it's me, Philip.'

'Oh darling, darling.' Then she sobbed so much that he couldn't hear what she was saying. He kept saying: 'Darling, keep calm, keep calm.' But she only sobbed the more. Eventually she quietened down and he said: 'Now tell me what's happened. Have you talked to your step-mother?'

'Yes.'

'What did she say?'

She started sobbing again. Then through her sobs she said: 'Philip, she says I cannot see you for a whole year. A whole year. Philip, I'll go mad. Imagine – a whole *year.*'

'Well, didn't you tell her you wanted to get married straight away? And that it was none of her business anyway?'

'Yes. But she wouldn't listen. I told her I loved you more than anything else in the world and I wanted to give up this nonsense here and just be your wife. But she wouldn't listen.' Sobbing more, she said: 'Then I said I would fly back to London and marry you just like that.

And she took my passport and cheque-book and money out of my bag. I said I'd still go and she said if I did she'd commit suicide. Philip darling, what am I to do? Tell me what to do. And she won't let me go out of this house without someone else. I tell you, I am just a prisoner here. Tell me what to do.'

'Well, I'll have to come over and get you, if she's behaving like that. What is your father doing about it?'

'No, Philip, don't do that. Papa's in Copenhagen just now. I think maybe tomorrow Beatrix will not be so firm. If you came here, I'd love it, but I think it would do us no good with Beatrix. You wouldn't be allowed in the gates. I think it would spoil everything.'

'What does she object to?'

'Oh she says I am too young and silly to know my own mind, and I would be no good as a housewife in London and that you are so poor you have to play at a night-club and that my responsibility is here with the château and everything. She just doesn't understand me. She never has. I don't *want* the bloody château. I want to get away from it all. I hate it, hate it, *hate* it. I've told you that before. Oh, darling, I do miss you.'

'Look, I'll write your step-mother a letter and see if that will help.'

'Yes, perhaps that will help. Do it tonight.'

'Yes, I will. And what about the baby – have you told her about that?'

'No, I thought we should keep that until all else seems hopeless.'

'Yes, all right.'

'And you will write the letter tonight?'

'Yes, my darling. Right now.'

'Be very careful what you say, darling. I must go now before I cry some more at hearing you and not being with you, which is where I should be. Don't forget me, darling.'

'How could I? Don't cry too much. We'll win in the end.'

'Yes, my darling. We *will* win, won't we? Goodnight, Philip, my love.'

'Goodnight, my sweetheart, and don't cry any more.' He put down the telephone.

He buried his head in his hands for some minutes, then sat down at the desk to write a letter.

'To the Duchess d'Alsace.

'Your Grace,

'I have the honour to write to you about the fact that your step-daughter Sabine and I wish to get married as soon as possible. We have known each other for some months and are very deeply in love. I know that you have not yet met me but the French Ambassador has met me several times and will give you the relevant details about my family background.

'At the moment I earn £3,250 a year, which is ample for a couple to live on in London. I also have the lease of my cousin's mews flat which will be a very comfortable home for us to start in. I can assure you I will do my very best to look after her in every respect.

'I look forward to meeting you and the Duc and hope that you will both see fit to give your blessing to an early marriage between Sabine and myself.

'I have the honour to be Your Grace's Obedient Servant
                          Philip Rodolphin.'

14

Next morning in the office Afdera Lassage telephoned.

'So that bitch is up to her tricks again with that poor girl,' she said in her clipped foreign accent. 'Meet me at 1 at the Mirabelle and we will have lunch to discuss what you can do.'

She was sitting at the table when Philip arrived, wearing a white pill-box hat and dark glasses. She was a striking figure. They ordered an Americano each and then she said: 'Now tell me – do you really love the girl?'

'Yes. Very much. I have never loved a girl so much in my life.'

'It is not just because she knows how to fock well?'

Philip laughed: 'No, Ambassadress.'

'Tch, tch, call me Afdera always. And it is not because of her money?'

'I earn quite enough for us both to live on even if she had no money. We have never discussed money except to agree on that. And the only knowledge I have of her money is that the papers keep calling her an heiress.'

'Well she could be quite rich if her father decided to leave the fortune to her. But if she runs away with you, she will probably get nothing. You don't mind that?'

'Not at all. I don't want her to run away because she would obviously be upset at publicity hurting her family, particularly her step-mother.'

'Ach, that woman Beatrix. She is a prize bitch. She has ruined many marriages and she is always beastly to this girl. She is jealous of her. Beatrix, the bitch, tried to wreck my marriage. That stupid idiot my husband fell for all her stupid talk. But I soon talked some sense into him.'

'What's Sabine's father like?'

'Ah, he is wet, a drip. He is not her father, you know. He is impotent. It was a marriage of convenience – for appearance's sake – the real father is some French gigolo whose name I can't remember. But the father spends most of his time at his Embassy in Copenhagen, and that bitch Beatrix lives at the château in the Loire. He just can't afford to have her with him as Ambassador in Copenhagen because she would cause too much trouble.'

They ordered their lunch. Afdera asked: 'You have talked to the girl?'

'Yes. Last night.'

'How was she?'

'In a terrible state.'

'What did you decide to do?'

'I have written a letter to the Duchess asking if we can get engaged. She is trying to stop us seeing each other for a whole year.'

'I think in the end the girl will just have to leave and fly over here and marry you without her step-mother's approval. Or you will have to go there.'

'But your husband the Ambassador said——'

'Ach, don't listen to him. He is still under that bitch's spell. Anything she says he will do to avoid a scene. You come to me for advice. I'll tell you what to do. I think that that girl *shall* marry you, to get her away from that beastly step-mother. We will work it out between us. But don't listen to Henri – he is hopeless. Just be polite to him and then come and ask *me* what to do. One thing you must do if you do marry the girl.'

'What's that?'

'See that she has more baths. She hardly ever has a bath. Disgusting. Didn't she smell?'

'Not that I noticed.'

'Maybe love confused your nostrils. I could smell her often. Or perhaps you like women with a touch of – how you say it? – BO? It can be very exciting, or so they tell me . . .'

*　　*　　*

Three days later, a letter with a French stamp addressed in elaborate Victorian handwriting in black ink arrived for Philip. The envelope bore a crown on the back. So did the top of the paper inside. The one sheet, written in that same ornate, old-fashioned script, read: 'Dear Mr Rodolphin. Thank you for your frank letter. Sabine had already told me of your desire to marry. However, as her step-mother I cannot agree to this immediately because I think, firstly, that she is too young to know her own mind. Secondly, that you have not known each other for long enough. And, thirdly, that you are not yet earning enough money to look after her in the proper style which I would expect. My husband agrees with me in all these respects.

'As you know, I have acted as her mother since she was two years old.

'I suggest that you do not see each other for a year and we then see what the position is. In the meantime please do not upset Sabine by doing anything rash.

'Yours sincerely,
　　Beatrix, Duchesse d'Alsace.'

Philip crumpled up the letter in fury, then smoothed it out again and put it carefully in his bedside-table drawer. He telephoned Afdera Lassage and told her of the letter.

'The bitch,' said Afdera predictably. 'I think you had better talk to the girl and decide what you can do. She must fly over here. That is the only thing.'

'I am talking to her tonight. I'll let you know what we decide,' said Philip. 'Thank you so much for your support.'

'Ach,' said Afdera, 'that's nothing. Anything to get the better of that unholy, four-flushing bitch Beatrix.'

*   *   *

That night he got back from playing at the Romeo as early as he could to be in time for Sabine's call. At 11.45 pm it came through.

'Hello, my darling Philip. How are you?'

'Fine but missing you, my love. How are you?'

'Not as depressed as before.'

'Why?'

'I had a long talk with Beatrix today. She was in a very good mood.'

'I got a letter from her this morning. It said we have to wait a year before seeing each other again.'

'What?'

'That's what she said.'

'She is quite impossible. She said to me she didn't really mean that stuff about a year's wait, and that she would soon fly over to London to meet you.'

'Well, the letter said quite firmly that you didn't know your own mind and that I wasn't earning enough to keep you properly.'

'Ach, she is a liar. She never said any of that to me.' She began to cry. Philip said: 'Now don't cry. That won't help at all. The only thing to do is for you to fly back to London and for us to get married. After all, what about the baby?'

'Yes, but Beatrix says she'll kill herself if I do that. I would have her on my conscience for the rest of my life. Philip darling, I just couldn't do it. I wouldn't dare. I'd never forgive myself if she did, and it would be a terrible start for our marriage.'

'Of *course* she won't kill herself. She's just saying that.'

'You don't know Beatrix. She might easily.'

'Of *course* she won't. It's just a threat. You go to her and tell her about the baby. *That*'ll change her mind.'

'But she might make me get rid of it. And I couldn't bear to do that, darling. It's ours, from our great love.'

'Well, you'll just have to refuse to get rid of it. It's all up to you, the whole thing.'

'Darling, don't say that. I can't do a thing. You don't know Beatrix.'

'All I know is that the only way we will see each other again is for you to fly back to London and say to hell with your step-mother.'

'But supposing she *does* kill herself?'

'She won't, I'll bet you.'

'But she might. And it would be too awful. Philip, I couldn't.'

'All right then: tomorrow you tell her about the baby and refuse to get rid of it, *whatever* she says.'

'Yes, darling, I will. And I will telephone you tomorrow night. Darling, I miss you and need you so much at nights I can't go to sleep and I have to do it by myself. Darling, is that wrong?'

'No, no. I miss you terribly, too.'

'Do you have to do it by yourself, too?'

'Yes.'

'And you think of me – not of anyone else?'

'No, of *course* not of anyone else.'

'Because I think of you being with me in the bed. Sometimes even in the daytime I have to go upstairs to my bedroom thinking of you inside me, which is where you belong, isn't it, darling?'

'Yes. I do so love you, my sweetheart.'

'And it will all come all right in the end?'

'It will if *you* play the right game with your step-mother.'

'Darling, don't be angry. I will do my best. You don't know Beatrix, you don't *know* Beatrix . . .'

* * *

The next night she called again at the same time. Philip said:

'How did it go with your step-mother?' She was crying again:

'Darling, I have something terrible to tell you.'

'What?'

'I woke up this morning and my days had come. So I'm not having a baby after all.'

Philip felt half-relieved, half-disappointed: 'Did you talk to your step-mother then?'

'No, I did not dare – she was in such a terrible mood. I think she hates me.'

'But you *must* talk to her and get her to stop this waiting for a year business.'

'I know, darling, I promise I will talk to her as soon as I can. In the meantime I will write to you every day.'

'Not telephone?'

'No.'

'Why not?'

'Because I am worried that someone is listening in. We must keep all this secret. No one must know. I will ring you lots of times, but not every day, darling. Will you write to me every day?'

'Yes.'

'You promise – every day?'

'Yes, my little love.'

'And tell me everything you do?'

'Yes, my little love . . .'

*   *   *

One evening when Philip was about halfway through his stint at the Romeo, in walked Mervyn Twankey. He looked as scruffy as ever, still in the same stained and crumpled grey double-breasted suit, dilapidated suede shoes, and frayed, dirty white shirt.

He sat on his own for a time with a drink, listening to Philip play and making him feel acutely uncomfortable. Then when Philip paused to sip the vodka gimlet which Twankey had sent over for him, he came up to Philip:

'Good evening, Mr Rodolphin.'

'Good evening, Mr Twankey,' Philip was icily polite: 'Thank you for the drink.'

'Have another.'

'No, thanks.'

'How are things going here? Enjoying yourself? Pity about your girlfriend having to go away so suddenly.'

The casualness of the remark almost caught Philip off his guard. He recovered his balance just in time to look suitably non-plussed: 'What? My girlfriend? Gone away?' Twankey carefully lit a cigarette, then stared hard at Philip with cold grey eyes:

'Yes. The Countess Sabine d'Alsace, the French heiress with a fortune and a château in the Loire Valley. You know her well, don't you? You saw a lot of her while she was here?'

'I did meet her once or twice – with other people.'

Twankey drew on his cigarette with an air of studied boredom, mingled with disbelief, and blew out the smoke towards the ceiling:

'I'd heard there was more to it than that.'

'Oh really?' Philip plucked at the strings of his guitar to hint that he ought to start playing again. Twankey kept picking at the wart on his right knuckle.

'Yes. I'd heard that you'd got engaged. That you had given her a ring. Rubies and diamonds.'

'I don't know what you're talking about,' said Philip hastily. 'Look, I must go on playing now. And I'd be grateful if you wouldn't write any of this nonsense in your newspaper.'

Twankey stubbed out his cigarette. He gave Philip a humourless grin: 'I won't write a word of it, dear fellow. Not unless I get it confirmed. And then it'll be on the front page. See you around.'

Twankey sloped out of the bar with his shuffling gait, still picking away at the wart on his knuckle.

*   *   *

The next evening when Philip arrived at the Romeo there was a girl sitting alone in the bar. He recognised her: it was Tamara Reno. She gave him a quick smile, then turned away to sip her drink. He didn't know what to do about her, whether he should go up and talk to her or not – and while she was the only person in the bar he felt a bit embarrassed about playing to her alone. He presumed she was waiting for Twankey, and dreaded his arrival.

She was certainly very glamorous: her long reddish hair fell decoratively down over her slim shoulders and bare arms, and she was wearing a short black and white 'op art' mini-skirt at least 8 inches above her knees. On her elegant legs she wore white Courrèges boots. She smoked Gitanes through a long black cigarette-holder.

Soon some other people came into the bar, so Philip was able to start playing without embarrassment. At his first pause she came over to Philip: 'We met one night before in here. I'm Tamara Reno.' Her speech was a bit slurred, suggesting she had drunk too much.

'Yes, I remember.'

'I was with Mervyn Twankey, then. The shit.' Philip looked questioningly at her. 'Yes, that *shit*. I'm finished with him. For ever.' She put her hands up to her eyes.

Philip put a hand on her shoulder: 'I think you had better go and sit down.'

'I want to talk to you.' She spoke from behind her hands.

'I can't talk to you now. I'm meant to be playing.'

'I'll wait till you have finished. Then can you talk?'

'Yes, I suppose so.'

'Thank you.' She walked dejectedly back to her table without looking at Philip, lit another Gitane and ordered another drink for herself and one for Philip.

At the end of his playing time she was still sitting there, drinking interminable gin-and-limes, smoking endless Gitanes. She looked definitely drunk. She could hardly walk straight, so Philip guided her to the door. 'Aren't you going to talk to me?' she asked pitifully.

'I can't tonight. I have a dinner date,' Philip lied. He didn't want a drunken Tamara Reno on his hands, especially as he didn't really know the exact state of her relationship with Twankey. Twankey was on his trail enough without alienating him still further by coming between him and his girlfriend.

He offered her a lift home in his car. She readily accepted. She shared a flat with another model off Bayswater Road. As he drove her there, she clutched his left arm as if for support. She did not speak, Philip suspected because she was too drunk.

As she got out she said 'See you tomorrow' and slammed the door, weaving an erratic path over the pavement to her door.

Every night for the next week she appeared in the Romeo bar. The pattern was the same. She always looked glamorous, dressed in a new mini-skirt outfit each night. She would sit drinking and smoking on her own, watching Philip, and then at the end of his stint she would ask to be taken home. Philip had to admit to himself that, in spite of Sabine, he was attracted to her: she was a very beautiful creature, although on close inspection the face was hard, merciless, covered with thick make-up. She wore long false nails and false eyelashes. For her to be so obviously lonely and unhappy struck pity in Philip. He wondered why it had bust up between her and Twankey.

On the seventh consecutive night that she appeared, he felt he must do something about her.

'If you're not doing anything after I've finished playing, how about having dinner with me here?'

Her face lit up: 'Oh I'd love that.' She tossed her hair to one side. 'I'd love that. Do you really mean it?'

'Yes. But you'll have to go back to your table now till I've finished playing.' She went back jauntily with a smile.

Going in to dinner, she took his arm. Every male face

in the restaurant followed her as she walked with Philip to his table. She was looking stunning that night. Philip felt proud to be with her. Even though, he had to admit, close up her face under the make-up was visibly pitted – probably from wearing so much make-up all day in front of the cameras and the hot lights.

After they had ordered their dinner, Philip said: 'What went wrong with you and Twankey?'

'Oh, he's a bastard and a shit. I hate his guts. And also he's a crashing snob. I just wasn't good enough for him, that's all. My name's not really Tamara Reno, you know. It's really Rita Scud. I come from Birmingham. Not exactly posh, that, is it?'

'Who cares about being posh?'

'Twankey does. He's got an obsession about it, he has.' With the effects of the alcohol she was lapsing into her old Birmingham accent.

Throughout dinner she told him her life-story, most of which he didn't listen to because he was thinking about Sabine. But he gathered she had been a shop-assistant in Birmingham until some perceptive rich tycoon had spotted her and told her she should be a model. After which she had come to London on the tycoon's money to enlist at the Mayfair Model Agency to be groomed. The treatment in her case had certainly worked.

'Twankey really put me on the map,' she said. 'I'll have to give him that. He did a piece about me in that Diary, with a picture. And the bookings flooded in. I was made. But it still doesn't stop me thinking he's a right bastard and a no-good shit. Now I haven't had any work for nearly two months. My face has gone out of fashion just like that. Or over-exposure. Have you got a girlfriend?'

'Yes, I suppose I have.'

'Why does she never come to see you play?'

'Because . . . she's away at the moment.'

'Where?'

'Abroad.'

'Oh. Is she coming back?'

'Yes.'

'When?'

'Soon.'

'What, you mean you don't know?'

'Not the exact date. But soon.'

'Would she mind you being with me then?'

'I expect she would. Girls do mind, don't they?'

'I think you need someone while she's away. A man's no good without a girl, just as a girl's no good without a man. That's why I came to you.'

'Why did you come to me?'

'Because I think you're attractive. And I wanted you. You know, to myself. But if you've got some other girl, then it's no good, is it?'

'Not on a permanent basis. No.' Philip, in spite of his stern resolutions, felt himself getting excited by this girl. And, he had to admit, he was flattered that she had singled him out.

'Why, you're engaged then?' she said.

'No, not exactly.'

'Oh, a sort of permanent mistress?'

'Yes, more like that.'

'Don't you feel you want me at all then?'

'Yes, I do. That's what makes it so difficult.'

'Why difficult? It makes it *easy*. Because I feel I want you.'

At the end of dinner he guided her out and said, as they were getting in his car: 'I'll take you home.'

As he got into the driver's seat, she said: 'I can't go home tonight. I've lent my bed to a friend.'

He looked at her and said: 'Well, where are you going?'

'Haven't you got a spare bed?'

He hesitated: 'Yes, I suppose I have.'

'Well, could I have that, just for one night? It would save me having to go to some draggy hotel. I'm broke, you see. With a huge overdraft. I spent all my earnings and now I've got nothing left to pay my taxes with.'

He took her back to his flat, hoping that Sabine would not ring. He left her with a drink in the sitting-room while he went next door and tucked the signed photograph of Sabine into his bedside-table drawer above the letter from the Duchess. He didn't want her asking any awkward questions about Sabine. Then he led her into the bedroom. He caught a whiff of her armpits.

'Where are you going to sleep?' she said.

'In the other room.' She put both her arms round his neck and kissed him on the lips. The smell of sweat was overpowering.

'I've been wanting to do that all night,' she said.

She kissed him again. Then she began to get undressed. He made as if to leave the bedroom.

'No, stay,' she said. 'I want you to stay.'

She said as she stepped out of her dress: 'I'm broke. Can you lend me some money? Just a hundred or two?' Philip laughed. 'I'm afraid I'm not rich enough for that. I'd love to but——'

'Oh come on. With this flat and all you must be well-lined.'

'The flat belongs to my cousin.'

'Oh. Where's he, then?'

'In New York.'

'Oh.'

186

Soon she was naked. She crawled languorously in under the bedclothes. Again he caught a whiff of her body odour: sweat almost covered up by scent and powder.

'Now you get in, too,' she said.

'But I'm sleeping next door,' he said halfheartedly.

'Give me one little goodnight kiss, then.'

He kissed her. 'I want you,' she moaned. 'Get into bed with me.'

In spite of her obviousness and her odour, he felt the need for her – for *someone*. He undressed and slid in between the sheets . . .

After their love-making was all over, he wanted to wash himself straight away to rid his body of the stigma of her touch. He had never made love to a woman with such a strong body smell. Before love it was not unattractive: now, afterwards, he hated it. As if reading his thoughts, she said: 'Now you must have a bath. Then I'll have one, too.'

He almost retched at her smell on him. It clung to his fingers and every part of his body. He went to the bathroom and turned on the taps. Soon he was lying in a warm bath, gladly ridding himself of that musty, insidious odour. He hated himself for making love to her. He was tainted, he felt: he had dishonoured Sabine. Tamara was skinny and small-breasted – the type of body he hated – and she was a cheap little whore, on the make, and he couldn't understand how he could have been attracted to her in the first place. He put it down to frustration at missing the daily love-making with Sabine, and flattery at the obvious pass she had made at him. And, outwardly at any rate, in spite of her dirtiness and her bad complexion, she was certainly a striking-looking woman. But that was no excuse, really.

He returned to the bedroom with a towel wrapped

round him. Just before he opened the bedroom door he heard a scuffle. She was lying on her stomach on top of the bed, naked. She stood up as he came in, saying: 'Now I will have a wash, too.'

Some sixth sense told him that something was wrong: she had not looked him in the eye. When she ran out to the bathroom, he looked round the room. He noticed first that his jacket had been hung up on the chair. Then he saw the drawer of his bedside table was an inch open. He opened it: the letter from the Duchess was out of the envelope *on top* of the photograph of Sabine – and he had put the photograph of Sabine *on top of the letter*. He went into the bathroom – she was just about to step into the bath. He said angrily:

'You have been looking into my private belongings.'

'What do you mean?'

'You have been looking into my bedside-table. The letter was in the envelope *under* the photograph when I last saw it. Now it is out of the envelope *over* the photograph.'

She lowered her eyes: 'I don't know what you are talking about.'

The real truth suddenly hit Philip.

'Twankey sent you here. I know he did.' Philip spat out the words: '*Didn't he?*' He shook her shoulders. She lowered her eyes: 'Yes,' she gulped. 'He did.' Then she shouted: 'And I'm glad he did, you silly little nit, for being taken in by me. I wouldn't look at *you* in a million years.'

Philip slapped her face hard. She put her hand up in pain and surprise.

'*Get out*,' he shouted. '*Get out*, you little bitch.'

She screamed: 'You'd have done it for a hundred quid too, you rich, posh, mean little bastard. I had to get it somehow. *You* wouldn't lend me any. And I went to bed with you, didn't I? You fucked me, didn't you? What *more* do you want?'

He said quietly, angrily, 'Get out before I hit you again.'

He waited in the sitting-room while she dressed. Without speaking he followed her down the stairs and slammed the front door behind her.

He cursed himself. Then he sprayed Airwick-mist all round the bedroom and bathroom to get rid of the guilty, all-pervading smell of her body.

15

Nothing happened for two days. The lull before the storm, thought Philip. He was still furious with himself for being taken in by Tamara. How *could* he have been so stupid? Sabine had called once the night after, but he could say nothing about it to her – after all, what could he say to excuse himself taking a girl back to his bedroom? It would immediately put her in high hysterics, if he knew Sabine at all. He had written to her each day as he had promised, her scrawled letters to him arrived faithfully each morning.

Then – as he suspected it eventually must – the bomb exploded: on Friday evening Twankey appeared in the Romeo. He did not look at Philip as he came in: he went straight to the bar and ordered a drink. The barman brought a vodka gimlet across for Philip: 'With Mr Twankey's compliments. He thinks you'll need it.' Philip looked across at Twankey: he was lighting a cigarette with a self-satisfied smile on his face.

Twankey did not bother to interrupt Philip while he was playing. He sat at the bar with his back to Philip, making little notes on a pocket note-pad. At the end of Philip's stint, as he was packing his guitar into its case, Twankey came over: 'Mr Rodolphin, I think you and I had better sit down and have a talk.'

'Oh, what about?'

'I think you know very well what it's about: about Sabine. There's no point in continuing to hold out on me. You see, I've spoken to the Comptroller of the Duc d'Alsace's household in France——' he consulted the sheaf of notes in his hand – 'a Count Pierre Malraux, and he has given me a long statement confirming the whole business of the romance and all that.' Philip stood still, too surprised to say anything. Twankey said: 'I think we'd better have another drink and a long talk.'

Philip blurted: 'I've got absolutely nothing to say.'

'Oh you needn't say anything at all unless you want to. Everyone else has said it for you. Or at least Count Malraux has. But you might want to answer some of the things he's said.' Twankey was at his smarmiest and smuggest: he had the upper hand and he knew it. And he was rubbing it in with an ill-concealed malicious delight.

They sat down at a table and Twankey ordered two more drinks. He said in a matter-of-fact way: 'This morning I rang the Duchess, but she refused to take my call. I asked to speak to Sabine but she was unavailable. In the end they put me through to Count Malraux, and I put to him that I knew the story of Sabine's romance, that she had been flown home to avoid any more contact with you, that she was wearing your engagement ring, and that the Duchess had written to you denying you access to Sabine for a year and refusing to let you get engaged.' Philip swallowed nervously: he was trapped – he did not know what to say or do. He merely knew he must say the minimum.

Twankey went on, consulting his notes: 'Count Malraux called me back this afternoon with this statement: "Mr Rodolphin has no money and no position. He certainly cannot marry the Countess Sabine. As soon as the Duchess d'Alsace heard of the romance she brought her step-daughter back from London home to the family château in France. The intention is that she will be prevented from seeing him again".'

Philip went cold inside. But he said nothing.

Twankey said coldly: 'Have you anything to say in answer to this?'

'Nothing. I have no comment to make at all.'

'Do you intend flying to France to see Sabine?'

'No.'

'But you are engaged and wish to marry her?'

'I have nothing to say.'

'Is that your final word?'

'Yes.'

'Well, I can't blame you. There's not much you really *can* say. Oh by the way this story will be coming out in this Sunday's *Echo*. I shouldn't worry too much about it.' Twankey was picking away at the wart on his knuckle. He grinned coldly: 'It'll certainly bring the crowds into this place. Goodnight, Mr Rodolphin.'

He rose and walked away. Philip sat for several minutes as if stunned. Twankey was on to a good story, and no philanthropic considerations could shake him off now.

He went to find Randi Ravello. Randi was sitting in the restaurant with a couple, waving his usual fat cigar and treating them to a silver chalice full of champagne. Philip sent a waiter to say to Randi that he wanted to talk to him urgently.

Randi came out: 'What is it, my boy? Something wrong?'

'Randi, there's a family crisis. I can't really explain it but I wondered if I could have Saturday and Sunday nights off, please?'

'Of course you can, my boy. Something serious?'

'Yes, it is rather.'

'Give my best regards to your grandfather if you see him and tell him I miss him in my modest little establishment. Tell him to come in next week for some free caviar and champagne.'

'Thank you, Randi.'

Philip just knew he must get out of London for the weekend. But where to go? He couldn't face going to his parents, nor explaining about Sabine to them. They would have a fit when they read the story in the *Echo*.

Then it struck him – his cousin Teddy, Uncle Marcus' eldest son by his first marriage, Gerald's half-brother and one of the brightest Tory MP's. He had always been easiest to get on with of all the Rodolphin cousins. He lived with his wife Debo and three sons in a large house at Knebworth, Hertfordshire, which he had said Philip could visit at any time.

Though it was nearly midnight, he telephoned Teddy's number. Teddy himself answered. 'It's Philip. Sorry to ring you so late. But I'm in a terrible crisis. Can I please drive straight down and stay with you?'

'Yes, of course. I'll wait up for you.'

'No, please don't do that. Just leave the lights on and a note telling me which room I'm in.'

'Are you in trouble with the police?'

'No. I'll tell you the whole thing tomorrow.'

Dear Teddy – he knew he could rely on him, even though he hadn't seen him since he had left the Army. Teddy would help – Teddy would tell him what on earth to do.

*   *   *

The next Sunday, on the front page of the *Sunday Echo*, beside a huge picture of Sabine, the story ran, under the headline of 'The Heiress and the Guitar-Player – Duchess forbids them to meet again': 'Countess Sabine d'Alsace, heiress to the Alsace château, vineyards and fortune and great-great-granddaughter of the Kaiser, has been forbidden by her step-mother, the Duchess d'Alsace, formerly Princess Beatrix of Wolfenbuttel-Schleswig, to see again or get in touch with the man she loves and wishes to marry.

'He is Mr Philip Rodolphin, grandson of Lord Rodolphin, head of the famous merchant bankers. He works in an advertising agency by day and plays the guitar in the bar of Mayfair's Romeo Club by night. The ban—and a letter from the château in the Loire Valley to a small mews flat in Chelsea – is the answer to Mr Rodolphin's request for permission to marry the Countess.

'The letter, answering one sent by him to the Duchess, tells Mr Rodolphin his request is "not possible".

'Count Malraux, Comptroller of the Duke d'Alsace's household, said in an official statement: "Mr Rodolphin has no position and no money. He certainly cannot marry the Countess.

"As soon as the Duke d'Alsace (at present France's Ambassador to Denmark, and Sabine's father) heard of the romance he and the Duchess brought the Countess back home from London. The situation is that she shall be prevented from seeing Mr Rodolphin again."

'Count Malraux said there was nothing in law to prevent Countess Sabine marrying Mr Rodolphin if she insists. She is 23 this year and needs no family consent.

'Countess Sabine was recalled from London a few weeks ago where she was staying at the French Ambassador's private residence to learn nursing at St Stephen's Hospital, Fulham.

'"She has seen her step-mother for only a short period," said Count Malraux, "but there is no ill-feeling between them." The Countess is the daughter of the late Princess Tsai of Thailand, the Duke's first wife.

'Mr Philip Rodolphin was laconic about this romance.

"I have nothing to say about it," he said. But it was clear from his attitude that he does not intend to let things end with the ban.

'Indeed in his bedroom is a signed photograph of Sabine with her written inscription "To Philip from your very own S. XXX."

'Note – the family motto of the Rodolphin family is "Amor Vincit Omnia" (Love conquers all).'

*   *   *

'Well,' said Teddy Rodolphin at Sunday breakfast, 'I must admit it looks tricky.'

Teddy had always been Philip's favourite cousin. Not only was he an eccentric and engaging member of the Tory Right wing – he was also a war hero: he had a wooden leg which he had earned – with the DSO – leading his squadron of tanks in the Guards Armoured Division in the Ardennes offensive. Philip loved him, and wished he could see more of him. With his curly black hair and tinted dark glasses, Teddy cut a dashing and colourful figure wherever he went. He was supremely good-looking, which probably explained why he always had at least two mistresses crazily in love with him – quite beknown to the beautiful Debo, his wife and mother of his three sons. She never seemed to care a jot how many mistresses he had, and she was quite right not to mind – for whatever mistress he had, Teddy was always the perfect husband and father. His enemies – and he had many – would say that he could never have got away with it if he hadn't been born so rich. But Philip suspected that Teddy's charm, Byronic good looks, and his sardonic wit would have made him exceptional, however poor he had been born.

Philip said: 'What do you think is the best thing to do?'

'Nothing,' said Teddy with a wild laugh. 'Absolutely nothing. Say nothing and just carry on as if nothing had happened.' They were alone together: Debo, heavily pregnant, was having breakfast in bed.

'What, you mean go to the Romeo tomorrow night?'

'Yes, of course.'

'But won't the whole Press be there?'

'Probably they will. But raise two fingers at them and just play on as if nothing had happened. Be oblivious of the whole thing. Be miles above it. Ignore them. Don't be drawn into argument or discussion with any of them. I know the way the Press works from my election experiences. And I can tell you the only way to handle this is to ignore them. Say absolutely *nothing*!'

Philip had told Teddy the whole story of Sabine, Twankey and Tamara's seduction. Teddy had laughed himself silly, much to Philip's consternation. 'You were really taken for a ride there,' Teddy had cackled. 'You shouldn't be so keen to go to bed with birds. They're always liable to be dangerous. You're old enough to know that, for Heaven's sake. Did she *really* smell awful?' Teddy just couldn't take the Tamara incident seriously at all. He laughed and laughed and laughed. Then he saw Philip's anguished face and became serious. 'Don't tell Sabine, whatever you do,' he said. 'She would never understand it. Women like Sabine don't understand that sort of thing, however natural it is. I mean, *I* understand it, but *she* wouldn't.'

'What do I tell her then, to explain how the Press knew about the letter and the signed photograph?'

'Tell her that your charwoman talked, or that someone got into your room. Tell her anything, but don't tell her about Tamara, whatever you do. I personally think that if the girl's got any gumption at all she'll say fiddlesticks to her step-mother and get on a plane to fly to London and marry you.'

'But her step-mother's threatened to commit suicide if she does that.'

'But that's just a typical threat, a typical meaningless threat by a jealous step-mother,' said Teddy decisively. 'Of course she would no more commit suicide than fly to the moon.'

'I agree. But how do I get Sabine to see that?'

'Well, she must be pretty stupid if she can't see it already. Is she stupid?'

Philip hesitated: 'I don't think so. She has never seemed stupid to me, except in her attitude towards her step-mother. But she has some deep-seated obedience and terror of her step-mother which you cannot beat, however awful her step-mother may be.'

'I think,' said Teddy, cleaning his dark glasses with his blue silk handkerchief, 'that the first thing you'd better do is to ring Sabine and see what's happening there. By the way, do your father and mother know anything about this?'

'No, nothing.'

'Hadn't you better tell them?'

'No. I couldn't face it.'

'Well, they'll be on to you like a shot on Monday morning.'

'I'll wait till that happens.'

'I should ring Sabine now. Use our telephone.'

Teddy left the room and Philip put a personal call through to Sabine on her private number at the château. He got through to her almost immediately.

'Darling?' she said. 'Is it you?'

'Yes it's me, Philip.'

'Where are you? I've been ringing your London number hundreds of times.'

'I'm staying in the country with my cousin Teddy. Darling, what's happened with the papers?'

'Oh, it's chaos here. There are masses of photographers and people at the gates, but we won't let them in. Darling, what started it all?'

'I don't know. A man came to see me——'

'But how did they know about the photograph I gave you, and the ring, and Beatrix's letter?'

'I don't know. They know everything.'

'But, darling, Beatrix says you must have told them to try to make her change her mind about the year's wait. That's not true, is it?'

'No, of course it's not true. I haven't told them anything.'

'Oh, darling, I'm so glad. Because Beatrix said if you had told them she would never let me marry you.'

'What the hell's it to do with her? And what's all this nonsense this Count Malraux has been telling the papers?'

'Oh, don't believe a word he says. He is an old fool. He knows nothing. Beatrix is furious with him for getting it all wrong. He is a silly old fool.'

'Well, he's the one who's caused all the fuss with his statements.'

'Yes, darling, I know. But don't listen to a word he says.'

'Do you love me?'

'Of course I do, darling Philip my love. But I wish that all this didn't have to come out in the papers. It makes everything so difficult with Beatrix. She is absolutely *furious*. Darling, how did they know everything?'

'I don't know.'

'Just as Beatrix was beginning to relent a bit about the

year's wait, all this has to happen. It's not fair.' She began to cry.

'Darling, don't cry. It will all be all right.'

'Yes, but everything is so difficult now. With everyone knowing about us. Darling, don't say a thing to any newspaper, will you?'

'No, not a thing. I haven't done so yet, and I won't.'

'I miss you and need you terribly, my darling. I am going nearly mad without you. And Beatrix is so difficult – I have no one to talk to. When will you be back in London?'

'Tonight late.'

'I will call you then, my darling,' she sobbed. 'And don't please say anything to the newspapers. Because of Beatrix.'

He said no and goodbye and put down the receiver. Teddy came in:

'Satisfactory?'

'Well, she's a bit upset because her step-mother's blaming me for all the press fuss.'

'That's inevitable. I shouldn't worry. Let it simmer. Women will always come to you if they want you enough. How about a strong Bloody Mary? You look as if you need one . . .'

*   *   *

After the two days of comfort and quiet at Teddy's house, Philip returned to an absolute furore in London. As he drove up to the flat at about midnight, he saw a group of cars filled with men waiting outside the flat door in the mews. The men got out of the cars as he stopped.

A galaxy of flash-bulbs exploded. Press men battled

round him shouting questions: 'Are you going to France?' 'What have you to say to Count Malraux's statement that you have no money and no position?' 'What stones are in the engagement ring?' 'Have you spoken to Sabine by telephone?' Still the flash-bulbs exploded. At the door of the flat Philip turned to the group and said 'I'm sorry, I can say nothing. I have no comment to make at all.'

A voice shouted: 'Are you going ahead with a runaway marriage?' Another shouted: 'Is Sabine flying here?'

Philip smiled wanly into the exploding flash-bulbs and retreated behind the front door with an exhausted sigh. He felt like a hunted animal, like a fox who hears the jabberings of the hounds outside his earth. He looked out of the sitting-room window – some of the reporters and photographers had left, some appeared to be pre-pared to sit out the night.

Next morning there was a long piece about him and Sabine in every paper with – and this infuriated him – extensive quotes by his father saying things like 'If the girl's got any guts she'll fly over and marry him and to hell with what Count What's-his-name says.' 'No position my foot. The Rodolphins have been prominent in English history for 700 years, which is more than you can say for the Alsace family in France. They were mere shoemakers until Napoleon made one of them a duke in 1807.'

That sort of remark is not exactly going to help, thought Philip. He silently cursed his father but realised the futility of telephoning him to ask him to be more discreet in his statements to reporters. His mother, he noted with relief, had not said a thing.

As soon as he arrived at BDP, still followed by three cars full of reporters, the Chairman sent for him. Philip was ushered into his office.

'Sit down, my boy. Sorry to read you've got yourself

into a bit of a pickle, one way and another. Looks an attractive girl, though. Can quite understand. What can we do to help you with the Press? Anything?'

'I don't know, sir. I'm being pursued at the moment but I think the best thing is to say absolutely nothing.'

'Absolutely right, absolutely right.' The Chairman offered him a cigarette which he refused. The Chairman lit one himself: 'The only thing that worries me is that this guitar-playing job of yours in the Romeo at nights makes it look as if we're not paying you enough.'

'Well, sir, you're not paying me very much yet because I'm still a trainee.'

'Quite so. Let me see——' he consulted a file on his desk – 'you're getting £750 a year at the moment?'

'Yes, sir.'

'Well, you have done very well, so they tell me, on your trainee scheme and so I think we'd better put the salary up to £1,250 a year. How would that do?'

'That would be marvellous, sir. But I'd still want to go on playing at the Romeo. It doesn't interfere with my work here, and they do pay me £50 a week. Which makes a lot of difference.'

'Um. I can see that.' The Chairman looked meditative. 'If you gave up the Romeo, you mean, you wouldn't be earning enough to marry the girl.'

'That's exactly it.'

'Well, I can't do any more than that financially at the moment. But if ever you want any help over anything, don't hesitate to come and see me. I know that dealing with the Press in your position is a very tricky business. But say nothing – absolutely nothing – and you can't go far wrong.' The Chairman rose to lead Philip out: 'The stepmother's being a bit difficult, is she?'

'Yes, sir.'

'Umm. Often happens. Hope true love conquers and all that. I'm sure it will.' He patted Philip on the shoulder: 'Good luck, me boy, young Lochinvar.' The Chairman chuckled into his double chin.

*　　　*　　　*

Philip did not go out for lunch that day because there was still a group of reporters and photographers waiting at the door of BDP. He had sandwiches alone in his office, brought by his secretary from the canteen. During lunch a messenger boy delivered a note to him: it was from the Editor of the *Echo* offering to pay Philip's air ticket to France to go and see Sabine. He crumpled the note up and threw it in the wastepaper basket.

During the afternoon he got a telephone call from Twankey. 'Look,' said Twankey in his greasiest voice. 'I've done all my stuff on this story and there's nothing else for me to write. I'm sorry if it's landed you in a bit of trouble but good stories are good stories.' Twankey chuckled in his cold way. 'What I'm suggesting is that I could give you a bit of advice on how best to deal with the rest of the Press. If I come to the flat when you're getting ready to go to the Romeo – I suppose you are going to the Romeo?'

'Yes.'

'I could advise you on certain things not to do.'

Philip, though unremitting in his dislike of Twankey, felt so vulnerable and incapable of dealing with the Press *en masse* that he thought Twankey's offer was worth accepting. After all, Twankey couldn't do any *more* harm. He said: 'OK then.'

Twankey went on: 'I'll ring three times on the bell and then you can let me in, and I'll tell you what sort of thing you should and should not say to other reporters. Believe me, there's nothing in this for me because I've done my story and I feel slightly guilty about landing you in all this mess.'

'OK,' said Philip, willing to clutch at any straw of support and completely unsuspicious of Twankey's motives.

At 5.30 he drove back to the flat still followed by three car-loads of reporters and photographers clamouring for an interview with him. He said nothing and gently closed the door in their faces. Inside the flat he poured himself a strong vodka gimlet. The doorbell rang constantly, but he ignored it. Then it rang three sharp times: it must be Twankey. Philip opened the door as little as he could, and Twankey slipped in, while the other reporters' shouts grew to a babble.

'Now what am I going to do?' said Philip when he had given Twankey a whisky and water in the sitting-room.

'Don't say a word to any of the others, whatever you do,' said Twankey. He looked all round the room, his head moving in little jerks as he took in the décor and furniture, picking at his wart as he did so.

'How long will this pursuit go on?'

'Oh, it'll all be off by tomorrow. They'll get fed up when you say nothing. I say, could I go and have a pee?'

'Yes, of course.' Philip showed him the bathroom. Twankey seemed away a long time. The doorbell kept ringing, but Philip ignored it.

Twankey returned, finished his drink in one gulp, then said: 'I must go now. Just say nothing to anyone else and you'll be all right. I'll let myself out. Oh by the way, that step-mother of hers must be a ghastly old bitch.' Twankey smirked.

A fat lot of use *his* advice was, thought Philip when he

had gone. There must have been some ulterior motive for him coming round. But he was not to learn the real purpose of Twankey's visit until the next morning.

After changing into his dinner-jacket for the Romeo, he looked out of the window and saw the group of reporters still waiting. He decided to dial the Chelsea police: 'Hello, my name is Philip Rodolphin and I'm being badgered by newspaper reporters and I'd like police assistance to get out of my flat.'

'What did you say your name was?'

'Mr Philip Rodolphin.'

'Oh yes. Address?'

'33A Pavilion Road.'

'Thank you, sir. We'll send a car round right away.'

Philip watched out of the window. Soon a police car drew up and a burly sergeant got out. Philip let him and a constable in: 'I'm sorry to bother you, Sergeant, but these reporters are becoming more than a joke. I have to go and play somewhere——'

'At the Romeo Club, isn't it, sir?'

'Yes. How did you know?'

'I read my papers, sir.' The Sergeant flexed his arms and fingers inside his police gloves. 'Just leave those reporters to me, sir. They are a blasted menace when they get on to something like this.' The Sergeant turned round to open the front door, then looked over his shoulder and said: 'Oh by the way, sir, hope you don't mind me saying so – but I hope you get your girl in the end.'

'Thank you, Sergeant.'

*　　*　　*

Philip arrived at the Romeo unfollowed: the Sergeant had blocked the end of the mews with his squad car and prevented the reporters from following Philip. But at the Romeo itself there were a lot of reporters waiting, all sitting drinking at the tables in the bar. He could easily tell they were reporters by the way they looked at him when he came in. Well – nothing for it but to accept them and play as he normally would.

Randi Ravello came in almost immediately. 'Look, boy, why did you not tell Randi you were in this business of marrying an heiress?'

'Well, what could you have done about it?'

'Randi can fix anything. Anyway, you at least fill up my bar.' He cackled with glee, waving a hand round the full tables. 'I tell you when you begin I will make you the most famous guitar-player in Europe. And *hey presto* I have done it.' He clicked his fingers and laughed delightedly, sucking ferociously on his huge cigar. 'The best thing that has happened to the Romeo for years. I immediately double your salary, OK?'

'Thank you, Randi, I'll need it.'

'Ah, not with *her* money you won't. But in the meantime you might.'

Randi left him to dispense *largesse* and chat round the assembled members of the Press. Philip noticed that as he started playing each new tune the reporters scribbled something – he supposed it was the song title – in their note-books. The only thing to do to lull his nerves was to drink – and Philip drank as much vodka as he could take. By the end of his stint he was too drunk to care about any reporters. As he packed his guitar into its case, they all gathered round him asking him questions about Sabine. He maintained a genial silence, smiling enigmatically at each loaded question. He was almost too drunk to answer, anyway. Most of them did not follow him out of the club: they realised he would not speak to them. A few badgered him getting into his car but unwillingly let him drive away.

At home in the flat he collapsed on his bed with strain and exhaustion. That night he ate no dinner – instead he took two sleeping pills left by Gerald in the bathroom cupboard.

The next morning the *Echo* splashed all over its front page 'an exclusive interview by Mervyn Twankey with Philip Rodolphin, the man at the centre of *the* romance of the moment'. It told how Twankey had got into the flat by 'a secret code of three rings on the bell', it described the flat in detail, even the bedroom and the photograph of Sabine on Philip's dressing-table (which Philip supposed Twankey must have snooped at when he said he was having a pee, or else had heard about from Tamara). Philip thought: what a double-crossing shit. What a fool I was to trust him at all. I will know better next time.

But it was too late. That night before he went to the Romeo, Sabine rang: 'Darling, it's all over the paper here that you let a reporter into your flat, and he saw everything in the flat and the photograph I gave you of me, and you spoke to him about us and everything.'

'I did *not.*'

'And he says in the paper here that you said awful things about Beatrix.'

'I didn't mention your blasted step-mother, darling.'

'Well, she is perfectly furious and says it shows you can't be trusted after you'd promised me you wouldn't say anything. Darling, *why* did you do it?'

'I didn't', said Philip weakly. He sighed . . . It was no use trying to explain.

16

During the next few days, though the Romeo bar was full every evening, the hue and cry of the Press dwindled away – mainly because Count Malraux put out an official statement. He said he regretted that his earlier remarks had been distorted, that there *was* a romance between Philip and Sabine, that there was no parental opposition by either the Duke or Duchess d'Alsace but that Sabine had agreed to her father's request that she and Philip should wait, separated, for a while so that 'the situation could be reviewed again in the not too distant future'. The whole statement was ridiculously woolly and full of meaningless officialese phrases which did nothing to lull Philip's suspicion about the Duchess's real motives. But he kept a discreet silence, refusing several requests for interviews and refusing to speak to Twankey whenever he appeared, which he did regularly, either at the flat or in the Romeo, always with that self-satisfied leering grin on his face, never looking Philip in the eyes.

One night Philip asked Randi Ravello if he would do him a favour and ban Twankey from the Club premises. Randi threw up his arms in horror: 'My dear boy, my dear dear boy, I know he is being a pest to you but he has given me a lot of useful publicity in the past, that boy Twankey. He stinks, I know; he is a bastard, I know. But Randi Ravello has been in this business too long to do a dam-fool thing like ban the *Echo*'s gossip columnist for no good reason. You see, boy, you see my difficulty, don't you? I mean, Twankey is no trouble in the place?'

'Except to me.'

'Except to you. Ah, my boy, but you are a well-known figure now and you will have to learn to deal with people like Twankey. You shouldn't go around marrying heiresses. And wasn't that Twankey's girlfriend who used to come in alone and buy you drinks every night? Didn't you give her dinner one night?'

'Yes, but——'

'Ah well, my boy, perhaps he is jealous.'

'Of *course* he's not jealous. Anyway, I don't see her any more.'

'Ah – hell hath no fury like a top-model scorned. Ha ha, ha ha, my boy, you listen to Randi.' He laughed loudly, enormously proud of his summing-up of the Twankey-Tamara-Philip triangle.

*   *   *

Early in the morning after the Twankey pseudo 'interview' had been published, Philip's mother telephoned:

'Oh, darling Philip, I have been so worried about you these last few days. Why didn't you tell me about all this going on? I mean, darling, is it true what we read in the papers – are you in love with that girl?'

'Yes, of course.'

'Well, why didn't you *tell* me? Is she nice? She looks very pretty in the pictures.'

'Yes, she's very nice. We want to get engaged. But her step-mother won't let us.'

'But, darling, have you known her long enough? I mean, it sounds a very good thing, but do you know her well enough?'

'As well as I'm ever going to, I would say.'

'And you really feel sure you want to marry her?'

'Yes, absolutely.'

'Would it help if I wrote to her step-mother? Or her father?'

'I don't think so. Not at the moment.'

'Well, what can I do? I feel so powerless.'

'Nothing. We'll just have to wait.'

'It all must be a terrible strain for you. Surely we can do *something*. Can't you fly over and see her?'

'No. She's particularly asked me not to as she says it would prejudice the situation even more.'

'Can't you meet her secretly outside her house somewhere?'

'She's kept like a prisoner in that château, watched night and day by her step-mother and this bastard Count Malraux.'

'Oh, I feel so sorry for you.' Philip heard his father's voice in the background. His mother said: 'It's Philip.' Obviously his father grabbed the receiver because his voice boomed loudly: 'What the devil do you mean by getting yourself splashed all over the gutter press? Why the *hell* can't you conduct your affairs with more discretion? Dammit, you've become a sort of poor man's Peter Townsend.'

'Father, it wasn't my fault——'

'Of course it bloody well *was* your fault. You shouldn't go around chasing some bloody Frog heiress. Dammit, I spent six years of my life fighting for the blasted Frog and trying to rescue him for chickening out in 1940 and now my son has to cap it all by trying to present me with one as a daughter-in-law. Bloody insult.'

'She's not a Frog. Her mother was Siamese.'

'Well, no better. Bloody Chink. And anyway, the Chinks are just as bad. Can't trust 'em an inch. Look what they're doing in Vietnam. Typical. Fine mixture, fine mixture – half-Frog, half-Chink. Anyway, why the hell doesn't the woman fly over here, marry you and get it done with? She would if she had any guts. A girl of that age being run by her step-mother. Bloody ridiculous, I'd say. I'd get out of it while the going's good. Give up the whole foolish idea. Wouldn't trust a Frog-Chink an inch, money or no money, Countess or no Countess. Anyway, titles over there don't mean a damned thing. Just means you've got more vineyards than the next man.'

'Father,' said Philip quietly. 'Sabine and I want to get married.'

His father exploded: 'All right, you silly cunt-struck little ass. Don't say I didn't warn you. If she won't fly to you, if she hasn't got the guts to stand up to that interfering Kraut bitch of a step-mother, then you'd better get on the next plane and bloody well *bring* her back. Go and rape the damned knickers off her: that's probably all she wants anyway, frustrated little Frog whore——'

Philip slammed down the telephone. It was more than he could take – from his own father at that.

*   *   *

Every day, as she had promised, Sabine wrote a letter to Philip. Her spelling was atrociously bad, completely phonetic. Hence 'enough' would be 'enuff' and 'come' would be 'kumm'. What with her childish, illiterate writing, it used to take him a long time to grasp the meaning of what she had written. Always in her letters and in her telephone calls she complained, often in tears, about the way in which her step-mother virtually imprisoned her, shut her off from all personal contact with the outside world except by telephone. Everywhere she went she had to be accompanied either by her step-mother or by Count Malraux. She wrote: 'I think Beatrix is doing it just to brake me down so that I say I do nott love Philip. But I won't do it, my darling, I won't do it. Even thoe I am going madd I won't do it, I promise you.'

As if in sympathy with Sabine, Philip imposed on himself a strict discipline of no girls. Not that he particularly wanted a girl – except possibly as an outlet for the physical passions that every call and every letter from Sabine fanned immediately into blazing flames. He could not talk to her or read her letters without feeling a growing excitement in his body until by the end of the letter, in which she had described how she slept naked in bed so she could feel herself like Philip had done, or until the end of the call when she was literally gasping with passion on the telephone, pleading with him to come and assuage her longing for him inside her – by then his ardour was quite out of control and he would run to the photograph of her and imagine it was she who was caressing him . . . It was like a permanent hunger in his guts, a hunger that made it difficult for him to concentrate on typography at BDP or at guitar-playing in the Romeo. He had never before felt this insatiable longing for someone's touch, for someone's mouth on him, someone's naked legs parallel to his own, winding themselves round him. Sabine was like a drug – as each day went by without her, he longed for her more.

So the weeks passed. From time to time little paragraphs would appear in the Press about Sabine, or a picture of her, always mentioning Philip at the same time. And each time such a paragraph appeared, Sabine would plead on the telephone: 'Darling, you must not allow the papers to write about us. Each time they do it makes Beatrix more furious and puts her more against you. It makes it so much more difficult. If only the papers would stop writing about us, Beatrix would cool down.'

Philip would vainly protest: 'But I can't *stop* the papers writing about us.'

'Well, darling, don't do anything to encourage them.'

'I don't. I do nothing. I never speak to anyone about us. Not even to my family. We can't go *on* like this – just being separated. When do your father and step-mother say we can meet again?'

'They say they won't allow us to meet while the papers go on writing stupid things about us.'

'Well, the longer we are kept apart, the more the papers are going to write. They must *see* that.'

Then one day the bombshell fell. Sabine rang just as Philip was leaving for the Romeo. Eventually she said: 'Darling, something terrible happened last night.'

'What?'

'I met Heini at a dinner party.'

'Well?'

'And I went back to his flat afterwards.'

'Alone?'

'Yes.'

'What happened?'

There was no answer. He repeated, more forcefully: 'What happened?'

She still did not answer. He said: 'Did you go to bed with him?'

'Darling, I couldn't help it. I'd been missing you so much lately that I thought I was going mad. And I just couldn't stop myself. I just had to lie with someone, some man, naked in a bed, and I thought of you the whole time, my darling, believe me. Please believe me . . . Are you angry with me?'

'Sabine, listen,' said Philip, his anger making the palms of his hands tingle, beads of sweat breaking out on his forehead at the thought of her in bed with another man.

'I'm telling you now – unless your father agrees to let us meet at some fixed time soon, or comes over here to see me to discuss it, I am not going on with it like this.'

She sobbed: 'But darling——'

He interrupted: 'You'd better speak to your father tomorrow morning and get something arranged. And you can call me tomorrow evening at the same time. Otherwise we'll have to stop this.' He didn't want to stop it, but he felt that her succumbing to Heini was the thin end of the wedge.

She sobbed: 'But don't you love me, darling Philip?'

'Of course I do. I love you too much, that's the trouble.'

'If you loved me really so much, you wouldn't say things like that.'

'If you loved *me* you wouldn't go back to Heini's flat.'

'Darling, I can't help it. Without you here I *need* someone, *need*, *need*, *need*. I am going *mad*. Heini was nothing to me – I proved that to myself last night. But I don't want it to happen again. And yet I'm afraid about it – without *you*.'

'Well, you'll just have to talk to your father or step-mother tomorrow morning. I mean this. You have got to *do* something. We can't go *on* like this.'

That night at the Romeo he had to drink a lot of vodka to quieten his anger and his jealousy over the Heini incident.

'Something wrong?' asked Joe the barman as he brought Philip his sixth drink: 'You look upset over something.' Philip shrugged his shoulders.

'Don't worry, lad,' said Joe kindly. 'You'll get her in the end. If she wants you enough. And if she doesn't, you're well out of it.'

The next evening, as arranged, Sabine telephoned:

'Darling, I have wonderful news. Beatrix is going to come to London to see you.'

'When?'

'On the seventeenth. Isn't that terrific? Aren't you proud of your little Sabine for fixing it? Darling, *say* you're proud of me.'

* * *

'I'm sorry to have to ask you to come round here,' said the French Ambassador in the Embassy two evenings later. 'I know how busy you are. But I have been in touch with Sabine's step-mother. And she is coming over to see you. I think that this bodes well for you and Sabine. I hope so, anyway.'

'Thank you, Excellency,' said Philip. They were sitting in the Ambassador's study.

'I must stress to you that no knowledge of this visit must find its way to the Press. You will be absolutely discreet about this, won't you? I'm sure I need not ask but——'

'Of course,' said Philip quickly.

'The Duchess wants to see you at 11.30 on Sunday the seventeenth.'

'In my flat, I presume?'

'No, not at all.' The Ambassador looked apologetic.

'At her hotel then?'

'No, not at her hotel. I must explain – she is anxious at all costs to avoid publicity and therefore she has suggested another rendezvous – the flat of a great friend of hers. It is 3A Connaught Close, a mews in Bayswater. You just have to ring the bell and you will be let in. My advice to you is to arrive slightly early. She is keen on punctuality. Most Germans are' – he added with a laugh.

The next morning Afdera telephoned Philip in his office: 'Can you lunch with me today? The Mirabelle at one?'

'Yes. I'd love to.'

'I have some things I want to say to you.'

At lunch Afdera was her usual explosive self: 'So that bitch of a step-mother is coming over to see you?'

'Yes.'

'That is good. But you must be tough with her. She is a hard woman. Do you still love the girl?'

'Yes, very much.'

'All right then. Has she been faithful to you?'

'I don't know——' Philip hesitated.

'I hear she has been seeing that awful Heini again.'

Philip looked up. 'Who told you that?'

'Oh, I have my sources. But he is a real devil. I think you should see her again as soon as possible. Does she write to you?'

'Yes. Every day.'

'And telephone?'

'Yes. Most days.'

'Has she mentioned this Heini?'

'Yes.'

'Does she still love him?'

'I don't think so.'

'But you never know with a girl like that. She has ants in her pants.' Philip looked up surprised. 'Don't mind what I say – but I know a girl like that when I see one. They just can't keep away from a man. And if the man they love is not there, they settle for the next best thing. I know because I'd do it myself. So would most women, though they don't admit it. My advice to you is: if you want that girl, marry her quick. She has – how do you say it? – a tiger in her tank. As long as you realise that——'

'She'd be perfectly all right without her step-mother, away from that château.'

'Maybe. I hope so – for your sake. But remember: what do they say? – the leopard cannot change his spots. Would you mind if she was unfaithful to you?'

'Of course I would. But I don't think she would be once I married her.'

'Not as long as you fock her plenty she won't. But remember – that girl needs focking. Plenty of focking. I can tell that. If you can do it, fine. If you can't, watch out. If she's anything like her step-mother . . .'

* * *

Philip arrived at 3A Connaught Close at 11.15 that Sunday morning. He sat in the car for ten minutes, checking that his tie was straight in the car mirror, brushing hairs and dust off his best dark-blue suit.

He rang the bell. The door was opened by a foreign maid who smiled and nodded and led him up the stairs to a small sitting-room. The maid gestured at an armchair. Philip sat down.

The room was stifling hot. He could feel the sweat forming on his forehead and running down his chest inside his shirt. He mopped his brow with a clean white handkerchief.

He looked at his watch. It was 11.35. He began to walk up and down the small room. Then he heard the doorbell ring, so he sat down again. He wiped the sweat off the palms of his hands on the arms of the chair. The clock on the mantelpiece seemed to tick very loudly.

He heard footsteps on the stairs. The door was opened by the maid and in walked a short grey-haired woman dressed completely in black – from her shoes to her gloves and handbag and her hat which sat neatly on her grey hair. Her eyes were flinty blue, her nose sharply aquiline, and her mouth a mere slit in her tight, white-parchment face. Her legs were slim and elegant, but her hips wide and cumbersome. With a strained smile on her face she stretched out her hand to Philip.

They shook hands in silence. She sat down in one armchair, propping her bag on one arm. Philip sat down in the other. Still no word had been spoken. Philip thought: in her younger days she must have been a very striking-looking woman; for that matter, she was still attractive.

She laboriously removed her gloves and placed them beside her bag on the arm of the chair. The ticking of the clock on the mantelpiece seemed extra loud in the strained silence. Philip looked at his shoes – he was determined not to speak first.

Eventually the Duchess cleared her throat and said: 'Isn't it a lovely day?' She spoke with a strong guttural German accent.

'Yes,' said Philip eagerly. Another long silence.

She said: 'Thank you for your letter.'

Philip mustered his courage. 'You must realise – Sabine and I want to marry as soon as possible. I earn enough money to keep her.'

She turned towards the window, fiddling with the ornate rings on her left hand. After a long silence she said:

'Sabine is not ready for marriage. You must understand that.'

'But she is nearly twenty-three.'

'I know. But she is very young in mind. In fact, she does not even know her own mind. Today she wants to marry you, tomorrow it is someone else. I know and I understand because I was just like her at that age.'

'This time,' said Philip quietly, 'I think she *does* know her own mind.'

'Ah – I can understand you thinking that. Because Sabine is a very attractive girl and she has told you a hundred times that she loves you, yes?'

'Yes. And I believe her.'

'Ah – but you must not believe everything she says. She is a mere child and does not know what she is saying.'

'I believe she does.'

'Well, I as her step-mother should know better, you agree?'

'No. Not on this particular thing. I think I know her better than you do.'

'Not at all. You will *never* know her better than I do.' The Duchess sounded dogmatic. 'It is as if she were my daughter and I know her better than anyone ever can.'

'The point is that we are in love and want to get married. Only you stand in our way.'

She sighed: 'My husband and I agree that you can get married on only one condition – and that is that you provide the kind of home for Sabine comparable to the one she has always known. What can you provide at the moment?'

'A very nice flat in Chelsea.'

'With servants?'

'No.'

'Who would do the cooking?'

'Sabine. But she says she enjoys cooking and does it very well.'

'Ah. That is what she says. Sabine can scarcely boil an egg. Because she has never had to. She doesn't understand what cooking means. You must not believe everything she says. She has a very vivid imagination, you know. And she does not always tell the truth. I wonder – you do not know her all that well, perhaps?'

'I think I know her as well as anybody,' Philip said firmly, clenching the arms of the chair and sitting up straight.

She smiled enigmatically: 'I don't think anyone knows Sabine well. She is a very – a very complicated girl. But tell me, Mr Rodolphin – ' her tone changed to one of metallic sweetness – 'where do you propose to live with Sabine if you do marry her?'

'Well, initially in my flat in Pavilion Road.'

'But that belongs to your cousin, does it not?'

'Yes. But he is away for two years.'

'Not much security, is it? And I am told the flat is not much bigger than this.'

'Certainly it is quite big enough for a couple to live in.'

'Is there room for servants?' She spoke with a sinister innuendo, as if she already knew the answer.

'No. But they can come in each day.'

'Ah, but Sabine will need living-in servants. She does not know how to look after herself. She has had, you must understand, a very sheltered upbringing. It would be unfair to expect her to cope just like any normal girl.'

'Sabine herself seemed to think the flat quite suitable to start off with.'

'Yes, but I told you – Sabine must not always be believed. What she says to you perhaps she does not always say to me. Or perhaps she does not think.'

'Has she said to you that the flat was not big enough, then?'

'She has, shall we say, implied it.' She smiled a twisted smile and fiddled with her gloves. Her mouth smiled, yet her eyes were cold as ice. 'You see, Mr Rodolphin – I know when to believe Sabine and when not to believe her. I doubt if you do.'

Philip was getting irritated by her constant implications that he did not know Sabine: 'You seem to think I do not know Sabine well.'

'I don't think you do. How could you have had the chance to do so? A few meetings – and then you say you want to marry her. It is not right.'

'You seem to forget that we met every day for several months.'

She frowned angrily: 'Every day? The French Ambassador told me that you only met a few times.'

'The Ambassador did not know of all the times we met. We kept them secret.'

'You met without Nicole?' She sounded insistent.

Philip saw no point in lying: 'Yes.' He could feel her mounting anger.

She said briskly: 'So you used deceit then?'

'Not deceit. We just didn't tell anybody. We thought it was the best way.' Her expression grew flinty and angry, her lips hardening, her mouth tightening into a sharp gash as her lips pursed.

'Mr Rodolphin, I must tell you that there is no chance of me agreeing to you marrying Sabine, my step-daughter, while you are not in the position of being able to give her the kind of home she is accustomed to. Your cousin's flat is simply not the kind of home I would like her to live in, nor is it one in which she would feel happy or *could* feel happy. I might tell you that in all this my husband agrees with me totally. So, although she may not tell you, does Sabine herself. When you have a home to offer which I consider fit for my step-daughter to live in, then perhaps we can have another talk. Until then, there is no point in further discussion. Of course I cannot stop you talking to Sabine on the telephone, but I must warn you that I think it unfair on her for you to continue to encourage her while you have no chance at all of providing a suitable home for her here in England. You must realise that eventually she will inherit the possession of the château in France——'

'But she says she doesn't *want* that,' said Philip desperately.

'Ah, that is what she tells you. But of *course* she is going to inherit it and she will have to live in it. That is the kind of nonsense she talks which someone who knows her well, like myself, has learnt not to take any notice of. I suggest quite frankly, Mr Rodolphin, that you think again.'

'But if I get a house that you consider suitable for Sabine, then you and the Duke are prepared to agree to the marriage?'

She thought a long time, then said: 'Yes. At least we are prepared to accept the fact that you are eligible to marry Sabine, which we are not prepared to accept at the moment.' She rose, to indicate that the meeting was at an end. The same flinty smile flickered round her tightened mouth, the same ungiving glitter lay in her eyes. She held out her hand. Philip shook it without saying anything and walked down the stairs, out of the door, to his car. In the car he laid his head on his hands on top of the steering-wheel.

I 7

That evening the telephone rang. It was Sabine: 'I have spoken to Beatrix, darling, and she likes you very much. She says as soon as you can find a bigger house for us to live in she and Papa will let us get married. Darling, isn't it fantastic? You must try at once to find a bigger house.'

'That won't be easy. But she said it was you who said the flat here wasn't big enough.'

'Darling, don't be silly – of *course* I think it's big enough. But Beatrix doesn't, and once she gets an idea like that in her head she is quite impossible.'

'She said you couldn't cook.'

'Darling, you *know* I can cook. I adore cooking. I took a course on cooking in Paris. I expect she said I needed lots of servants, too.'

'Yes.'

'Oh, she's always saying that. I *hate* servants hanging about. I'd much prefer to do things myself. She will *never* understand, it does irritate me so. But, darling, you did well, I am sure – because she liked you very much. And once you have got a bigger house, everything will be all right. She promised me that. Do try, darling.'

'Well, I'll try. But I don't know how I'll get one. I'll only be able to afford it if I go on at the Romeo.'

'Well, that's all right. I love you playing at the Romeo. It's so romantic. Darling, do you still love me and miss me terribly? . . .'

*　　*　　*

Philip deliberately did not tell his mother and father about the Duchess's visit to London. After his father's outburst on the telephone, Philip thought it wiser to withhold any news about developments in the romance until there was absolutely no chance of his father wrecking them, either by direct approach to the Alsace family or by an indiscreet explosion to some reporter like Twankey, who was always sniffing round for a story. Twankey had gone down to Philip's parents' house one day with a photographer and pursued the Colonel as he rode round exercising the hounds – much to the fury of the Colonel who had apparently flung obscenities at both Twankey and the photographer and threatened to use his riding-crop on them if they didn't clear off. A picture of the Colonel on horseback had appeared subsequently in the *Echo*, side by side with a picture of Philip playing the guitar, to show the widely different pursuits of the Rodolphin family.

In the absence of discreet and reliable relations who would understand his delicate and difficult position, Philip, increasingly pent-up and nervous, felt a desperate need for a confidante whose advice he could ask without fear of the information being passed on. The only person to fill that bill was Teddy. On the evening after his meeting with the Duchess he rang Teddy at home in Hertfordshire. Teddy immediately gauged Philip's distress and arranged to have lunch with him the following day, Monday, at Buck's.

Over a roast pheasant and a decanter of Buck's best claret, Philip told Teddy all about the meeting with the Duchess: 'She gave nothing, she promised nothing. She was tight-lipped and frosty the whole way through. Oh, she was polite all right. But in a cold, totally ungiving kind of way. I can see exactly why Sabine has so much difficulty with her. I didn't realise fully until now just what a formidable step-mother she must be. I'd be absolutely scared stiff of her.'

'Didn't she give you the slightest bit of hope?' Teddy asked. 'Not the glimmer of a concession?'

'Well,' said Philip resignedly, 'she said if I got a house fit for Sabine to live in instead of the flat, she would allow us to get married. But how on earth could I afford to get a house, with servants, to be compared with that bloody château she lives in now? You'd have to be a millionaire to——'

Teddy gripped Philip's arm: 'Listen. I think I know the answer. It's a fantastic coincidence. Do you know Vincent Morgan?'

'The Welsh property tycoon whose father was a miner?' Teddy nodded. 'I know of him from the papers.'

'Well he lives in a huge house in Richmond Park. He was shooting with me last weekend in Hertfordshire and happened to ask me if I knew anyone who'd like to live in the sort of lodge-house-cum-dower-house at the end of his drive in Richmond Park. I never thought of you because I didn't know about this old bitch making this a condition of her approval. But I gather the house is quite big, four bedrooms, two bathrooms and a servants' flat, a nice garden – and the great thing from your point of view is that he doesn't want any rent for it, just the maintenance and upkeep. It's Queen Anne. He says he wants someone he knows to live in it, not paying any rent because he's so rich anyway that it would all go in tax.'

'But how could I possibly afford to furnish it? Put carpets down and so on? They cost a fortune.'

Teddy thought for a moment, then said: 'Listen: I'll speak to the Morgans, see if they like the idea, then you can see the house – and if you like it, go ahead and take it. It's too good an offer to pass by.'

Philip persisted: 'But what about the furnishing? And paying the servants? Presumably one would need a couple – a man for the garden and a cook-housekeeper for the house?'

'Yes.' Teddy sipped his claret. 'Listen, Philip – I'll lend you the money. You can pay me back in monthly instalments when things get better.'

'No no——'

'Yes, I mean that. I'd like to see you beat this domineering bitch. And after all, Sabine's got money of her own – plenty of it – hasn't she? I think this house of the Morgans might be the answer. They're both crashing snobs and would love to have you at their lodge gates. You could cope with the upkeep and servants and so on, once you moved in, couldn't you?'

'As long as I'm playing at the Romeo – I suppose yes.'

'Well, you'll just have to keep on at the Romeo. BDP don't mind, do they?'

'No. Not at the moment anyway.'

*   *   *

Two days later, Teddy telephoned Philip at BDP: 'I've spoken to Priscilla Morgan and she is delighted at the idea of you living in the Dower House. She said she'd read all about you in the papers. I told you they are both crashing snobs, and though I didn't tell them the exact position with the Alsaces, I hinted at it enough to whet their appetite. I could hear her preening herself at the thought of you and Sabine living at the end of her drive. She says she'll meet you at the Dower House at eleven o'clock on Saturday morning to show you round, and they've both then asked you to lunch.'

Philip did not tell Sabine of this unexpected lucky break over the house – he wanted to clinch the deal first before raising her hopes. Teddy had explained the route to the Dower House, so punctually at eleven o'clock the following Saturday morning he parked his car outside the gate and waited for Priscilla Morgan to arrive.

Five minutes later she appeared on foot up the drive, smoking a menthol-tipped cigarette, accompanied by two white poodles and an Alsatian. Philip got out of his car and shook hands.

'How do you do, I'm Priscilla Morgan.' The dogs sniffed his trousers. 'Vincent and I are so glad you are interested in living here. I think it would be perfect for you.' She led him up the steps and unlocked the front door with a large key on a ring with a lot of smaller ones. The heavy wooden door swung back with a creak. She said laughingly:

'It's very old, but we lived in it ourselves for a bit while they were putting the central heating into our own house. And we found it very warm and cosy.'

After she had shown him round the house, she said:

'We both would love to have you living here. Will you drive me up to the house? The dogs can run behind the car.'

She guided him to a large white modern house with a courtyard outside the front door. A butler in a white coat opened the door before they reached it. The dogs rushed in ahead of them. She gripped Philip's arm as they went into the sitting-room. A small, fat, balding man in a brown tweed suit rose from a chair by the fire. He did not smile. 'Vincent,' she said, 'this is Philip Rodolphin. I've just shown him round the Dower House. He loves it.'

Vincent Morgan shook hands with Philip, still without

smiling. He waved towards the drinks tray on a table by the window. 'Help yourself to a drink.' His voice was unmelodious and rasping, his face unchangingly hard. 'Get those bloody dogs out of here,' he said to Priscilla. 'They're dirtying the carpet.'

*   *   *

Lunch was a strain. Priscilla Morgan prattled nervously on about this and that, mainly about her hunting experiences with the Enfield Chase, answered by gruff rebuttals and contradictions from Vincent. Philip felt most uncomfortable.

Then the butler came in and whispered something to Vincent Morgan. 'It's Fred,' said Morgan to Priscilla. 'I must go and talk to him.'

'It's Fred Stark, his greyhound trainer,' Priscilla Morgan explained as her husband waddled out of the room. 'Vincent thinks about nothing except his business and his greyhounds. He's going through a bad patch at the moment. None of his dogs seem to win.' She changed the subject: 'It *is* exciting about you coming to live in the Dower House. When can you move in?'

'Well, almost any time. As soon as possible.'

'When do you think you'll get married?' Philip looked up quickly. Priscilla said nervously: 'I mean, Teddy explained it was for you to get married in and I just wondered . . .'

'I don't know. Soon, I hope.'

'Oh, I *do* hope it's soon. It would be such a nice house to start off your married life in. I've read *all* about you in the papers. I do think it's exciting. She looks a terribly attractive girl.'

Vincent Morgan came back into the room muttering

'Damned fool, damned fool.'

Priscilla said: 'Vincent, I've been asking Philip when he can move in to the Dower House.'

'Oh yes,' said Morgan. 'We'd better have a talk about that.' He sat down and laid out his napkin on his knee. 'Now you do realise,' he turned to Philip, 'that I'm not charging you no rent our of sheer charity? I'm doing it because at my rate of tax it is ludicrous. I'd just pay it all back in tax, so it becomes pointless. But I'd rather have someone I know about living in the house. I don't want a bloody stranger on my doorstep.'

'Yes, of course,' said Philip. 'It's very kind of you to——'

'It's not kind at all,' growled Morgan. 'It's sheer bloody economics. But I'll expect you to be entirely responsible for all the upkeep and maintenance of that house and the garden. Rates, drainage, repairs, the lot. You can deal with my agent Major Scamp about all that. I don't want to be bothered. Clear?'

'Yes, of course,' said Philip.

'Oh darling, don't sound so business-like,' laughed Priscilla nervously.

'You've damn well *got* to be business-like in this world,' said Morgan gruffly. 'Otherwise you for one wouldn't be sitting here enjoying the luxury that you do.' He turned to Philip: 'When can you move in?'

'As soon as is convenient.'

'I'll get my lawyers to get in touch with you.'

'Your lawyers, darling?' said Priscilla surprisedly.

'Yes, of course. Got to have the arrangements on a proper legal basis. Never know what might happen. But I'm telling you' – Morgan turned to Philip – 'there are only two eventualities in which I'd want you to get out of the house – a major war or my death. So you needn't worry – I hope. Let's go and have coffee in the sitting-room.'

Priscilla said to her husband as they left the dining-room: 'What did Fred want?'

'Camberwell Beauty's gone lame. Damned nuisance. Can't run him on Monday at White City.'

*   *   *

'I've got a wonderful surprise for you,' Philip told Sabine on the telephone that evening.

'What is it, darling? Tell me.'

'I've got a house.'

'You *haven't*? Oh darling, you are brilliant. Where?'

'In Richmond Park. It's Queen Anne. Four bedrooms and a servants' flat. A lovely garden. And I don't have to pay any rent.'

'Oh darling, Papa and Beatrix will be delighted. They can't object to us getting engaged any more. They promised that when you got a house they would agree to everything. You are clever. When are you moving in?'

'I should think early next month. When I have got everything sorted out with Gerald about the flat, and got some furniture for the new house.'

'Darling, can you afford it?'

'Yes. I told you, we don't have to pay any rent. And I'm getting all the furniture at a second-hand store in Euston Road. My cousin Teddy's very kindly lending me some money for the carpets and curtains and things like that.'

'Is that the Teddy you've told me so much about in your letters?'

'Yes.'

'He sounds divine. Thank him from me, darling, will

you? But don't borrow too much because it will be such a bore to pay back when we are married and need it most. Why don't you have to pay any rent?'

'Because the people who own it, the Morgans, are so rich that any rent would all go in tax.'

'Darling, you are so very clever to find it. I will tell Beatrix tomorrow morning.

It will be ideal for us. Near enough central London, yet in the country. It couldn't be better.'

'Oh, my darling Philip, I am so excited. All our problems are now solved. Beatrix simply *cannot* object any more. Darling, I love you so much for being so clever and finding a house for us . . .'

*　　*　　*

In the next two weeks Philip signed the legal document prepared and sent to him by Vincent Morgan's solicitors, bought a lot of antique furniture in Euston Road, fixed up credit accounts with local tradesmen recommended by Priscilla Morgan, and went with Belinda Caterham to choose curtains and carpets at John Lewis's.

He had taken Belinda down to see the Dower House beforehand so she would know what the rooms were like. She had been thrilled with the house.

He also spoke to Mrs Drinkwater, the daily at Pavilion Road, told her of his plans, and asked her if she would come and live in at the Dower House as cook-housekeeper. Mrs Drinkwater, a widow, immediately said Yes, she'd love to, she'd always preferred the country.

He wrote to Gerald in New York, explained to him the situation including his purloining of Mrs Drinkwater, and Gerald wrote back saying he quite understood, to go ahead and let the flat furnished. His solicitors would take care of all that.

At last the day for the move arrived – a Saturday morning. Philip was to drive down to the Dower House first thing in the morning with his own luggage, meet the Army and Navy Stores removals van with the furniture and then return to pick up Mrs Drinkwater in Fulham while they were unloading. The carpets and curtains were not due to be put in until the next week.

He had deliberately told as few people as possible about his move to Richmond Park: if the news got out into the Press, it would only cause renewed speculation about the romance and harden the Duchess d'Alsace's heart still further. Who were the people who knew? He counted them off in his mind as he drove down that Saturday morning: Teddy – well, *he* was quite safe. Belinda Caterham – he had sworn her to secrecy; Mrs Drinkwater; the Morgans – he had to trust to luck with them – that was the lot. Oh and Gerald, but he was in New York. Philip had not even told his parents for fear of another outburst from his father. The security couldn't have been much tighter, he thought, as he pulled the E-type into the Dower House driveway.

He unloaded his own suitcases and odds-and-ends and took them into the house. The key was where Priscilla Morgan had said it would be – under a flower-pot to the right of the porch. He left his stuff in the hall and wandered round the garden. It was a big garden: he wondered how much the Morgans' gardener would cost him. The morning was clear, fresh, dewy, the birds singing: he suddenly felt at peace for the first time for months, as if the Dower House provided the passkey for him and Sabine to find happiness at last.

There was the sound of a heavy lorry in the drive. He

went round to the front door to see a large furniture van pull in to the gate and draw up with a jerk. Two men in brown overalls jumped out: 'Mr Rodolphin?' said the larger one.

'Yes, that's me.'

It was only then that he saw parked behind the lorry a black Ford Cortina. Out of it, a self-satisfied smile on his face, his suede shoes crunching on the gravel, stepped Mervyn Twankey.

18

It was as if the Serpent had just slithered into the Garden of Eden. A wild fury flared inside Philip. Twankey said: 'So sorry to bother you just at this moment, but——'

'What the *hell* are you doing here?' Philip's voice quivered with anger. 'How the *hell* did you know about this?'

Twankey smirked: 'I have my contacts, you know. Listen: there's no point in getting angry. Cool off, old fellow.' Twankey casually lit a cigarette. 'Quite a nice little nest you've found here.' He airily looked round the garden: 'Good lawn for croquet. How did you get it?'

'Listen: I'm not saying one word to you, so you had better go. Why the hell can't you leave me alone? No one's interested in what I do. Yet you go on and on and *on* putting in absurd little titbits in the paper——'

'You're wrong there, you know. Our readers, the great British public, *are* interested. What do they say? – all the world loves a lover: especially when he loves a beautiful foreign heiress. You must face up to reality, old cock.'

Twankey looked down at his wart which he had been picking and began sucking it. He went on in that silky tone of voice that Philip had learned to fear and to hate: 'But I'm prepared to play ball with you over this. I'll have to write the story, of course. It's too good a story to miss. But I won't say in my story where your new country house is. Then you won't have the other papers bothering you. I won't even tell the people in my own office where the house is, so that way there'll be no leaks. And we'll have the story exclusive to us. OK? Fair do's?'

Philip saw that any further anger was pointless. He said resignedly: 'Do you have to print the story at all?'

'Oh yes. Surely you understand that.'

A sudden movement in Twankey's car caught Philip's eye. A long telefoto lens was protruding out of the front window. Twankey saw Philip's reaction: 'Oh, you don't mind my photographer taking a few photographs, do you? Just for the files.'

'Yes, I do,' snapped Philip, quickly stepping back behind the furniture van.

Twankey called to the photographer: 'All right, Jack. That's enough.' He turned to Philip: 'Obviously I can take it you won't make any statement?'

'No. Nothing.'

'Not even a few words about why you took the house?'

'No. Absolutely nothing. I would be grateful if you and your photographer would now go and leave me to get on with supervising the unloading.'

Twankey shrugged his shoulders, sucked his wart for a minute, then said: 'OK, OK. We've got what we came for. See you around sometime.' He got into his car, backed down the drive and drove off.

In spite of the cool freshness of the morning, Philip had to wipe the sweat off his forehead.

'Cocky bastard,' said one of the furniture men who had been listening to the conversation. 'Who the flipping hell does he think *he* is, anyway, barging in like that on someone's private property? Now, sir, let's get on with the work.'

By the time Philip had to leave for the Romeo that evening, all the furniture was in the correct rooms and Mrs Drinkwater installed in her quarters. The tradesmen had all made their first deliveries and everything was as organised as could be expected – less, of course, the carpets and curtains.

As he left the bar, after playing, to walk to his car, the hall-porter stopped him: 'Excuse me, but Lady Caterham left a box for you. She said to tell you it was a moving-in present.'

On the table in the hall sat a large wooden box with wire netting over the top. Philip peered in – inside, fast asleep on straw, was a yellow Labrador puppy. The hall-porter smiled: 'Only six weeks old, her ladyship said. And would you please telephone her tomorrow and tell her what you're going to call it.'

*   *   *

He had a long lie-in that Sunday morning and called Belinda Caterham from his bed.

'It's Philip. You are angelic to give me the puppy. He woke up when I lifted his box out of the car and I took him for a run round the garden last night. Mrs Drinkwater thinks he's wonderful – which is lucky because she'll have to clean up the messes. But I've put him in that passage between the back door and the kitchen, and it's a stone floor, so it won't matter if he does make the odd puddle.'

'Oh I'm so glad you like him. I couldn't think what else to get you, then I remembered you telling me that

235

Sabine loved dogs. So I thought a Labrador would be the perfect answer – especially with that lovely big garden to run around in. What are you going to call him?'

'I don't know yet. I'll have to talk to Sabine about it. She'll be thrilled.'

'By the way, have you seen the *Sunday Echo*?' Philip feared the worst:

'No. I haven't seen any of the papers yet today.'

'It's that odious Twankey again. On the front page. All about you moving to a new country house in preparation for the engagement. There's a picture of you standing by a furniture van. Luckily he doesn't say where the house is. How did he get all that?'

'He turned up here with the furniture van. I don't know how the hell he found out. I dread to think what that bitch the Duchess will say about *this*. I'll get blamed again, I suppose. What's so unfair is that it's entirely because of *her* attitude and the ridiculous statements of that Malraux idiot that Twankey is so interested in the first place. If they let Sabine and me behave like any other normal couple who want to get officially engaged there would be nothing *in* the story for Twankey.'

Almost as soon as he had stopped talking to Belinda, the telephone rang: it was Sabine. She was in tears.

'What's wrong, Sabine love?'

'It's Beatrix again. Because of the story about your house – our house – in the newspaper today. She's absolutely furious. She says you must have deliberately told him.'

'What is the *point* in me telling them when I know perfectly well that all it does is to infuriate her and make her more difficult?'

'Darling, please don't get angry with me. It's not my fault.'

'It *is* your fault. You should stand up to her when she talks this nonsense. You should explain to her that the Press is bound to take some interest in us when she takes this tough line and won't let us get engaged when we both want to.'

She sobbed: 'Darling, now even you are turning against me. Everyone is against me. I have no one to talk to.'

'I am *not* against you: I am against your step-mother. She is being deliberately destructive. Can't you talk to your father?'

'Och, he is never here and anyway he is hopeless with Beatrix. She completely rules him, like she rules everyone.'

'Well, you'll have to get her to see sense. We just can't go on like this. The more she stops us, the more it will be in the papers. Don't you *see* that?'

'Yes, of course *I* see it, but Beatrix doesn't.'

'I think she deliberately does it so that there *will* be stories in the newspapers and then she can complain about me.'

'Darling, she *likes* you. She said she did.'

'She may like me, but she doesn't want us to get engaged. That's as plain as anything.'

He heard her sob more. Then she said: 'Oh do tell me what to do. Please tell me.'

'Tell your step-mother and father unless they let us get engaged you will get on a plane and come over to London and marry me.'

'But she said if I did that she'd commit suicide. I *can't* do that, I really *can't*, darling – you must understand. Please understand. I want her to give her blessing to our marriage. It would be awful to start off knowing that Beatrix was against us – or had committed suicide because of us.'

'Of course she won't commit suicide. She's only saying that to frighten you into obeying her. It's typical of her devilish mind.'

'Darling, don't turn against Beatrix.'

He changed the subject: 'Not a very happy conversation for your first call to our new house, is it?'

'Oh darling, I forgot, with all this fuss about the news-papers. How are you in *our* new house?'

'Fine. No carpets or curtains yet. But everything else is in. By the way, Belinda Caterham has given us a moving-in present.'

'What?'

'A Labrador puppy. Yellow.'

Her voice changed to a tone of happiness: 'Oh, how wonderful. How old is it?'

'Six weeks. What shall we call him, my love?'

'Umm – ' She thought: 'Something that has a special meaning for both of us.'

'Something to do with our special music we always played together?'

'Yes, darling. What was that Sinatra record? – Oh yes, "Songs for Swinging Lovers". The one we always talked and danced to. The one where you said the arrangements were so brilliant. What was the man's name who did them?'

'Nelson Riddle.'

'Yes, that's him. Let's call him Nelson, darling. Then he will always remind us of those evenings when we were alone together and when we found each other's love. I think of those secret evenings so much now, my darling Philip – they are always in my mind. When will we spend another evening like those?'

She sobbed again. He said rather brutally: 'When you can get that damned step-mother of yours to see sense.'

'Don't blame Beatrix too much. It's not her fault. She just wants what's best for me. She just doesn't believe I love you enough to give up everything for you.'

'Well then it's up to you to change her mind. My love, it's only you who can do it. I can do nothing more. She said we could get engaged if I moved into a suitable house for you. I've done that now.'

'I know. But the newspapers spoilt it all. Instead of being pleased, she is very angry with you.'

'I give up.'

She said loudly: 'Darling, don't say that. Don't you love your little Sabine any more?'

'Yes, of course I do. But it's your step-mother – ' She interrupted quickly:

'I will try to speak with her, darling, I promise you. Today. I will say we can't wait any longer. I promise I will. But, darling, please don't ever say you will give up. I think I'd go mad. And you will keep writing every day?'

'Yes.'

'And I'll write and telephone each day.'

'Don't telephone between 6 and 7 because now I change for the Romeo in the office. It's too far to drive back here in between.'

'Then I'll call at about midnight, when I'm tucked up in bed and longing for you to be beside me. Darling, after talking to you in bed I can never get to sleep until I do what you used to do to me. Sometimes I feel I am going mad when I put down the telephone: it's like a terrible ache in my tummy. I need you, Philip, my God I need

239

you . . . And Nelson. Give him a kiss from me, my darling – I can't wait to see him. And you.'

* * *

The annual office party at BDP was, for most of its 600 employees, the social highlight of the year. A bumper dinner was held, usually at Grosvenor House, followed by speeches, dancing to Joe Loss's band, and a cabaret by members of the staff in which most of the directors were wittily lampooned.

Philip asked Randi Ravello's permission to be absent from the Romeo for one evening. 'Yes, my dear boy,' said Randi. 'Anything you ask. You are my star attraction and my customers who come on your night off will probably come again specially to see you. Good for business, eh, eh?' He laughed his loud laugh and waved his cigar in the air.

On the evening of the party, Philip warned Mrs Drinkwater he probably wouldn't be back home until very late.

'That's all right,' she said. 'I'll put Nelson out about eleven and then tuck him up in his basket. See you in the morning.'

He arrived at Grosvenor House at 7.30, parked the car and went straight to look at the seating plan. His eyes widened: either by sheer chance or by some devilishness of the party committee he found he was sitting next to Shirley. He had not seen her or talked to her for months: he wondered how their renewed acquaintance would thrive during the evening. Still, he felt, although the general standard of looks among BDP secretaries was very high, he would rather sit next to Shirley than anyone else he knew in BDP. In spite of Sabine and his wild love for her, Shirley's warmth and beauty still lingered in his memory. After his first glass of sherry, he found himself keenly looking forward to seeing her again. He thought: I wonder, does she have a new boyfriend? She must do – surely an attractive girl like her could not go without a regular escort for long? Probably she would leave early to meet someone else.

The gong rang for dinner. He had not seen her in the crowd by the bar. He went to his table and stood by his chair. Suddenly he saw her coming through the ballroom door: she looked even more beautiful than ever. She wore a pale blue satin mini-dress with a low neckline and shoes to match; her long blonde hair was swept up in a chignon. She was, Philip thought, far and away the most attractive girl in the room.

'Hello,' she said, smiling. 'Fancy being next to you!'

'I count myself very lucky – you look marvellous.'

She was visibly pleased: 'Thank you. I thought I'd better doll up a bit in case I have to seduce a director.'

They sat down. Philip looked at the card on his other side: it read 'Deirdre Cowan'. She was an intense-looking brunette with spectacles, in a pink crinoline dress with sequins on it. Philip had never met her, nor any of the others at his table except the Chairman, who was on the other side of Shirley. He nodded at Philip and said 'Good evening', then immediately started talking to Shirley. Philip turned to Deirdre Cowan: 'What do you do in BDP?'

She giggled: 'I'm a comptometer operator in the Research Department.'

Philip looked at her with renewed respect. She giggled again: 'But don't let's talk about comptometers. I know everyone wants to. But I'm on a night out and I'd like to forget them.' She took a long sip of the sherry that had just been poured out by a waiter.

Philip said: 'I'm a trainee for the Art Department.'

'Oh I know all about you,' she said. 'I read the papers, you know.'

Philip blushed: 'Don't believe everything *they* say.'

'Why, isn't it true, then?'

'Well, some of it. But let's talk about you.'

'Oh, there's nothing to talk about. I'm one for the quiet life. I live with my Mum and Dad in Cricklewood, see my boyfriend at the weekends, and that's about it.' He looked at her left hand and saw a ring on her engagement finger.

'So you're engaged then?'

She saw him looking at the ring: 'Well, we've been going steady for three years now. But I don't dare take the plunge. He keeps on at me – but . . . well, I don't know, I don't think I'm quite ready for marriage. Not yet, anyway. One day, maybe. He's a nice boy, all right, but . . . oh well, I just don't know. Perhaps I'm waiting for someone else to come along out of the blue. But I don't expect he will.

'Doesn't a long engagement get on your nerves?'

'No, not really. I hate making up my mind, you see. Orson, that's my boyfriend, well he gets mad at me, but I can always cool him down in the end.' She giggled and finished her glass of sherry. One waiter handed out the fish while another filled the glasses with white wine.'

'So you're not sure you really love Orson then?'

'Really, what a question! Of *course* I love Orson. But I just don't know that I want to spend the rest of my life loving him. Maybe I can find something better.'

'What does he do?'

'He's a mechanic at the Blue Star Garage. Not exactly a Prince Charming. Comes out with his fingernails full of grease and smelling of petrol. But he's nice. Well, *quite* nice. Good enough to be getting along with, anyway. Mum and Dad don't like him much, but then I don't think they'd like *anyone* I brought home. I'm an only child, you see. Problems.' She took a long sip of her white wine: 'Coo, good wine, ain't it? Could drink this all night. Orson never buys me wine like this. Can't afford to, I suppose, on his pay. Coo, who'd marry a mechanic, I *ask* you! No money problems with *your* girlfriend, I'll bet. An heiress and all. I wish some nice rich heir would come along and sweep *me* off my feet. I wouldn't raise a finger to stop him.'

Philip felt a nudge from Shirley. She whispered: 'The Chairman's changed sides. Aren't you going to talk to me?'

Philip said to Deirdre: 'I think you'd better talk to the man on your right now.'

'Oh, fed up with me already,' said Deirdre huffily. 'All right – I can take a hint.' She turned round with a flourish and knocked the waiter's arm as he was serving the chicken off a large silver platter to the man on her right. Bits of chicken flew all over the table. Shirley tried to stifle her laughter, Deirdre put her hand up to her mouth in horror and apologised to the waiter. Philip wanted to laugh but dared not.

'There now,' said Shirley when the bits of chicken had been replaced. 'Look what a state you've got her into, with your subtle boyish charm.'

'Don't be sarcastic. She's been telling me all about her boyfriend Orson who works in a garage.'

'Well, I'll bet Orson isn't a patch on you.'

'You're very complimentary tonight.'

'I feel like it. I haven't seen you for so long. But I've thought about you a lot – and missed you very much, surprising though it may seem.'

'You *missed* me?'

'Yes, I know it sounds odd, especially after the stupid way I walked out on you. But I thought you'd come back to me. And you didn't. I suppose because you met Sabine.'

'Yes.'

'Tell me about her.'

Philip hesitated, looking down at his plate. Shirley said hurriedly:

'Of course I don't want to pry or anything like that. I just thought you might want to get something off your chest.'

'I'd love to talk about her. But not here. Too many people about. What I would say would be just for your ears, not for anyone else's. Listen – What are you doing after this, after the dinner and the cabaret which I suppose we have to stay for?'

'Nothing.'

'Well, will you come on with me to a night-club? Then we can talk. Just us.'

She squeezed his thigh under the table: 'Yes, Philip darling, I'd love to. Be quite like old times, won't it?'

*   *   *

After the speeches, the balloons, the spotlight dances, the forfeit dances and the cabaret, Philip started looking for Shirley. He had spent most of the evening at the bar with Greville Whitfield, avoiding the company of Deirdre Cowan who seemed quite set on attaching herself to Philip for the evening. Luckily, at an earlier stage in the evening, she had started swaying and moaning: 'Oo, I'm woozy after all this wine. I think I'm going to be sick.' Philip had quickly organised another girl to escort her to the Ladies', where she had accordingly remained unmoved for hours.

Philip had watched Shirley: she was rarely off the dance-floor. She looked easily the most attractive girl there, and from directors to messenger boys they were all queuing up to dance with her. Philip wondered if he would ever get her away. He began to feel the old attraction for her rise again inside him as he watched her; it was only by drinking that he could silence the little nagging voice of guilt that kept whispering 'Sabine' in his ear. Soon he was rationalising to himself: 'Damn it, Sabine isn't here – and Shirley is.'

Eventually he spotted Shirley in the throng on the dance-floor and waited at the side, trying to catch her eye. She noticed him, nodded and walked towards him. It was then Philip noticed that she was dancing with the Chairman.

'So you're going to take this lovely creature off my hands, eh, Rodolphin?' boomed the Chairman. 'You're a lucky fellow.' He patted Philip's shoulder and walked off to the bar.

Shirley raised her eyes to the ceiling and said: 'God, let's go. If I have my bottom stroked by one more lecherous old man, I think I'll throw something at him.' She tucked her arm into Philip's and they made for the door. On their way out, several men came up and reminded Shirley she had promised them a dance. 'Sorry, *so* sorry, but it's too late now and I'm going home. Save it till next year,' she laughed.

Philip said quietly: 'I can't tell you what an honour it is to be taking home the Belle of the Ball.'

'Well, you do have a certain edge over every other man here, don't you? I'm a faithful girl at heart, you know, and you're the only man in that room I've been to bed with – or for that matter would even *consider* going to bed with. Now – where are you taking me?'

'The Blue Lagoon?'

'Fine.'

*　　*　　*

'Good evening, Mr Rodolphin,' said the head-waiter at the Blue Lagoon. 'You're quite a stranger. Haven't seen you for ages, sir. Welcome back.'

Philip and Shirley were ushered to a corner seat by the dance-floor. When they had ordered their drinks, Shirley said: 'Now, lover boy, tell me the whole story about you and Sabine. I want every detail.'

Philip started at the beginning . . . When he had finished, two drinks later, Shirley sat in silence for a while. Then she said: 'That step-mother sounds a real bitch. But why on earth doesn't Sabine just fly over to London and marry you?'

'Because she wants the blessing of her family – without it she thinks a marriage would get off to an unlucky start. And because she is frightened her step-mother will commit suicide.'

'But of *course* she won't. It's just a threat.'

'I know. I've told her that but she won't listen.'

'Is she very good in bed – Sabine, I mean?'

'Yes. Wonderful.'

'Better than me?'

'Well, you only once let me go to bed with you, didn't you?'

'I know. That was my fault. All due to my stupid ideas.

246

I realise that now. I did it with the best intentions, but I won't fall into the same mistake again. If I'd let you more, would you have . . . have not fallen in love with Sabine, who *did* let you?'

'I don't honestly know. How can one tell?'

She clasped his hand with both of hers: 'Philip, I'm a bit drunk, but I have to tell you that I think I still love you.'

He looked into her eyes, which were sparkling in the candlelight. He leaned forward and kissed her: she opened her mouth wide for him. At the end, she was breathing quickly. 'Let's dance, for God's sake,' she said hurriedly, standing up.

It was the first time he had danced with anyone since Sabine had left. Shirley danced close, weaving her body into his, kissing his neck. He began to feel all the old excitement. Yet all the guilt he had felt previously that evening was still there, buried inside him. Hell, what did it matter? – it was only one night out on the town with an old flame after the office party. Surely that was excusable?

There was a sharp, sudden flash. Philip said: 'What was that?'

'Oh, I don't know,' Shirley said sleepily. 'Probably someone lighting a cigarette. Hold me tight again – it's wonderful. . . .'

As they walked back to their table after a long, intimate dance, Philip saw a face momentarily lit up by the light over the head-waiter's table: it belonged to Mervyn Twankey.

'Come on – we're going,' he said abruptly. 'I'll pay the bill at the desk.'

'Why, Philip? Don't you want to dance with me again?'

'We've got to go now. Come on.' He spoke firmly, grabbing her arm.

She finished her drink in a gulp: 'Will you come back to my flat?' Philip hesitated. 'Please do,' she said. She looked more beautiful, more fetching, than ever. 'All right. I will,' he said. But that nagging voice inside him still repeated: 'Sabine, Sabine. . . .'

*　　　*　　　*

In the car she did not speak. She clutched his left arm firmly. At the flat she led him in silence straight to her bedroom and put an LP on a small portable record-player. It was Frank Sinatra singing 'Blues in the Night'. She began to get undressed, throwing her clothes casually into an armchair beside the dressing-table. He watched her till she was naked. She stood for a moment in front of him, then kissed him, sliding one knee between his legs.

'It's what we both want, isn't it?' she whispered. Then she got into bed and closed her eyes. He could see her legs moving rhythmically under the bedclothes. He began undressing. His stomach felt hollow in anticipation of her touch. . . .

Sinatra's voice came wafting over Nelson Riddle's brass: *But when the sweet talkin' done, A woman's a two-face, A worrisome thing who'll leave ya t' sing The blues in the night.* . . .

Soon he slid in beside her, shuddering as he felt her cool body clamber avidly over his. She said:

'This time I'm having all of you, every bit of you, just as I want it. Just as Sabine did.'

'But——'

'But nothing. You deserved all of me months ago. Now you'll get your reward. And I'll make it worth waiting for. Kiss my tits like you used to – they haven't been touched by a man's hand since you. Oh *Philip* . . .' she moaned.

All the pent-up passion from months of frustration without Sabine welled up in him. He revelled in her entwining body, biting her, squeezing her, stroking her, licking her, sucking her, crushing her.

'You see,' she gasped, 'you see how much we need each other . . .'

. . . *'But when the sweet talkin' done* . . .'

*   *   *

They lay still and silent. Then Philip got out of bed. 'Where are you going?' she whispered.

'To get dressed.'

'Why, Philip, why? I want you to lie here beside me – like you used to.'

He said nothing while he put on his clothes. Soon she asked from the bed:

'Do you hate me for seducing you?'

'No. I hate myself for letting you.'

'Why?'

He was fully dressed now and sat on the end of the bed: 'Because . . .' He choked and the tears came into his eyes. He spoke through his sobs, burying his head in the bedclothes: 'Because I have let Sabine down. I wanted to prove to myself that I could wait for her. Now I know I can't.'

'But you love her more than me, don't you?' She stroked his hair.

'I thought I did. Now I'm not sure. If only I could see her again I know it would be all right. It's all this un-natural separation. It's all that bloody step-mother. Sometimes I even wonder to myself whether I do love her or not. Sometimes I wonder if it isn't just the fact that she's so marvellous in bed. Oh I don't know . . .'

He groped for her neck and caressed it, still with his head buried in the bedclothes. She continued to stroke his hair.

'Philip, you'll have to decide all these things for yourself. No one else can tell you the answers.'

He sat up and looked down at her, the tears running down his face: 'Don't tell me – I know it. But if only I could see her, I would know it. It's this terrible business of being kept apart, like prisoners in two separate prisons.'

'Can't you go over there?'

'Not unless I'm invited. That would wreck everything. I could *kill* that *bitch* of a step-mother.' He slapped his hand hard on the pillow.

'Philip, sweet, go and get a drink and bring a whisky for me. Then we can talk.'

He went to the sitting-room, poured out a strong vodka on the rocks for himself and a whisky for Shirley, then returned to sit on her bed.

She said: 'Was I a failure to make love to?'

'No. You were wonderful. That's what makes it so difficult. I thought I'd forgotten all about you. But obviously I haven't.'

'I *knew* that I hadn't forgotten about you. I just thought that you had gone from me for ever. Entirely because of my own stupid behaviour, too. God, I was a fool. But I'm not out to make difficulties between you and Sabine – don't think that. After all you've been through, I hope you win her and have a marvellous life together.'

He gazed at her nestling on the pillow: she looked so soft and appealing. He put down his glass on the bedside table and kissed her. After a long kiss she whispered:

'Take off your clothes and get in beside me again. Then we can go on talking.'

He pondered for a second, then began undressing. As soon as he felt her nakedness beside him, they began making love again with all the old crazy passion.

At the end of it he hated himself even more. Again he immediately got out of bed to get dressed. While he was dressing, she said: 'Tell me, why did you leave the Blue Lagoon so suddenly, just when we were beginning to have fun?'

'Because I saw Mervyn Twankey, that pest of a reporter from the *Echo*.'

'What harm could he do?'

'You never know. He follows me around like a leech. Every time there's something in the papers, that bloody step-mother takes it out on Sabine. She uses it as a bargaining lever with Sabine. She pretends not to realise that it's nothing to do with me when the papers print things. Shirley, little love, I must go now.'

'Do you have to?'

'Yes.'

'Well, I understand, in a way. I would have liked you to stay all night. So that I could wake up beside you. But I won't stop you.'

He kissed her gently on the forehead and said: 'Thank you for being so understanding. You are a great comfort.'

'I need you, Philip, because I love you. Remember that . . .'

As he drove home to Richmond through the grey light of a spring dawn, with the touch and smell of Shirley warm on his skin, he thought to himself: 'Why did I do it, why did I do it? I have betrayed Sabine.'

*   *   *

251

The next morning's *Echo* contained a large photograph of Philip dancing in the Blue Lagoon with Shirley. Both his arms were tightly round her, and she was kissing his cheek. The caption by Twankey questioned whether Philip was going back to Shirley, his 'previous girl-friend'.

So *that's* what that flash had been. Blast that menace Twankey. How foolish of him, how *idiotically* foolish of him to go out with Shirley at all.

Now, what would Sabine say? And, worse still, what would that blasted Duchess say?

19

Almost as soon as he arrived back at the Dower House that evening from the Romeo, the telephone rang. He knew who it was before he picked up the receiver.

'Darling?' said Sabine.

'Yes, it's me.'

'Darling, what have you been *doing*?'

'What do you mean?'

'That picture in the papers of you and that girl.'

'Shirley? She's just an old friend of mine It's nothing.'

'Are you sure?'

'Of course. She works in the same firm and we just went on together to a night-club after the office party. I told you I was going.'

'Darling, are you sure there's nothing more to it than that?'

'Of course not.'

'Did you go to bed with her?'

'No, no. Why should you think that?'

'Well, she looks very attractive and you told me all about her before. Darling, I couldn't bear it if you went to bed with her now, when you're waiting for me.'

'There's no need to worry,' he said flatly. He heard her sniffle as if she'd been crying. 'She's just a past flame. You know that.'

'Darling, I was so upset when I saw that picture that I saw Beatrix and said we couldn't go on like this. It wasn't fair on either of us.'

'Well done. You should have said that ages ago.'

'Darling, don't be hard to me. I am doing my best.

And Beatrix said you could come over here and Papa had said we could get engaged straight away. Isn't that wonderful?' He checked, amazed:

'It's sensational. Did they *really* say that?'

'Well, I was in such a state over that picture, and she was so furious with you for letting the picture be taken——'

'I did *not* let the picture be taken.'

'But, darling, how did they take it?'

'I don't know It's that same man who's always tailing me. The night-club must have told him I was there – or something. I didn't even know it had been taken until I saw it in the paper.'

'Darling, you must be more careful. I am so jealous of that girl dancing with you like that when it should have been me.'

'My love, I wish it had been you.'

'Here am I, all shut up like a jailbird, never seeing anyone, and you can go out dancing with a pretty girl like that. Darling, she was kissing your neck.'

'I know. That's just the way she dances. It meant nothing. When can I come over and see you, though? Let's talk about that. That's the best news I've heard for ages. It's wonderful.'

'Darling, now don't be angry with me, but there's just one little thing you have to do before Beatrix will agree. It's quite a small thing——'

'What is it?'

'You have to give up playing at the Romeo.'

Philip was momentarily stunned: 'But – but how will I be able to afford to keep the house going and look after you if I *don't* play at the Romeo? I get £100 a week there. I couldn't possibly afford things on my salary from BDP. It's only £25 a week. She must be mad.'

'Darling, don't get angry. We will work everything out all right in the end. Darling, if you really love me and want to marry me, you will do as Beatrix says. It's the only way, believe me. You can always go back to the Romeo and play after we're married, if the money is difficult. But I have some of my own which will probably make it all right.'

'When do I have to give up the Romeo then?'

'As soon as possible. Tell that Ravello man tonight. Get it all fixed. Darling, you will, won't you? I do want you to come to me as soon as you can. I have been such a good little girl, waiting for you. It's torture. But it will be all right in the end if only we can get married. It will be worth all the agony and the waiting. Tell Ravello tonight, darling, won't you? . . .'

* * *

During Philip's playing-time at the Romeo that night in walked Twankey. He came straight up to Philip: 'Sorry to bother you, old boy, but I wondered if that picture of you and Shirley meant that you had finished with Sabine?'

'Look, for Christ's sake can't you leave me alone? There must be thousands of other people you can write about.' Several heads in the bar turned round at the angry loudness of Philip's voice.

'Don't get worked up, old boy. I keep telling you you're news. Just tell me that one thing and I'll leave you in peace – is it all over between you and Sabine?'

'I'm not saying a damned thing.'

'OK, OK, just as you want it. It merely means I'll have to find out elsewhere. Like a drink?'

'No thanks.' Twankey raised a nonchalant arm and

padded out on his tattered suede shoes. Joe the barman winked encouragement at Philip, as if to say 'Well done.'

At eleven o'clock Philip packed his guitar away and went to find Randi Ravello. He was in the restaurant, dispensing champagne in silver chalices to favourite clients and waving his cigar about as he shouted at waiters.

'Randi, can I talk to you for a moment?'

'Yes, my dear boy. Let us sit down at a table. Waiter' – he clicked his fingers – 'champagne for Mr Rodolphin at my table in the corner. Now what is it, my dear boy?' he asked as they sat down.

'Randi, I don't know how to say this because you've always been so kind to me but——'

'Don't tell me, don't tell me. You've been offered more money to play somewhere else. Don't listen to them for a minute.' He banged on the table. 'Not for a minute. I will raise you to £150 a week.'

'It's very kind of you, Randi, but it's not that.'

'£200 then. How much you want? Say it and Randi will pay.' The waiter poured out the champagne. Philip sipped it and said:

'Randi, I just have to stop playing altogether. Just for the moment. Maybe I will come back soon. But for the moment I must stop.'

Randi pulled a white handkerchief out of his breast pocket and began snuffling into it as if he was crying. He spoke in broken sobs:

'Philip, you are like a son to me. Would you leave me, now, now, just when I have built you up?'

'Randi, I don't want to leave but——'

'You would leave me in the lurch,' he sobbed, 'just when my modest little establishment most needs you – at the beginning of the season? You would bite the hand that has fed you all these months,' he sobbed again more loudly, 'and leave me without anyone to play in the bar?' He buried his face in his handkerchief and felt for Philip's hand which he held. Through the handkerchief came more muffled sobs and a plaintive: 'Randi is like a father to you. Would a son leave his father like this?'

'Randi, it's not a question of leaving you in the lurch. I just have to stop playing for a *bit*.'

'Why? You don't like Randi any more?'

'For purely personal reasons. I can't explain.'

Randi looked out from under his handkerchief: 'Is it that girl – the Countess?'

'In a way, yes, I suppose it is.'

Randi brightened up immediately: 'Ah listen, dear boy. Randi would never stand in the path of true love. When you have married her you will come and play for me at whatever you want a week. Is that a deal?'

He offered his right hand for Philip to shake.

Philip laughed as he shook it: 'Yes, it's a deal.'

'Waiter,' roared Randi. 'Quick, boy, quick. Some caviar for Mr Rodolphin. Quick, boy, *quick*.' He slapped Philip on the back and puffed so hard on his cigar that sparks flew from the end.

*   *   *

The next morning in BDP Philip was summoned to see the Chairman.

'Come in,' said the Chairman. 'Sit down. Take a cigarette. Look – I don't want to pry into your private affairs, but your private affairs seem to be becoming a bit public these days, what?' The Chairman guffawed at his own joke. 'I mean this' – he held up the picture in the *Echo* of Philip and Shirley dancing. 'Now what you do outside this office is absolutely no concern of mine. But I wondered – in confidence, of course – if you could put me in the picture about the whole situation. And then maybe I might be able to be of some help. Or the company might. Of course it's absolutely up to you. If you want to tell me politely to mind my own bloody business, I will quite understand. But if you can't even go to a night-club with a girl without having a great picture in the papers of you snogging on the dance-floor, it looks as if you're in a bit of a pickle, what?'

Philip was warmed by this gesture of kindness and goodwill. Shirley was the only person to whom he had been able to tell the full story of Sabine, and in the absence of his parents he welcomed this opportunity of unloading himself to the father-figure of the Chairman, such an obviously generous and well-meaning man.

'Can I start at the beginning, sir?'

'Please do. Take as long as you like. And remember – this is in complete confidence between you and me. So don't mind what you say: it will go no further than these four walls.'

When Philip had finished, the Chairman inhaled deeply on his cigarette: 'Not a pretty story, is it?'

'No, sir.'

'And you've given in your notice at the Romeo?'

'Yes, sir. Last night.'

'Why do you think the family's insisting on that as a condition?'

'I think it's disguised blackmail – so they can now turn round and tell me I'm not earning enough money to support their daughter. Which, on the basis of my salary here, would be quite true.'

'You get no money from your parents at all?'

'No, sir. My cousin Teddy loaned me some money to move into the house with. And I'm going to write to him to ask if he will guarantee my overdraft now that I'm stopping playing at the Romeo.'

'Listen now – I'd like to help, and I think I can to some extent. First of all, you've finished your trainee's course with flying colours – I talked to your group-head this morning – and so now you're becoming a fully-fledged art director we can give you a substantial rise in salary.'

'Thank you very much, sir.'

'Well now, wait a minute. I don't think we can put it up above £1,750 without being unfair to your colleagues. And I daresay the family wouldn't regard that as enough for you to keep the girl on, either.'

'No, I don't think they would.'

'What about the daughter's own money? The papers always call her an heiress.'

'I've never discussed money with her. Maybe she doesn't get it till her father dies or something. She never appears to have much money. And maybe her step-mother would stop it altogether if she married me.'

'That bloody step-mother sounds capable of anything – if you'll excuse me saying so. I don't envy you having her as a step-mother-in-law.'

'Well, she'll be in France.'

'Yes, that's one blessing. Can't the father help at all?'

'No. He's completely ruled by the step-mother, and anyway he spends all his time at the Embassy in Copenhagen. You see, he's not Sabine's father at all.'

The Chairman looked wide-eyed: 'Good God – additional complications. What a mess of pottage. Look, old boy, do you have any personal debts?'

'Only the tax I'll eventually have to pay on my earnings at the Romeo.'

'Have you been saving up at all?'

'No, sir. With all the expenses of the new house I haven't been able to. Especially now that I have to pay a housekeeper and a gardener.'

'Well, listen – now you must keep this entirely between ourselves. Not a word of it must be breathed to anyone. But I think you've had a raw deal and would like to help you. And I'll say this: I'll be happy to lend you the money you will have to pay in tax when you get the demand in. You can pay me back in small instalments when things get better. No hurry.'

'You are very kind, sir. Thank you very much indeed.'

'It's nothing. Nothing. Just don't tell anyone, that's all. And keep me posted on developments, will you? And, yes, one more thing: I shouldn't go out dancing any more with Shirley again. Not at the moment. Attractive girl though she is.' The Chairman chuckled. 'Wouldn't mind going out with her myself—but not with a bloody *Echo* photographer on my tail . . .'

*   *   *

The following Saturday Philip got a letter from Teddy in reply to his own letter requesting a guarantee for his overdraft. Teddy wrote saying he quite understood Philip's position and would gladly guarantee the overdraft, if it would help put a stop to Sabine's step-mother's gambits.

Philip's spirits quickly rose with Teddy's letter. It gave

him renewed confidence that he and Sabine were at last winning their long battle. It was a warm morning, so after breakfast he took Nelson out for a romp in the sunlit garden.

He was interrupted by a call from Mrs Drinkwater out of the sitting-room window: 'Telephone for you, sir.'

'Who is it?'

'Madame Lassage or someone. Says it's urgent.'

Afdera – what could *she* want? He hurried in.

'Hello?'

'Philip, it's Afdera. Can you lunch with me at the Mirabelle today? It's urgent. I have things to tell you. Nicole's been staying with Sabine.'

'I know. Sabine told me.'

'And what she says you must know. One o'clock at the Mirabelle then?'

'Yes. OK.' He hated the thought of his Saturday being interrupted, but Afdera sounded so agitated that he thought he had better agree to see her.

'I'll be out to lunch, Mrs Drinkwater,' he called.

Afdera was waiting in the Mirabelle when he arrived. She was wearing a large floral hat and dark glasses, sitting at her usual table.

She kissed him on the cheek as he sat down beside her. He said: 'Now tell me: what's all the flap about?'

'Nicole swore me to secrecy but to hell with that. I just had to tell you. We've got to beat that bitch Beatrix. You still want to marry the girl, don't you?'

'Yes, of course. Why do you ask?'

'Well, after that picture last week of some blonde seducing you on the dance-floor——'

'That was just a quiet reunion with an old flame.'

'I don't wonder. I should think you need a few old

flames after all these months of waiting. But that bitch Beatrix was furious about it, and yet she *loved* it because it gave her an opportunity to show Sabine that you were being unfaithful to her.'

They ordered lunch and two Americanos. Philip said: 'I explained all about it to Sabine on the telephone.'

'You don't suppose that bitch Beatrix believed what you said, do you? She has said you must give up playing at the Romeo, yes?'

'Yes. And I have given in my notice.'

'And now she is going to say that you don't have enough money to keep Sabine – so Nicole tells me.'

'Ah, but I have arranged that. My cousin Teddy has guaranteed my overdraft and I have had a big rise in salary from my firm.'

'Does Sabine know that?'

'Not yet.'

'Well, you'd better tell her quick. Because Beatrix, the bitch, thinks she has won. She is all out to stop you and Sabine. And do you know why?'

'No.'

'Because you are English and she has found out that your grandmother was a Jewess. And you know that in the war she was on the side of the Nazis? *Madly* pro-Nazi?'

'I'd heard about it but never believed it.'

'It's true. Her brother was one of the German Navy's most fanatic U-boat commanders. He loved machine-gunning British sailors swimming in the water after he had sunk their ship, rather than take them prisoner. He even got the Iron Cross for it.'

Philip looked appalled: 'Is that really true?'

'Of course it's true. And that's not all I have to tell you. Do you trust Sabine?'

'Well, yes . . . of course I do.'

'What has she been saying to you about this Heini she used to know?'

'She told me she saw him once.'

'Only once?'

'Yes.'

'Well, Nicole tells me she has been secretly seeing him almost every day. She says she must because she is so lonely. You know he is a famous seducer with the reputation of having the biggest prick in Germany?'

'Sabine had hinted at it. But——'

'Well, he's been staying near the château and she sneaks out unknown to Beatrix to see him nearly every night. She pretends she is seeing a girlfriend.'

Philip felt a cold hand clutch his stomach. Afdera continued: 'And since that picture appeared of you and that girl, Sabine has been saying that, if you can go out with a girl, why shouldn't she see Heini. I told you she was a whore. All she is interested in is being focked.'

'Nonsense. If you were shut up like a prisoner in that château, with that step-mother guarding your every move, you'd feel the same urge to get out. After all, she's an attractive girl and you can't blame her for wanting to see a man.'

'I tell you, this man Heini only wants to see her because he knows he can fock her whenever he likes. He is just a playboy with a big prick, and he knows how to use it. If that bitch Beatrix ever finds out about Sabine and this Heini, you have had it. Because it will prove to her that Sabine is not in love with you: she *couldn't* be if she goes out every night to be focked by this Heini.'

In spite of his doubts, Philip couldn't believe Afdera's story: 'I can't believe it. She would have told me.'

'Whores are born liars,' said Afdera finally. 'If you

want to marry that girl – and I think you are mad to do so because she is by nature a whore – then you had better do something quickly. I only tell you all this to help you not to make a big mistake.'

Philip pushed away his plate of scampi, unable to eat it.

* * *

When he arrived back at the Dower House, he waited for Sabine's call: she had promised to telephone before he left for his last engagement at the Romeo.

At 5.30 the telephone rang.

'Darling, how are you? I've been missing you so much.'

'Fine, thank you. This is my last evening at the Romeo.'

'Oh that's wonderful. Beatrix will be so pleased. Now she can't stop us getting engaged.'

'And I've had a big salary rise from the firm.'

'Oh, marvellous, darling. I'm sure we will have enough money. How is Nelson?'

'He is very well. Almost house-trained now. How was Nicole?'

'She was such fun. It was lovely for me to have her here. I never have any company. And we talked a lot about you. Every night we spent hours talking about you.'

'Sabine, have you been seeing Heini again?'

There was silence on the line. Then she said: 'Darling, why do you ask that?'

'Have you?'

'Well . . . yes. I have seen him a few times. Did Nicole say something then?'

'I haven't seen Nicole. How much have you been seeing Heini?'

264

'Oh, once or twice at dinner parties. Nothing special. Darling, why are you asking me this?'

'Have you been to bed with him?'

Her voice rose: 'Why are you asking me all this? You know I would tell you.'

'Have you or have you not?'

There was silence, then a sob. He repeated his question: 'Have you or have you not? Tell me. Now.'

A sob, then a quiet: 'Yes, darling. But it was only because of that picture of you and that girl. I was so desperate. I *had* to do something. It meant nothing to me, nothing at all. I think of you the whole time I am with Heini, imagining it is you and not him. You mustn't blame me, darling, please don't be angry with your little Sabine. You're not angry with me, are you, my darling?'

A cold fury gripped his throat: he could not bear the idea of her being in bed with another man, of his hands on her nakedness. He said softly, menacingly:

'Sabine, I am telling you this now. Listen, because I mean it. When you call tomorrow, unless your step-mother has agreed a definite date for me to come over and see you and get engaged, I am not going on with this.'

She sobbed several times and said: 'No, no, no.'

He spoke louder to drown her: 'I mean it. Tomorrow when you call me, you must have agreed a date with your step-mother when I can come over. I mean it, I mean it. We've been through enough of this idiotic shilly-shallying. Now I'm going – I've got to get changed for the Romeo. Do you understand me? Do you understand me?'

Between her tears she moaned: 'You don't love me any more. You——'

'I do. That's just why I'm saying this. I *do* love you.

265

But I'm not going on in this way. I will talk to you tomorrow. Goodbye, Sabine.'

As he slowly put down the telephone he heard her choking with sobs. He buried his head in his hands and wished he didn't have to be so brutal.

20

Philip's last evening at the Romeo gave Randi Ravello the perfect opportunity to indulge in some typically flamboyant pieces of showmanship and sentimentalism.

First, Randi arranged for a bottle of champagne in a silver chalice to be beside Philip all evening on top of the grand piano, for him to fill up his glass whenever it was empty – which, needless to say, it never was, because Randi kept flitting in and out of the bar like a fat dragon-fly, filling up Philip's glass each time he passed.

Then at five to eleven Randi came up to Philip, put his hand over the microphone and whispered: 'Can you play "Bye Bye Blues"?'

Philip nodded. Randi swept round to the audience of about thirty people drinking and clapped his hands twice: 'Ladies and gentlemen,' he shouted, 'forgive me for interrupting your conversation but there is something I would like to beg your forgiveness for. This is, for a very special personal reason, one of the saddest nights in the history of my modest little establishment.' He choked on the words, pulled a huge white handkerchief out and mopped delicately at one eye. 'So I would like to record my emotion, my deep emotion, by singing to you my favourite song' – Joe the barman dropped the top of his cocktail shaker and threw an astonished look at Philip – ' "Bye Bye Blues".' He beckoned to Philip for an introduction and took hold of the microphone. Philip played a chord: Randi's voice croaked through the loudspeakers as he waveringly found the correct note. Joe the barman closed his eyes in mock prayer. Several of the customers put their hands slyly up to their faces to hide their laughter.

'Bye Byeeeee Blooooooose,' wailed Randi hopelessly flat, puffing at his cigar between lines, eyes shut, one hand hugging the microphone which even picked up the clicking of his false teeth as he opened and closed his mouth.

As he got to the last line, his voice cracked on the first 'Bye', broke into a sort of wheeze, then he let go the microphone, put his handkerchief over his eyes and stumbled blindfolded from the room. There were bursts of clapping and cries of 'Encore, Randi, encore.' Randi appeared again at the door and bowed low, the tears running down his face.

*   *   *

Philip did not leave the Romeo till 3.30 am that morning. Randi insisted on giving him a five-course dinner with a menu printed specially for the occasion, followed by some 1906 brandy. Randi spent most of the dinner in tears at Philip's departure, mopping his eyes in between his angry shouts at whatever waiter was in his ken.

Randi eventually guided him to the door, gripping his elbow tightly.

'Philip, you are like a son to me. You are an honorary life member of my modest little establishment. You will come back, dear boy, you will come back to old Randi?'

'Yes of course. Thank you for being so kind. And for singing . . .'

Randi suddenly embraced him, kissed him on both cheeks and turned away moaning: 'I hate goodbyes. It is only au revoir. Only an au revoir.'

As Philip got into his car, he heard Randi barking at

someone: 'Boy, you wouldn't get a job at focking Wimpey's.'

He sat down on something hard. It was a little black box tied with a red ribbon. He opened it: inside, wrapped in tissue paper, was a tiny silver guitar on a black stand. The plate on the stand was inscribed: 'To Philip from the Romeo – R.R.'

*　　*　　*

Philip spent all that Sunday nervously waiting for Sabine to telephone. In a way, he was still furious with her, both for giving in to Heini and for being so powerless with her step-mother. But he knew that, in spite of his fury, he still loved her and desperately needed her: he almost understood and condoned her weakness with Heini – after all, hadn't he behaved in the same way with Tamara Reno? And with Shirley? What was the difference? And Sabine had at least confessed to her misdemeanour, while he had lied. The guilt of making love to Shirley still rankled in him: perhaps that was why he had been so tough with Sabine on the telephone. He felt confident that, in the end, given the right opportunity, he could conquer Sabine's need for Heini. What he was not so confident about was whether he could win over the Duchess and break the almost hypnotic hold she seemed to have over Sabine. . . . And what did Sabine's father really think about the whole affair? Perhaps he should write direct to the father? No – Afdera had said that the Duke was a mere cipher and putty in the hands of the Duchess. If he knew – which he presumably did – that he wasn't Sabine's father anyway, probably he wasn't taking much interest in her romances – how could he be when he spent most of his time in

Copenhagen and his wife and Sabine lived at the château?
What a rum set-up it was.

For the hundredth time Philip found himself re-
questioning his own motives: was it, *could* it be, just
Sabine's money that made her so attractive to him,
that made him tolerate her unfaithfulness and weakness?
He asked himself, and his subconscious assured him the
answer was No. The answer was, and he knew it already
even though he sought reassurance for it, that it was
Sabine's body that was the fascination for him, not her
money. He had seen nothing of the money anyway:
he didn't even really know for certain that she would
inherit it. Only the newspapers said so. Yet . . . perhaps
it was just as wrong, too, to be so fascinated by her
physically? No. That couldn't be wrong. Physical harmony was surely a cornerstone of a relationship between
a man and woman. And the physical harmony he had
with Sabine had been, up till now, the most rewarding,
complete and thrilling experience of his life. He had
tested that with Shirley, hadn't he? There was just a
special something about *touching*, merely *touching*, Sabine
that simply didn't happen with other women . . . what
did the French call it – *l'attraction de la peau*? A force
so potent that in his case it seemed to have the effect not
only of allowing him to forgive Sabine for her infidelity –
but also, paradoxically, of actually increasing his love
for her because of that infidelity. In an inexplicable way
her weakness made him keener than ever to protect her,
to rescue her from the stagnant and ineffectual life she
was forced by her step-mother to lead.

If only he could get her away from that bitch . . . she
would be a new person, alive, laughing, gay, unrestricted,
a constant joy to be with – instead of the hopeless, helpless, neurotic creature that living in the prison of that

270

château turned her into. He knew it, he *knew* it – he had
seen so many glimpses of what Sabine was really like
on the countless secret trysts they had had while she
had been, albeit momentarily, free to be truly herself
with him, her lover . . . His memory dwelt longingly
on some of those magic hours that now seemed so long
ago.

The telephone bell made him jump. It was Sabine.

'Darling?' She sounded wonderfully happy. Was it
good news?

'Yes, hello, my love.'

'Oh darling, I have such wonderful news for you. I
have spoken to Beatrix and she has *agreed* with me that
you should come over here.'

'How marvellous. When?'

'Next month. On the 7th. For five days. Papa will be
here, too. Darling, isn't it absolutely wonderful? Oh I
am so happy, so very happy. Aren't you proud of your
little Sabine for fixing it? Darling, say you're very proud
of me. Beatrix is writing to you today. But, darling, you
will keep it very secret, won't you? She doesn't want
anyone except the Lassages to know. They will fix everything for you. But don't tell *anyone* else – not even your
family. Darling, promise? . . .'

*   *   *

Two days later, a curt, non-committal letter arrived
from the Duchess, merely saying that she would be pleased
if Philip would visit the château as the family's guest
from 7th–12th and that all arrangements would be
handled by M Lassage, who would be getting in touch
with Philip. There was no mention of Sabine, no mention
of a possible engagement: her writing, in that Victorian

copper-plate style with strong Teutonic overtones, even managed to *look* cold. Still, it represented considerable progress – perhaps even the breakthrough. He wondered how Sabine had achieved it: when he had asked her on the telephone exactly what she had said to her step-mother, she had been vague and elusive.

'But has she said we can get engaged?' Philip would insist.

'Darling, she wants us to wait till we see each other again before making up our minds. Of course I am sure *I* want to, darling, but for Beatrix's sake let's agree to wait.'

The next day the Ambassador telephoned Philip at BDP asking him to come to his office that evening. At 5.30 pm his chauffeur-driven Citroen was waiting at BDP's front door.

Philip was ushered by the same liveried footman straight into the Ambassador's study. They shook hands and Philip sat down by the fireplace in the same chair he had sat in before.

'Now your trip next month,' said the Ambassador. 'It must be arranged in the utmost secrecy. That is the Duke and Duchess's wish. And I think it would be advisable for you too. So I have booked a seat for you on a scheduled flight to Paris on the 7th in the name of one of my staff: Monsieur Saton. You will be picked up at Paris by Count Malraux's car and driven to the château.'

'Did the Duchess say anything about an engagement being announced, Excellency?'

'No, I fear she did not. She merely mentioned that her husband the Duke would also be in residence at that time. I think that that piece of information indicates well for you.' The Ambassador smiled, rising from his chair. 'Forgive me for bringing you here for this short talk, but I think it better not to discuss these things by letter or on the telephone. Too many other eyes and ears are interested, no? I wish the best of luck to you, Philip.'

He held out his hand for Philip to shake. His eyes were enigmatic above the half-lensed spectacles.

'Thank you, Excellency.'

*　　　*　　　*

The weeks leading up to his visit to Sabine were trying ones for Philip. He found that he missed the nightly diversion and distraction of playing at the Romeo. Apart from a few dinner parties, he mainly sat at home watching television, waiting for Sabine's telephone call. He dared not risk taking a girl out to dinner: Shirley was the only one he would have liked to take out, but he was afraid that another burst of publicity about him going out with Shirley might cause the Duchess to change her mind about letting him visit Sabine. He had spoken to Shirley on the telephone several times, he had even looked in at Reception to talk to her; and she had been very apologetic about the trouble she had caused him. Sweet Shirley . . . he sometimes wondered, if Shirley had not acted so strangely after their night together on the train, would he have ever left her and fallen in love with Sabine?

He had lunch with Afdera who, needless to say, in spite of the Ambassador having stressed the need for the utmost secrecy over Philip's visit, had succeeded in finding out all the relevant details.

'That Beatrix: she is a bitch. I hear she even suggested putting private detectives on you to try to find out something shady about your past life at school and in the Army. You will have to be tough with that bitch. And cunning.

Cunning as a fox. She will do her best not to give in, you wait and see. Don't think that just because she has agreed to you going there she has given in. The only answer is for the girl to come back with you. If the girl loves you as she says she does, why doesn't she?'

'I don't know – except that I know she doesn't want to upset her step-mother any more,' Philip had answered helplessly.

'Well she's not going to *marry* her bloody step-mother, is she? Who does she want to spend her life with – her step-mother or you? Pah, the girl is an idiot, an absolute *idiot*.'

But, in spite of the inarguability of Afdera's point of view, Philip was determined to give Sabine this one last chance to prove her love: after all, he knew what difficulties she was going through – he'd had enough trouble with his own parents, though he'd taken the easier, perhaps more disloyal, way of cutting off contact with them and leading his own life in his own way, unbeholden to, and independent of, them. Sabine obviously could not, in her position, do that quite so easily.

As the day for Philip's visit approached, Sabine grew more and more happy in her letters and telephone calls. Sometimes on the telephone she would cry with joy, saying: 'Now everything's going to be all right. Beatrix finally understands I mean what I say and know what I want. Oh, darling, come soon . . . I can't wait.'

On the morning of the 7th, the car from the Embassy arrived to take Philip to the airport exactly as the Ambassador had promised. At London Airport a tall man in a grey suit opened the car-door and said: 'Mr Rodolphin? Please come with me. Your luggage will be taken care of. Give me your passport and ticket, please.'

The man handed over the passport and ticket to an air hostess and led Philip upstairs to a sitting-room. 'Sit down here and have a drink while you wait,' said the man. 'Whisky?'

'Yes, please. With water.'

The man poured out the drink and excused himself, saying he had to check that the passport and ticket got through all right. Philip watched the planes moving around on the tarmac outside the window. He thought: They've certainly organised it well this end. After some minutes the man returned with Philip's ticket and passport.

'Now, Mr Rodolphin, will you come with me? We'll take you to the plane ahead of the other passengers.'

Philip followed him down bleak corridors of offices until they eventually came out above the Main Building. They went down some stairs and along a stone-floored corridor running the whole length of the building. The right-hand wall was glass, looking out on to the tarmac and the waiting aeroplanes.

At the end of the corridor was a wooden arrow-sign pointing right and marked 'F'. Beside it stood a police-man. As they approached the sign, another figure in a British Warm overcoat and dilapidated suède shoes came out of a door beside the policeman and stood waiting. He was smiling at Philip.

It was Mervyn Twankey. Twankey. The policeman asked him something and he showed a card. The police-man nodded.

As Philip passed, Twankey stepped in beside him.

'Sorry to break down the security, old man, but I gather you're going to Paris. Any statement?'

'No,' said Philip, looking straight ahead.

'I tried to get a seat on the same plane but it's all

booked up. However, I'm coming on the next one an hour later. Have a good trip.'

*   *   *

How *could* Twankey have known? Philip asked himself on the plane. Now he, Philip, would be blamed by the Duchess for telling the Press, and she would inevitably manage to produce some new obstacle to postpone the engagement. Hadn't Sabine stressed that the whole visit must be held in the utmost secrecy, otherwise her step-mother had said she would not co-operate? He harboured a growing sense of doom about the whole trip. Only the thought of how much he wanted to see Sabine again kept his spirits from plunging into despair. He was *determined* to win this time – against the Duchess, against Twankey, against *everybody* . . . he *would* win, he *must* win . . . the farce had gone on long enough.

The air hostess leaned over and interrupted his thoughts: 'Mr Rodolphin? We've just had a message from Paris. When we arrive, would you let everyone else disembark first, please, so that you go off last? Apparently it will make things easier.' She smiled, Philip nodded. 'An immigration official will stamp your passport on the plane,' she said. 'To save you going through the barrier. May I get you a drink?' She smiled again: she was pretty.

'No, thank you.' When Philip lit a Philip Morris after she had gone, his hands were shaking. . . . .

As the aeroplane taxied up the runway towards the main building, Philip could see a dark-blue Citroen parked on the tarmac. Beside the car was a cluster of cameramen being herded into a group by several police-men.

The door was opened and the other passengers filed out. The air hostess came up to Philip with a uniformed man. She said: 'Your passport, please, Mr Rodolphin.'

The official stamped the passport. A man behind him in a black leather overcoat said: 'Can I please have your baggage tickets? I am Count Malraux's chauffeur.'

Philip tore them off his air-ticket and gave them to the chauffeur.

'Venez avec moi,' said the official. As Philip descended the steps, a battery of flash-bulbs exploded in his face. The official led him between rows of policemen to the waiting Citroen, while the crowd of press photographers shouted questions at him.

He jumped into the front seat of the car and the official closed the door behind him. In the driving seat was a middle-aged man with a square face dominated by a huge black moustache.

'I'm Count Malraux,' he said in a strong French accent, revving up the engine. 'Welcome to France. Now let's get rid of these pests the Press.'

He hurled the Citroen through the crowd of photographers so that they had to jump clear, and drove fast towards the exit gates.

'But what about my luggage?' said Philip.

'Ach, mon homme will fetch it,' grunted Malraux as the Citroen swung with screeching tyres round the corner into the main road.

Malraux looked in the rear mirror: 'Ach, les stupides are following. We will lose them, oui?' He trod on the accelerator and the Citroen leaped forward into the eighties.

Philip shut his eyes.

21

Count Malraux did not speak on the nerve-racking journey. He was too engrossed in handling the car. After what seemed to Philip like an eternity of screeching tyres and taking corners on two wheels, the car drew to an abrupt halt at a large pair of ornate iron gates. Count Malraux angrily pressed his horn several times and flashed his headlights on and off. A man ran out of the house beside the gates, shielded his eyes against the headlights, and then opened the gates when he recognised the car.

Malraux shouted something at the man in French as he drove through. The gates behind the car clanged shut in the face of the convoy of Press cars that had still been successful in following Malraux's Citroen in spite of the breakneck speed at which he had been driving.

'That will fix them,' said Malraux. Philip breathed a sigh of relief that the hectic chase had at last finished. A huge castellated château appeared from behind some trees.

'That is the château where the Duke d'Alsace lives,' said Malraux proudly. 'An impressive building, si?'

'Yes,' said Philip. But instead of driving up to it as Philip had expected, Malraux took a sharp turn left down a narrow lane and pulled up at a much smaller house in the grounds.

Philip said: 'But aren't I——'

'You are not staying at the château, mon ami,' said Malraux as he switched off the engine. 'The orders of the Duchess. You are staying avec ma femme et moi. I trust you will not be too uncomfortable. Come in, oui?'

He opened the door and got out. Philip followed. As they walked up the stone path, the front door opened and a hugely fat woman in a shapeless black dress appeared in the doorway. She had a lined, sad face and her hair was swept austerely back in a bun.

'This is my wife,' said Malraux curtly, walking past her into the hall. Philip shook hands. 'She cannot speak English,' Malraux shouted over his shoulder. The wife grinned helplessly and pointed to her mouth, shaking her head.

Malraux said: 'I'll show you your room when your baggage arrives. It shouldn't be long. Is there anything you'd like to do?'

Philip said hesitantly: 'I'd like to telephone Sabine, please.'

'Of course.' The Count led Philip to his study: 'There is le telephone. Use le private line to le château. Here: I will do it for you.'

He picked up the telephone, pressed one of the row of buttons, asked for Sabine by name and then handed the receiver to Philip. As Philip waited, Malraux noisily left the study.

' 'Allo?'

'Sabine? It's me, my love.'

'Oh *darling* Philip. How wonderful that you are here. You sound very near. Not like in London with those crackling lines. Was your trip all right?'

'Yes, thank you. But, darling, when can I see you? Why am I staying here with Count Malraux and not with you as you promised?'

She sighed: 'Darling, I tried my best but Beatrix would not allow it. She refused absolutely to let you stay here. I tried and I tried, but it was no good. She is hopeless when she is like that.'

'Well, then, when can we meet?'

'Not till tomorrow morning, darling.'

'*Tomorrow morning?*' Philip almost shouted.

'Darling, now don't get angry. You see, Beatrix is out this evening and——'

'You mean you're in that vast château all alone?'

'Yes. But she wanted to be here when you came so that she could meet you. I asked if I could go to the Malrauxs' for dinner but she said No.'

'This is quite ridiculous.'

'Darling, you are *here* – that is the main thing. It is almost a miracle. I never thought it would happen. So I am thankful for just that. Waiting till tomorrow morning won't make that much difference, will it, my darling Philip?'

'I just object to being treated in this childish way. Having come all the way from London, it's quite idiotic being a few hundred yards away from you and not being allowed to see you. Especially when you are sitting there all alone. I've a good mind to walk out of the house and come over——'

'No, darling, don't do that. There are guard-dogs round the house and they might attack you.'

'Well, can't you come over here?'

'Malraux would tell Beatrix and she would be furious.'

'By the way, I might as well warn you that I was recognised at the airport and the Press know I'm here. They chased us the whole way from Paris.'

'Oh darling, how *could* they know? Now it will be in all the papers tomorrow and Beatrix will lose her temper again. She was determined to keep it a secret.'

'When will she *ever* learn that it's hopeless trying to fool the Press? They always find out things if they're interested.'

'Yes, but why should they be so interested in *us*, darling?'

'Mainly because your step-mother has behaved in such a foolish way. If she had been sensible and let us get engaged when we first wanted to, there would have been none of this fuss.'

They talked for several more minutes, and Sabine promised to ring next morning after breakfast.

At dinner that evening, Philip had to listen to Count Malraux's complete war reminiscences. His wife never spoke a word throughout the whole meal.

Philip went early to bed, with a sleeping pill. Even then he found it difficult to sleep.

*   *   *

Next morning the English newspapers arrived shortly after breakfast, and in every one, mostly on the front page, there were photographs of Philip over a story suggesting that an engagement between him and Sabine was imminent.

'The Duchess is furious about the Press,' said Malraux. 'There are lots of them in cars at the gates. They stayed all night. They have offered the gate-man lots of money to let them in. I have told the local police and they are going to put a policeman there. What a curse they are. Why cannot they leave people in peace? The Duchess even suggested that you should go back to London and visit here another time——'

Philip looked up, astonished.

'But it's all right. I think Sabine must have persuaded her to let you stay. I am to take you up to the château at eleven o'clock. We will walk as it is so near.'

Eleven o'clock was striking on the château clock-tower

as Malraux led Philip across the gravelled forecourt in front of the huge building. It was even more impressive at close quarters than it had looked the previous evening at a distance.

The front door opened as they walked up the steps. A liveried footman clicked his heels and bowed to Malraux. Inside, Philip immediately smelt the musty smell of decay: there were large tapestries hanging on the walls of the hall, frayed at the edges, and swords arranged in crescent shapes with Army helmets above them. Their footsteps echoed on the cold stone floor as they followed the footman towards the main staircase.

They were ushered into a large room with a high ceiling. The walls were covered with large framed pictures of men in uniform, presumably ancestors.

'This is the ante-room,' said Malraux in an almost reverential whisper. The footman knocked on the tall double doors at one end. A female voice on the other side said 'Come in' in French. The footman went in, then reappeared, fully opening one of the doors to allow Malraux and Philip past.

At the far end of the room, in front of the fireplace, stood the Duchess Beatrix. She wore a triple row of pearls and an old-fashioned plain black dress. Her hair was swept back, like Countess Malraux's, in an austere bun. Count Malraux marched the whole length of the room, clicked his heels with a little jump, took her hand and bowed low. Philip followed and shook her hand in the usual manner.

'Welcome to the château,' she said. She was smiling with her mouth, but her eyes were stony-hard. 'I am sorry but my husband who was coming from Copenhagen today has just telephoned to say that he is unable to come. So he will not have the pleasure of meeting you.'

'Oh, I am sorry,' said Philip.

She turned and talked angrily in French to Malraux. After some minutes of conversation she turned to Philip and said: 'I am sorry. But I have just been complaining about all these wretched reporters trying to get in the main gate. I have given strict orders that none of them are to be allowed in. How did they know you were coming, Mr Rodolphin?' Her question was phrased with sinister emphasis.

'I don't know,' said Philip. 'One of them was at London Airport when I left.'

'Well, I must say that it is not a very happy start to your visit, which I had hoped would be quiet and pleasant for everyone.'

She talked again in French to Malraux, interrupting her conversation only to ask Philip if he understood the language.

'No,' he said. They continued talking, completely ignoring Philip, who felt most ill at ease. He looked round the room. A large framed photograph on the piano caught his eye: it was of a blond-haired young man in Luftwaffe uniform with a swastika on his arm. There was a written inscription across the bottom which Philip could not read.

Count Malraux clicked his heels, bowed and left the room. The Duchess said: 'I will call Sabine now.' She buzzed on the internal telephone and spoke peremptorily.

She saw Philip looking at a large portrait over the fire-place of a dark-moustached man in military uniform.

'That is my great-grandfather,' she said. 'He was commander-in-chief of the German Army.'

'Oh yes,' said Philip, not knowing quite what more to say.

The door at the end of the room opened and Sabine came in. She was looking quite beautiful, hair down but beautifully combed, in a well-cut, dark-blue coat and mini-skirt. She caught Philip's eye and smiled: Philip noticed that her eyes were red and puffy: she must have been crying. She advanced, smiling, towards Philip. Beatrix suddenly spoke sharply to her in French. She checked, looked at her step-mother, then turned and ran out of the door.

The Duchess turned to Philip with an acid smile: 'It's those clothes. I have told her countless times they are not suitable to wear here. But she will not listen. Now she will change and come back . . . I do hope you are comfortable with Count Malraux.'

'Yes, thank you,'

'I thought it better that you should stay with them. To save unnecessary complications.'

Philip did not know what to answer: what complications? There was an awkward silence. He felt a deep dislike for this bullying woman and the way she had so cruelly humiliated Sabine in front of him.

But one fear he had been nursing was lulled: the fear that, when he saw Sabine again, he would not find her so intriguingly attractive as he had once done. As she had entered the room, all that fear had evaporated: he felt a quickening of his blood as she had tried to come near him. The intensely provocative face, the languorous, exciting way of moving, the beautiful hands, dusky face, slanted eyes, and long, carnal legs that soared up to her hips.

The Duchess interrupted his thoughts: 'We expect you to stay to lunch and dinner.' She said it more like an order than an invitation.

Philip felt like saying: that's jolly big of you when I've

come all the way from London at your invitation. Instead he said: 'Thank you very much.'

There was another awkward silence. Then Sabine reappeared, this time in a sloppy grey sweater and black jeans. She looked hesitantly at her step-mother for approval. As no outburst came, she smiled at Philip and clasped his hand tightly as he kissed her on the cheek. She held on to his hand after the kiss as if frightened of letting him go.

'Now what are you going to do with Philip?' said her step-mother officiously. 'What plans have you made?'

Sabine looked wide-eyed at her, like a rabbit hypnotised by a stoat. She said haltingly: 'I just want . . . to be with him. To show him around. To talk.' She turned nervously to Philip, seeking his agreement.

Philip said firmly: 'We have a lot to talk about.'

The Duchess ignored him. 'I think,' she said to Sabine, 'you had better show him round the state rooms. You know where the key is.'

'Yes, Beatrix.'

'And make sure you tell him all the history about them.'

'Yes, Beatrix.'

'Do you remember it?'

'Yes, I think so, Beatrix.'

'*All* of it?'

'Yes, I think so.'

'At lunch I will ask Philip to see if you have told him right. Now away you go. There's a lot to see.'

'Yes, Beatrix.' Sabine nodded at Philip and they left the room. As soon as they were in the passage, they fell into each other's arms, hungrily searching for each other's mouths. They kissed for a long time, holding each other closely. They they heard footsteps and broke apart. The door opened and the Duchess stood there, eyeing them with a hard, caustic smile.

'Not making much progress are you, Sabine? Would you like me to guide Philip round myself?'

'No, thank you, Beatrix,' Sabine stammered, walking quickly away down the long, high passage. As they turned the corner at the end, Philip looked back: the Duchess was still standing in the doorway watching them – but that bitter smile had changed into an undisguised sneer of contempt.

*　　*　　*

'My love – ' said Philip. Sabine turned and put her finger to her lips. She opened a door into a linen room where there were several maids busying themselves about. She took a large iron key from a nail on the wall, nodded at the maids and shut the door.

'Sabine – ' Again she turned and put her finger to her lips to bid him be silent, then ran along the corridor till she came to a large double oak door with a brass crown above it. She opened the door with the key: it made a loud creaking sound as it turned. She beckoned Philip inside, closed the door and locked it from the inside. The room smelt musty: it was the ante-room to a suite, with an ornate desk and sofa, and heavy red curtains on the tall windows. Sabine pulled out the key and beckoned Philip into the next room, through another tall double-door. This was a large bedroom with a bow window: in the middle of the room stood a large four-poster bed with crowns embroidered all round the tapestry pelmet and a large brass crown over the bed-head. There was an ornate Regency dressing-table with candelabra, two large armchairs, a sofa, and two chests of drawers: the carpet was faded Aubusson. Still the same musty old smell.

Sabine turned to Philip, threw the key hard on the floor, and flung her arms round his neck: 'Oh, darling, darling, my darling Philip, I can't stand this.' She began crying, her shoulders heaving as she sobbed into his neck. He could feel the warm wetness of her tears running down into his collar.

'Sh,' he tried to comfort her by stroking her head. But the sobs got worse till she was almost gasping for breath between them. He guided her to the sofa and made her sit down. But still she wept, uncontrollably.

'What are you crying for?' he said softly. 'It's all going to be all right. I'm here. We're going to win.'

She just shook her head violently and carried on crying. Then he said, trying to change the subject: 'What is this room?'

Between her sniffs and her snuffles, she said: 'It's the state bedroom. Where Napoleon slept. It's been left unchanged since he slept here. Even the bedclothes.' She took her hands away from her eyes and looked at him, with the tears shining on her cheeks: 'Darling, I want you. I can't go on like this. I need you because I love you so much that it kills me not having you.'

He said: 'What about me? Don't you think I feel the same way, too?'

They kissed again. She pulled him roughly towards her on the sofa, then rose and went to the four-poster bed and threw the covers off. 'Darling, I won't feel normal till you make love to me,' she said. 'I can't help it, I just won't.'

Then with a sudden movement she drew off her sweater and threw it on to the floor. Next her bra, and her jeans and her shoes. She stood naked then, for a moment, stretched her arms upwards. Then she fell face downwards on Napoleon's bed, her arms round her head. 'Philip,' she called. 'Philip, come to me.' Her voice was muffled. He looked at her naked body squirming on the embroidered bedspread. He began undoing his tie . . . His blood racing in his veins, he climbed on to the large bed and gazed down at her. She turned over on her back as she felt him beside her and grasped his thighs with both hands, an almost animal fierceness in her touch. She gently scraped him with her fingernails.

She was not crying now. Not any more. He touched her breasts: with a jerk she pressed herself up into his hands.

Then she called out for him so loudly that he had to put one hand over her mouth. Gently she bit the flesh of his hand as her long legs twined hungrily round his waist. . . .

'I wonder what Josephine would say if she could see us now?' said Philip.

Sabine laughed and sighed: 'I bet she never had such a wonderful feeling on this bed as I've had. Darling, it was wonderful and I feel almost myself again. Before, I thought I was nearly going mad. Was it wonderful for you, too?'

'Yes, it was worth waiting all this time for. Was it better than with Heini?'

'Oh, darling, don't be so stupid. I told you – with Heini it was nothing. I thought of you all the time. And what about you with that girl?'

'What girl?'

'Darling, I know you must have been with that girl Shirley. Was I better than her?'

He saw no point in lying further: 'Yes, my love. When I was with her I thought all the time of you, too.' He looked round the room: 'When is this room used?'

'Never. Except when we are open to the public. It is

kept locked and just as it was when Napoleon stayed. Beatrix always makes me show it to her guests. I used to hate coming in here. But now I will love it because it will remind me of you.' Suddenly she sat up on one elbow: 'Darling, I am worried.'

'Why?'

'Because Papa was coming here to see you and then Beatrix put him off.'

'Put him *off*?'

'Yes, I know she did. I heard her talking to him on the telephone. And I think it's because she is not going to let us get engaged now because it's come out in all the papers that you are here.'

'Look,' said Philip firmly, 'sometime today or tomorrow we are going to talk to your step-mother and tell her that we want to get engaged now. *Aren't* we? And anyway, why aren't I staying in the château with you?'

'That's another of Beatrix's ideas. Just to stop us seeing each other. If you were here, we could spend the nights together, darling, couldn't we? Well, that's what Beatrix is trying to stop. She knows my mind, I can tell you. She knows how much I want you to be with me. That's why she is being so difficult.'

'Well, this difficulty of hers has got to be stopped. We are going to get engaged, aren't we, my love? *Now?*'

She hugged him close: 'Yes, darling, now.'

'Whatever she says?'

'Whatever she says. I can't wait to come and live with you in your little white house with Nelson and Mrs Drinkwater, and to get away from this *awful* château that I hate so much. It's like a prison, I tell you, darling, it's like a prison. With Beatrix here I am not myself. It's no better when Papa is here – because Papa is so weak with Beatrix. I *must* get away, *please* help me to get away –

because I do love you, my Philip, I do love you so much. Oh, I wish I could start a baby by you, then all this would be solved and Beatrix and Papa would *have* to say Yes. Darling, kiss me more.'

He kissed her open mouth. As they fought and struggled in passion, pressing their naked bodies into each other, there was a creaking noise from the next-door room. They lay suddenly still: it was the sound of the door-handle being slowly turned.

'Sabine?' A voice called softly. It was the Duchess.

'Quick,' whispered Sabine. 'Get dressed and go out through the other door.' She pointed to a door at the other end of the room. 'I will follow you when I have tidied up the bed.'

Philip dressed quickly and ran out through the other door, down some stone stairs and into a dark passage. After what seemed like hours, Sabine appeared dressed, grabbed his hand, and they both ran down the stone passage to another door that led into the front hall. She unlocked the door with the same key, then locked it again behind her.

In the hall she said: 'Do I look tidy?'

He looked her over, adjusted her hair slightly: 'Yes.'

'Now we tell Beatrix this,' she whispered. 'We went to Napoleon's bed-room, then Josephine's study. And I showed you all the pictures in the gallery. Then we went for a walk in the rose-garden and we came in. You go up to Beatrix's sitting-room and I will take the key back to the maids' room. I will see you in a few minutes.'

She ran away. Philip climbed the stairs to Beatrix's sitting-room.

He opened the door and walked in. Beatrix looked up from her armchair where she was reading a letter and said: 'Where's Sabine?'

'Getting ready for lunch.'

'Where did she take you?'

'To Napoleon's bedroom, Josephine's study, the picture gallery and the rose-garden. They were fascinating.'

'Which did you find the most interesting?'

Before he had time to answer, there was a knock on the door and in came Malraux, whom Beatrix rose to greet. The Count bowed to her deeply. Sabine came in from the other door, looking rather flushed.

'Do you understand French?' said Beatrix to Philip.

'No, I'm afraid not.'

'Then I suppose we'll all have to speak English,' she said with a smirk.

'Oui,' said Malraux heartily.

The Sabine that came in was completely different to the vibrant, vital, positive creature Philip had just made love to: now she was cowed, frightened and negative, darting looks at her step-mother every few seconds with a kind of terror in her eyes, saying nothing.

A footman announced lunch and they all went into a small adjoining dining-room. During the lunch Philip tried to talk to Sabine but she seemed incapable of saying anything except Yes or No, still looking every few seconds at her step-mother. Beatrix and Malraux monopolised the conversation, both of them seemingly deliberately avoiding bringing Sabine or Philip into it.

Eventually Beatrix turned to Philip and said: 'What did you think of Josephine's study?' Philip paused, then said:

'Very interesting.'

'Which picture did you admire the most?'

Again Philip hesitated. Sabine interrupted: 'The one of the Cavalier over the fireplace, Beatrix.'

'Oh really,' said Beatrix with heavy irony. 'Why?'

'I don't know,' said Philip. 'It just seemed to be the most interesting and colourful picture in the room.'

It was like a game of cat-and-mouse – with Beatrix trying to catch out Sabine and Philip. Luckily Sabine always intervened before Philip could reveal his ignorance of the state rooms and the rose-garden. But as the lunch went on, Philip could detect a new confidence growing in Sabine, a kind of effervescence that enabled her to stand up to her step-mother's incessant spiky questions. This was more like the old Sabine, the one he had known and fallen in love with in London – the Sabine he knew in their secret, stolen hours together. In the intimate looks that constantly passed between them, he tried to instil more strength in her.

At the end of lunch the Duchess said to Sabine: 'I want you to go riding this afternoon, to exercise that horse of yours. It's getting too fat.'

'Philip, do you ride?' Sabine asked.

'Not any longer,' said Philip.

'Philip can look at the pictures in the picture gallery,' the Duchess interrupted bossily. 'I will give him a catalogue. Now go and change into your riding clothes.'

Sabine shrugged her shoulders and left the room, throwing one last pitiful glance at Philip.

The Duchess and Malraux began talking softly in French, while Philip, feeling completely excluded, played mindlessly with a Fabergé box on one of the tables.

Eventually the Duchess noticed him and said: 'Ah, the catalogue.' She produced a thick white booklet from her desk drawer: 'This should interest you all afternoon. The picture gallery is the first door on the left down the long passage.'

Looking at pictures was not a pastime that Philip

particularly enjoyed, especially since he wanted to be with Sabine. But it seemed that the Duchess was determined to allow them as little time as possible together.

After about an hour of thoroughly bored gazing at dull pictures of the Duchess's Prussian ancestors, he decided he had had enough. He went back into the sitting-room, but no one was there. He heard low voices coming from the Duchess's small study which opened off the sitting-room. The door was unlatched, so he pushed it gently open without knocking. Malraux and the Duchess were standing by the fireplace, their arms round each other, their mouths pressed together in a fervent kiss. Philip quietly pulled the door shut again.

He went out of the sitting-room into the passage, deciding to go down to the stables to find Sabine, who should be back from her ride by now. He thought: so *that's* it – that's why the Duke never comes here: because the Duchess is carrying on with Malraux. What a sordid set-up . . . No wonder Countess Malraux looked so pathetic and neglected: she obviously knew exactly what was going on.

He found the stables without difficulty: he had seen them from one of the windows through the trees.

The main door was open. He went in. There was a row of looseboxes on the left, each with a horse in it. He walked down the row admiring the horses. Then he saw that the last loosebox door was slightly open. In it, he could see through the railings there was no horse, only bales of hay.

That was funny – all the horses were back and no sign of Sabine.

Something made him look round the door of the last loosebox. There, lying on the hay, her shirt open to reveal her bare breasts, was Sabine. Beside her lay a thin blond young man in a blue check shirt and rough working trousers which were down about his knees. Philip stood there, too shocked to move or speak.

Sabine suddenly looked up and saw him. She gave a little shriek, then jumped up, hurriedly tucking her shirt inside her johdpurs. The young man stood up and turned away with his back towards Philip, buttoning up his trousers. Philip rushed forward in a fury, intending to hit him. Sabine threw herself at Philip, grabbing wildly at his arms, screaming: 'No, no!'

He roughly pushed her out of the way so that she sprawled on to the bales of hay. With all his strength he hit out at the man's cheek. The blow knocked the man to the ground. The man put up his hands to ward off another blow to the head, but Philip kicked him hard in the stomach. He sprawled headlong, then clambered up on his hands and knees and scrambled panic-stricken out of the loosebox on all fours.

Sabine was on her knees, watching the scene with horror, hands to her head. His fury still unabated, Philip went over to her and slapped her as hard as he could on the side of the face. She put up her hands to cover her face. Again and again he slapped her, muttering: 'You bloody fucking little whore. You filthy soiled whore. Whore, whore, whore!' he shouted as his open hand struck her.

Blood welled up on her hands and cheeks where his signet ring had torn the skin. He pulled her roughly up and shook her hands free from her face. Surprisingly, she was not crying. There was a kind of bright excitement in her eyes.

'I needed that, darling,' she said. 'You were quite right. I *am* a whore.'

The blood dripped off her cheekbone and her knuckles.

Philip walked quickly out of the stable door.

She ran behind him. 'Philip,' she pleaded. 'Philip, listen to me. Philip, please *listen* to me. It was nothing. Nothing, I promise you. Philip, please *listen* to me. Listen . . . just *listen* . . .'

22

Sabine had to run to keep up with him. He strode on, shaking her hands off his arm, refusing to look at her, a mixture of anger, jealousy and horror churning inside him How *could* she behave like that, with some stable-lad, especially after this morning?

'Who was that man?' he said tersely.

'Pierre, the groom. Philip darling, it was nothing. Believe me, it was nothing.'

'You had your hand on his cock, didn't you?'

'Yes – but he made me do it to him. That's all I do.'

'So you've done it before?'

'Yes. He makes me. He never touches me, he just makes me do it to him.'

'Your shirt was open.'

'Yes, because he makes me undo it. But never anything else. Please, Philip, believe me. I don't love him at all. I only love you.'

'Then why do you behave like that with Pierre, especially when I made love to you only this morning?'

'Because he makes me. I can't stop him. And I never let him go inside me or anything like that.' She was hysterical now, crying, grabbing at Philip's arm to stop him walking so fast. Each time he angrily shook her off.

She wailed: 'What are you going to do?'

'Talk to your step-mother.'

'No no. Please, darling Philip, *please* don't tell her.'

'She's not much better herself. I caught her doing much the same thing with Malraux.

'Oh, that's been going on for years. Beatrix is like that.

And I am like Beatrix. But *you* can *stop* me being like that. It's only because I can't have you all the time that I am like that. If only I had *you*——'

'You made love to me this morning. And now this afternoon I catch you with Pierre.'

'It was the last time. I told him it was to be the last time. But he *made* me do it and I couldn't stop him. I was frightened.'

'Nonsense. You could have if you'd wanted to.'

'No, he *made* me. He *made* me. Darling, please don't tell Beatrix. I promise it was the last time.'

He turned, grabbed her by the shoulders and shook her violently: 'Now listen. I am going to tell your step-mother that we have got to get engaged now or else I am going back to London. I am not standing for this any more. Most men would break off the whole thing having seen you behaving like that with Pierre. But I am bloody stupid enough to still love you in spite of that. And I want to get you out of this awful life in this ghastly prison with your ghastly step-mother: because it's this place and that woman that makes you behave like this.'

'But, darling,' she said in a frightened voice, 'Beatrix will never agree to an engagement unless Papa's here.'

'Right – well, you will telephone him now and tell him to come here at once otherwise you will run away with me to London.'

The blood and tears were still staining her face She said meekly: 'Yes, darling. Can you really still love me after this?'

'Yes, I *do* love you. I wouldn't be saying all this if I didn't. I'd have got on the aeroplane to London by now. But all this shilly-shallying has got to stop. If it doesn't, then I am getting out.'

'Darling, I will telephone Papa right away.'

'And accept no excuses. Either he comes here tonight, or I go back to London. With you or without you.'

'Yes, darling, I agree with you.' She kissed his cheek. Her face was all bloody: 'It must be done. But we must see Beatrix together. I will meet you in the Picture Gallery after I have spoken to Papa. And, darling, please forget about Pierre – it was nothing, I promise you. Nothing at all. What shall I say about the cuts and bruises?'

'Say you fell off your bloody horse,' he said coldly.

* * *

The three of them were sitting having tea – the Duchess, Sabine and Philip. Sabine had changed out of her riding clothes into the clothes she had worn for lunch. The Duchess had accepted the story about Sabine falling off her horse without question.

In a lull in the conversation Philip said: 'Duchess, there is something important we both want to say to you.'

The Duchess looked at him surprised, but said nothing. He continued: 'Sabine and I wish to get engaged *now*, without any further delay. We are not prepared to wait any longer. We love each other and want to get married, and we want your blessing on our immediate engagement.'

The Duchess turned away and looked out of the window. After a long pause, she said: 'I understand your point of view, but I'm afraid there can be no announcement of an engagement without Sabine's father being here.'

Philip said: 'He is coming. By the plane tonight. Sabine has telephoned him.'

The Duchess swung round and stared at Sabine with fury in her eyes. 'Yes, Beatrix,' said Sabine, looking down at her tea-cup. 'I have spoken to Papa. He understands. And he is coming here tonight. He told me to tell you.'

'Ach,' said her step-mother with irritation and walked to the window. After a long silence, she said: 'Then we will wait to hear what your father says.' She put her tea-cup sharply down on the tray and walked out of the room.

Sabine burst into tears and ran to Philip saying: 'She will never allow it. I know she will never allow it.'

'It's up to your father and you, Sabine,' said Philip sternly. 'If she doesn't allow it, then you must come to London with me. Otherwise it's finished, absolutely *finished*.'

'No, *no*, my darling,' she clutched at him and pulled his head down to hers. 'Without you I am nothing. I cannot be without you.' She held up her engagement ring: 'Look – I am yours. You can't leave me now.'

'I won't leave you,' said Philip. 'But you may have to leave here. It's either me, or here. Make up your mind. I'm sick to death of seeing you in tears. That woman is wrecking your life – don't you *understand*?'

The only answer was a sob from Sabine as she buried her head in his shoulders and clutched him tightly to her.

*　　*　　*

When the Duke d'Alsace eventually arrived, he spent a long time closeted alone with the Duchess in his study. He then sent for Sabine and spent some more time alone with her.

After a long wait, he sent Sabine to ask Philip to see him. Sabine would give no hint of her father's attitude. 'Wait till he sees you,' was all she would say. But she kissed him fondly outside the study door.

Philip went into the Duke's study. Only the desk lights

were on. Behind the desk sat a thin, gaunt, fair-haired man of about sixty, with a balding head and sharp nose. He was in an immaculate black suit and stiff white collar and white shirt. He rose as Philip entered and shook hands, beckoning him to sit down in an armchair beside the desk.

'I am sorry,' said the Duke in perfect English, 'that your first visit here should be under such difficulties. The Press are besieging the gates with such ardour that I could scarcely get into the park myself. Naturally under these conditions nerves tend to get a bit strained and tempers frayed, and matters tend to get a bit out of proportion. But I am glad I came because that has given me a chance to meet you. Now that we are alone together, please would you tell me exactly what are your own feelings in the present position? And please tell me everything.'

Philip cleared his throat: 'Sir, Sabine and I have been in love for some time now and wish to get married. She is over twenty-one, and I am earning quite enough money for us both to live on comfortably. I have got a charming house in Richmond Park. I have given up the mews flat which the Duchess considered unsuitable for Sabine. I have given up playing the guitar in a night-club as the Duchess requested. We are both still very much in love and have decided that, unless we can announce our engagement this time, Sabine will come back with me to London and we will get married on our own without your blessing or that of the Duchess. It's not fair on Sabine: she is in a highly nervous state as it is.'

Philip was out of breath when he finished, so fast had his words poured out. The Duke fiddled for a moment with a glass paper-weight. He sighed. Then he spoke: 'Believe me, I quite understand your feelings. You are in a very difficult position. So is Sabine. But I have spoken to Sabine, and she quite understandably does not want to

300

get married without her step-mother's blessing – in spite of what she has promised to you. She feels it would bring bad luck to her marriage, because they have always been very close. And I can understand that, because she never knew her mother, and no daughter really likes to defy her family over so important a step as marriage – especially in Sabine's case, when there would inevitably be a lot of publicity and it would become even more of a *cause célèbre* than it has been already.

'I have also talked to my wife. Her feelings are these, and I think we must respect them: she is worried about the amount of publicity your visit this time has received, and she feels somehow that she is being forced into allowing you to marry Sabine now. In a month's time it will not only be Sabine's birthday: it will also be our wedding anniversary. And my wife has suggested that she would be grateful if you would allow her her deep wish – that you and Sabine announce your engagement on that date. You can come back here, Sabine can meet you at the airport, and you can stay here in the château, officially engaged. Then everyone will be happy. I know it means you have to wait another month, but only a month. And don't you think it would be worth it for everyone to be happy – and especially for *Sabine* to be happy?'

Philip thought for a few minutes, looking at the carpet. Then he said: 'If Sabine has agreed, I will agree. For her sake only. Not because *I* want to.'

'Sabine has agreed. Not because *she* wants to either. But mainly because of her step-mother's wishes.'

'Then let us wait for one month. But for one month only.'

'Thank you, Philip. I think it will be for the best.'

*   *   *

Dinner that evening was a strained, unhappy affair. The Duke sat almost totally silent, and the conversation was dominated by the Duchess, who spent most of the time complaining about Sabine's jewellery, dress, looks or behaviour in some form or another. By the end of dinner Philip could see that Sabine was close to tears. At times his anger almost reached boiling-point and he had felt like shouting abuse at the Duchess in an effort to stop her merciless humiliation of her step-daughter. But he had always managed to control himself in time: he reckoned that it could only make relations worse for him to have a slanging-match over the dinner table with the Duchess, however much she was so obviously gloating over her victory in delaying the announcement of an engagement for yet another month.

After dinner there was stilted conversation for a while between Philip and the Duke. Then the Duke suggested that Sabine should show Philip the way back across the park to the Malraux's house. Sabine's face lit up; the Duchess's lip curled in distaste as she turned away.

'I have told the dog patrols not to start until you are back,' the Duke said to Sabine with a smile.

'Thank you, Papa,' she said softly, smiling and clutching his hand in gratitude.

*   *   *

Philip and Sabine left hand in hand by the front door. As soon as they were outside, they stood and kissed hungrily and long.

'I've been waiting all evening for that,' said Philip when eventually they broke free.

'So have I,' said Sabine. 'At times I could have shouted out, I wanted you so much.'

They strolled, with fingers entwined, up the drive. It was a warm night with a full moon almost bright enough to read by.

'I know where we'll go,' Sabine said.

'Where?'

'To the summer-house by the swimming pool.'

She led him by the hand through the trees till they came to a little white cottage beside a large swimming-pool that shimmered and looked cool and inviting in the moonlight.

'Don't turn on the light,' she said as they went in. 'Beatrix might see it from the house.' But the moonlight was bright, even inside the summer-house, which had large windows on all four sides and wide skylights on the roof.

'Oh it's so wonderful to be with you outside the château. I don't feel myself in there,' said Sabine.

'Nor do I,' said Philip. 'Not with that step-mother of yours watching every move we make. Your father's fine. But your step-mother – God preserve us.' His hands joined in prayer.

They sat down on one of the couches on wheels inside the summer-house.

Philip said: 'I have decided one thing: I am going back to London tomorrow.'

She looked at him with hunted eyes: 'Darling, why? Why?'

'I decided during dinner. There's no point in staying here under the present arrangement. It only makes life terrible for both of us. It would be much better if I left tomorrow and then came back in a month as we all agreed, with everything finally fixed. Then maybe your step-mother will be more pleasant.'

'Darling, it doesn't mean that you're running away from me? That you don't love me any more?'

He hugged her to him: 'Of course not. Though I'm still angry about this afternoon – you and Pierre. How *could* you do that?'

'I've *told* you, Philip my darling. I was frightened. He'd made me do it to him before. And I told him this was to be the last time. It was awful of me, I know, but you must forget it and forgive me. Will you, darling? Can you?'

'I'll try to. But don't you dare do the same thing during the next month till I come back. I should have killed Pierre, there and then.'

'No, I couldn't let you do that because it was all my fault, not his. And he's smaller than you, anyway.'

'You just said it was *his* fault because you were so frightened.'

'Yes, darling, because I suppose I should have run out of the stables. Anyway, let's forget the whole horrid incident. I promise it will never happen again. It makes me thoroughly ashamed of myself: to do that when I love you so much and need you so much. How *could* I have done it? Oh, I am *awful*.'

She put her head in her hands and sighed deeply: 'What can I do about it? It's like a madness. Only you can help me by always being there for me when I want you. I've never felt so much need for someone as I do for you. That's what makes it so silly when I do these idiotic things with Heini or Pierre. It means nothing to me with them, I promise you.'

Philip felt all the old excitement at her presence returning. It did not seem to matter if she was unfaithful to him: he was obsessed with her – she had some magic power over him.

'Get undressed,' he said quietly, squeezing her hand. She looked at him questioningly.

'Stand up and get undressed,' he repeated.

'Wait,' she said. 'There is a radio in here. I will put on some music.' She opened a wall cupboard. Soon the music from a Continental late-night dance-music programme filled the summer-house. She placed the radio carefully on a window-sill. Then, standing in the brightest shaft of moonlight, she slowly began to undress in time to the music, throwing off her garments one by one like a professional strip-tease dancer.

So much energy did she put into it, so much did she undulate and writhe, that by the time she was naked she lay on the rush-matting floor gasping for breath.

Philip quickly threw off his own clothes and lay beside her. She squirmed into him, whispering: 'Bite me. Hurt me for what I did this afternoon. Bite them, yes, go on and bite them. Punish me. Bite my shoulder. Force it in me so that it hurts. I need to be hurt.'

'You're a little whore, do you know that?'

'Yes. Don't you like me being a whore?'

'As long as it's only with me.'

'You do need me, don't you? Because you're like an animal with me. I love you being an animal. Bite me again. Harder.'

She yelped at the sharpness of his teeth. 'Go *on*, go *on*,' she shouted, breathing more quickly than ever. Her thighs wound round his hips like two snakes, winding and unwinding. He bit her neck and her shoulder till she cried out.

'I could kill you,' he whispered. 'I could do this until you died out of sheer agony. I ought to, after what you've done to me.' Her fingers pinched the flesh of his thighs, then she ran her fingers savagely up his back so that her nails tore the skin.

'Go on, hurt me, hurt me,' she shouted.

*   *   *

Afterwards she wouldn't let him move. She made him lie just as he had been while they were making love. Every time he moved, she held him tightly with her athletically strong legs and arms. Eventually he forced himself out of her grip.

'Is the pool heated?' he asked.

'Yes. Why?'

'Because I'm going for a swim. Come on – you too.' He pulled her up by the arm. She embraced him and they walked out into the moonlight. Philip dived into the pool. By the time he surfaced she was beside him. The water was wonderfully warm.

He swam on his back with her floating on her stomach between his knees. They kissed with open mouths as the water lapped over their faces. After some time of gentle grappling and holding each other, they sat together in the shallow end. The warmth of the water, the intensity of Sabine's touch, the excitement of their watery nakedness . . . Philip kissed her violently, forcing her head under water until they both had to come up gasping for air.

'I want you again. Now,' he said.

'Then you'll have to catch me,' she laughed, struggling out of his arms and swimming away with fast strokes towards the deep end. He caught her in no time, grappled with her laughingly for a few moments, then pulled her back to the shallow end by her hair.

'Let me sit on top of you,' she said. She got astride him.

At that moment a torch flashed straight in their eyes from the edge of the pool. The Duchess's voice spat out in its most icy tone: 'Sabine, what are you *doing*? You will come back to the château at once. At *once* – otherwise I will set the guard dogs loose.'

The torch-light played around their naked bodies for a

few seconds, then went out. By the time their eyes had again grown accustomed to the moonlight, the Duchess was nowhere to be seen.

Sabine climbed out of the pool and ran to the summer-house, her sobs echoing through the quiet night air.

23

The next morning, having told the Maulrauxes of his plans to return to London by the midday plane, Philip telephoned Sabine to say goodbye. It seemed that the previous night her step-mother had got worried by her long absence, had gone out with a torch, heard noises from the swimming-pool, and gone to investigate. Sabine had not seen her step-mother when she had got in, nor this morning.

'But it's only for one month, darling. Then we will be together again for ever,' she said.

'Don't cry, whatever you do,' said Philip. 'Just be brave and strong. Stand up to your step-mother. And no more Heini, no more Pierre, otherwise——'

'No, I promise you I'll be the perfect little girl, absolutely good from now on,' she assured him. 'I'll telephone you tonight when you are back . . .'

*   *   *

At London Airport there was a platoon of Press photographers and reporters to meet Philip. He said nothing. But the next day all the popular papers wrote that the romance between him and Sabine must be over, because of his premature return with no announcement of an engagement. Sabine continued to write and to telephone every day.

But on the following Saturday morning he got a call from Vincent Morgan asking him to their house for a drink before lunch to discuss 'something important'.

He arrived at the Morgan house at 12.15 pm. The butler let him in. Vincent Morgan was alone in the sitting-room. After the usual formalities of introduction, Morgan said: 'Look, sorry about it and all that but we want the Dower House.'

Philip looked astonished: 'You mean you want me to get out?'

'Bluntly speaking, yes.'

'But you said I could have it unless there was a war or unless you died.'

'Yes, but something's cropped up. Sorry and all that, but there it is.'

Philip said: 'Mr Morgan, I'm getting engaged in three weeks' time. And unless I remain in the Dower House, I won't be able to.'

'Engaged? Who to?'

'To a French girl.'

'Not this d'Alsace girl the papers talk about?'

'Yes. To her.'

'But they said your engagement was off.'

'I know they did. But they were wrong.'

'Oh well, that puts a different light on it. I'd no idea. In that case of course you can keep the house. I mean, we can't turn you out just when you're going to get married, can we?'

He laughed a brittle, metallic laugh with no humour in it at all: 'Have a drink, old boy.'

*   *   *

As the three weeks went by, Philip became more and more introspective about his feelings for Sabine. Why did he put up with all this delay? he asked himself. Why did he tamely put up with the Duchess's deliberate malice?

Why did he tamely put up with Sabine's flagrant infidelity?

The answer was, he supposed, that he was utterly obsessed with Sabine and had to win her, whatever the obstacles. Pride came into it, too, he had to concede: after all this speculation in the Press about their romance he just had to win through. Or was it in reality just the appeal of her money? No, it couldn't be. She could well be cut off without a penny if she married him and refused to live in that château and inherit her title. It *couldn't* be her money: it was her self, her physical self. He had to win her in front of the world, to prove himself to the world and to himself. Even now it gave him a hollow feeling in his stomach to think about making love to her, about her nakedness wrapped round him, about her mouth touching his body. He felt she needed him to rescue her, to protect her, to love her. She was the perennial, definitive, maiden in distress.

One morning in the office at BDP, Shirley had rung up.

She said: 'I thought you might like to see me.'

'Why?'

'After what I read in the papers.'

'Don't believe what you read there.'

'So it's not all finished between you and Sabine?'

'No.'

'Oh.'

'Why?'

'Well, just remember that if at any time you need me or want me, I am here. I still love you, Philip, I can't help it but I still do. I need you terribly. But there's not room for me *and* Sabine, is there?'

After a pause:

'No, I'm afraid not. Might as well say it straight out.'

'Goodbye then. Just remember what I said. Goodbye, Philip.'

She put down the telephone without waiting for an answer.

Hell, he thought: *he* needed Shirley, too, in his own way – but he must remain faithful to Sabine, especially when he had made such a fuss about her own infidelities. With Shirley . . . with Shirley it was somehow less complicated, less angry, but less fulfilling, less intense, less vibrant than it was with Sabine. But still it was a near thing: if Sabine hadn't been there, he would have never let Shirley go. If only it was as uncomplicated with Sabine as it was with Shirley – no Press reporters, no bitchy step-mother, *none* of the problems. He had one of the usual explosive telephone calls from his father. 'All this bloody balls in the papers – why don't you get *on* with it and rape the arse off this little Frog? Or else give up the whole thing? Making a bloody ass of yourself and the family in front of everybody. . . .'

He couldn't possibly explain the intricacies of the situation to his father, so he said nothing. In the end he had to put down the telephone to cut short the angry obscenities.

At last the day arrived when he was to fly to Paris. Sabine had telephoned the night before, lyrical, passionate in her expectation of his arrival the next day.

The radio-taxi for London Airport arrived early. After he had loaded his luggage into it he went back into the Dower House to shut up Nelson with Mrs Drinkwater. The telephone rang. Who *could* it be – at this time? He deliberated whether to answer it, then decided he had better do so in case it was the air-line telling him the flight was delayed or cancelled or something.

'Hello?'

'This is Paris calling. A call for you. Hold on. . . . Your call to England.'

'Hello, Philip?' It was the flinty voice of the Duchess.

'Yes, it's me.'

'Philip, I had to ring because Sabine is not well.'

'What's wrong with her?'

'Oh, just a kind of flu. Nothing serious. But I don't think you had better come.'

'*What?* Why not?'

'Because she is not well. We think you should put off your visit until she is better.'

'Has she a temperature?'

'Yes.'

'How much?'

'Oh just a slight one.'

'Can I speak to her, please?'

'I don't think you had better. Not today. I think you must put off your visit, though.'

'I'd like to speak to her, please.'

'She is ill.'

'But not ill enough not to speak on the telephone.'

There was a pause. Then the Duchess said: 'All right, hold on, and I will put you through.' Another pause. Then Sabine came on the line. Her voice was all snuffly and muffled. She had obviously been crying.

'What is wrong with you?' said Philip. 'You were perfectly all right last night when we talked.'

'It is nothing, nothing.'

'Then why can't I come as arranged and promised?'

'Because——'

'Because what?'

'Darling, don't be difficult,' she said between sobs.

'Do you want me to come?'

A long pause. Then she said: 'I don't know. It's

Beatrix. *She* doesn't want you to come. And I don't know what to do.'

'Haven't you got the strength of character to stand up to that bitch?' he said angrily. 'For months now we have been at the mercy of her obstructive, selfish whims. She has made everything as difficult as she can. She has tried to poison our relationship. She bullies you, she tries to bully me. We would already be engaged if it wasn't for her malicious bloody machinations. How long are you going to let this go on? When are you going to stand up to her? Have some guts?'

The only answer was the sound of her sobbing. He went on: 'I'm fed up with being made to look a fool in front of the whole world – as if I was chasing you for your blasted money. I'm *fed* up with waiting for you. I'm *fed* up with your whorish antics with Heini and Pierre. Make up your bloody mind. Make it up now. My luggage is in the taxi. But I'm not coming *near* you unless you guarantee you're going to stick by me and defy that bitch your step-mother. Are you – or are you not?'

'I don't know,' she sobbed.

His voice was as hard as granite. He said: 'Well, make up your mind. Now.'

'I don't know,' she whined through her tears.

'I'll give you *one* more chance,' he said. 'Are we going to get engaged this time? Or are we not? Tell me. Yes – or no?'

'I don't . . . I don't know.' Her sobs grew louder.

His fury exploded. 'You're a bitch and a bloody little whore,' he said through quivering lips: 'I have stuck by you through thick and thin for months. And now when the crunch comes you haven't even got the guts to stand by me. Just because of your fiendish step-mother. You've shown I can't trust you, what with Heini and Pierre. And now your step-mother. It's too much. You can go and *stuff* yourself stupid, go and rot in your bloody château with your bloody bitch of a step-mother and toss off Pierre for the rest of your life. I'm *sick* of you, I've had enough. Get stuffed, you bloody whore, you fucking bitch. I'm going now.'

'But what shall I do with your ring?' she pleaded hysterically.

He said: 'Stuff it. Or send it back. You've cost me a bloody fortune as it is. Now I really am going. Goodbye, Sabine, you fucking helpless, hopeless little bitch. You despicable little whore.'

The only sound he heard as he slowly put down the receiver was her violent sobbing, and cries of 'No, Philip, no.'

He looked at the telephone for a long time after he had replaced it. Though his hands were shaking, the calm and silence and peace was wonderful. His brow and palms were wet with sweat, yet suddenly he felt intensely relaxed and relieved, almost *cleansed* – as if he had just walked out of a sauna bath into the cool air. He had shrugged off a skin, a skin which he secretly must have suspected for a long time didn't really fit him, in spite of all the humiliation and trial he had borne to wear it.

He went out, tipped the taxi-driver and told him and Mrs Drinkwater to unload the luggage. Then he changed into an old sun-shirt and jeans, called Nelson, picked up a pair of secateurs in the hall and went out into the garden to prune some shrubs.

Some fifteen minutes later he came in and dialled Shirley's home number.

'Hello?' she answered.

'Do you still need me?'

'Oh, it's *you*. Yes, of course. Need you ask?'

314

'Well, now *I* need *you*.' She answered very softly:

'I somehow had a hunch you might sooner or later . . . Tell me what I should do, then.'

'Be ready in half an hour's time. I'll come and pick you up. All right?'

'Shall I pack my night things?'

'Yes.'